THE FORT

A NOVEL BY

JOAN VASSAR

PROLOGUE

FORT INDEPENDENCE
MARCH 20, 1864

Black's eyes popped open from a dead sleep at the sound of booted feet in the corridor just beyond his bedroom. Sunday was pressed into his side with an arm thrown over his chest. Slowly, he untangled from her before swinging his legs over the side of the bed. Once on his feet, he moved about in the darkened chamber. His wife groggily murmured his name as he was strapping on his gun.

"Nat?"

Walking to the bed, Black leaned over and kissed her. "Go back to sleep."

"What time it is?"

"Almost dawn," he answered, then kissed her again.

When his wife dozed, Black turned heading for the door. Stepping into the unlit hall, he pulled the knob until he heard a soft click. James broke the silence.

"Ant come to me and Elbert. He was gon ring the bell, but we told 'im–no."

Elbert added. "Ain't no since scaring the women and children."

"It's a carriage in front the gate. Ain't no one got out–it's just there." James continued.

"The men patrolling?" Black asked.

"They say when they come 'round one time, it wasn't there–next time, it was." James explained.

Black nodded. It was dark, so his brothers couldn't see him. "Let's go to the gate."

The men moved through the dark house as though it were daylight. In the hall leading to the porch stood Paul with an oil lamp and shotgun. Once they stepped onto the porch, the old man locked the door behind them. At the bottom of the stairs, the twenty-two waited; Frank, Lou and Anthony held the torches. Black descended the steps; Elbert and James followed. The posse moved as one to the front gate.

The temperature held frost and though it was after winter, it was still before spring. As they walked the path to the front of the fort, Black tried to think through every scenario. He was drawing a blank. When they reached the gate, the men on guard looked agitated. Philip stepped forward to explain.

"Good morning, Black. The carriage been out dere a hour–ain't no one got out. We called out–nothing."

"Thank you, Philip." Black replied as he moved to the door beside the gate.

His brothers stepped out behind him. James carried the torch and Elbert, his gun–the hammer already cocked back. Black reached for the torch and James relinquished the dancing flame in favor of his own gun. When Black heard James cock his weapon, he approached the vehicle. The two horses attached to the carriage didn't seem uneasy or skittish. Black stepped with caution toward the door of the vehicle. Under his boots the ground crunched. He did no more than glance around the darkness to see if anyone lay in wait. His mind considered ambush, but his men were still patrolling.

Torchlight, though better than nothing, offered limited visibility. Breathing in sharply, Black placed a hand on the door handle and James hissed. "Now!"

Black yanked the door wide at his brother's command. The cab was empty. Still, closer scrutiny shook him to his core. It was Elbert who summed up Black's racing thoughts. "Damn."

The brothers leaned forward in one fluid motion: the sight before them gruesome, even in the absence of a body. Blood soaked the interior of the carriage. As Black tried to process what he was seeing, James added. "Whoever was in there ain't make it."

Black agreed, but he could find no words. He was working through the questions floating around in his head. Who had been in the carriage? Where did the carriage come from? Why was it left outside the gate? How did his men miss the arrival of the carriage? What the hell did all this mean? He had begun recycling the questions when James spoke his name.

"Black?"

"I don't know." He answered before his brother could say more. "I don't know..."

The twenty-two took control of the gate, while the brothers stood about in complete darkness. Black had extinguished the torch, so they wouldn't be vulnerable to attack; still, they did not leave the carriage. Two hours passed in silence and daybreak found Black standing on the side of the vehicle, arms folded over his chest. As the sun chased away the murkiness of night, Black circled the vehicle. He noted the obvious while thinking out loud.

"The carriage came from the east and there are no wheel marks leading away."

"Shit," James mumbled.

Black examined the horses. Lifting their hooves, he looked for the groove placed on all the shoes by their smithy; there were no identifying marks. Next, he assessed the driver's seat and found a sizable blood stain. At the back of the vehicle, he stooped down to look beneath the frame. He found an "F" branded into the undercarriage.

Standing, Black faced his brothers. "The horseshoes have no marks from our smithy. Looks to me like someone went through the trouble of re-shoeing the animals."

"What is you sayin'?" James pressed.

"I'm saying these are our horses. The animals came home." Black clarified.

"The carriage?" Elbert asked.

"Belongs to us." Black replied.

"I figured as much." Elbert said as he looked to the trees.

"What next?" James asked.

"We count the people." Black replied, his tone grim. "See who's missing."

* * *

Ten Miles from the Fort
One Day Earlier

Virgil reached his small farm well after dark. He had closed the store hours ago; still, he meant to avoid an argument by completing unimportant tasks instead of heading home straight away. The weather held a chill that invigorated, which was in direct contrast to spending the day in his suffocating office. A full moon sat high in the sky, and the bare branches that canopied overhead appeared to be touching its yellow surface.

The moment his horse stepped into the clearing of his secluded farm, Virgil noted several things that caused him unease. One: the house was dark, offering no signs of life. Two: the stable door was shoved wide and lantern light spilled from the entrance. Three: there was an unidentified carriage parked haphazardly at the door along with several horses. They never entertained guests. His life was in town, and no one ventured onto his land. His world was private, and he liked it that way.

Virgil had been contemplating backtracking into the underbrush when a man's cry of pain spurred him forward. As he drew near, three white men stepped from the stable. Two were holding torches, the scene before him distorted by the flickering firelight.

"Percy!" Virgil shouted as he brought his horse to a skidding halt before swinging down from the saddle and sprinting for the stable door.

The torch holders stepped back, and a fourth man emerged from the stable. Virgil had been about to draw his weapon, when yet another man appeared and stood in the torchlight. He was older and thin of frame. Virgil didn't have to wait long, the last man to the party addressed him.

"Mr. Virgil, we been waiting for you."

"Who the hell are you?" Virgil queried. "And where is Percy?"

"It's fixing to be a long night and I can say for certain you won't ever forget it. Now about your gun..." the man continued, his southern drawl both coaxing and threatening as he ignored Virgil's questions.

"Get Percy out here–now." Virgil demanded. He drew his weapon and to his shame, his gun hand shook.

"Your gun, Mr. Virgil–I won't ask again." Percy cried out just as the man issued the warning.

"Percy!" Virgil yelled as he ran for the entrance. His unwanted guests closed ranks, grabbing, and then dragging him back from the door. He tried to get eyes on Percy, but there was no visual to go with the cries of distress. This left his imagination to work overtime. Raising his hands in the air, Virgil bent at the waist and placed his gun on the ground before him.

"Good," the older man praised. "Now we can move forward."

Virgil's focus was on the stable, so he didn't see one of the men pull at the carriage door. A commotion started to his right causing him to turn his attention to the vehicle as a colored woman was yanked from the cab. She yelled out in pain, but her sobs were weak as if she couldn't catch her breath. Inside the dark carriage a man hollered.

"Please! Don't hurt her... please!"

Virgil couldn't reconcile the events, or how he and Percy had become unwilling participants in this nightmare. While he grappled to understand what was happening, two of the five men climbed into the carriage, promptly silencing the man within... the man Virgil couldn't see. This moment made clear why the first screams he'd heard hadn't sounded familiar. The woman, who had appeared incoherent, came to life when the man's cries stopped abruptly.

"Don't hurt him!" she shrieked. "Stop! Don't harm him... damn you all!"

One of their captors' backhand slapped her–stunning her for seconds. Virgil sprang into action on her behalf only to be wrestled to the ground. The woman flew at the perpetrator, scratching, biting, kicking, and punching him; the man howled in agony before she was subdued. She wept softly and Virgil wanted to comfort her. He reached out to her, but someone stepped on his fingers grinding the digits into the dirt.

Virgil refused to cry out, and his defiance was met with swift reprisal. He looked on as Percy was pulled from the stable and beaten right before his very eyes. One man held him up while the other issued blow after blow; and when Percy fell to the ground, both men stomped him until he groaned.

"Nooo!" Virgil sobbed. "No more... please!"

All went silent save for the wind as it rustled the tall grass running the perimeter of the property. The older man spoke, and his words were both enlightening and perplexing. "You can save everyone here this night, Virgil, by simply telling us what you know about Hope."

The woman answered as if to cut off his response. "We don't know no Hope."

The older man, who had up until this point displayed nothing but control, stepped to the woman and kicked her in the head. Virgil watched as her body went limp–still. His dick shriveled up in his long underwear for he was not as brave as she. He could not continue to watch her suffer and neither could he bear Percy's pain.

"What is it you want to know?" Virgil asked, his gaze fixed on Percy's lifeless form.

"Everything," the man replied.

CHAPTER 1

FORT INDEPENDENCE
MARCH 1864

The gate groaned as it was being pulled open by the men of Fort Independence. Black watched as Philip led away the horses pulling the bloody carriage to the westside of the fort. The men were looking to him for answers, even as they understood that he was late to the situation. Black did what he always did–he offered leadership while trying to work through the burden of being in charge.

"I want the horses corralled separate from the other animals." He paused for a beat, then went on. "Take the carriage to the old quarantine area and take it apart."

Five men broke from the crowd to follow Philip, and Black continued to issue orders. "The fort will be on lockdown with Simon and James controlling the gate. Elbert and the remaining twenty-two will meet at my house in thirty minutes. We are behind in understanding the facts–the hours of natural light are crucial and must be productive."

Spinning on his heels, Black strode in the direction of his house; Elbert fell into step beside him. As they moved along in silence, Black experienced a feeling of calm overtake him. Threat had come to the fort, and he realized there was only one way to deal with the issues facing them as a people–he would have to back away from worry. He could not engage in any thought that went against the safety of the fort.

"You have a plan?" Elbert asked.

"The plan is the same as it's always been–we protect what is ours."

"Yeah," Elbert replied.

The early morning sun washed over the land in yellow and white rays. A chilled wind disguised as a breeze pushed dirt around on the trail. People had begun emerging from their homes moving toward the chores of the day. As the brothers neared the bottom of the hill facing the house, Black heard sounds of iron striking iron.

"Bring me the blacksmith."

Elbert turned heading in the direction of the smithy. Black watched him go before bounding up the stairs and into the gloomy hallway. The natural light from the kitchen window spilled into the corridor along with the aroma of strong coffee. When he reached the entrance of the kitchen, Black found his mama sipping from her favorite white cup. Big Mama was staring out the window.

She wore a brown dress with a beige sweater that was buttoned all the way up. The house still held a coolness that wouldn't recede until his mama started cooking. Her silver hair was parted down the middle and braided in two fat cornrows. She didn't look his way, but she did engage him verbally.

"Heard ya brothers come for ya dis mawning. I been up ever since."

Black hesitated for a beat unsure of how much he should divulge. "The men found a carriage at the gate."

"Who was in dere?" Big Mama asked, her lips poised to sip the steaming black liquid. She continued gazing out the window.

"No one," Black replied and what went unsaid seemed louder than his spoken words.

Big Mama turned her eyes on him. "So, trouble done found its way."

Leaning back against the doorframe, Black stood with one foot in the kitchen and the other in the hall. He folded his arms over his chest and offered steady eye contact. "Yes, Mama, it would seem so."

She offered a weak smile before turning her gaze back to the window. Black walked over and kissed her on the cheek before moving down the hall toward his study. Seating himself behind the desk, he pushed through his day. He was ordering supplies when the first of the men wandered into his study. Jeremiah was followed by Josiah, Horace, Frank, and Lou. When the study filled with the twenty-two minus Simon and James, Black stood and moved to the center of the room; glancing from man-to-man, he gave orders.

"Each of you will head to the barracks and break the men down forming several groups of patrol. You all will be responsible for your own men." Black paused for seconds and when no one spoke he went on. "I want the uninhabited parts of the land heavily guarded making the inhabited parts that much safer."

Spinning in place Black made certain to look each of his men in the eye. "You will all report directly to Elbert, James and Simon, who will report to me–all urgent matters will start with them."

"The women…" Elbert said, his voice strained. "What will we tell them?"

Black chuckled. "The women will report directly to me."

Elbert nodded and Black went on. "The morning is getting

away from us. Report anything that gives you pause; Simon and James are at the gate."

As the men filed out, Elbert remained and when they were alone, Black asked. "The smithy?"

"Is waiting in front of the house."

Black nodded, then followed Elbert out of the study. In the kitchen Big Mama was peeling potatoes and looked up from her task to smile. His brother kissed her cheek and when Elbert backed away, Black spoke. "I want to meet with the women in the late afternoon."

"Sunday, Callie and Cora is seein' 'bout the children. I'll make sho' they knows." Mama replied.

At his mama's words Black continued through the kitchen, down the hall and out onto the porch. Descending the stairs, he moved to face the smithy. He noted that the man before him was tall and thin. Dressed in dark brown trousers with a tan homespun shirt, the blacksmith held eye contact and Black saw it as a good sign.

The smithy was dark of skin with thick knotted hair, bushy eyebrows, and a wide nose. He neither smiled nor frowned and per his occupation–he smelled of smoke. Black gauged him to be more than forty winters because everything about him appeared haggard; to assess him by summers seemed too kind judging by the creases around his eyes and mouth.

"Mawning, Mr. Black. Elbert tell me ya wanted to talk wit' me. I come directly to you, but I smells of fire–so I waited out chere for ya."

"Good morning, Odell," Black replied. "Yes, I wish to speak with you."

"Yes, sah," the smithy replied.

The sun had changed positions in the sky and the cold that held the early morning eased. It was yet another indication that the natural light could not be wasted. Allowing his gaze to scan their surroundings, Black saw that the people of Fort Independence were well into their workday. The act of dismissing the smithy while engaging him at the same time was a tactic meant to shove the other man into uncertainty. In the distance Black could see one of the women sweeping her porch and though it appeared that she was his focus–it was the smithy who held his attention.

"How many carriages and horses did you sell in the last year?" Black asked.

"I give three carriages away and I sold two." The smithy answered without hesitation. "I give seven horses away and I sold two."

Black's eyes fell on the man before him. Odell did not fidget. "The vehicles and animals given away…"

"Went to the orphanage like ya say."

"Where did you make sale?" Elbert asked.

"Went to town–sold the horses and carriages behind the store. Mista Virgil what owns the establishment Everythang is always obliging."

Black continued in his scrutiny and still the smithy remained at ease. "Thank you, Odell."

"Yes, sah, Mista Black."

When Odell turned to leave, Black stopped him asking two more questions. "Do you know who purchased the carriages and horses? Do you re-shoe the animals before selling them?"

"Three white men paid the coin for the animals and carriages. Cain't says I know 'em. Naw, sah, I don't re-shoe the horses unless I has to."

Black nodded and the smithy went on. "Cain't says I paid much attention to the mens what buy our goods, but these men… they refused to work wit' me. Mista Virgil had to step in."

"Do you remember what they look like?" Elbert asked.

"Naw, sah–shit, I tries not to look too hard upon white men who thanks Imma damn boy. Ain't nothin' but trouble down that dirt road."

Black chuckled and Elbert dismissed the smithy. "All right, my friend–we might have need of you later."

"Yes, sah, Mista Black–Mista Elbert." And with that Odell turned on his heels and strode away.

Black, followed by Elbert, turned in the opposite direction moving toward the area of the old quarantine. The brothers walked in silence for a bit until Elbert asked. "What you think about the smithy?"

"Nothing," Black said shrugging his shoulders. "He's not part of this trouble."

"How can you know for sure–he ain't part of this shit?" Elbert asked.

Once between the trees, Black slowed, then stopped walking. He faced his brother. "I can't be sure, but this is what I see. When questioned, Odell held eye contact and gave direct answers. Being looked upon as a man is important to him. The smithy likes it here and takes pride in what he does for the fort. Checking his words is as simple as speaking with Virgil. No, the smithy ain't part of this trouble."

"Shit," Elbert hissed.

Black laughed. "You see it the same."

"You ponder too much–I don't wanna be thinking 'bout shit all the time. Sucks the life right outta ya." Elbert countered.

Sobering, Black stared up at the clear blue sky before replying. "Yeah–it does."

Putting one foot in front of the other Black pressed on to the westside of the fort. Elbert fell into step on his right. The brothers didn't follow the well-worn path; instead, they kept on through the dense foliage until the unused barn came into view. Philip and the men were there disassembling the bloody carriage.

The large wheels lay flat on the ground, side by side. Leaned against the front of the barn were both carriage doors; the black cab itself sat upside down with the sun glinting off the metal axle. In the middle of the chaos, the interior and driver seats lay to the right of the cab. If Black had not known the inside of the carriage was brown, he wouldn't have been able to decipher the color–there was so much dried blood. As he stared about, the grisliness of the situation seemed magnified by the sunshine.

Black walked between the carriage parts, his eyes studying each piece with careful deliberation. Reaching into his pocket he retrieved a piece of charcoal and a folded slip of parchment; immediately he began sketching the scene before him. When he stooped to look inside the cab, Philip called his name.

"We brung ya some work gloves."

Standing to face Philip, Black replied. "Thank you."

It was all he could manage before turning his focus back to the task at hand. He stood for hours lost in his head trying to make clear the facts; while there were several issues he was sure about–there were just as many questions that left him baffled. Using a stick, he poked at the interior seats and found that more blood seeped to the surface flooding the fabric. In the same instance the driver's seat did not offer seepage. This act of violence, Black was certain happened within the last day. He would check the horses again, but the animals appeared fresh.

One of the cab doors had a small piece of pink fabric wedged in the joint–where the mechanism engaged the lock. The material, though small, was free from blood stains. This detail alarmed Black: he took it to mean that a woman was present but removed from the cab before the bloodshed happened. All he could do was surmise, and yet the possibility of rape and death having already befallen her was real. He shook his head as if to clear it, but the thought clung.

"Ain't you suppose to meet with the women?" Elbert asked.

Black turned to find his brother standing in the doorframe of the barn, flask in hand. Philip and the other men were gone; he hadn't even missed them. Looking to the sky, he realized from the position of the sun, it was moving toward late afternoon. The expression on his face must have shown the morbidity of his thoughts.

"What?" Elbert pressed.

"There was a woman in the carriage." Black answered.

"How you know?"

Black, who was standing in the middle of the wreckage, pointed to the door with the pink fabric stuck in the joint. "See for yourself."

Elbert placed his flask in his back pocket and moved in to examine the door. "Pink–no blood."

"I think the woman was removed from the carriage before the bloodshed took place." Black said.

"Or her dress was closed in the door after she got in the cab. No blood because this piece was stuck in the joint before the killin'."

Black stared at his brother; Elbert shrugged before adding. "Imma go to the barracks while you see to the women."

"Yeah," Black responded.

Elbert didn't wait, he rushed away as if to avoid hearing Black's thoughts. Folding his arms over his chest, Black continued to linger–to think. As the sun dimmed with the onset of evening, he heard voices. The crunch of booted feet on the dirt path snagged his attention before Philip and the men appeared.

"Elbert say–yous late." Philip said.

Black nodded, then gave orders. "Place the carriage pieces in the barn and lock up."

"Sho' thang, Black."

After offering each of the men with Philip eye contact, Black turned and headed for home. He took the long way because he wasn't thrilled about disrupting the lives of their women. But he was clear that keeping them ignorant to an issue of this magnitude would serve no one. Delegating duties to the twenty-two extended his power beyond the barracks, pushing even the tradesmen to stand up and take notice. Having their women report to him would give him insight into the lives of the women and children of the fort. He would also have a better accounting of the people by sticking close to their women.

His gait was lazy, not at all reflective of the fact that the women were waiting for him. As he moved along the path, he noted the season change and the trees coming back to life. He could see two women working–one in her garden and one removing laundry from the line; not too far away, men worked on the roof of a cabin, readying the occupants for the rainy season. The sunshine now offered an orange hue, signaling the end of the natural light. People waved and called out to him. Black did his best to appear untroubled by the events of the early morning.

When his home came into view, so too did the women who waited for him. Morgan spotted him first, pointing in his direction. Collectively the women turned and filed into the house. Once he reached the stairs leading to the porch, he stood for moments trying to ready himself. His intake of air was sharp before he took the steps two at a time. He found the kitchen empty, and he was sure that the older women were tending the children.

Black continued to the opposite hall; his study door was open, and the buzz of light conversation drifted into the corridor. Stepping over the threshold caused all manner of discussion to cease. He maneuvered between the chairs until he stood facing the room. In the front row sat his wife, Morgan, and Beulah–Horace's woman. Behind his wife sat Anna, his brother Elbert's woman who had recently given him a new son. James' woman Abby, and Tim's woman Sarah also sat together. Mary, Carrie, and Hazel–Gilbert's woman sat on the gold couch. On the right side of the room sat Molly, Callie, and Emma. Even E.J.'s women were present sitting to the left of the room.

The soldiers seated before him wore an array of colors–from green to blue to pink. The fabric of their dresses rustled with the slightest of movements and for Black, the sound was unsettling. He wondered if Simon had felt uncomfortable when working with the women. Sunday smiled at him and he found that he needed the push.

Clearing his throat helped him find his voice. "Good eve, Ladies."

The women responded in unison. "Good eve to you, Mista Black."

Black's arms were folded over his chest, his posture stiff and his feet were braced apart. "This morning a carriage appeared at the front gate."

"Who come to the fort?" Morgan asked.

"There was no one inside. It seems…" he said, looking for the right words, "as though someone was killed in the vehicle."

"You said ain't no one was in the carriage." Beulah countered; her eyebrows pressed together as she tried to understand his words. She was a brown skinned woman with a mole in the center of her nose. Horace's woman wore her hair pinned back from her face with a large puff at the back of her head.

"The amount of blood…" Black answered, then cleared his throat. "Too much blood."

"So we's here cause the carriage belongs to the fort." Sunday stated, rather than asked.

"We're gonna have to count the people." Anna said to the room at large.

"Me and Abby keep a list of people's comings and goings," Mary said.

"I has the list," Abby said.

Black listened as the women went back and forth. Emma–Anthony's woman asked, "Wouldn't we know if someone what lives here been killed?"

"I would like to think so… I would hope so." Black answered, hating that he couldn't offer more.

While he was working through Emma's words, Hazel asked. "You all right, Mista Black?"

"Shit," he muttered causing a burst of giggles. Black was

annoyed that they would have to check on him–instead of vice-versa.

"You gon have to get used to us." Morgan said, giving him a smile.

"Yeah," he agreed.

Sunday, his beautiful wife stood, her green dress swishing as she moved to stand next to him. Morgan followed suit in a blue dress. Both women wore their guns holstered at their upper left sides–each positioning themselves on either side of him.

It was Sunday who spoke first. "Abby and Mary, please see Philip; he got him a list of the folk what been comin' and goin'. Won't be easy–some cain't write they names. Match it as best ya can."

A small amount of discussion started, but when Sunday held up her hand, the room fell silent once more. His wife went on. "Callie will be in charge a da children. Emma and Molly will do as Callie directs."

Morgan chimed in. "Hazel, Carrie and Beulah, we needs you to check wit' the womenfolk. See what they knows that we don't. Me and Sunday will help Black count the menfolk."

Turning to Netti and Suzanne, Sunday said. "Netti, you gon help Shultz wit doctorin' and Suzanne, you gon help Mary wit' schoolin' for the older children."

"We starts in the mawnin'," Morgan said. "Brang yo babies here when ya has to work. The older women will keep 'em fed and the younger women will keep 'em safe."

And with that the women had their orders. They stood and filed out leaving Black alone with Sunday and Morgan.

"All right, Nat. What ain't you tellin' us?" Sunday asked.

Morgan, Black noted, secured the door behind the last woman. Leaning back against the edge of his desk, he stared between them.

"Sunday, you are correct, the carriage and the horses belong to us. It would seem the animals came home." He answered.

"And..." Morgan pressed.

"I had the men take the carriage apart. We found a piece of a dress stuck in the door of the carriage–pink."

"Well... we has work to do," Sunday said.

Black couldn't help but notice that neither woman flinched at his words.

* * *

At three in the morning, Black stepped into his study to find the twenty-two waiting for him. He figured only Simon, Elbert and James would be present, but they were all accounted for. Moving to the front of the study, Black leaned against the edge of his desk. Morgan and Sunday soon appeared, and the men parted so the women could pass. They sat behind his desk, Sunday in his chair and Morgan in a chair that Simon produced for her. The room settled and Black nodded.

Frank gave an accounting. "Each of us has ten men."

"That number includes some of the farmers and tradesmen," Elbert said.

James inserted. "Some of 'em doubles in they duties; but a big number of the men is only tradesmen or farmers."

Black nodded. "The men who aren't soldiers have been made to understand that the women and children are their first responsibility."

"Yeah," Lou said. "They knows what they gotta do, while we moves in and outta the gate."

"Good," Black replied before issuing orders. "Now that we are prepared, I want the land around the fort for two miles inspected–report back what you find. You are looking for anything that explains the carriage."

Morgan spoke up. "We ain't needin' the peoples to work today."

"I sees it the same. We needs to disturb thangs inside the gate so we can tally the peoples." Sunday added.

"Anthony, you and your men go to each cabin. The men need to report behind the barracks now, and after daybreak the women and children need to report to the school," Black said. Turning back to the women, he asked. "Have I missed anything?"

"No," they replied in harmony.

* * *

Sunday stood at the backdoor of the barracks where the early morning cold was biting. She wore a thick brown overcoat and gloves; her husband, who stood a few feet away, wore nothing to ward off the chill. His shirtsleeves were rolled up, revealing powerfully veined forearms; on his bald head he wore a leather brimmed hat–pushed back just enough to see his eyes.

The light from the early morning sun spilled in through the backdoor on an angle. They had come to the barracks in the dark and had been counting the men for hours. The system in place was simple and there were three checkpoints. Morgan, Sunday, and Black did the counting and they did it four times. The tally was two hundred and ninety-five men, with each man who had a family giving a count of his household. This gave insight into the expected numbers happening at the school where the women and children were being tallied.

As always, Sunday found the menfolk to be polite, but in her husband's presence they were subdued with her. She suspected that Nat didn't want her in the barracks, but he wouldn't say such a thing. He respected what she did for the people and that meant much to her. And so, the men made certain they didn't smile, chat too much or cross a line that she couldn't see. They spoke among themselves as they moved through the line to be counted. The route was in through the backdoor and out through the front.

A series of questions were asked of each man: What's ya name? Do ya have family? How many lives in ya cabin? Are ya a tradesmen, farmer, or soldier? The answers varied from man to man. As the morning hours ended, the men moved back into their normal work routine. When she and Morgan finally left the barracks, everything went back to business as usual.

Nat walked behind them carrying the ledger in which they recorded the numbers. The change in temperature had Sunday carrying her overcoat, her gloves now jammed into the left pocket. They didn't go to the school in the center of the fort where Sarah and Anna were counting the women and children; instead, they headed for the house. Nat went straight to his study, while she and Morgan checked in on the children. Sunday found the children three summers and younger were napping. The older children were helping Miss Cora and Big Mama in the garden. She could hear Little Otis and Nattie talking and laughing from the kitchen window.

"Imma go see 'bout lunch for Simon," Morgan said.

Sunday turned and beamed. "Mama made stew and cornbread–has some for you and Simon. I's 'bout to brang some for Nat."

Morgan nodded and the women moved around the kitchen preparing lunch for their husbands. Sunday called over her shoulder as she headed toward the study, tray in hand. "See you 'round the same time we met yestaday. The others should be 'bout done wit' they task."

The sigh that emitted from Morgan caused Sunday to stop, turn and look at her. Morgan had leaned against the sink and was staring down at the floor. Her black boots peeked out from beneath the hem of her brown skirts. She toed the wood floor nervously.

"Letti?" Sunday said, using Morgan's real name. The other woman's head popped up, offering a sad smile. Sunday pressed. "What's the matta?"

"We tries to keep the fort safe. My heart finna be broken if'n one of the peoples is missin'."

"It's been in my head too, 'bout what the others is gon find when they's done countin'. I ain't wantin' to think on it neither."

Morgan sighed again before adding. "We cain't hide from it–won't help us none."

"No," Sunday agreed. "We cain't hide."

Placing the tray on the table, Sunday stepped forward and gave Morgan a hug. Each woman took strength from the other before going their separate ways. Sunday walked down the shadowed hall toward the study. Sunlight splashed into the corridor where the door sat open. She paused for a moment trying to collect her emotions; she didn't want her husband to worry. Bracing herself, she stepped into the doorway to find Nat standing in the middle of the study staring at her.

He came forward and removed her burden. After placing the tray on the desk, Nat turned back to where she stood in the doorframe. Taking her by the hand, he pulled her into the study. Sunday heard the lock *snick* at her back. Pressing herself against the cool wood of the door, she looked up into her husband's eyes.

"Brung ya somethin' to eat." Her voice was breathy.

"I see."

She would have suggested that he sit and eat but he placed his palm flat to the door. Nat leaned in and kissed her. It was a deep fusing of their mouths which caused her to moan involuntarily. Upon the slightest parting of her lips, he pushed his hot tongue into her mouth. The action was both emotional and lusty. When she thought he would have pulled back for air, he bit her bottom lip to keep her in place. Reaching up, she cupped his face and his eyes drifted shut. He kissed her again allowing his tongue to rub sensually against her own. She felt a pang of need pool between her legs when he pulled back and whispered in her ear.

"I love you, Sunday, and I promise to keep you safe."

"Oh... Nat."

He stepped back from her while blocking her from the room at large. His scrutiny was intense; still, she did not drop her gaze. Nat was dressed in brown trousers, black boots, and a tan homespun shirt. A black leather holster held his gun in place at his upper left side. His hands were shoved into his pockets as if to keep himself from reaching for her. He was bald again and menace dripped from him. Yet his words were needy–uncertain.

"You wanna sit and talk?"

Eyebrows furrowed, Sunday asked. "What is you wantin' to speak on?"

Nat shrugged his massive shoulders, then laced his fingers behind his head. The tension in his person visible.

"Shit…" he muttered. "Anything you want."

Then it hit her–what was happening; Sunday grinned. Nat was jealous about her time at the barracks. She had forgotten all about it.

"You ain't like me at the barracks?" she asked.

"No."

"Thank you for appreciatin' what I has to offer," she whispered.

"Yeah," he replied dropping his arms to his sides.

"You should know…" Sunday replied. "The menfolk ain't like me being at the barracks neither."

Nat smirked. "Come eat wit' me."

The task of counting the women and children was finally complete. Black sat behind his desk while the women chatted among themselves. In this meeting, Elbert, James, and Simon sat in the back row to listen to the findings. He went through the numbers twice; there were two hundred and ninety-five men and three hundred and sixty-three women and children. Each man accounted for his family and the reverse was true for the women. All the women accounted for their children and men.

When he was finished going over the numbers, Black laid his fountain pen down and stood. Walking around to the front of his desk, his eyes landed on Anna. The room went silent as he allowed his gaze to move to Sarah–Tim's wife. He thought of Morgan's advice; he had to get used to working with the women.

"Anna–Sarah, is there anything that gave you pause?"

Anna smiled. She had always been shy, so Black was shocked when she said, "We had three of the women claim the same man. These women weren't as agreeable as Netti and Suzanne."

Netti leaned forward in a fit of giggles. Suzanne patted her back; she too was laughing. Black, used to the banter of men, was not ready for the women. Sarah chimed in adding, "Two of the women had full bellies."

Black's eyebrows shot up and he turned to look at Elbert, but it was James that spoke up. "Ain't funny one bit. Ole Vernon be lookin' awful tired."

Simon put his head down trying to hide his mirth, and Black coughed to bring the room to heel. The gathering fell silent once more and he could feel the anxiety rolling around the room. The women were attempting to ease a tight situation. Propping his right hip on the edge of his desk, Black began speaking through the numbers.

"Sunday, Morgan, and I counted two hundred and ninety-five men. Each man gave an accounting of his family. Yes… even ole Vernon. The count of women and children tallied to three hundred and sixty-three." Black said. "The women have the same accounting of their families. Even the unattached men and women could speak to the wellness of his or her neighbor. I'm happy to report there is no one missing from the fort. We are officially on lockdown."

"While it's a relief ain't nobody been killed, I's more disturbed we cain't say who been hurt in that carriage." Molly, Lou's woman said.

"Still could be peoples we know," Hazel said.

Black was about to comment when Jeremiah and Tim appeared in the doorway. Simon stood upon seeing them and stepped into the corridor. James and Elbert were about to follow, but Black called out to them.

"Simon!"

When Simon reappeared in the doorframe, his expression was grim. Black addressed the men when he demanded, "Come in and close the door–we are all in this together. Jeremiah, tell us what is happening."

The women swung their gazes to the back of the room. In truth, Black wanted to dismiss them, but he was sure that wouldn't go over well. He suspected Jeremiah, James, and Elbert felt the same. Simon was broader in the area of seeing the women as soldiers. Black knew Simon stepped into the corridor because the men were uncomfortable. Jeremiah stood at the back of the study, the late afternoon sun causing him to squint.

The black cracker cleared his throat. "Found a woman about a mile out–dead."

"Do we know who she is?" Black asked, afraid of his own question.

"No." Tim answered, but his eyes said something else.

"The men is bringin' her here–thought you might wanna look before we move her," Jeremiah said.

"Yeah," Black answered. To the women he said, "Do you want to meet when I'm finished? I can't say what that time will be or in the morning."

"The bad news will hold til mawnin'," Morgan said.

"I sees it the same," Sunday said.

Black reached for his hat before following the men out of the study. The men moved in silence back through the house, out onto the porch and down the stairs. Once they reached the path leading to the gate, they stopped walking.

"Tim?" Black said.

"Some of men think they know her–others ain't so sure," Tim said.

"Which group of men do you fall in?" Black asked.

"I think I met her before."

"So, you think I know her as well." Black said.

Tim's voice was low when he answered. "I'm sure you know her."

Black stared at Tim for moments. He refused to ask Tim to identify the woman. "Let's head out–we are losing the light."

CHAPTER 2

MEMORY LANE

On horseback, Black followed Tim and Jeremiah east once outside the gate. James rode on his left, with Simon and Elbert bringing up the rear. He could see the men moving about carrying out his orders to search a two-mile radius around the working parts of the land. The property line went much further than what was walled in–most of the land he purchased and some he took. It was the way of the world.

Spring was now upon them making the foliage thick and the trees heavy with fat green leaves. The speed at which they galloped along wasn't breakneck, but neither was it slow. A breeze blew causing the vegetation to bend and sway. Black could smell a storm coming, but they had time; the natural light was still happening. Out ahead of them, Lou, Frank, and Anthony stood shoulder to shoulder, and he couldn't see beyond them. It was as if they were attempting to ease him into the situation.

Black brought his horse to a stop, then swung from the saddle.

He vaguely heard Simon say, “Keep on wit’ yo’ duties, we got dis here.”

A few feet from where he left his horse, Black saw Shultz leaned against the side of the wagon. The doctor never gave him eye contact. When the area cleared out, Anthony, Frank and Lou parted allowing the tragedy to come into full view. On the ground, a short distance from the path lay a small form. It would seem at least two of the men removed their overcoats to cover the body. Still, one bare, scraped up leg was visible.

Before focusing on the problem, Black took in the surrounding area. The grass didn’t seem overly disturbed and neither did the shrubs. Turning to Anthony, he asked, “What else did you find?”

Anthony shook his head, but Frank answered. “Some horseshit was on the path–a ways up; too cold and dried up. It ain’t come from our animals.”

Silence fell. Stepping past the men to the body, Black stooped and lifted the overcoat that covered the face and upper torso. While he was no stranger to violence and death, he was ill prepared for the vision that greeted him. The woman’s features were almost unrecognizable. Her eyes were swollen shut; her nose was broken, and the right side of her head was caved in. Reaching out two fingers, he tipped her chin back noting the choke marks and missing skin about her neck. She was naked and there were slashes on both breasts.

Pushing back the second overcoat, he saw that one of her legs still donned a pink stocking and her foot, a black shoe. Licking the pad of his thumb, Black rubbed to the right of her navel to clear away the blood marring her midnight skin; regrettably, he found the identifying mole. His eyes smarted and when he looked away, he found his men standing with their backs to him. Covering her once more, he stood.

“Let’s move her to the fort,” Black said.

Frank and Lou pulled the pine box from the back of the wagon.

The doctor came forward and asked. "You want Miss Ruby buried today?"

"In the morning," Black replied, his voice unnatural and void of emotion. "I need time to think."

"I'm sorry, my friend," Shultz said.

"Yeah… me too."

Shultz and Anthony placed her in the box. Frank and Lou loaded her onto the wagon. The doctor checked the area where the body lay to make certain they missed nothing. Black stood with Simon, Tim, Jeremiah, Elbert, and James down by the horses. As the wagon pulled away driven by a disgusted Shultz, Anthony, Frank, and Lou mounted up to see the doctor safely home, leaving Black and the others to stand about in shock.

"Ain't no word come to ya from Spike?" James asked.

"No."

"Spike wanted her… if no word came from him, he's dead too." Elbert surmised.

Black feared no word came because anyone that knew how to contact him was dead. As the men around him tried to piece together the events–for Black, an image was emerging, and it was sinister. He didn't give voice to his thoughts, he needed to ponder. His ability to contemplate and consider had been the real weapons he used to keep the people safe. Yet this series of incidents seemed to mock and point out his fails.

"Black… is you listenin'?" James asked.

"I'm sorry–what?"

They were all staring at him and he wasn't sure for how long. Jeremiah took the lead suggesting, "Let's head home. My men will be headin' back soon. I wanna hear what they found."

"Yeah," Tim agreed.

Black nodded. It was all he could offer to the discussion. He was having trouble focusing, but he was aware that Elbert rode on his left and James, his right. When he nudged his horse toward home, his thoughts wandered back to the last time he saw Ruby. He remembered trying to needle Spike for the fun of it.

"I'm guessing you would prefer I not be alone with Miss Ruby." He had asked Spike.

"You would be guessin' right," Spike shot back.

"Spike!" Ruby had been embarrassed by Spike's forwardness.

"I ain't start it, Ruby; Hope did. I ain't 'shamed neither. I be here for ya every day, but ya ignores me for him." Spike had grumbled.

Ruby had been annoyed. "Why would I chase wit' you, Spike? Yes, you come every day to see me and leave every night to be at that damn whorehouse. I ain't sharing wit' no whores."

Black could remember Ruby all fired up with her hands on her hips.

"That ain't fair, woman. I would do anythin' ya ask of me, but ya keeps pining over him. Ya keeps this place like he gon' walk through the door any minute. Hope ain't so damn special," Spike had said, pointing an angry finger at him.

Ruby yelled. "Hope owns the place!"

Black could still see Spike scowling at him. He had played the innocent when he replied. "I don't own the place anymore. But you are incorrect about one thing..."

"Yeah, and what that is?" Spike had growled.

"I am special." He had said to make Spike angry.

Ruby burst out laughing, and he hugged her while smirking at Spike over her head.

"Be safe, Hope, and thank you for everything," Ruby had whispered to him.

"You be safe too, Ruby." He remembered saying, and now...

Black shook his head trying to remove the image of Ruby from his thoughts. What of Spike and the people of Montreal? He hated to think on it, but they must be dead. Spike would have come himself if he had been able; Black was sure of it. All of this left him in a major dilemma–did he ride out with his men or stay with his women? There was much to weigh.

The sun had begun its descent behind the hills and trees. Once inside the gate, Black swung down from his horse and a stablehand took the beast away. An unrest had settled over him as he headed for the barracks taking the shortest route. When he reached his destination, he didn't enter through the front with the other men; instead, he walked around to the back of the structure to linger in the dark. Elbert and James followed, but they did not attempt to engage him. His brothers allowed him to think, to grieve and accept that which he could not change; hours passed in silence.

"They are attempting to count us." Black said aloud to no one in particular. "Pull the men inside the gate, we will patrol the fort from within. Go–make the men aware of my wishes."

The retreating sounds of booted feet on the dirt path signaled their departure. Once alone, Black revisited the incidents. Pushing the scenes together in his head, he now understood them to be one event. He continued in thought until the wee hours. Shultz came to check on him, but no words passed between them. Later, Simon appeared and like the doctor, he gave quiet support. The black cracker showed up at about two in the morning–more silence. It was James, who disrupted his musings.

"You got the womenfolk in a lil bit and they ain't like us–they gon ask questions." His brother reasoned.

"I want to speak with Virgil; tell him I say come posthaste." Black countered, stepping over James' statement about the women.

"The twenty-two will ride out at first light to collect 'im." James promised.

Black leaned against the colossal oak that sat between the mess hall/laundry and the bathhouse. And though the backdoor of the barracks was ajar, the light from within offered no relief. He couldn't see his brother, but he could hear the stiffness in James' voice. Black sighed because he too wanted to experience the simplicity of anger and not the complications of grief. Heartache caressed his whole person like an unwanted lover. Untangling himself from the tree that he was propped up against, he walked away.

As he rounded the side of the barracks heading for the front, Black finally felt the drastic drop in temperature. The darkness was complete, yet instinct coupled with memory propelled him along the path. Reaching his home, he climbed the stairs and turned the knob. The house was cold, but warmer than outside. He passed through the kitchen on to the second hall; his footsteps were light so as not to disturb. At his bedroom door, he hesitated for seconds before entering.

Firelight danced in the hearth; the warmth of the chamber embraced him as he stepped over the threshold. A single oil lamp sat atop the small table in the corner where he took breakfast with his wife when time allowed. The wick was turned down low; moving to the lamp he outed the flame. Black undressed, hanging his gun on the wall by the bed. His expression softened as he stared down at the shadowy bundle that was his wife. Sunday was snuggled deep in the blankets.

Removing his clothing, he placed everything in the basket on the floor at the foot of their bed. When he was naked, he stood in front of the fireplace to warm his skin but being in his bedchamber hadn't given him peace. He figured it was the trust his wife displayed in his ability to keep her from harm–indicated by the way she rested without a care.

It was almost time for him to rise and meet this day. He considered dressing once more and heading for his study, discontent his latest companion. The dying embers caused him to toss another log into the fire. When the blaze leapt to life at his tending, Black stood back folding his arms over his chest.

"Nat?" His wife whispered; her voice sleep stained.

Black didn't respond verbally. Walking to his side of the bed, he climbed in. "Wooow…" Sunday breathed. "You's cold."

Pushing her onto her back, Black settled between her thighs. An unexpected feeling of desperation filled him; taking himself in hand, he angled his dick–just so and pressed forward to the hilt. Sunday was tight, hot, and moist. She let go a low moan as her muscles rippled around him. Black didn't move, but he did drop his forehead to hers. He wanted to mindlessly rut, but her words caught his attention.

"I's safe wit' you," she panted.

He took her mouth in a searing kiss. Capturing her bottom lip between his teeth, he then suckled her tongue and licked at the delicate curve of her jaw. Sunday was his everything. She changed the angle of their joining by wrapping her legs about his waist. He sank deeper into her body and had to break their stormy kiss to groan.

"Have me, Nat," she purred. "I's all yours."

He went up on his hands and knees to take some of his weight from her; the action caused her legs to fall from his waist. Pulling out to the tip, he slammed home and her cries of pleasure mingled with his own. He set a rhythmic pace of in–out–shove, in-out–shove. And when he felt himself approaching frenzy, he pulled out trying to prolong the inevitable. Black pressed his full body to hers, trapping his dick between them. He took her lips in another raging kiss before plunging into her once more.

It was the stroking, the friction, the ecstasy–the tightening of his testicles that confirmed two truths for Black: First–the mother of his children, his wife and best friend was safe in his arms. Second–she saw herself as protected in his care. He thought he would have more time to enjoy their connection, but Sunday's muscles clenched and spasmed. Orgasm took him by surprise and his stride faltered. He became frantic as he wedged himself within her as far as he could go.

"Black… Black..." Sunday sobbed.

In private and during tender moments, his wife addressed him as Nat. Her use of the name Black caused his dick to pulse, jerk, and spill. The euphoric haze of their lovemaking seemed unending. Sunday pulled him to her for another kiss. She wrapped her arms and legs around him–welcoming his weight. Black spun them until he was on the bottom. As he slipped from her body, he felt the gush of his seed flow from her, and it was better than good. She nuzzled his neck, kissed his jaw, his cheeks, and his nose. Black needed this time with her. They didn't converse and he appreciated that she hadn't demanded answers. As he dozed, he had a last thought. He could not live without Sunday.

His wife thought she was second to the fort, but nothing could be further from the truth.

* * *

Black hadn't slept long; next to him a light snore emitted from his wife. Swinging his legs over the side of the bed he moved about the chamber. He tended to his morning grooming as the early morning sun crawled through the window. Strapping on his gun, he bent to kiss Sunday's cheek. She stretched and opened her eyes.

"You ain't sleep none." She accused.

He kissed her again before stepping back from the bed. "I will meet with you and the other women later."

Black saw her concern for him, but Sunday only nodded. Turning on his heels he headed for the cabin where Shultz saw patients. He would face Ruby one last time before letting the men place her in the ground. The kitchen was empty, and he was thankful. He didn't want to be questioned by Mama. The older women must be tending the children, so the younger women could report to him.

When Black stepped outside, he found Abby on the porch. She smiled up at him. "Mornin', Mista Black."

"Miss Abigail," he replied, while stepping aside to let her in the house.

"I ain't going inside–already been. Big Mama got my baby, I was waitin' on you."

"Me?" Black asked, his surprise evident.

"The doctor is wantin' me to brang ya to 'im."

Black stared at her. He couldn't bring himself to ask, but he wondered if Abby had seen Ruby. He swallowed hard before advising. "You can point me in the right direction… Miss Abigail, you don't have to…"

"I don't mind," she said, her voice soft.

Black stared at her some more; he was trying to figure out how to make her go inside with the women. Abby wore a blue dress with a matching sweater. Her skin was flawless, black and spoke of health. She wore her hair in two fat braids; her brown eyes held his gaze.

"After you," he conceded.

Abby nodded, stepped to the landing, and kept on until she stood on the path. Black took a deep breath, then followed. When he joined her at the bottom of the stairs, she led the way. They strolled along for a few moments without discussion, until Abby interrupted the quiet.

"The doctor brung the poor lady to another cabin, not one what he sees patients in."

So, she *had* seen Ruby, Black thought. When he didn't reply, Abby went on. "The doctor likes to keep the livin' wit' the livin'. He say it fights sickness."

They walked a good distance turning down one dirt path after another. Shultz stood on the porch of the last building on the lane. The doctor appeared to be staring off unseeing, clutching a tin cup in his right hand. At the sound of their approach, he tossed his drink back and grimaced. Setting the dented cup on the railing, he gave them his full attention.

"Black."

"Doctor."

Abby didn't stop; she kept on into the cabin. Shultz looked, to Black's way of thinking, like he felt. The smell of whiskey on the doctor's breath said much at this hour.

"Shall we go inside?" Shultz asked.

Black stared off into the distance. He didn't know which was worse–viewing Ruby again or viewing Ruby again with Abby present. He shook his head, but still followed the doctor inside. The sun which fell through the window on a slant was coupled with three oil lamps for brightness; there was nowhere to hide. Once over the threshold, Black took in his surroundings. In the center of the one room sat a sturdy wooden table. On the surface lay the small form of a person covered by a pea green blanket.

Shultz stood at the end of the table by Ruby's head. Black moved to stand to the left of the table, opposite the window. Abby stood on the right side of the table down by Ruby's feet. Behind Abby, Black noticed for the first time the pine box that was used to transport his friend. To the left of the coffin was a stack of white sheets. Reeling in his focus, Black turned his attention to Shultz. Needing no further prompting, the doctor spoke.

"When you gave the order not to bury the young miss, I had her brought to this cabin and moved her to the table from the box. I figured you wanted to better assess the situation."

"Yes," Black said.

Shultz reached out a hand to pull the blanket back and Black cleared his throat. The doctor met his gaze and Black let his eyes drift to Abby. She in turn allowed her gaze to bounce between them. The doctor shook his head before clarifying. "Miss Abby has seen worse."

Black was sure she had seen worse, but it was his goal that she or the other women not have to deal with such atrocities. Shultz continued. "Miss Abby's job over the past few years has been to help me with the living and the departed."

He conceded with a curt nod, and Shultz pulled back the blanket to reveal a battered but cleaned up Ruby. Even with the swelling of her face, the removal of the excess blood made her features legible. It looked as though Ruby's hair had been freshly braided; her arms were folded over her chest fostering the illusion of peacefulness. She was so still that Black couldn't reconcile the lifeless form before him with the woman who had shared her body with his younger self.

There were many scrapes and bruises and he committed each to memory. Black wanted answers–no he needed to know who would be so bold as to leave her at his doorstep in such a state. In the name of modesty, the doctor covered her torso once more before stepping to the opposite end of the table to uncover her legs. Black cringed. There were more superficial wounds marring her skin. It meant she had suffered.

"The young miss suffered." Shultz said, snatching the thought right from his head.

Shultz didn't speak her name and Black appreciated the discretion. The use of Ruby's name while in the company of the women could only diminish this tragedy by causing questions regarding the irrelevant. Black wanted the doctor to leave and take Abby with him. He needed this time with her–he didn't want an audience. But before he could make the request, Abby addressed him.

"On the plantation, I took care of the dead for the slaves and the mast... I means to say the owner."

Unclear how to respond, Black nodded.

"A person what cares for the dead comes to see thangs not the same. Look here..." she said, gesturing for him to come stand next to her.

The bottom of Ruby's left foot bore more cuts and abrasions. Shultz came to stand behind him, but off to the right; Abby went on. "She tried to run–seen dem wounds on slaves before. Some slaves ain't had no shoes–some ain't had good shoes– same thang, I suppose. But the young miss's right foot ain't had no wounds. I took one shoe off her."

Abby pointed to a brown basket on the floor by the pine box. Inside sat one black shoe and a torn pink stocking. Black was still staring at Ruby's feet when Abby spoke again. She was now standing between the table and the window.

"This right here, ain't nothing I seen before," Abby said, pointing to Ruby's hands. "She tried to fight 'em off."

There was awe in Abby's voice and Black's eyes bounced up to meet hers. She shrugged her slender shoulders. "If'n you gon die anyhow…"

Abby's words offered comfort and Black smiled; still what Abby didn't realize was that all of this was his fault. If what he surmised was correct, it was his presence at Ruby's eatery two years back that caused her death. Black had climbed so far up in his head–he didn't hear Abby and the doctor take their leave. He looked up in time to see Shultz close the door behind himself. Turning back to Ruby, he sighed.

"I'm so sorry, dear friend." Black whispered.

Reaching out a hand, he caressed Ruby's cold cheek allowing the morbid reality to settle in his bones. Against the far wall sat two wooden chairs and Black pushed one up to the table. He turned down the oil lamps before seating himself to face the window… and her. Propped up by his forearms at the edge of the table, he pressed his forehead into his hands and exhaled. He remained at Ruby's side for one hour; and while he paid his respects, he did not plan or scheme. It was all about her.

The sound of horse hooves and a squeaky carriage spring brought him out of the peace he was feeling. Beyond the door he heard the murmurs of Shultz and Abby; their voices soon mingled with that of Philip and Chester. Finally, Black stood and made his way to the door–pulling it wide. Four sets of eyes landed on him.

"Is you ready?" Abby asked.

"Yes," Black replied.

Stepping onto the porch, Black squinted against the brightness of the sun. The doctor and Abby had gone inside; both shuffled about as they readied Ruby for the cemetery.

"Morning, Chester–Philip."

"Black," The men responded in unison.

Each man stood on either side of the doorway and Black stared between them into the distance. All that was visible were the tall trees and a dirt path that led to the graveyard. His voice was relaxed when he offered direction.

"You men come to take the woman?"

"Yes," Philip answered. Chester only nodded.

"Cover her but don't close the grave," Black said.

"Sho' thang," Philip replied.

Black's gaze touched the older men one last time before he stepped down off the porch and walked away. He would meet with the women and wait for the men to bring Virgil to him.

The store Everything was on the outskirts of town, yet close to the other establishments. Elbert rode on horseback with James at his side, while the other men fanned out watching all the roads leading in and out of town. They tethered their animals to a hitching post in front of the establishments. Stepping up on the planked boardwalk that led to the storefront, Elbert glanced about. James moved to stand next to him and neither man spoke.

The day was sunny but held a chill that was synonymous with springtime. Elbert noted that while it was early, he could see patrons already strolling the aisles of Everything through the large window. In the distance, he also noted more people milling about the walkways. After assessing their situation, he turned heading for the end of the boardwalk. Stepping down onto the soft earth, he continued around to the back of the establishment.

Virgil was a real businessman and three times a week he made coin by allowing local tradesmen to sell their wares in the back of his store. Each merchant paid a percentage of their earnings to Virgil, while increasing foot traffic to his place of business. It was a win for all involved. Folks came from far and wide for the opportunity to make market behind Everything.

Elbert wasn't shocked when he and James made it around the

weather-beaten building to find rows of merchants already in place. There was a mixture of folks, both colored and white, as Virgil's only aim was coin. The backdoor to the main structure was thrown wide and Virgil himself leaned against the frame sipping from a porcelain cup. His brown hair was wet and combed back from his face. When his blue gaze fell on Elbert, he didn't smile or offer greeting; Virgil turned and walked into the building.

"Go on. I got it out here," James said.

Elbert nodded before following Virgil inside. A small cluster of patrons stood discussing a painting that hung on the wall at the front of the store. In the back-left corner of the showroom, the office door sat open. Maneuvering himself between two large, black wood burning stoves that were for purchase, Elbert crossed the space to the office. Upon reaching the entrance he found Virgil seated on the end of his desk–arms folded over his chest. He wore a white ruffled shirt, blue trousers, and black boots. Virgil's pallor was off and under his eyes were dark smudges from lack of sleep.

There was no need to shut the door–there would be no sensitive conversation. Elbert extended the invite that was really no invitation at all. "Black wishes for you to lunch with him."

Virgil grinned. "And if I ain't hungry?"

"You'll come anyway... you ain't gotta be hungry." Elbert countered and he didn't smile.

The exchange caused Virgil to chuckle. "I will tell my help that I have suddenly become ravenous and will be gone for the remainder of the day."

"Frank and Lou will meet you out front with the carriage." Elbert said, then walked away.

As he made his way down the aisles of parasols, dresses, and boots, Elbert stepped out the store and back onto the boardwalk. Looking up the dusty roadway, he spotted Lou driving the carriage and Frank climbing up next to him, even as the vehicle moved in his direction. Once it was clear the twins spotted him, Elbert followed his original path back around the building. He found James where he left him–on the perimeter of the market.

"Let's go, the twins got Virgil."

"Yeah," James said, but he never looked away from the crowd or the beehive of activity.

"What?"

"Making market is gettin' bigger and bigger. Most of these folk–I ain't seen before," James said. "The white folk is downright hostile."

"Virgil told Black he was having trouble wit' some of his white patrons and merchants because he bought and sold–to and from coloreds."

"The war is spillin' into Canada." James replied with alarm in his voice.

Lowering his voice, Elbert said. "Canada is a place where slaves took their freedom. The war had to come here to dispute our claim to liberty."

"You gettin' to be like Black."

"I do be thinkin' too much." Elbert replied, while cringing with distaste.

* * *

During his meeting with the women, Black concluded that he really didn't understand the fairer sex. They listened intently as he explained that a young miss was found dead two miles from the main gate. When he assured them that he and the men were looking into the matter–the women nodded collectively. He felt sympathy emanating from them, but like his wife, the women appeared unfazed by the implied danger.

As he pondered their reactions, his gaze bounced from woman to woman. It was Morgan who asked, "Is we gon stay on lockdown?"

"I think it best for now." Black answered.

Anna, who sat third row, second chair to the right, piped up. "Me and Beulah will see about the old folks."

"Me and Sarah will check on the younger women... make sure they ain't fretting," Hazel said.

"Callie and me will tend the children down at the school," Emma said, and Callie nodded in agreement.

Sunday spoke up. "Me and Molly will see what Mama, Cora and Iris needs."

"Me and Mary will go on to the barracks," Morgan said.

"Miss Abby asked me and Netti to help her and the doctor," Suzanne said.

The ladies stood and backed away from the chairs in which they sat. Black realized with some amusement that the women were dismissing him. But when they would have filed out of his study, he stood, raised his hands, and spoke; his words brought the impending exodus to a sharp halt. The women were gathered near the door and all eyes swung to him.

Black cleared his throat. "So–I am not doing a good job of working with you all."

Silence met his statement–*fair enough,* he thought. "Jeremiah is a man that can shoot with both hands–he and Morgan will set up a schedule for lessons. You will breakdown into two groups. Lessons will begin at first light on the morrow–rain or shine."

The women moved back to their seats and Black continued. "Ladies, you will alternate between the barracks and the gate. Sunday, you will work with Simon and James to set a proper schedule."

"I will." His wife answered.

"Anna, Beulah, Callie, I see that you ladies are not wearing a weapon." Black looked about the study before adding. "Every one of you will wear a gun at all times. Are there any questions?"

A collective "No" sounded around the room. Black leaned back against the edge of his desk and looked around. "If I catch any one of you without a weapon–you will not be pleased with me."

Someone from the back row giggled, but he ignored it. "The men have gone into town to fetch the owner of the establishment Everything. I will meet with him to see what has been happening that we may not be aware of."

"You think he know who kilt the woman?" Morgan asked.

"I have asked Virgil here because I would be remiss as a leader if I didn't. I have no answers." Black replied.

"Seem to me–whoever hurt the young miss got them a heap of scratches and bruises just the same. I ain't sho' anyone could miss the one what tussled wit' her." Abby said and again, Black noted the pride in her tone.

"Good for her," Suzanne said.

"Damn right," Hazel added.

"Shit," Both Sarah and Sunday said at the same time.

"All right, ladies, you are all dismissed," Black said. As the women took their leave, Elbert appeared in the doorway. His brother had removed his leather hat and kissed Anna's cheek before she disappeared with the other women.

"Virgil is at your cabin." Elbert said.

Black nodded and headed for the door. Once outside, the brothers went their separate ways... Elbert to the barracks and Black to the cabin he shared with his wife. Following the dirt path around the outside of the main structures, Black walked for a few minutes before coming to his destination. Frank and Lou stood on the porch. Virgil waited beside the carriage. The situation was a tight one and Black could feel it even as he approached. A woman had been killed... a woman with whom his men were acquainted.

As Black drew nearer, Virgil looked up and his expression was blank; he looked like shit. His guest was troubled, that much was obvious. Addressing the twins, Black said, "Virgil and I will walk to the gate when we have completed our visit."

The twins offered nothing as they stepped down from the porch, climbed into the carriage and drove away. When they were alone on the path, Black stared at Virgil, who cast his eyes back to his feet. He didn't move to escort his guest inside the cabin, for Virgil looked as though he would toss his belly right where they stood.

"You ill, my friend?"

Virgil's eyes snapped up to meet his own, and Black could see his fear. "You shouldn't have demanded my presence."

Black moved his head from side to side, studying his longtime associate. Virgil had always been an ally, but his fascination with coin left Black leery about his loyalty. He had never betrayed the fort, but then Black never put himself in a position to find out if Virgil's allegiance was for sale to the highest bidder.

"So, you know who killed the woman?"

At the mention of Ruby, Virgil crossed the dirt path and stepped into the grass that lined the edge of the trail; he tossed up his belly. Black felt the same, but he managed nonchalance as he waited for Virgil to gather himself. The other man was still hunched over hands to knees–panting and retching. When his guest finally straightened and crossed back to where he stood, Black offered the smallest of courtesies.

"There is a pump behind the cabin." It was the best he could do, given he wanted to beat the hell out of the other man.

Virgil nodded before heading to the pump. A warm breeze blew, and Black's exhalation was slow. At this very moment he struggled with anger, sorrow, and impatience. Crossing his muscled arms over his chest, Black cast his eyes in both directions. The sun was adjusting in the sky as the hour moved past noon. He had been about to turn his attention back to Virgil when his brother stepped from between the trees. But James didn't move toward him, instead he disappeared back into the thicket.

Behind him, Black heard Virgil's unsteady gait as he walked through the grass and dried twigs. Turning toward the shorter man, Black remained quiet, refusing to repeat himself. Virgil took the cue, growing paler in the face of his scrutiny. His guest was nervous, speaking in sentences that went nowhere as far Black was concerned.

"It started when your smithy came to make market. The war between the states is spilling over into Canada. Some of my white patrons don't want me doing business with slaves..."

When Virgil stopped speaking, Black did not fill the silence. He waited, giving Virgil time to think on his words. Black did keep eye contact, almost daring the other man to look away. Virgil went on.

"I stepped in on behalf of Odell against three white men. I thought the issue resolved, but they came back. And not to Everything–they came to my home. I have a colored hand who has been with me for about five years–they beat him, bad."

Black recalled meeting the field hand that Virgil spoke of and if memory served, his name was Percy. What Black found interesting, Virgil raised chickens, that was it–no real farming took place on his land. "Your field hand... is he on the mend?"

Virgil's eyes watered. His voice was thick with tears; he didn't answer the question of Percy's well-being. "I moved him from my land to the room above the store. It's safest for now."

When Virgil coughed to cover the fact that he was about to cry, Black looked away. The pain he witnessed in the other man's eyes ran deep. But how did all this translate to his world... to Ruby? He had been about to voice his thoughts when Virgil started rambling.

"Eight men came to my home a few nights ago. Three of them were involved in the sale with your smithy from a year ago. I had forgotten who they were–but they had not forgotten me."

Virgil stared off as if remembering, and then he broke down. A loud sob ripped from him and though Black wanted answers, his guest it appeared had a question of his own.

"D-Did you..." Virgil stuttered, then tried to collect himself. "Did you find the man that was with her?"

"Man?" Black replied.

"She begged them not to hurt the man with her. The man, in

turn, pleaded with them for her life… shit–to no avail." Virgil choked, turned his back, and wiped at his eyes. "They killed him in the carriage–the woman, they dragged away with rope about the neck. She swore she didn't know anyone named Hope."

Black was dying inside; Virgil's words painted an image far grizzlier than he had anticipated. Hearing about her loyalty—

"I confessed to knowing you," Virgil said, interrupting his thoughts. "I thought it would save her…"

Black squinted up at the sky, his own eyes stinging. He wiped at them quickly. Virgil still had his back to him, and Black was thankful for the few seconds of privacy.

"She fought them–as for me…" Virgil continued in disgust. "Well–I told them where you could be found." Virgil turned to face him, tears streaming down his cheeks. It seemed his guest had given up on trying to hide his emotions. "It did no good. She is dead, and they beat Percy to keep me talking."

"What did you tell them?" Black asked, the timbre of his words thick with hurt.

The question Black posed caused his guest to become irate. Stretching his arms out in defeat Virgil glared at him. The other man's indignation was large, but Black showed no reaction as he assessed. Virgil's right lapel was stained with spittle and his blue suit coat wrinkled. His brown hair was untamed and hanging in his blue eyes. The brightness of the sun added so much detail to the situation that Black could not miss the accusation radiating from the other man.

"What could I tell them? You introduce me as a good friend, but you don't trust me. Our friendship consists of business only and though I have helped you in small ways in the past–you have never trusted me. I thought to save the woman; still, she is dead, and now Percy is damn near dead."

"You want my help, Virgil?"

Rubbing his hand over his clean-shaven jaw, Virgil stared at him for long moments. His musings fell flat in the space between them. Virgil was thinking aloud rather than answering the question. "I suppose it could be argued that I'm guilty of not allowing anyone to truly know me."

Black understood what Virgil did not say about the relationship between he and his field hand. But he had a purpose, and it was to maintain freedom, the people, the land... the fort.

"You can't help me, Black. Cavorting with my kind is considered unnatural, and it is punishable by death–not even you can fix this."

Black did not respond to Virgil's declaration, so one minded was he. "You will point these men out and you will do it today.

"Eight men came to my home, but I am sure there are more," Virgil said, and Black could feel the fear that rode him.

Black chuckled, a mirthless sound that was filled with promise. "You have only one choice at the moment."

"And that is?"

"Are you more afraid of them or me?" Black asked as he folded his arms over his chest; he didn't need Virgil to reply–there could be but one answer.

"They watch me." Virgil whispered. "They watch the town."

CHAPTER 3

MONTREAL

Campbell R. Penn was put in place by the Preservers of Southern Life to accomplish that which his predecessors had not. He would not capture and then ransom Lincoln–no, he would kill the president of the union army. And unlike the past group, he would not be made to suffer distractions. Most important, he would not be bested by slaves.

There was one major problem, and it was an enormous miscalculation on his part; the remedy would be no easy fix–these things never were. Campbell had undertaken a series of interviews; some of which were held in polite settings and others that came to a violent end. The goal, however, was the same in either situation–to find where his countrymen had failed and do the opposite.

It was his interview with John Booth that caused him to underestimate the situation. Three white men had infiltrated the ranks of the Preservers of Southern Life–a Dr. Morgan, his cousin Willie Morgan and a Brit called Bainesworth. Campbell's common sense had allowed for the possibility of a rival organization that was against the southern way of life; this he could handle. But when he began squeezing the darkies in these parts for information, the stories they told scared him... twenty niggers, collecting and gathering facts about their enterprise.

Armed with his findings, Campbell had traveled to a small, uneventful place outside of Ottawa; a town dubbed Independence by the dark locals. He traveled with thirty guns for hire only to discover that the slaves in question had amassed an empire–in plain sight. This propelled him to local government to find the name of the current landowner. Campbell had paid the oily clerk a few coins to gain the name of a *Hope Turner,* which told him less than the darkies of Montreal.

"Who exactly is this Hope Turner?" Campbell remembered asking.

The clerk, a white man of mid age with brown hair and brown eyes stared back at him. He wore thick spectacles that he kept adjusting and a white shirt with a blue vest. His hands were heavily stained with black ink, a testament to his position as recordkeeper. The slighter man offered no participation in what Campbell had hoped would be an enlightening conversation.

And so, it began. His trying to hire the proper number of men to see this matter through, even as word spread throughout the organization that their men had been left rotting in a carriage in Washington, DC. It had been a public humiliation, and Lincoln, of course played the clueless leader. But Campbell knew the union president was duplicitous, for the spies they placed at the executive mansion had gone missing–never to be seen again.

A knock at the door stopped Campbell's thought train, though he never did turn from where he stood watching the main thoroughfare below. The rooms he occupied on the second floor of the Grand Hotel faced the front of the establishment giving him a bird's eye view of all the happenings. Behind him he heard light footsteps and waited for her words.

"Sir, breakfast is served," Penny said, her voice soft–throaty.

Most southern gentlemen traveled with a valet, but Campbell journeyed with a female slave–who saw to all his needs. At her words, his attention swung from the window to Caroline. She was slender, almost six feet and dark of skin. Her lovely face featured large chestnut brown eyes with thick lashes and full pouty lips. She wore her long hair in two fat braids pinned at the top of her head. Caroline's mode of dress was formal and always in four bland colors–blue, black, gray, or brown; today was a blue day.

In the light of day every decency was observed, she was his loyal body servant. Caroline was older than his thirty-four years by five summers, though she looked much younger. Together, they had grown up on the Penn plantation in Georgia–him being the rightful heir and she, a house slave. His everyday life was hectic and filled with the pressures of maintaining during the war. At night, she was his company and they never spoke of his days. Campbell also never addressed her as Caroline, preferring to call her Penny; it was a play on his own last name and the fact that she belonged to him.

"I'll have coffee–Penny."

"Yes, sir."

When she would have taken her leave, he stopped her. "I will take my noon meal later in the day. Please have enough served for four."

"As you wish, sir." she replied, stopping to give him eye contact.

"That will be all, Penny."

"Yes, sir."

Campbell had already turned back to the window, falling back into thought.

* * *

Caroline assessed Campbell from the set of his strong shoulders to the stiffness of his stance. He was troubled and though she would never say, she thought him wise to be concerned. She'd heard tell of slaves who had escaped to Canada, but she couldn't understand how they managed once free. The life she led as Campbell Penn's maid/companion was charmed–she wanted for nothing. She had no reason to seek freedom. In his company she had become a well-traveled slave that partook in the finer things that life had to offer.

When she examined her feelings for him, there were times when she fancied herself in love and other times when she was no more than fond of him. She had been about five summers when Campbell was born, and it had always been her job to care for him. She took a deep cleansing breath, which must have translated to his ears as a frustrated sigh. He turned back to her, his piercing brown eyes searching her face.

"What is it?" he asked.

"Sir?"

"You're still here... What is it?" he queried.

She studied him. Campbell stood six feet with a mop of unruly brown curls. The bridge of his nose still held the gash from when she had dropped him as an infant–*she* still held the scars from the beating she had sustained because of it. He was broad of shoulder and well-muscled. Campbell dressed fashionably, but his style was neither gaudy nor overstated; he was no fop. The man before her controlled everything about her life. He was plain at first sight, but to glance again was to be engulfed by his appeal.

Unbidden, her thoughts wandered back to the year of her nineteenth summer. She had hoped to be granted permission to marry. Jasper, a stablehand had shown interest. She wanted so desperately to jump the broom with him; but when Jasper had asked the senior Penn for permission to make a family with her–he was sold posthaste. Jasper's mama never got over the heartbreak and blamed her. The loss was acute causing her to rethink her status as a slave.

After the Jasper incident, she was then given to Campbell to do with as he pleased. As the son of a prominent plantation owner, Campbell traveled in the richest of social circles. Along the way, he enjoyed the company of many southern belles, who were considered his equal in society. The master had only one rule where she was concerned; she was allowed no suitors.

Caroline hated herself for asking, but she needed to know. "Will Miss Beacham be joining you for dinner, sir?"

A slow smile crossed his face. "Why, Penny, are you jealous?"

It took some effort, but she remained expression free. Caroline was even careful with the inflection of her response. "What answer will be acceptable for you this morning, sir?"

Campbell barked out a laugh, she did not. "I would like the truth as you see it, Penny."

"Miss Beacham can be particular, sir. I wanted to make certain dinner was something she would enjoy."

He stared at her for long seconds before replying. "So, you think Miss Beacham–difficult?"

"I think no such thing, sir." She answered, conveying her boredom with the situation. "Miss Beacham threatened to lash me if she is served another lacking meal."

It was his turn to sigh. "Miss Beacham will not be joining us again."

"You..."

"You... what?" Campbell said, urging her to continue.

"You–sir... Miss Beacham takes dinner with *you*–not me."

Campbell eyed her; he was a cross between amused and annoyed. "You are dismissed, Penny."

"Yes, sir."

Caroline left his chamber heading for her chores of the day, which involved directing the hotel staff away from Campbell. She was disgusted with herself, for not only was she jealous–the very thought of her master laying with another hurt. At this moment in time, she was fancying herself in love with him. Her only saving grace was that she never discussed how she felt with Campbell Royce Penn. He was a thinking man, and Caroline was sure he would use such musings to her disadvantage. Being a slave meant she too was a thinker–constantly trying to stay two steps above those in the field. She cringed at the thought of living outside the comforts that had become her norm.

* * *

The suite of rooms where Campbell was staying at the Grand Hotel consisted of a master bedchamber, a smaller bedchamber, an office, and common area. It was the equivalent of a mid-size flat, equipped with plush blood red carpeting, a mint green settee and two matching chairs that sat facing the settee. Thick, red velvet drapes were pulled back from the windows and tied with black stays. His rooms dripped of elegance and his visitors took notice.

Campbell sat at the head of the polished oak table with two of his guests at his right and one at his left. Placed appetizingly before him on a white porcelain plate trimmed in gold were small portions of roasted duck, garlic potatoes and carrots; all of which he hated. He had to fight not to smile, Caroline's anger was apparent. She had him served foods he disliked making clear her unhappiness. There was no question, she deserved a lashing.

"Who appointed you, Campbell?" Carlton Renfro asked, and there was no missing the malice in his inquiry.

Both the question and the tone brought Campbell up short. He had allowed his thoughts to wander. Carlton sat to his left; the natural light from the windows was unkind. His guest had salt and pepper hair with a well-trimmed beard. Carlton's dark eyes were disconcerting; the right drooped, while his left eye, ever focused, glared about the room–counting the coin in Campbell's pocket.

He'd dealt with Carlton on many occasions, and it was always the same. Carlton's major worry seemed to be that others might get something meant for him. Campbell didn't understand such a concern because Carlton was one of the richest slaveholders in the south. Placing the fork beside the plate and dabbing his face with his napkin, Campbell gave unflinching eye contact.

The tension in Carlton's person was evident by the way he clenched his napkin. The white shirt he wore was travel stained and his gray suit spoke of his lengthy time in the saddle without benefit of a place to tidy up. Carlton Renfro was not happy, and he would make certain everyone knew it.

Across the table, Roderick Styles cleared his throat causing Campbell to look his way. Rod was around Campbell's age with blond hair that he wore pulled back in a ponytail. His brown eyes were dull, as if he'd rather be elsewhere. Roderick had eyebrows that were so faint Campbell wondered if he shaved them. His nose was sharp, and his lips were turned down in a constant frown. Rod was dressed in a blue suit that had seen better days.

Next to Roderick sat Jared Clinks, and like the other two men, he too seemed to be taking inventory of the hotel suite. Jared also had blond hair; his eyes were blue, and he had a snout for a nose. Campbell could see up his nostrils and the sight was unpleasant. They never said, but Campbell believed Rod and Jared related. Clinks and Styles were from Mississippi–Carlton Renfro was from Alabama. Campbell watched as Jared pushed back from the table and moved to stand in front of the windows. His brown suit wrinkled.

Clearing his throat once more, Roderick said, "You never answered Carlton's question, Camp."

"No, I didn't, but you are all free to leave the organization if you so choose," Campbell said, and there was no hostility in him. His words were matter of fact. "I am in place to see that all duties are carried out."

"So, the men who put you in charge have more money than Roderick, Jared, and me–is what you mean to say," Carlton said, rephrasing the conversation.

"I said what I meant, Carlton. I am here to distract, so that those in place can do their job. I have my own coin, gentlemen," Campbell's gaze swept over his guests. "There is no need for me to be concerned with your purse strings."

When Roderick would have spoken, Campbell raised his hand, pushed back from the table, and stood. He didn't walk away, but he did feel the need to be more upright. Campbell couldn't relax with his sitting and Jared standing. "This discussion has no value... let's not continue. What I want to know is did you all complete your tasks?"

His inquiry was met with a type of silence that bordered on obstinance. Clasping his hands behind his back, Campbell stared between the men. He cocked a brow and Carlton cleared his throat.

"When you left us in Independence, we started with the store owner as agreed."

Jared turned to face the room at large. "The owner of the establishment–Everything gave us Hope's whereabouts. We dumped the woman where she could be found."

"The man called Spike... where is his body?" Campbell asked.

"In one of the carriages we purchased behind the eatery," Roderick said.

The conversation lulled and Campbell took the opportunity to get the men focused on the goal. "Gentlemen, our purpose here is to keep the runaways distracted. It is to keep them from interfering in the Lincoln matter."

When the men nodded their agreement, Campbell went on. "How many men did you leave to keep watch?"

"None – they will have to travel to Montreal." Carlton said, and he looked exhausted.

"Good," Campbell said. "Three rooms have been acquired on this floor. Go rest, gentlemen."

Carlton stood, picked up his plate and started for the door. "I will be in my rooms."

They all watched him go and when the door closed behind him, Jared said with an air of annoyance. "Renfro is too old for this."

Campbell agreed with Jared's assessment of Carlton, but he wouldn't say such a thing. He didn't want to sow discord between the men. Roderick and Jared soon followed suit with Roderick taking his own plate and Campbell's untouched food. The meeting might have proved difficult, but they were now on to the next step. Life was about to get interesting in Montreal. He would send word to those that put him in charge.

* * *

Richmond, Virginia
March 1864

Jeff Davis removed his spectacles. Pinching the bridge of his nose and rubbing at his eyes, the confederate president leaned back in his chair and exhaled. He was exhausted, and it was only midday. His home office was part of a suite of rooms that was changed from a bedchamber–there was no door. The sound of booted feet along the corridor outside his office caused him to look to the open doorway. Burton, his personal secretary appeared, and he was anxious.

"Sir, a telegram has come."

Waving the thinner man forward, the president reached out a hand. Burton surrendered the message and waited for instruction. Davis' eyes scanned the one line:

OUR LITTLE ONE HAS TAKEN HER FIRST STEPS

The president read the line twice more before looking to Burton, who wore a blue waistcoat that buttoned to the left of his chest with matching trousers. His brown hair was parted in the middle and his eyes were dark–perceptive; his secretary was concerned.

"Mr. President?"

Davis smiled, then shooed the younger man away. "Go on back to work, Burton. I have no response."

When the younger man retreated, Jefferson stood and walked around his desk. He listened to the sounds of his house. The nanny was corralling his three older children, and his wife could be heard giving direction; his newest child was crying. The president reveled in the noises of his family, it helped him think.

As he paced his office, his thoughts raced. He had a new plan in place–one that could not fail a second time. The brown drapes were pulled back with tan stays. A white lace hung over the pane to keep out prying eyes. The day was overcast and dreary, but his mood was much lifted. Wandering over to the intricately crafted globe in the corner, Jefferson sent it spinning on its axis.

The president had not been hungry and so disregarded the meal brought at midday. This small win made him ravenous. Pulling out the black wooden chair pushed up to the table, he sat and ate. The meal consisted of squab, sweet potato, and cranberries. As he chewed and swallowed, one thought came to mind. All is fair in war.

CHAPTER 4

FORT INDEPENDENCE

The sky became heavy with dark clouds as the men mounted up at the gate. Frank and Lou would drive the carriage with Virgil as their passenger. It was well past midday when the gate yawned from being pulled wide. The twenty-two rode out as the rain began to fall and at the fork in the road the men split up. Black headed for Virgil's home with ten at his back. The remaining eleven headed for town and the establishment called Everything.

Black was discouraged by the weather; it meant the facts would be harder to discern. Still, he and the men rode for over an hour until they came upon a yellow farmhouse. Under normal circumstances the men would have left their horses in the overgrown brush at the edge of the property. But Black stepped his horse into the clearing without a care, trotting straight up to the front porch. The men fanned out taking every precaution that he did not. His brothers flanked him and as Black swung down from the saddle, Elbert offered a warning.

"Watch yerself–Hope."

"Yeah," Black replied, but he didn't look at Elbert. His next words were morbid and necessary. "The men we seek aren't here–I'm certain of that. Have the men search for Spike's body."

Elbert rode off with the other men, but James swung from the saddle and followed Black up the stairs. The first three steps of the white porch were mud splashed; the roof stuck out far enough to protect them from the steady downpour. Producing a skeleton key from his pocket, Black made quick work of the lock. Removing his hat, he shook the water from the brim before crossing the threshold. James did the same.

Black moved to the oil lamp on the table and lit it, immediately casting the room in equal parts light and shadow. Virgil's home was a step above a cabin. There was a great room that consisted of a living area, dining room and kitchen. James moved to stand next to him at the table, lighting the second oil lamp. The extra light brought a plaid couch into view that faced an unclean fireplace. Deep in the right corner sat a black wood burning stove with two pots on the surface. A small, white, round table with two matching chairs stood a few feet to the left of the fireplace.

At the back of the house were two doors and both were open. One door led to an office with an oversize cherry wood desk, weighed down by stacks of parchments. The drapes were closed, and Black had to hold the lamp up to inspect the space. The next room was a bedchamber and like the rest of the house it was furnished simple. A massive bed dominated the center of the room and it was unmade; the quilt and sheets were tangled, and both sides of the bed looked used. There were two night tables on either side of the bed–one held a glass of water, while the other held a glass pitcher.

"Black..." James called out.

Backing out the bedroom, Black found James standing in front of a bookshelf. In his hand was a piece of decorative parchment. When James handed the paper to him, Black's blood ran cold.

Holding the oil lamp and the paper closer together, his eyes scanned the page.

Montreal's Buckingham Theatre Presents

Romeo and Juliet
Friday: April 14, 1861

John Wilkes Booth........................ Romeo
Anna Marie Stone.........................Juliet

"The dates from a while ago," James said.

"But the threat is meant for now." Black countered. Spinning in place, he looked about Virgil's humble abode before giving James eye contact. "We are feeling the consequences of interfering on Lincoln's behalf."

"Yeah," James answered.

Folding the playbill and shoving it in his pocket, Black headed for the door. When he stepped onto the porch, he noted the rain had stopped. The sound of water running off the roof into the puddles around the house was the background noise to the scene before him. Nine men on horseback, dressed in black leather hats and coats to ward off the chill, waited for direction.

"Ain't no one here," Simon said.

Black wasn't surprised, but he had hoped to bring Spike home and bury him with Ruby. Nodding at Simon's words, he and James moved down the steps to their horses. Once in the saddle they headed for the fork in the road. Black and the men lingered in what was now complete darkness, until the squeaky carriage driven by Frank and Lou came rattling around the bend, accompanied by the thunder of horse hooves. The posse reunited and rode for the main gate of Fort Independence.

When the gate closed behind the twenty-two, the rain had once again begun falling in a light drizzle. The horses were led away by the stablehands; Frank and Lou parked the carriage in front of a cabin with an oil lamp flickering in the window. Black, Simon, and Elbert arrived on foot prepared to assist, but the twins and Anthony were already helping Virgil. The doctor was instructing them.

An oil lamp sat on the floor inside the doorway of the cabin, and Shultz carried the extra light. "This way... easy–don't jostle him too much."

Virgil handed the injured man out of the vehicle, while Anthony and Frank got him upright. Lou took hold of his feet and walked backward up the stairs. Virgil hovered on the periphery of the situation and per the lantern light–he was distraught. As the scene unfolded, Black realized he wouldn't get much from Virgil until Percy was stable. Stepping into the well-lit cabin, Black removed his coat placing it on the peg by the door. He dropped his hat on the chair pushed against the far wall.

The cabin they occupied sat alongside the cabin Shultz used to see patients. Looking to his brother, Black gave a curt nod in Virgil's direction and James took the cue. "Virgil, come on wit' me to get the buckets filled."

Virgil was shaking his head in the negative when the doctor spoke up. "Yes, I need clean water and my bag from the carriage. We need to get this place warmed up."

"I'll get the fireplace and the stove going." Black said, walking to the stove first.

Virgil gave in taking the bucket by the door and following James into the night. When he had the stove lit, Black turned to speak to the doctor and found Percy staring at him from the bed. Shultz was staring at Percy. Black had thought the patient unconscious, but he was alert. Virgil's field hand was a large man with weather roughened brown skin. If he were standing, Black estimated that he would be taller than his own six feet, three inches.

Percy's face was swollen and discolored from the beating he took. Black couldn't gauge an eye color and his bottom lip was split. His black beard was scruffy and though short, his hair was knotted and unkempt. Percy wore brown homespun trousers with a tan bloodstained shirt; he also smelled foul.

"Do you remember the men who did this?" Black asked.

"They killed the woman. I will never forget them." Percy replied. His speech was learned; he shook his head as if trying to unsee his own thoughts. His voice was thick with hurt when he continued. "She didn't deserve to be treated with such disregard."

"Names?" Black asked, trying to stay focused and not dwell on Ruby.

"They didn't use names, but I will never forget their faces…" Percy said, before looking away. "I failed her."

Black turned his attention back to getting the fireplace lit; he found that he was no longer interested in this man's thoughts. In the background, he could hear Shultz speaking with Percy about his injuries. The front door suddenly swung open with James and Virgil lugging in the water. Upon seeing Percy awake, Virgil put the bucket down in the middle of the cabin and rushed to his side.

"Oh, love, I've been so worried. Are you feeling any better?" The cabin went silent as they all witnessed the emotions stirring between Virgil and his field hand. Percy gasped.

It was the doctor who remained centered on the matter and to Percy, Shultz said. "Let's get you cleaned up, so I can assess the situation."

Like most of the cabins at the fort, there was a full-size bed in the corner, a small wooden table, and a black potbellied stove. The window on the back wall was covered with homespun drapes of tan. Beneath the window, a large tin tub sat upside down. James dragged it to the middle of the room before pouring in the water from the bucket Virgil left in the center of the floor.

"I'll get ya some more water, Doc," James said as he headed for the door.

Shultz grunted.

When the fireplace came to life under Black's skilled hand, he turned to Shultz. "You need help?"

Shultz shook his head. "I think we can manage."

"I'll be at my cabin when you're done here," Black said before grabbing his hat from the chair and his coat from the peg by the door.

"All right," Shultz answered.

As he reached for the doorknob, Virgil spoke. "Black..."

At the sound of Virgil's voice, Black turned to face him. Virgil's eyes were red, but there were no tears. His skin was pale, and his clothes rumpled. He pushed his fingers through his hair displaying the anxiety he was feeling; still, he managed to get out two words.

"Thank you."

Black was used to being emotional with his wife–not the men. All eyes were on him, but he couldn't muster the words, so he nodded. Turning back to the door, he stepped onto the porch to the sight of Simon, Elbert, Tim and Bainesworth. A lantern was left on the planked floor of the porch. It was the ambassador who spoke first.

"I'm afraid I've caused you all some serious trouble."

"We are in this together, Ambassador." Black replied. "We have no time for regret."

"What next?" Elbert asked, as James returned with the water.

Tim opened the door for James and stepped in to help the doctor. When the door shut behind them leaving only Simon, Elbert and the ambassador, Black spoke.

"We go to Montreal." Black finally answered.

"Ya want me to stay wit' the womenfolk?" Simon asked.

"No," Black said. "I'll stay with the women."

"We got us two problems, don't we?" Elbert asked.

James and Tim had rejoined them, each with two empty buckets in hand. The flickering light from the inside of the cabin became large, then disappeared with the opening and closing of the door. His brother and Tim stood next to Elbert as if waiting for Black's answer.

A chill clung to the air and in the lantern light Black studied the men before him. Each man's expression held the grim reality of Ruby's demise. The rain had stopped, but the dampness only added to the cold. Black knew they were waiting for him to have all the answers, but he deflected leaving Elbert to explain what he saw as two problems.

"You see two issues?" Black asked.

"I do... we bein' used as pawns," Elbert said and then he paused as if to gather his thoughts. "White folks wit' somethin' to lose gon kill Lincoln, and we can't stop it. They killin' our friends and the innocent to keep us in line."

"I see it the same." Black replied. "I will take a stand with the women. You all will go to Montreal."

"Is Virgil wit' us or against us?" James asked.

"He's not anything." Black countered. "In this situation he's a victim who got caught up in our punishment."

"But can he be trusted, my good man?" Bainesworth asked.

"We will see what Shultz says..." Black replied. "What the doctor sees will help me to see the matter a little sharper. In the meantime, tell the men to add this cabin to the patrol."

"Yeah," Simon said, before walking away.

"I brought his field hand here as an extra precaution," Black said. "In case I'm reading him wrong."

At those words no one spoke, so Black continued. "I'll be at the cabin when the doctor finishes here."

As he stepped from the porch onto the trail, he heard Elbert say, "Montreal will be another cleanup."

And to Black's way of thinking, Elbert was right.

* * *

It was almost dawn when the doctor showed up to Black's cabin followed by the twenty-two. He knew it was wrong to have this meeting here and not at the house, but Black didn't want Ruby discussed in front of the women–his wife in particular. Shultz began his report.

"Percy has several broken ribs and three broken fingers. He was beat about the face and neck pretty bad. Virgil, I suppose wasn't beaten because he's white and they needed someone to convey their message."

"What now?" Jeremiah asked.

Shultz cleared his throat and Black took the cue. "Let's hear it, Doctor."

"Virgil fears for their life. He hasn't said directly, but his apprehension is evident," Shultz said.

"You think him a liar, Doctor?" Black asked.

"No… ahhh." Shultz turned red. "He and Percy…"

Black cocked a brow. "So, he's worried that when I have no use for him or his field hand–I will kill them for buggery."

"Yes," Shultz answered, and he appeared relieved not to have to explain the specifics.

Jeremiah chuckled and asked facetiously. "Is you saying they ain't brothers–like me and E.J.?"

The men laughed and it was Elbert who spoke his own thoughts from months ago. "Shit, I thought Simon and Morgan practiced buggery when I first met them. I ain't know Morgan was a woman."

"Da hell wit' you, Elbert." Simon said on a chuckle. "Was you thinkin' not to work wit' us causin' ya thought we practiced buggery?"

Elbert sobered. "My only concern is can a man pull his own weight when we are away from the fort."

"I sees it the same," Frank said.

"If'n we kill Virgil's ass–it's gon be causin' he against us," Lou said.

There were grunts of approval around the room before E.J. spoke up. "We locked up his store–he understands he can't go back for now."

"The doctor is correct. Virgil was truly frightened." Bainesworth added. "His disquiet about the field hand is genuine."

"They waitin' for us in Montreal," James said, bringing them back to the real problem. "When is you wantin' us to leave?"

"Let me think," Black answered. "I just know it has to be soon."

At Black's statement there was no more discussion; the men dispersed, leaving him to plan. His next move would be Montreal–the goal, to see how far this calamity extended. He would send word to Lincoln, but what he did in Montreal would not depend on the union president's response. This undertaking would be to acquaint himself with anyone who could enlighten him about the Preservers of Southern Life. *Yes,* Black thought–*they would take hostages.*

Now that he could see his way to the next step, Black turned his mind to reconciling the ledger. When the morning sun eased through the window, he dropped his pen back in the inkwell at the edge of the desk. Pushing his chair back, he stood. Outside, the air was cold, the earth wet and the trail leading to the gate, soft under his boot. As he approached, Black could see that Anna, Morgan, Hazel and Beulah were among the men patrolling.

Black stood outside the activity waiting for James or Simon to notice him. His brother walked over first. "Elbert's at the barracks."

"Turn the gate over to Morgan. The men need rest, Montreal won't be easy."

"I'll get word to the men." James replied, before turning on his heels and walking away.

Simon stepped to him next. "Shultz is wit' Virgil. Percy caught a chill."

Black nodded. "The doctor will stay here with me. But you, my friend, will be riding out for Montreal. Get some rest. Morgan's got the gate."

Simon looked back at his wife, and Black continued. "I'm keeping Shultz here for the women and children... go rest."

Black understood Simon's worry; still Simon responded. "I's ready."

The men trekked down the hill but before they could reach Black's home, Simon made a right on the footpath headed for his own cabin. As Black watched the blooming foliage swallow up Simon's large form, he realized that he too needed rest.

* * *

When Black made it to his bedchamber there was a bevy of activity. Big Mama was seated in the rocking chair laughing at the scene before her. His wife was chasing their son Daniel, who was holding on to the side of the tub trying to get away. Ben-Ben, his twin was naked and peeing on the carpet.

"Boy is ya tee-teeing on the floor?" Big Mama asked and then commented. "Ya daddy used to do me that way."

Nattie, his daughter spied him and squealed. "My daddy!"

She ran to him and Black scooped her up, kissing her with a buzzing sound that made her giggle. Looking to his wife, he could see that she looked frazzled; he asked, "You alright?"

Sunday scowled at him before accusing. "You used to pull yo nappy off and pee on the floor?"

"I'm sure Mama is mistaken." Black replied, deadpan.

"No, I ain't neither." Mama added with a cackle.

Sunday smirked. "I's tired and tryna get them ready to be with Callie and the other women."

Black nodded. "Let me help."

He dressed Nattie in an orange dress with matching ruffled pantaloons. Mama braided her hair, while Sunday tended the boys. Out in the hall Black could hear his nephew running and calling out for Nattie. Little Otis appeared in the doorway followed by Elbert, who was carrying Junior. Black chuckled, his brother looked weary too.

"They couldn't wait to see Nattie and the boys." Elbert explained. "Me and Anna gonna sleep upstairs. Dennis been up the last few nights, and Anna wants to be near for feedings. She been up all night between the gate and the barracks."

Black nodded. "Good... see me when you wake."

"Yeah," Elbert answered.

Junior squirmed from Elbert's grasp to join the other children. Cora appeared in the doorway joining the fray after kissing Elbert on the cheek. And that was how Black passed the morning helping with the children rather than resting. The women pulled two shifts, rotating between the barracks and the gate, while trying to maintain babies still at the breast–he could do no less.

In the late afternoon, Black decided to sit on the couch in his study for a moment. He was awakened by Elbert and James. Opening his eyes, he noted that darkness had fallen and the oil lamp on his desk was lit.

"What time is it?" Black croaked; his throat was dry.

"'Bout ten," James answered. "We just gettin' up too."

"Give me a few minutes," Black said and headed for his bedchamber.

His bedroom was empty, and he hated that his wife was out patrolling rather than resting. He freshened up and changed his shirt before meeting his brothers back in the study. The men didn't speak as they walked through the quiet of the house and out the front door. Their first stop was Simon's cabin. Elbert banged on the door.

The door was yanked open to reveal a frowning Simon. "If'n ya wakes the baby–you gon be dealin' wit' her."

In the light spilling from the cabin, Black saw Elbert shrug. Simon stepped over the threshold, shutting the door behind him.

Darkness engulfed them once more, and on instinct the men formed a circle and Black spoke his thoughts.

"You men will ride out for Montreal tomorrow at midnight."

Black's words were met with silence. He went on. "Tim, Bainesworth and Virgil will ride with ten extra fort men. These men will be in place to help you transport hostages but make no mistake… this is a cleanup."

"Virgil?" James said.

It was Elbert who answered. "We keep Percy for peace of mind."

"I thought ya said he ain't had nothing to do wit' it." Simon stated, confused.

"He knows for sure the men you seek. I can't let him sit and send you all off blind. I don't think he is duplicitous here…" Black replied trying to find the correct words. "But I would be negligent if I didn't consider the playbill we found in his house could mean something else. It could mean he is involved."

"He ain't gon wanna leave the field hand." James added.

"If he refuses my offer…" Black said, then decided not to finish the thought. He meant to have satisfaction in this matter. Virgil wouldn't be allowed to block him from the truth.

Elbert got to the root of the matter. "Can we trust stayin' in the colored sector?"

The concept broke Black's heart, still he answered honestly. "I don't know."

"Seems like we got us two jobs," Simon said.

"Find out what happened in the colored sector; why ain't no word come," James said.

"Ferret out who killed Ruby and Spike," Elbert added.

"I'm going to let you all work out Montreal. I have but one request." Black concluded.

"Anything," they all said in unison.

"Remain upright–life first."

Plan in place, the four men headed for the cabin Virgil and

Percy occupied. When they turned onto the lane, three figures stood in front of the cabin. As they drew closer, the light from the window revealed Frank, Sunday and Lou standing on the path. Black shook his head and turning to Elbert, he whispered.

"Our women's lives have been turned upside down. Montreal is cleanup–don't forget it."

"Yeah," Elbert grunted.

At the front of the cabin, Black greeted. "Sunday... Frank–Lou."

"Black," they all responded in one voice.

It took effort for Black not to ask his wife if she was cold. In order to respect her contribution, he didn't linger; instead, he moved on up the three stairs and pushed at the cabin door. The scene before him: Shultz seated in a chair against the wall with his head slumped down into his chest, fast asleep. Virgil sat to the table with his fingers wrapped about a bottle of whiskey. The owner of Everything appeared freshly bathed as he took up vigilance over the man lying still as death in the bed.

Virgil's eyes bounced up to meet his own, and Black knew the other man had been expecting this visit. The doctor opened his eyes, but he didn't get up or speak.

Black watched as his guest stood and moved toward the door. Virgil never let go of the whiskey bottle and with his free hand he reached for his coat on the peg by the door. Black preceded him onto the porch where his brothers and Simon waited. The twins and Sunday were gone, and Black tried not to be annoyed.

They didn't leave the porch, instead moving in front of the window. The dim light from within the cabin didn't offer much, but it was enough for Black to gauge Virgil's facial expressions.

"You will ride out with my men tomorrow at midnight."

Virgil's eyes widened as he breathed. "You would have me leave Percy... at a time like this."

"I would have you identify the men who killed the woman." Black countered.

"When you offered your help, you knew these men wouldn't be in town. You planned to hold Percy hostage." Virgil hissed.

Black remained calm as he explained Percy's status at the fort. "Your field hand can be a welcomed guest or hostage; it's all based on how you wish to carry on."

"I have done nothing to warrant this type of treatment. This happened to me because of you, Black. How could you ask me to leave his side?" Virgil responded and his tone was pleading.

"Two people were killed; your very own field hand was beaten damn near to death. Do I really have to explain the need to have these men pointed out?" Black asked.

The night was chilled but not freezing and there was no wind. Black noted that though Virgil had retrieved his coat, he never put it on. He stood there in the dim glow holding his garment in one hand and the whiskey bottle in the other. Lifting the strong drink to his mouth, he took a deep swallow and grimaced before nodding in defeat.

"Elbert will kill you if he finds any deceit where you are concerned," Black said.

Virgil looked over at Elbert and nodded once more. Black went on. "The Buckingham Theatre in Montreal–have you ever been there?"

"No," Virgil replied woodenly.

Black detected no anxiety at the posed question. "Lay off the whiskey, eat and get some real rest."

He didn't wait for an answer. Black walked away followed by his brothers and Simon. As the night swallowed them up, the men stopped when Black spoke.

"I'll send word to Lincoln, but he is not the authority here. You men are to do as you see fit."

"Yeah," Elbert replied.

The plan was simple, it would be organized chaos.

CHAPTER 5

THE BURDEN
APRIL 1864

Torches offered unsteady lighting as the men readied themselves to ride out. The temperature was mild, and Elbert hoped the weather held up. The route they chose would extend travel, still it was the best way to proceed into hostile territory. They would stop only to rest their horses and when they drew nearer to the goal–they would rest their bodies.

Bainesworth, Virgil and Tim had already moved out hours ago, along with ten extra men. It would be their job to find a place to camp out while the eighteen scoured the city for answers. The possibility of being recognized by members of the Preservers of Southern Life meant Bainesworth, Tim and even Virgil would be almost invisible. Elbert understood the plan; he would meet up with Tim and then bring the men together when it was safe.

He was standing between the horses when Black walked up, James at his side. Black appeared troubled and his words reflected his demeanor.

"The man who killed Ruby..."

"We will set everything to rights." Elbert reassured.

Black nodded and James clapped him on the back before backing away to effortlessly climb into the saddle. Elbert could see that Black hated staying behind, but his was an important job. Once in the saddle, Elbert said as much.

"My family is in your hands."

"Yeah," Black responded.

Turning his stallion toward the gate, Elbert rode out with seventeen at his back. The darkness was complete and while Montreal wasn't far, they would also only travel at night. Giving the horse his head, Elbert allowed himself to wallow in the fact that he didn't get to spend intimate time with his wife before leaving. Anna had her duties and the children; he had not really even glimpsed his wife the entire day, save for a few stolen kisses behind the barracks.

They rode for hours away from Montreal before riding toward it. James who had been bringing up the rear moved in beside him. Speaking above the sound of the horse hooves, James grumbled, "I ain't get no time wit' Abby before I left. I better not get killed–shit."

Elbert chuckled and shook his head, but he didn't comment. He was feeling a weight about his neck that had not been identifiable until they rode away from the fort. Black had shrewdly placed him in charge without using words and the men had conceded. He hoped he could live up to such expectations; shit, he hoped he didn't get killed either.

It was near dawn when Elbert rode into a small railroad town, alone. The men had broken down into several groups and fanned out for the purpose of safety. He was tired and so was his beast. As he took in the scene before him, Elbert noted the railcars which sat on incomplete tracks. The doors of some cars were pushed wide, giving him a glimpse of the people who lived this life. Along the edge of the tracks were crudely made cabins and tents. It was a shanty town, and the morning fog made the place eerie.

Elbert swung down from the saddle giving his horse a much-needed rest. The cloak of night was starting to recede when he noticed a lone figure walking toward him. He tensed, then realized that he recognized the gait of the man coming his way. Tim was dressed in black trousers and a brown overcoat. The temperature had dropped significantly, leaving Elbert to surmise that they were close to a body of water. When they were face to face, he stepped a tad to the left to keep his eyes beyond Tim.

"We couldn't get closer?"

"I ain't even try." Tim replied and the weariness of his tone caused Elbert to focus in on him.

"What is it?"

"Virgil…" Tim sighed. "He's struggling–he ain't made for what we do."

Elbert nodded as his horse nudged him in the shoulder. Mindlessly, he reached up patting the animal's black and white nose. Getting to the root of the matter, he asked, "Are we good here?"

"As good as can be expected," Tim replied. "The people ain't askin' no questions. It's mostly a colored town; it will pick up and leave wit' the railroad."

"Yeah."

Upon further assessment of his surroundings, Elbert saw there were some women, some children, and a lot of men. The people looked hard and it reflected their life. Rows of cabins and tents lined the acreage to the left of the tracks. The cabins seemed to be for the women and children while the tents were for the men. Behind the living space were lean-tos for the animals. Several of the makeshift shelters housed a few men who were bedded down with their horses. It was how he and James had existed when they first left the plantation.

"How long these folks been here?" Elbert asked. He had traveled much with the eighteen and the twenty-two; he didn't remember this settlement.

"They been here about three months." Tim answered. "Railroad cities don't last long."

As the sun rose, so too did the temperature. Elbert didn't want to waste another minute; he had a plan and when night fell again, they would begin problem solving.

"This way," Tim said, before turning to walk away.

They followed Tim in a straight line–first Tim, then Elbert and then the horse. Thankfully, Tim led them to a space a good way from the outhouses. Bainesworth and Virgil were hard at work pitching a tent; neither looked his way. Elbert was removing supplies from his saddlebag when Chester, Mamie's man, and Odell the blacksmith approached. They helped with his tent, then blended back with the men from the fort.

While the smithy tended his horse, Elbert crawled into his tent. Closing his eyes didn't shut down his thoughts. He ruminated over the distance to Montreal, Ruby and what could be waiting for them. Finally, he fell into a calculated rest; the plan tossing over and over in his mind. James and the men would be along soon–the thought gave Elbert comfort.

* * *

Jeremiah stood in front of Elbert's tent with E.J. and James. It was early afternoon and the sun shone bright. The persistent odor of burned metal hovered, while the sounds of men yelling, children playing and women chatting overstimulated. It appeared no one paid them any attention, but Jeremiah knew better. He felt watched and he could not shake the feeling. Allowing his eyes to lazily scan the scene before him, he glanced from person to person; he found nothing.

E.J. and James passed the flask between them as they, too, surveyed the situation. James' attempt at appearing nonchalant while guarding Elbert's tent fell short. E.J. suggested that he rest before nightfall, but Jeremiah ignored his brother; he would not be treated fragile. The weather was mild according to the other men, but Jeremiah felt a chill all the way to his bones. He wore full underwear beneath thick black trousers and a brown shirt. His overcoat was also brown and though he was cold, he left the garment open revealing two revolvers at his hips and one at his upper left side. He was making clear that he was open for business.

Jeremiah decided to move about continuing his evaluation of the railroad town. When he made to walk between the tents, cabins, and lean-tos, his eyes fell upon the source of his unease. A young colored woman and man stood together in front of a large gray tent. The woman nodded as the man spoke, but her focus was on Jeremiah. The man's back was to him, still the woman was in full view. She wore clunky black boots, a brown dress that looked well used and a too big black overcoat.

His appraisal was interrupted by the sound of E.J.'s voice and footsteps catching up with him. Jeremiah stopped but didn't look away from the woman who held his gaze. She looked to be about twenty summers, maybe younger. Her head was shaved and her skin dark; the girl had huge eyes and he guessed them to be brown from this distance. Abruptly, the man standing with her turned, following her line of vision. The man's expression held a measure of scorn when his eyes landed on the black cracker.

Where the girl's skin tone was dark, her companion was light. The man speaking with her also had a shaved head. He was dressed in mud splattered black trousers and a matching overcoat. There was no more time to gauge the matter; the man turned back to the woman, grabbed her by the arm and dragged her away. The man's hostility toward her caused Jeremiah to take a step in their direction, but E.J. placed a restraining hand on his shoulder.

"No."

The black cracker turned his eyes on his brother for seconds before looking back to where the couple had been standing. E.J.

was right. He couldn't go off half-cocked, they needed this place for the purpose of hiding in plain sight. Jeremiah decided to take his brother's advice on self-discipline and rest. Going back the way they came, Jeremiah strode to the gray tent next to Elbert's and crawled in.

Once inside Jeremiah saw there were many blankets and pillows. He wanted to punch E.J. for coddling him and though he would never say, the black cracker felt both comfortable and warm; he did rest, but he did not sleep. His mind was fixated on the plan and the sunlight that eased through the gaps in the fabric where the tent was tied together. He lay staring at the ceiling until the natural light faded.

He could hear the town gradually coming to rest even as people milled about. E.J. poked his head through the flap of the tent. "Jake and I are ready."

Getting to his feet Jeremiah stooped over, exiting the cloth shelter. On the left of the tents and lean-tos for the fort men, the eighteen stood in a circle. Elbert was at the center with Frank and Lou holding the torches. His words were clipped and to the point; he did not rehash the plan.

"You all are to remain upright. Life comes before all else." Elbert paused. Spinning slowly on his heels to engage all the men, he went on. "Trust no one."

At those words, the men separated once again breaking down into five groups: two groups of three and three groups of four. The townspeople gathered around the fires to eat and make merry. As the evening progressed, Jeremiah noted their men disappeared into the night. When it was his turn, Jeremiah walked with his brother to the border of the railroad town. Jake was waiting for them with the carriage; E.J. climbed into the cab and the black cracker climbed up on the driver's bench next to Jake –shotgun across his lap.

* * *

Elbert, Simon, and James stood in the darkness staring at the saloon/pussy parlor where Spike was known to spend his evenings. The atmosphere was the same as it had been when last he was here with Black. Piano playing and loud talking floated on the night air. Light spilled onto the boardwalk from the entrance of the establishment and Elbert felt it–a lawlessness that hovered in the space between him and the swinging doors; his blood thrummed.

Flanked by James and Simon, he crossed the uneven roadway and stepped up on the boardwalk. The crisp wind whipped about causing him to pull the black knitted cap Anna made for him down over his ears. Behind him, he heard James grumbling about the cold. Simon chuckled. Elbert stopped at the entrance looking into the saloon over the top of the doors. He was also giving Frank, Lou, Anthony, and Josiah time to get in place–they were the invisibles.

Pushing at the doors, Elbert walked into the night life of Montreal's colored sector. When he had come with Black all those many months ago, the bar grew hushed at the sight of his legendary brother. But tonight, though he felt watched, the patrons carried on displaying only a mild curiosity in him. Strolling up to the bar, he noted that the barkeep was not Sidney. The man before him looked to be about thirty summers, skinny and dark of skin. On his left cheek was a jagged scar and his hair was wild-knotted. His eyes radiated intelligence and the spectacles he wore magnified the fact that he was doing some assessing in return. He was dressed like most, in brown homespun trousers and a matching shirt; the barkeep was unfamiliar.

"What'll it be?"

"Whiskey," Elbert replied, dropping a few coins on the polished bar.

He looked beyond the bartender to the crudely made shelves, which housed the shot glasses. Elbert had no real intention of partaking, so he turned his back to the bar to evaluate the room at large. Everything looked the same as it did when he had come with Black; the collage of brown faces, the scantily clad women, the music… even the piano playing. But when he had come with Black, his job had been to gauge the situation, so while things appeared the same–they were different.

Elbert listed the differences. The barkeep was not Sidney; the piano player was not Jimbo, and the tables that occupied the great room now had two chairs; the changes were subtle but evident. He glanced to the doors where Simon and James were posted up. Simon stepped into view and nodded. Taking a cleansing breath, Elbert turned back to the bar.

"I'm lookin' for Spike."

The barkeep's eyes widened. "Who askin'?"

"Me," Elbert countered. "Is he in the office back there?"

The bartender slammed the shot glass on the counter and dropped his eyes. "Yeah–Spike back there… go on back."

Elbert grinned, stepped back from the bar, and shoved his hands in his pockets all in one motion. Reaching under the bar, the other man came up with a revolver already cocked. His hand shook, but the bartender had Elbert firmly in his sights. Behind him, Elbert heard the music abruptly stop and other than a few gasps from the women, the saloon/pussy parlor grew hushed.

"Fenton!" a man from Elbert's left called out; the sound of at least two more guns cocking sounded.

"Bastard askin' after Spike." Fenton, the barkeep growled.

Elbert noted Fenton's agitation and the unsteadiness of his gun hand. He nodded toward the door where the barrel of Simon's gun was visible. When Fenton's whole body started shaking, Elbert spoke up.

"Easy, my friend–put the gun down."

Simon pushed at the swinging doors, stepping into the saloon; his gun trained on the bartender. On his left, a tall older man moved into Elbert's view.

"Who is you?" the man asked.

Elbert eyed him; the man's clothing was of a higher quality than what he usually saw in the colored sector. While Simon waited for him to work this out or shoot this out, Elbert gauged the older man. He wore dark trousers, a crisp white shirt, and black boots. The man was light of skin with deep creases around his dark eyes and mouth. His hair was cut close; he never broke eye contact.

"Hope sent me." Elbert replied.

At the mention of Black, the bartender un-cocked his gun and laid it on the bar. In the background Elbert heard the clicking of the other two guns. Simon didn't move. The older man looked about, confused with the turn of events. Elbert narrowed his eyes.

"You new to these parts?" Elbert asked the older man, noting his southern drawl.

"I am," The man responded. "From New York."

"The tongue you speakin' wit' say you from the deep south." Elbert countered.

"Been free a little bit now. I don't ponder on my time in the south." The man said with a shrug of his shoulders.

The bartender waved his hand, and the music started up again causing Elbert to glance his way. Turning back to the taller and older man, Elbert asked. "What's yo name?"

"Folks call me–Petey."

"Petey?" Elbert tossed out. "How long you been in Montreal?"

One of the whores walked up, stealing Petey's attention. She was a dark-skinned woman wearing all red; Elbert didn't assess her. Petey turned to the woman and walked off mid conversation. Elbert would have stopped him, but the bartender cut him off.

"Let 'em go–he ain't one of us." Fenton, the bartender said.

"Spike?" Elbert asked.

Fenton shook his head, and Elbert continued. "Who is in the office?"

"Charlie!" The bartender called out.

Fenton walked to where the wood could be lifted on a hinge

and stepped out from behind the counter. Charlie, one of the patrons, took his place tending bar. Elbert eyed Simon, who nodded ever so slightly as Fenton started for the office. James remained posted up out front as Elbert followed the bartender down a small passage. Lamplight flickered from beneath a door marred by two bullet holes. When the bartender's stride faltered, Elbert offered threat and encouragement.

"Keep going."

Fenton looked back at him; although the space between the office and great room was shadowed, Elbert saw his uncertainty–his fear. Before they could push at the door, Lou yanked it open to reveal Frank standing to the left of the room with his gun aimed at the bartender. The office was simply furnished with a scarred russet desk and rickety chair. In the corner on the floor were several bottles of unopened whiskey. The window behind the desk was open as far as it could go, allowing a chill to settle over the space. Lou stepped out, closing the door behind him. His job was to cover Simon, leaving Frank, Elbert, and Fenton to talk.

"I thought you say Hope sent ya." Fenton inquired, standing with his hands up, palms facing out. "Hope wouldn't treat us so."

Elbert ignored Fenton's worried tone and got down to business. "What's been happenin' in the colored sector?"

"The southerners is here lookin' for help wit' dis damn war." Fenton replied with disdain. "Colored folks is divided."

"Divided?" Elbert asked and he was incredulous. "You sayin' colored folks don't understand the reason for this war. How could they be separated from the real issue?"

"They understands that freedom and coin is the matter..." Fenton answered. "But they being told when the south wins, they can stay free. The people is being told, specially the old folks, that they is still slaves."

Elbert stared at the other man feeling all at once defeated and pained for his people. He shook his head realizing that he had to address the whole problem. Allowing his thoughts to stray from the course for a moment, he envisioned himself punching Black. Sighing, Elbert stepped to the window. Whistling into the night, he waited until Anthony and Josiah appeared.

All eyes and one gun were on Fenton. Elbert did the questioning. "How many whores you got here?"

"Ten."

"How many rooms on the upper level?" Elbert continued.

"Five."

"When you say–Petey ain't one of us..." Elbert said, repeating Fenton's statement from earlier.

"He ain't one of us–he a newcomer."

"Spike?" Elbert pressed.

"Is dead–but ya knows that already."

"Ruby?" Elbert asked.

"Miss Ruby, Spike, Jimbo and my little brother Freddy been missing for a few weeks. Spike only one we found–he behind the restaurant rotting in a carriage."

"Names?" Elbert pushed.

"I ain't got no names, but that theatre and that hotel is where the southerners be."

Elbert nodded, he remembered going with Spike and the men to meet Freddy behind the Grand Hotel. One of the staff present that night had to be the cause of this. Jimbo, the old piano player–missing. Elbert couldn't even fathom how he figured into this debacle. Grabbing at the back of his neck, he shook his head. Battling the beast that was slavery was made that much more complicated by the ignorance of his own people. Shit, standing in for Black gave him pause... enlightenment, he found, was a burden.

"Who runs this place wit' Spike gone?" Elbert asked.

"I do," Fenton replied. "Me and Spike split the coin, but he wanted Ruby more than this place."

Turning to Anthony and Josiah, Elbert spoke. "We changin' the plan–I want all the men here tonight. Leave E.J., Jeremiah and Jake in place."

"Yeah," Josiah replied.

Elbert closed the window and pivoted on his heels. When he faced Fenton once more, he said, "You are no longer in charge here... I am. We will kill you if you get in the way."

Fenton gulped, then nodded.

"Your patrons?" Elbert asked.

"They's all regulars, but that newcomer. He nice enough, but he strikes me as one of dem highhanded niggas. The kind what gets that way by seekin' praise from white folks and wit' Spike gone..." Fenton did finish.

"The women, can they be trusted?"

"No."

Elbert chuckled. "When do ya close?"

"Lotta the men ain't got no home–they works and sleeps whereva 'round the place. Business ain't been good since Spike left. Got worser afta Spike and Jimbo went missing. It's like a damn boarding house now," Fenton said, his disgust evident.

"So, the people are scared to do business here?" Elbert countered.

"Why it don't make no sense that the newcomer wanna be here. Shit, we don't wanna be here," Fenton said.

Elbert didn't respond, instead he walked to the door and pulled it open. He needed to start taking control. Turning back to Frank, he ordered, "Bar the window–make sure no one else can enter through it."

"Yeah," Frank replied.

Allowing Fenton to go first, Elbert followed him into the corridor. Looking over the shorter man's shoulder, he spied Lou and Simon. He addressed Lou in low tones as Fenton kept on to the great room.

"Go watch James' back."

"Yeah," Lou answered as he headed for the doors.

When Lou stepped into the night, Elbert made his way over to Simon. "Change in plans. We gonna set up shop here–Ant and Josiah went to inform the men."

Simon never made eye contact as Elbert spoke. He watched the room at large. "Petey is a problem–ain't no mistaken. What we gon do wit' him?"

"We gon let 'em leave," Elbert said.

"I sees it the same." Simon replied.

Turning their attention back to the situation, both men took in their surroundings. Elbert counted nine men, including the piano player. The music was playing, and Fenton had gone back behind the bar. Charlie had gone back to sitting with a few men around a table. It seemed the women and the men were waiting for the other shoe to drop.

Elbert was deep in thought when Simon asked, "Ready?"

"Damn Black," Elbert countered for Simon's ears only.

But before Elbert could address the saloon/pussy parlor, Petey stood placing his hat on his head. His words couldn't be heard over the music; still Elbert was clear he was taking his leave. The older man walked up to Elbert and Simon, who stood to the left of the doors.

"Imma be on ma way."

Elbert shrugged and Simon nodded. Petey was asking permission and they were granting it. Elbert grinned causing Petey's eyebrows to press together. "Which one of the whores is worth the coin?"

Relief shone in the older man's eyes when he answered. "Trudy–she be worth the coin and the time."

Elbert chuckled; Petey nodded, then disappeared through the swinging doors into the cold of the night. Simon stepped to the entrance while Elbert strode up to the piano player and placed a hand on his right shoulder. When the brown skinned man looked up, Elbert shook his head; the man ceased playing.

Spinning in a complete circle, Elbert allowed his gaze to

bounce from person to person. His voice was smooth yet laced with hazard. "We are taking this place over, and I will not tolerate acts that undermine my authority."

Still slowly spinning in place, Elbert asked. "Who among you ain't understanding my words?"

When no one spoke, Elbert issued his first order. "Women to the right side of the room and men to the left."

Chaos ensued for moments as the people did his bidding. When two lines were formed, whores to the right and patrons to the left, Elbert turned to the women. "Which one of ya is Trudy?"

The dark-skinned woman in red stepped forward; she purred. "I's Trudy."

She had calculating eyes, thick lips, and a flat nose. Trudy wore her hair in two braids pinned atop her head; she was shapely. Elbert assessed her and found her to be a handsome woman; still, his words left no misinterpretation of their positions.

"You, Miss Trudy, are my first hostage." She gasped and Elbert ignored her to speak freely to the men. "As for you men–we will not be taking any hostages."

* * *

James had moved further into the shadows and Lou took his place at the entrance of the saloon. Once they were in place, a man rushed from the building, sprinting into the night. The darkness was complete in the colored sector and only three things saved the situation for James. First: his quarry tired quickly. Second: as they moved into the more affluent white area, lampposts dotted the streets; and while visibility wasn't perfect, it was better than nothing. Three: his travels with the men had prepared him for such a task.

He couldn't see Lou, but he was sure he was nearby. They followed the man to the back of the Buckingham Theatre which was across the roadway from the Grand Hotel. The hour was late, so the place was deserted. At the back of the theatre complete darkness engulfed them once more. Three raps on the wooden door in quick succession caused James to stop moving. Lou touched his shoulder confirming his whereabouts.

The door made a grinding sound against the frame as it was being pushed open. James turned his attention to the noise as a large white man held a lantern up to identify the man they had been following. James noted their conversation was familiar.

"Campbell–they is here. They's at that run-down saloon."

"Not out here, Petey, come in... come in." The man called Campbell urged.

Once the men went inside and closed the door, James whispered. "Go–bring three men from the fort and a carriage. We got us our first hostage."

Lou didn't respond, instead he disappeared into the night while James lay in wait. He imagined himself wrapped up with Abby speaking about everything and nothing at all. This musing distracted him from the chill and smell of trash. It had turned into a kind of cold with no wind, and still, he didn't move. The time was well past midnight but not close to dawn. Lou had been gone for two hours and James was starting to lose the feeling in his feet when the theatre door opened once more.

"Don't go back to the saloon." The white man was saying. "We'll handle it."

"I ain't finna go back that way." Petey answered.

When the door closed shoving them back into the inky blackness of the night, James relying on instinct caught his quarry off guard from behind; he tackled Petey–winding him.

"What the hell..." Petey yelped.

James had a knee in the man's back. Cocking his gun with quick, efficient movements, he ground out in low tones. "Quiet 'fore I blow yo' fuckin' head off."

As he was going over in his head how to tie Petey up, the darkness leaving him at a disadvantage made him consider staying like they were until his backup arrived. But Lou's voice floated on the chilled air, and James felt relief flood his person.

"We got dis here," Lou said reassuringly.

With the help of Lou and the other men, James shoved a handkerchief into Petey's mouth and tied him up. They carried him like a struggling log and tossed him into the carriage. Odell and Chester climbed in with their hostage, while Jack, a field hand from the fort, drove the carriage. This freed up Lou and James to back Elbert.

CHAPTER 6

THE MATCHING OF WITS
FORT INDEPENDENCE

Black stood to the left of the gate as it was being cranked open by the fort men. It was early evening and day three since the eighteen rode out. There was yelling as the men calculated how far to open the gates and how much to expose the people. He watched as the black carriage pulled by a team rumbled through the passage. Odell brought the team to a halt in front of a storage cabin and hopped down from the driver's bench.

When the smithy was close enough, Black greeted. "What have we got?"

"James sent ya dis one," Odell said, pointing over his shoulder with his thumb. "He name Petey."

Black looked to the carriage in time to see Chester and Jack drag a struggling man from the cab. Four men who worked the gate closed in with the torches, shedding light on the situation. Odell began speaking again, and Black turned his focus back to the smithy.

"Elbert done took over a saloon in the colored sector. James say to tell you that he spittin' mad 'bout havin' to fill yo shoes. Say the peoples is scared, so Elbert gotta address the whole problem."

Between the torches at the gate and the ones being held by the men in front of the storage cabin, he and Odell existed in a place betwixt murkiness and clarity. Still, Black could see the other man was exhausted. After all, the men were riding a long route away from the fort before coming home. It was a safety precaution.

"So, the saloon is the base of operation?" Black inquired.

"Yeah," Odell confirmed. "We sent yo' message on–like ya wanted."

Black nodded. "When will you leave?"

"When night come again."

"Go find your bed," Black said as he stared over the smithy's shoulder. "We got it from here."

"Yes, sah." Odell said before turning and striding away.

The evening temperature was mild, an indication that spring was afoot. Taking in the scene in front of the storage cabin, Black shook his head, then moved toward the commotion. The women stood in a semi-circle eyeing the structure. Black moved between them and the cabin but before he could speak, Chester and Jack stepped onto the porch. Upon seeing him, the men headed in his direction.

"James tracked 'em to that theatre–say he spoke wit' a man named Campbell." Chester explained.

"Elbert say the peoples is scared," Jack added. "Reckon he tryna ease they worries."

Black's eyes bounced from man to man. "See me before you leave."

"Sho thang, Black," Chester answered.

When Chester and Jack faded into the night, Black turned his attention back to his newfound warriors. The women, tired of being cold, were now dressed like the men in all black. Morgan, however, who had lived life dressed as a man for years continued in the frill of dainty clothing; she would have none of it. At this moment she wore a green dress with her gun strapped to her upper left side.

Black issued orders. "Morgan, Sunday, Hazel and Abby–you four will take the first shift. Sarah, Anna, Carrie, and Beulah–you four will take the next shift. Ladies, you will always guard this man with two inside the cabin and two on the porch. No one is to see the prisoner but me."

The women stood about as Black's voice rang out into the night. He grew quiet for a beat giving his soldiers a moment. "I will not question him right away–it is a tactic meant to leave a man up in his head."

There was silence, so Black went on. "Sarah, Carrie, Anna and Beulah, get some rest, report back here in five hours. I will not insult you all by repeating the need for caution. You are to remain upright–nothing is more important."

Black saw that the women were nodding before they scattered to do his bidding. Hazel and Abby posted up on the porch, while Sunday and Morgan went inside. Orders in place, Black began his trek around the fort. He needed to move to clear his head and ponder the fact that Elbert set up shop at the saloon. The situation must be more dire than he thought.

* * *

Inside the cabin, Sunday and Morgan took up their positions at the opposite ends of the room. Morgan stood by the front window, right in the prisoner's field of vision. Sunday stood behind the man, essentially hiding from his scrutiny. Although she would never say such a thing, Sunday was unnerved by the situation, while her counterpart, Morgan, appeared unfazed.

When she entered the cabin after Morgan, she rushed past the prisoner, pressing her back to the far wall. She didn't look his way for fear he would be able to detect her frailties. The setup of the cabin added to her stress–the atmosphere was meant to intimidate. There were wooden crates stacked in the corner and the floor was littered with blood-stained hay. A lantern hung from one of the ceiling beams to the right of the door. Sunday was so engrossed in assessing her surroundings that the suddenness of the man's voice caused her to jump.

"Who the hell is you?" he snapped; his words hit like the nasty recoil of a whip.

Morgan, who was facing the window with her hands clasped behind her back, offered no reaction when she turned to face him. Her tone was even when she replied. "Imma be the one doin' the askin' here. What yo' name is?"

"I ain't done nothin' wrong! Untie. Me. Now!" Their captive bellowed as he struggled in his restraints.

Sunday saw that his hands were cuffed behind his back and his ankles were shackled together with an extra chain joining both set of restraints. She hadn't experienced real threat since she married Nat; still, this situation was emotionally taxing. As she dealt with her anxiety, Morgan's words pulled her from her self-pity.

"Shut yo' ass up."

"When I get loose from here..." their hostage growled. "Imma kill both of ya."

Trying for calm, Sunday focused in on Morgan. Her friend wore a forest green dress with bone colored lace at the throat. The bodice of the garment was fitted and showed off Morgan's slender form. She also wore a bone-colored overcoat that went well with her dress. Sunday thought her friend was dressed for tea with the womenfolk rather than patrolling. Morgan couldn't cook or sew, but she could handle a gun as good as any man.

"Untie me!" the man yelled again.

Morgan looked over his head; her words were nonchalant as she offered instruction. "We's women, so he tryna frighten us. It ain't neva gon be yo' job to match strength wit' a man. He weighs a few stones more than us and he taller–though we both seen bigger men."

Sunday gasped at her boldness.

Morgan chuckled, then went on. "When you's in doubt–out his light. The men will send us another hostage to be sho'."

The cabin grew quiet at Morgan's statement, save for when their hostage called her a bitch under his breath. Sunday watched as Morgan pulled her gun from the holster and running at their prisoner, she busted him upside the head with the pearl handle three times. Blood stained her overcoat; the immediate threat was neutralized.

"Shit," Sunday breathed.

"He not dead, but he gon wish he was when he wakes," Morgan said, then she grumbled. "Blood on my damn overcoat."

The rest of their time on duty was uneventful.

* * *

It was almost dawn when Black made his way to his bedchamber. He patrolled with the men, forcing himself to stay away from the cabin where the hostage was being held. The women needed to get used to handling the ugly, and *he* needed to get used to them handling the ugly; thoughts of Ruby cold in the ground were sobering.

Reaching his bedroom and finding it empty caused him to backtrack. His office was also unoccupied. He was about to go to Mama's room to see if Sunday was with the babies, but as he passed his studio, he noticed light flickering from within. Pushing at the door, he found his wife gazing out the window.

"Sunday."

She startled at the sound of his voice and the blood iced in his veins. "You alright?"

His lovely wife offered a weak smile. "I's fine, my love."

Black kept his tone coaxing. "Then why are you in here?"

"I's tired–but sleep won't come."

Stepping further into the studio, Black moved to stand beside her at the window. She kept her attention on the receding darkness. Sunday was avoiding him.

"You are unnerved."

She didn't react to the statement, and he saw that she was prepared to sidestep the conversation. Never turning to face him, Sunday replied. "Is you askin' me if I's afraid?"

"I'm asking if you need me, wife."

His words made her look at him; her response was soft. "I always need you."

Black opened his arms and his favorite person in the whole world stepped into his embrace. Sunday buried her face against his chest while hugging him tight. She was trembling and it caused his heart to squeeze.

"I do feel unnerved," she said with her face still buried against his chest. "But I understands ya cain't ask the peoples to do what you cain't do."

Black smiled as he held her; Sunday was the perfect partner for him. His wife was what the people needed. After a time, he released her, holding her at arm's length so he could look at her. She wasn't crying, but her eyes were wet.

"Let's go to our room."

Taking his wife by the hand, Black led her to their bedchamber. He helped her undress, and she did the same for him. Sunday climbed into bed, while he lit the fire and placed the grate in front of the hearth. After turning down the oil lamp, Black climbed in next to his wife. When he was comfortable, he allowed the coziness of their space to wash over him. The only sound that could be heard was the crackling and hissing of the fire.

"Morgan don't be nervous at all." Sunday whispered.

"It's one of the things Simon loves so much about her but hates about himself."

Sunday turned on her side to look at him. She was frowning. "I don't understand."

"Simon views Morgan's life with him as hard. He sees her having to live on the run as his failure."

Sunday sucked her teeth. "Morgan being able to handle herself ain't no fail on Simon. She is to be respected, and Simon is a good man."

"I agree... it's why I taught you to shoot. It's why Morgan is your right hand."

"The prisoner scared me." Sunday admitted. "But Morgan ain't study him naw bit."

Black grinned at his wife. "So, he was yelling and actin' a damn fool–trying to intimidate you all."

His wife's eyes widened. "Yes."

Black chuckled. "Shit, is he still alive?"

"Morgan clanked him upside the head. I thought he was dead." Sunday explained. "She was upset 'bout the blood on her new overcoat."

Black attempted to stifle his mirth, but his wife's face was so serious that he failed. And when he burst out laughing, Sunday eyed him until she too started snickering.

"It ain't funny, Nat," she tried to scold.

"Do I need to wait for another hostage?"

"He ain't dead." Sunday reassured, shaking her head.

Propped up on one elbow, Black stared down into Sunday's face. He felt better because he could see that she felt better. Turning the conversation back to the serious matter it truly was, he began teaching his wife.

"His name is Petey. James sent him."

"What is it we's tryna get from him?" Sunday asked.

"Whatever we can," Black replied. "James found him meeting with a white man named Campbell–that's all we know. It's our job to compel him to speak."

"After we get what we needs... what we gonna do wit' 'im?" Sunday asked.

"The men will deal with him once we get what we need."

Sunday stared at him for several heartbeats, then nodded.

While he hated that his wife had to deal with the ugly, Black also understood that being colored women left them no choice but to be strong. In his time as a slave what forced him to the path of abolitionist... he couldn't stomach the treatment of their women and children. There was no question he would do violence in their defense. Still, Simon had the right of it; he could not allow his need to protect the women stand in the way of their ability to safeguard themselves.

Black heard what his wife did not ask, and he wouldn't soften reality. "You are safe... Petey is not."

The sun shone through the window, a testament to the strange hours they now kept. Black decided that he was done speaking and thinking about business. Pulling back the covers he took in the sight of Sunday in all her naked glory, draped only in the light of the early morning; it was a sight to behold.

As they lay on their sides, Black pulled her until her back was flush against his chest. She turned as if looking over her shoulder to offer him her lips, her tongue, and her body. Black accepted all she had to give and lifting her top leg, he eased into her snug channel from behind. He tasted her moans of pleasure and couldn't get enough. Sunday was engaging all his senses.

Black strummed her clit, and when he applied the correct amount of pressure, she tore her mouth from his, panting. "Please, Nat... don't stop."

His wife squeezed around him, and Black allowed her orgasm to happen. This connection was about her and gritting his teeth against the sweet friction, he rocked into her again and again. His fingers skated through her dewy folds as he ordered. "Give it to me, Sunday."

And his wife did. She pushed back, impaling herself on him–

meeting him thrust for thrust. The tightness of her channel and Sunday's pleading words caused his dick to pulse. "I need this... Nat. I needs you inside me."

She became frenzied in her movements, her desperation tangible. It was sensation overload that pushed him right from the cliff. "Shit, Sunday, kiss me... I'm there..."

Their kiss was stormy–rough and as Black emptied himself within her, his thoughts were choppy, yet clear when he grunted. "Damn... Good."

The lovers didn't attempt to clean themselves up. They lay in a tangle of limbs, and as he dozed, Black could feel the very essence of him dripping from her sweetness; the thought made him hard again and he was grinning when sleep claimed him.

* * *

Sunday was still unsettled when she entered the storage cabin with Morgan for their shift with the prisoner. The only difference, tonight she wasn't hiding. She posted up at the window right in Petey's line of vision while Morgan played the back. It was as Sunday had predicted, Petey went straight for the intimidation factor.

"When I get loose from here... Imma kill both of ya." He growled as he pulled violently against the restraints.

Sunday feigned indifference when she turned and did what Morgan had done the night before; she lent all her attention to her friend, who smiled encouragingly. "I don't think they needs him anymore... Campbell say he finna lie anyhow."

Morgan's grunt was less than ladylike, yet there she stood wearing a rose-colored dress; the pale green sweater she donned had a collar that was shaped like the petals of a flower about her throat. The scene was perfect, and their hostage took the bait.

"Masta Campbell ain't here." Petey sneered.

Sunday didn't acknowledge their prisoner, treating him as if he weren't present. She had come to understand that Petey was simply attempting to save his own life. Self-preservation was to be respected–it would do no good, but it truly was to be admired.

Morgan added the extra carrot to sweeten the trap and her demeanor was perfect. "I has thangs to tend and nannying his ass when they has another hostage don't make no sense."

Sunday snickered as Morgan came to stand next to her. "We needs to do what we's told. The menfolk is tired of you changin' what they puts in place."

"Our hostage is colored." Morgan huffed. "I ain't fixin' to listen at what no white man they done caught say. I ain't in charge, but if they gon ignore us then I's done with dis here."

Turning back to the window, Sunday exhaled. "You's right."

"Damn right... I's right." Morgan snapped. "The mens is always tryna keep us busy, so we don't be under foot. I ain't no child. If'n the white hostage is tellin 'em what they wants to hear–why is we mindin' this one?"

When Morgan stepped toward the door, Sunday displayed the right amount of angst. "Where is ya goin?"

"Let the menfolk deal wit' this... I's tired."

Sunday nodded, then moved in behind Morgan as if to leave; Petey spoke up. "I ain't finna lie. The masta don't know what Imma say."

Morgan stopped, but Sunday kept stepping toward the door. Reaching out, Morgan grabbed her wrist before saying with exaggeration. "Wait."

"Is ya not listenin'–the menfolk ain't finna hear him or us."

"Yo' man ain't always right," Morgan said with an air of annoyance. "Least we could hear what he got to say."

Sunday stared at Morgan for long moments; her posture and the slight tilt of her head saying much. But before she could offer her thoughts, Petey said. "I ain't did nothing but ask questions 'bout some slaves."

Both women turned their eyes on him. It was Morgan who pressed. "Slaves… this is Canada, ain't no slaves here."

"Masta say all coloreds is slaves." Petey shot back.

"I ain't no damn slave," Morgan said. "Yo' masta in the next cabin finding out the same go for the men. Prolly why he blamin' yo' ass for every little thang."

"I ain't did nothin' but ask questions." Petey reiterated, his words laced with dread.

Sunday took the time that Morgan spent engaging their prisoner to study him. The man was older and light of skin. Along the right side of his face was a black and blue bruise from when Morgan had roughed him up. The eye on that side of his face was also swollen which made his returning gaze lopsided. His hair was cut close and barring the blood on his shirt, his clothes were kind of fancy to Sunday's way of thinking. Petey was perspiring, and oddly she felt no remorse. After all, he had warned that if he got loose, he would kill them both. She tuned back into the conversation when it seemed to heat up.

"When ya say ya just asked questions–what that mean?" Morgan inquired and her voice stepped up in pitch. "What questions did ya ask?"

"We asked after the twenty slaves what come to the Grand Hotel." Petey explained. "Masta wanted to know what the darkies knew."

Sunday dropped her hand from the doorknob. "What do the coloreds 'round them parts know?"

Petey shook his head. "They say Hope is the slave wit' the power. The coloreds say the fault belong to Freddy and Hope."

Neither woman offered a reaction to his words; the truth was, they didn't know what the hell Petey was talking about. The cabin fell silent and for the women, it was a tactic. Sunday was sure that what was being revealed had value, but she wasn't sure of its worth. Morgan picked up the thread of conversation.

"Freddy..." she didn't phrase it like a question. Morgan simply repeated the name, and her gaze was accusing.

"I ain't kill 'im," Petey said. "The masta did cause he say Freddy wasn't honest wit' him."

"So what you sayin' is–ya stood by while a colored man was murdered." Morgan's laugh was sinister. "Now yo' masta puttin' the blame on you."

"I wasn't there... I swears it," Petey said and his voice cracked. "I ain't never killed nobody."

"Ain't killed nobody..." Morgan mocked. "How long ya been helpin' Campbell plant fear wit' ya own peoples?"

Their prisoner had the grace to look away. Sunday didn't expect an answer, and Petey didn't give one. The lack of response made it clear that the old man had been a traitor for a long time. As part of the confusion that both she and Morgan were sowing, it was now her turn to appear his friend. Morgan changed courses; pulling her gun, she cocked and aimed at him.

"Wait!" Sunday said stepping between Morgan and Petey. "The menfolk gonna be riled if'n ya out his light."

"You hear what he is sayin', don't you?" Morgan snapped.

"I hears him sayin' he willin' to give us the truth." Sunday countered.

"I'm is," Petey said, his relief evident.

Sunday turned her back on Morgan and facing their hostage, she said. "Freddy is dead–who else Campbell lying 'bout?"

Petey's eyes bounced between her and Morgan; he shook his head. "Turn me loose."

It was as if Petey suddenly understood he was being manipulated. He shut down after his request to be unshackled went unanswered. Sunday tried to engage him. "Who else you and Campbell speak wit'?"

Petey ignored her inquiry and demanded. "Turn me loose and I'll give names."

Morgan rolled her eyes before turning back to the door and

pulling it wide. Sunday looked up in time to see her husband step over the threshold.

* * *

Black moved to stand between his wife and Morgan. Folding his arms over his chest, he locked his gaze on the prisoner. Sunday gave an accounting.

"Petey say he only asked questions in the dark sector. He say he ain't kill nobody."

Morgan countered. "He say Campbell killed Freddy. But I believes if'n ya check his hands they's stained wit' the blood of his own peoples."

At Morgan's words, everything came to a grinding halt in Black's head. He took a step forward dropping his arms to his sides. Dread slid over the prisoner's face as Sunday added, "Petey say the coloreds in Montreal fault Freddy and Hope for they troubles."

A vision of Freddy standing in the sparse lighting behind the Grand Hotel came to Black's head. He could hear the exchange and see Freddy's nervousness.

"I heard a ya, Mista Black. But I cain't thank of a damn thang I know that would interest ya." Freddy had told him.

"Let me be the judge of what's interesting, Fred. I'd like you to come with us, away from here, so we can speak freely." Black remembered responding.

"Yes, sah. Give me one moment." The trusting young Freddy had replied.

The silence in the cabin pulsed; Black stepped away from his thoughts and the past. Threat hung in the air between the men and when Black spoke his voice was cold–empty. "I'm Hope."

Black did not cajole; instead, he waited as the blood drained from his prisoner's face. Looming over the seated man, he watched as Petey bent his neck back to look him in the eyes. This was the part Black was good at–dominating the quiet.

"The masta took rooms at the Grand Hotel. We started wit' the colored staff first, that's how we learned 'bout Freddy." Petey explained. "It was a girl what told the masta 'bout you."

"What girl?" Black asked.

"Lucille… she were part of kitchen help." Petey answered. "Freddy say he ain't know a slave called Hope, but some of the colored staff say the girl was the one tellin' the truth."

"So, Lucille and Freddy are dead?" Black pressed.

Petey's gaze dropped to the floor and he looked like Black felt–defeated. "After the hotel, we turned toward the colored sector. We started wit' Ruby's Eatery and then the saloon. Campbell say he needed me for the saloon, and he would take care of the eatery."

Black was careful to show no reaction when he asked. "How long has this Campbell been at the Grand Hotel?"

"Few months… we come from Georgia and did some staying in Virginia." Petey replied.

"At the hotel, what room does Campbell occupy?" Black asked.

Petey furrowed his brow as he leaned sideways in his chair trying for eye contact with the women. Black stepped to the left blocking the prisoner's view of Morgan and Sunday. "You will not look to the women when I am speaking."

"You ain't caught the masta," Petey said and his tone was accusing.

Black eyed the other man for seconds. When he spoke, his voice held a type of menace that could not be missed. "What is Campbell's room number?"

"225," Petey whispered.

Black addressed the women. "Go inform Odell of what we have found, he will be leaving soon."

Looking back to his hostage, Black listened for the rustling of Morgan's skirts and Sunday's booted feet as they struck the planked floor; the cabin door closed behind him with a bang. And when the two men were alone, Black shared his grief with Petey.

"The people of Montreal are correct about the fault falling to me. I forget that there are those with skin like mine who have embraced bondage and therefore make the struggle for freedom that much harder."

Petey refused to meet his gaze, but Black was done with him. The cabin door creaked open and in walked two men who normally worked the gate. Zeke was about six feet and very dark of skin. Albert was the complete opposite; he was about five feet, nine inches with bright skin.

"You needin' us?" Zeke asked.

"Yeah. The women have other matters to tend." Black answered. "I will come for him later."

"Sho' thang, Mista Black," Albert said.

Turning for the door, Black didn't look back. Lamplight spilled from the window as he stepped from the cabin onto the porch to face the women. Hazel and Carrie were posted up on either side of the door, while Sunday and Morgan stood on the path in front of the storage building.

"Odell been told 'bout the room number." Morgan said.

Black was fuming, but he attempted to portray calm when he ordered. "Go find your beds and start again tomorrow."

The women did not argue, confirming their exhaustion. When the small gathering dispersed, Black stood about for an hour in the quiet of the mild night. He would give the women another thirty minutes before he stepped back into the cabin to extract what their hostage had not given freely. He would inquire about Ruby before he put Petey down.

CHAPTER 7

MONTREAL

Jeremiah stared down at the darkened roadway from the windows of the room E.J. had secured for them. Jake was sprawled out on the black couch. His brother was asleep in the matching armchair directly across from the couch. The space consisted of two bedchambers and a small dining area. He and Jake were playing body servants to E.J.'s whiteness.

The third-floor suite boasted of high-quality furnishings, thick, forest green carpeting and complementing drapes. A grandfather clock stood at attention in the corner; when it struck midnight giving a series of chimes, both Jake and his brother sat straight up from a sound rest. The black cracker waited as Jake and E.J. readied themselves. There was no conversation; they had been warned that the walls had ears.

Jake pulled the heavy wooden door wide, and E.J. stepped into the corridor. The plush burgundy carpeting traveled the long hall and the staircase as the three made their way to the lobby. Once on the main floor Jeremiah took in his surroundings. Behind the front desk stood a skinny white man dressed in a navy-blue bellboy uniform that boasted of large brass buttons. Given the late hour, the lobby was deserted.

Jake walked in front of E.J. and Jeremiah brought up the rear. There was no mistaking that they were E.J.'s personal protection. They continued through the lobby until they reached the entrance. When Jake pulled the door wide, E.J. slowed and Jeremiah stepped into the night first. On the walkway in front of the Grand Hotel, he noted two interesting facts: the mildness of the spring weather and all the lampposts on the opposite side of the roadway were out. The lighting from the hotel and the lampposts on their side of the thoroughfare only reached so far.

The Buckingham Theatre sat diagonal from the hotel, dark and imposing. Jeremiah stood to E.J.'s left and Jake at his right. The men gave E.J. enough space, while crowding his person. E.J. had been about to stroll down the walkway away from the front of the hotel and Jeremiah made to follow. His brother's steps were leisure until four white men stepped from the darkness into their path.

E.J. squeaked at the sight of the men, his temperament nervous and nonthreatening. "G-Good evening, gentlemen."

Jeremiah almost chuckled watching his brother present as incompetent. The group closed in on E.J. who took a fumbling step back. Jake caught him before E.J. could take a spill while Jeremiah observed the exchange. The taller of the men broke the silence–his grin shit-eating. "I believe the best phrase for such an hour is good morning."

"Y-yes, I suppose it is." E.J. stammered while trying to right his clothing.

"Awful early to be going for a stroll," the taller man said, his southern drawl suspicious.

E.J. turned to Jeremiah and requested in a strained voice. "My glasses."

The black cracker pushed open his overcoat to reveal three weapons–two at his hips and one at his upper left side. Reaching in his vest pocket, Jeremiah handed E.J. the glasses he did not need. Once his brother awkwardly placed the spectacles on his face, he mumbled a response.

"I am Hunter Edwards; folks call me Edwards. Who might you all be?"

"John Booth... actor extraordinaire."

The black cracker went for the assessment as his mind remembered the playbill Black had discussed. Jeremiah thought the actor a plain fellow with dark hair, a handlebar mustache, and a thin build. The lighting, though dim on the boardwalk, showed the actor to be less than fantastic. The man standing next to the actor was average in both stature and height. He too had a big mustache and dark thinning hair.

"The name is Sam Mudd."

"Rod Styles," a fair-haired man added.

"Jared Clinks," said the taller man and his tone held annoyance.

E.J. sensing the strain, breathed. "John Booth... the John Wilkes Booth. I saw you perform at the opening of Thalian Hall in 1858. You were brilliant."

Jeremiah watched as the actor took a mocking bow–all full of himself. His brother continued in his awe. "Come have coffee with me, I have trouble finding sleep. Your company would be a wonderful distraction. The great John Wilkes Booth... oh my."

E.J. clapped his hands together in glee and Jeremiah glanced over at Jake who remained stoned faced. While his attention was on Jake, the tallest of the men addressed him.

"You boy... what is your name?"

Jeremiah offered no reaction and no answer. It was his brother who answered the question, while the black cracker did his best to appear bored but trained.

"This here is Otis." E.J. explained then he pointed at Jake before introducing him. "And that there is Jake. They have been with me for years... they keep me safe."

"Safe from what?" The man called Clinks pressed.

"I'm a merchant, and there are times when the profession calls for peace of mind." E.J. answered.

It looked as though Clinks was going to continue, but the actor broke into the conversation wishing to get the dialogue back on him. "I would love a cup of coffee."

E.J. once again squeaked with pleasure as he turned for the hotel entrance. The actor fell into step alongside E.J. causing the men with him to follow. Jeremiah turned his back on the entrance as if giving himself a moment. Staring into the darkness on the opposite side of the roadway, the black cracker offered two curt nods before he abruptly turned on his heels and strode into the lobby.

James, Frank, Lou, and Anthony stood in the shadows on the opposite side of the roadway watching the exchange between their men and the four white men. Jeremiah had given the signal, there would be no contact this night. James spoke into the silence.

"Least we laid eyes on 'em."

The four headed back to the saloon. They would try again tomorrow to make contact.

Once in the lobby, E.J. picked one of the burgundy chairs with the huge, clawed feet; the actor sat next to him. Jeremiah stood to the left of the room out of earshot of his brother and Booth's conversation. Jake had taken up a position much closer but offered no reaction to the words happening between the men.

The southerners that entered the hotel with the actor stood about for a time then made their way up the carpeted stairs. There were sudden bursts of laughter between E.J. and Booth before they would go back to quietly talking with one another. The lighting in the hotel gave the black cracker a better view of the actor and his companions; still his assessment was the same–they were unremarkable.

It was just before dawn when the actor called it quits. Booth issued an invite. "I'm going to rest and then break my fast with friends in the dining hall; will you join us?"

"Absolutely," E.J. replied with enthusiasm. "What time shall we say?"

The actor grinned. "Around seven."

E.J. nodded and they all made for the stairs. Booth separated from them on the second floor and the trio continued on to the third landing. Once in their suite the men did not speak, but they did rest. And when the light of dawn trickled through the open window curtains, they readied themselves. His brother dressed in blue trousers, a crisp white shirt, and black boots. The frock coat he wore was gray. Jeremiah was reminded of E.J.'s time as a plantation owner. His brother, he thought, would fit in well.

Jake was dressed in a tan homespun shirt with matching trousers and black boots. His gun was harnessed at his upper left side, hidden only by a thin brown overcoat. Jeremiah was dressed the same, the only difference, he carried three weapons. When his brother stood heading for the door, Jake stepped in front of him pulling the door wide. The black cracker stepped into corridor first followed by E.J. and then Jake. The men moved as one, and when they reached the landing, Jeremiah found it to be crowded with hotel guests headed to break their fast.

* * *

Jake stared around the dining room, and like Jeremiah his facial expression registered boredom. He preferred roughing it when he rode out with the men and though he didn't talk much–not speaking at all was getting to him. He and the black cracker had been handpicked by Black for this ruse because they were both shorter than E.J. Black had explained that while Canada represented freedom for many coloreds, hatred still abounds.

E.J. found the actor seated to a table with a group of people who it seemed were of the arts. The conversation was animated with E.J. smiling and looking awestruck. At a nearby table were the actor's companions from the boardwalk incident. The men ate in a polite silence and their interest in E.J. appeared to have waned. The dining room was a formal affair with many round tables covered by white cloths. In the far back corner were a set of black swinging doors with a steady flow of colored staff moving about to do the bidding of white patrons. The clinking of silverware and the light conversational buzz became the backdrop to Jake's circumstance as he tuned out everything and everyone. He looked to the windows at the left of the dining hall and lent his attention to the sun spilling through the panes.

About thirty minutes passed when he felt a sudden shift in the atmosphere. The change, Jake noted was felt by all the men, both white and colored. Anticipating a commotion, he turned in time to see a tall white man enter the eatery. Jake assessed the new arrival and found him plain and uninteresting. But when he would have turned his attention back to the windows, his eyes fell on her.

A colored woman stepped out from behind the white man, her skin a deep chocolate. She wore her hair in two fat cornrows and her slim but shapely frame was right at six feet. Jake's breath caught at the sight of her, and he could not look away. She wore a dark blue dress with a collar that accentuated her slender neck. Her downward cast gaze dragged the floor as she strolled along in the man's wake. Jake wished she would look up so he could truly see her.

As if she heard his very thoughts, her head snapped up and large brown eyes, fringed with thick lashes, focused on him. Her intense gaze lasted for only seconds, but Jake felt it physically. The man before her continued maneuvering through the throng of tables, waitstaff, and patrons until he came to the group of men from the boardwalk. Based on distance and expressions, Jake gauged their dialogue to be benign. After a few moments, the white man moved on to a table for two, where he sat without pulling out the chair for the woman.

She strode toward the swinging doors and spoke with a much shorter woman. Jake watched as she gestured to the man. The shorter, plumper woman nodded then hurried off in the direction of the kitchen. Turning, she headed for the exit, and he was hypnotized by the sway of her hips and the way her blue skirts danced with her every step. Jake thought her perfect in the physical and majestic in her femininity. When she disappeared into the crowded lobby, his eyes lingered on the space she last occupied. Finally accepting that she was gone, he turned to reassess the man she came with… the man was gauging him in return.

Jake saw the possessiveness and challenge in the other man's eyes, and damn him–he couldn't look away. In his periphery he spied a swift movement at one of the tables. An angry E.J. stepped into his line of vision and spoke in low tones.

"When I step back drop your gaze. This ruse can work no other way."

"Yeah," Jake responded knowing E.J. was correct.

In one fluid motion, E.J. presented as angry and Jake as submissive. Once back at the table with his newfound friends, E.J. could be heard apologizing for the forwardness of his nigger… while Jake who kept his eyes cast to the floor plotted on how he could steal the tall, dark, beauty.

* * *

Elbert stood at the window gazing out into the early morning sun. He was listening as Lou, Anthony, James, and Frank gave an accounting of the exchange between their men and the four white men that exited the theatre after midnight.

"We ain't hear the words betwixt them but it was sho' hostile for a time," Lou said.

"Yeah," James confirmed. "Seem like E.J. got shit to settle down."

In the backyard of the saloon, the men set up camp between the barn and the main structure. A few chickens wandered about along with two goats. The men had to clean up the area to make it fit for themselves and their animals. Elbert had ordered the swinging doors removed and, in their place, a solid wood door was set. As he watched the men from the window, he realized he could delay no further and neither could he compromise the position of Jeremiah, E.J. and Jake.

"We'll start wit' the church," Elbert said.

"Yeah," James replied.

"The natural light is important." Elbert continued as he made his way to the door of the office. Lou, Frank, and Anthony had already passed through the frame out into the corridor that led to the bar. Before he could follow, James placed a hand on his shoulder causing Elbert to turn back and look at him.

"You alright?"

"Leading ain't easy like Black makes it look." Elbert answered.

"We in dis togetha."

Elbert could only nod, and James did the same before they stepped from the office into the plan. Walking into the lounge, the brothers found the patrons lined up. Nine men stood facing him and Elbert assessed them all to be before forty summers. Two of the men didn't look well and according to the whores they paid good coin to stare at the pussy.

Melvin, Oscar, Milton, and Emil were brown skin men of average build and height. Rufus, Gus, Fenton, Wilbur, and Cleveland were dark of skin and all at about six feet. Cleveland and Emil were the men who didn't look well. The latter were given less strenuous tasks; both were posted up at the window and the door to watch the activity outside the bar. Elbert had decided not to shut down the comings and goings in the area because he was looking forward to visitors; still, it had been four and a half days with no activity.

"See Simon." Elbert grunted and the men scattered.

Following the men through the dimness of the small kitchen out onto the rickety, weather beaten back porch, Elbert squinted against the morning sun. He observed the women tending the livestock; they feared him, and he pretended not to notice. Since he took over the saloon/pussy parlor the women no longer attempted to engage the men and at his request they were fully clothed. When they needed something, they sought out Simon, and Elbert was fine with the chain of command. Miss Trudy, his one true hostage kept to herself. When questioned she didn't respond; between them was a standoff and Elbert was losing.

Per his orders, the men were broken down into five groups of seven. Simon would man the bar with sixteen men. He would take six men and head to the church. James would take six men to Ruby's eatery–they needed to lay eyes on Spike's body. The remaining seven would continue to observe the Grand Hotel and Buckingham Theatre–those men would also watch Jeremiah, E.J. and Jake from a distance.

The barnyard was a bevy of activity as the men readied themselves for the next few hours. Elbert would take three men from the bar to help navigate the situation and three of his own men for the trust factor. Gilbert, Emmett, and Horace would see to his back while he watched Melvin, Fenton, and Gus.

Moving away from the back of the house, Elbert leaned against a tree to the right of the newly repaired chicken coop. A light breeze carried an odor of animal, earth, and spring; it was unpleasant. Simon, Tim, James and Bainesworth had formed a circle, speaking with one another in low tones. Virgil appeared at the entrance of the barn, his hair wet, and his face freshly shaved. The morning sun emphasized his paleness and lack of well-being. He was dressed like all the men in a tan homespun shirt, matching coarse trousers and black boots. In Virgil's right hand was a tin cup, a flick of the wrist sent the contents dashing to the ground.

Elbert assessed as Virgil, cloaked in resentment, walked toward him. Virgil spoke first. "I see the smithy and the other men made it back from the fort."

"They did."

There was a pleading in his tone. "Do they have news of Percy?"

Elbert turned to the thinner man and eyed him for seconds allowing discomfort to fill the space between them. When he spoke, it was to ask a question for which he expected a response. "Do you wish to ever feel safe again on yo' land?"

Virgil turned his back for moments; when he turned back, he offered a curt nod. Gilbert, Simon, James, and Tim approached just as Virgil strode away.

"We ready," James said and the rest of the men echoed the same sentiment.

Elbert didn't respond; instead, he swung into the saddle and moved out with six men at his back. Giving the stallion his head, he took in his surroundings. The establishments in close vicinity worked in conjunction with the saloon. Across the roadway was Sarah's dry-goods and next door was Mortimer the shoemaker. The enterprises weren't fancy, but they obviously served the community and a purpose. Several boarding houses also dotted the strip, and the men spent their hard-earned coin between the businesses.

It was clear that Montreal had grown since he'd been here last with his brothers and the men; the ex-slaves in these parts still operated from a place of mental bondage, and Elbert considered himself just smart enough to realize that he was no exception. He wondered how Black managed the role of leader in the face of the people's fear. His brother was longsuffering when dealing with the struggle of enlightenment; sadly, he was not Black. Elbert had one goal for this particular endeavor… *he would not manhandle his people.*

As they burst through the trees on horseback, a white church came into view. The stained-glass windows made the box structure appear human. A dirt path snaked through the tall grass right up to the front steps. At the right of the church, several horses were tethered to a hitching post. Further to the right sat a collection of well used carriages, buggies, and wagons; the morning gathering was full.

When Elbert brought his beast to a halt, he was greeted by the sounds of singing and piano music. Swinging down from the saddle, he stared up at the green double doors; the matching stairs showed fresh paint. Giving himself a moment, he turned taking in the field of wildflowers and the blue sky kissing the treetops. His inhale was slow and steady–his exhale was in the same vein. He ambled up the eight stairs two at a time and Gilbert followed. At the landing, it was Gil who spoke.

"We got it out here."

"Yeah," Elbert said before shoving the doors wide.

The music and singing stopped but it wasn't abrupt. Half the choir stumbled then stopped even as the other half followed causing the old woman playing the piano to look up. At the front of the church the preacher man and choir members were bedecked in gold and white robes. Suddenly, a collage of brown faces swung in his direction. Elbert didn't hesitate, he stepped forward onto the polished wood floor and made his way down the aisle; his booted feet echoing with authority.

When he stood facing the preacher man, he went for the assessment. The older man in the pulpit was brown of skin with salt and pepper hair; his perceptive eyes never faltered as he evaluated Elbert in return. Clasping his hand behind his back, Elbert tried for nonthreatening; his voice was strong–sure.

"I am Hope's man."

"We knows who ya is, son." The preacher man replied as he shuffled to the left trying to make room.

Elbert didn't move toward the podium; he was no preacher.

Turning, he faced the congregation. "I am here because Hope cares–because I care."

And with those few words everyone started speaking at once; raising his hands, the room quieted. "I can't hear all of ya at one time."

An old woman stood at the end of the second pew on the left. Elbert gave her his undivided attention. She gripped a cane in her right hand and held onto the back of the pew with her left. Her brown skin was creased, and her eyes were glassy. She had a chuff of cotton white hair and the dress she wore was a dark green; the fabric rustled as she steadied herself.

"They done kilt Ruby," she said, her pain visible.

But before he could respond a young man stood, and Elbert gauged him to be on the brink of manhood. "They dragged my grandpa away from our home."

"Who is yo' grandpa?" Elbert asked. "And who is they?"

"Jimbo," the young man answered, and his tone was laced with anger. "Some white men what wanted to know about Hope come for 'im. Grandpa ain't tell 'em nothin'. Now he gone like Freddy… like Spike… like Miss damn Ruby."

"The old piano player?" Elbert asked, trying to understand what he was hearing.

"Yes, sir."

"And your name is?" Elbert inquired.

"Folks call me Clem."

A dreadful silence fell over the church, and Elbert knew the next move had to be his. "I am here to serve you and deliver your concerns to Hope."

A line formed down the middle of the church at Elbert's affirmation and the problem became easy to see. The line represented who would speak with him and who would not. Elbert suspected that many would have left, but Gilbert posted up at the entrance was a deterrent. Horace and Emmett were posted up in the back securing the situation.

There were more women than men and more elderly folks than young. In the eyes of the older people, Elbert thought he saw relief. The younger people were another matter entirely–they appeared to be a mixed bag of suspicion, anger, and apprehension. Elbert saw much in their expressions; they knew what the elderly did not, and he was sure of it.

* * *

James took off on foot in the early morning headed for Ruby's eatery. The six men at his back split up with Ephraim and Josiah driving a carriage. Odell, Chester, Ralph, and Herman were on horseback. Elbert thought it best that this matter be handled by their own men–it was safest. The roadway held a light flow of flat wagons and scuffed up carriages that must have doubled as farm equipment and Sunday go to meeting transportation.

In the colored sector, James was sure word had spread that Hope's men had taken over the saloon. It was evident in the way folks watched him as he made his way to the southside. When he tried for eye contact, folks would instantly avert their gazes while calling out greetings to one another. James understood the plight of his people; he felt no insult.

As he neared the eatery, he observed that the structures in the area were in better condition though not by much. The establishments were an assortment of brown and gray buildings that were spaced out by the amount of land each business owned. It was Sunday, so many places of trade were closed for church. He feigned leisure while making certain not to look over his shoulder for his men; he trusted they were nearby.

James stepped down off the boardwalk and crossed the roadway. When he made it to the opposite side of the thoroughfare, he realized his mistake. His stride faltered as Ruby's came into view and three white men stepped from the building. James didn't have time to react, a man came up behind him digging the barrel of a gun into his side.

"Been waitin' on you, nigger." The man rasped against his ear. "Get yo' ass movin'."

James didn't look around–there was no need. This was going to be more than a seven-man job. "Turn me loose–ya got no cause to treat me this a way."

His captor shoved him in the direction of the eatery, and when he would have put up a fight, the man behind him threatened. "Betta look about..."

Doing as the voice in the background suggested, James allowed his eyes to scan the area. There was no missing the two-armed white men dressed in suits standing at the entrance of an establishment that sold animal skins. James continued glancing about, but it was his own men he was searching out. Most disheartening was the sight of colored folks rushing away in fear–trying to avoid capture themselves; his men were nowhere to be found.

James allowed his thoughts to wander to Abby and his children. Unbidden, his mind summoned up images of Mary during the time of Otis' demise. He didn't want that for any of the women, and he really didn't want it for his woman. When he glanced about once more, James counted five guns trained on him–six if he counted the one pressed painfully into his side. He took comfort in two thoughts. One, his brothers would care for his family. Two, his brothers would see Montreal burned to the ground in the face of his death.

"I say move yo' ass."

His goal was to remain upright, and so James permitted himself to be shoved along to the entrance of the eatery. Two blond men with thin builds stepped away from the doorframe so the man behind him could push him over the threshold; the third man lay in wait as he stumbled into the dining area.

James was met by a tall shadowy figure that stood facing him amid overturned tables and the smell of rotted flesh. Sunlight spilled into the restaurant from both the front and the back doors; the cross ventilation only made the smell of death stronger.

"Tie him up." The taller man commanded as he stepped from the murkiness showing half his white face and brown hair–his demeanor, haughty.

James' hands were yanked behind his back quite painfully and tied with the intent to stop circulation. He was then tossed into a chair that was positioned in the sunlight, while his captors remained in the shadows.

"I believe I know the answer, but I will ask the question just the same. Is Black and Hope Turner the same slave?"

James stared into the gloom offering no response.

CHAPTER 8

THE GRAND HOTEL

There was much that Campbell did not comprehend in his quest to protect the Lincoln matter. But the one thing he was certain of– the slave they captured had value. Pacing the common area of his suite, he contemplated his next move. Feelings of anxiety and accomplishment overwhelmed him; still, he had no other choices. Toppling the union president from his throne would have to be complete to save the south.

It was during those early fact-finding interviews that an image emerged of twenty niggers. And while he couldn't prove it, Campbell believed that the three white men Booth had spoken of were co-conspirators. It was his nasty exchange with the slave boy, Freddy that helped bring matters into perspective. He soon came to realize that while Freddy could speak of three white men, Booth had no knowledge of a band of slaves.

The key to this circumstance lay with the Brit called Bainesworth; he was sure of it. Spinning on his heels to retrace his steps through the common area, Campbell had yet another troublesome thought. The concept was so simple in its foundation that it could be overlooked with ease for a more complex idea. England was selling weapons to the south while also supporting the north. The queen was instigating this war and recruiting niggers in the process.

Campbell stopped pacing to run to his office where he retrieved the notes he had been keeping. He had to get the facts as he saw them down on parchment, so that he could bring his fuzzier thoughts into focus. When he finished jotting his musings, he moved to the window and gazed out. The midday sun was bright as he watched the people below strolling about. Across the roadway, the doors of Buckingham Theatre sat open. One thought tumbled over in Campbell's head as he stared off in the distance. What had the world come to when a common slave held the secrets of two countries?

A soft voice floated into the quiet. "Master, you have a guest."

Turning toward Penny, Campbell was brought up short by the vision she presented. Penny wore a dark pink dress with a tight-fitting bodice; the skirts belled out and danced with her every move. White lace trimmed the collar, sleeves, and hem. On her feet she wore black leather boots that were shined to perfection. Even her hair was different–she wore the thick kinky mass pulled back in a bun with decorative combs holding it in place. His Penny was a sight to behold, and Campbell didn't like it one bit. Narrowing his eyes, he was about to question her reason for dressing so drastically different. Campbell had been about to tell her to change and never do this again; but life happened, and it could not be ignored.

"Camp!" Renfro roared from the next room before he barged into his office.

Penny stepped back to keep Renfro from plowing into her. The older man drew his attention, and Penny rushed out leaving him to his business. Renfro continued. "We have us a problem."

Campbell stared after Penny for seconds before turning his mind to the issue at hand. "Renfro?"

"Did you hear what I said?"

"I did," Campbell replied. "Please get to the matter."

Renfro, he noticed, looked better–not travel haggard. His gray suit didn't add much to his complexion, but he did appear healthier. The older man paced before stopping abruptly to turn his lopsided gaze on Campbell.

"I think we caught one of *the* runaways from the town outside of Ottawa."

"I agree," Campbell said as he shoved his hands into the pockets of his blue trousers.

"They are a scary bunch... every southerner's nightmare," Renfro said while shuddering. "I believe we have poked a beehive."

Campbell agreed with the assessment. Renfro went on. "We should kill him and head south. The message will be unmistakable."

The problem to Campbell's way of thinking was much deeper. If they picked up and left, there was nothing to return to. The country was war-torn and there was no getting around it; even Richmond bore the marks of conflict. England recruiting organized slaves to do her bidding was dangerous on all levels. Turning tail could mean losing the war and their way of life.

"We can't leave," Campbell's tone was matter of fact. Renfro paled, and he saw it as a good sign. "We're too far in, and the situation is too grim."

Renfro appeared perplexed, but Campbell continued. "We will squeeze the runaway for information, and I do mean squeeze. There is no other option, and we will not leave until we have razed that damn town to the ground."

The older man nodded, then cleared his throat. "We moved the runaway like you ordered, through the tunnel we widened under the barn."

"Good... keep him alive for now. I want answers." Campbell replied.

Renfro nodded, then turned on his heels and quit the office.

When Campbell heard the snick of the suite door, he went in search of Penny, who was nowhere to be found. Striding over to the couch with purpose, he planted himself in the middle and waited. Seventeen minutes had gone by before Campbell heard the scrape of the skeleton key in the lock.

Penny stepped over the threshold and offered a polite smile at the sight of him. After placing her matching parasol in the bin by the door, she turned her attention back to him. Her words were brittle and mindful of their stations.

"Master, are you ready for your noonday meal?"

"Where did you come by this dress?" Campbell asked, fighting the urge to growl.

"You purchased it for me, sir."

"That is what I thought… What are the rules, Penny?"

"I am only permitted to dress up for you, sir."

"So, you are clear on the rules…" Campbell replied, his anger barely controlled.

"Are you hungry, Master?" Penny inquired as if she were bored with his inquiry.

Campbell leapt to his feet and stalked over to her–peril dripping from his person. He could not afford this distraction. She was making him break the rules. Snatching her by the hair, he angled her face up to his, their lips only inches apart.

"I will whip the hell out of you, Penny." He promised, his ire hot. "What is the meaning of this?"

Penny's eyes watered, and her breath caught. "I wanted to be beautiful today."

Campbell released her unexpectedly, causing her to stumble. She grabbed hold of the back of the settee to steady herself and he glared. As he watched her regain her footing, he backed away from her to give himself a moment.

"Go to your room and do not come out."

The bun she wore in her hair had come loose; the lashes framing her large, brown eyes were wet and her carriage stiff.

Penny floated past him on the blood red carpet as if he didn't exist. When the door to her room closed behind her, Campbell found himself wrestling with yet another alarming thought. Did his lovely Penny dress up to capture another man's interest? This thought was more disturbing than his concerns regarding England.

Campbell turned his mind back to the slave they captured. He simply could not afford this upset.

* * *

It was early afternoon when Elbert swung down from his horse at the back of the saloon. His time at the church was taxing. Simon and Tim approached; their expressions troubled.

"James been took," Simon said.

"We think the Preservers of Southern Life got 'im." Tim added.

Elbert turned to the men that rode out with his brother. "What happened?"

Josiah stepped forward, his brown skin dripping with sweat and gave an accounting of the events. "Me and Ephraim took the carriage. Odell, Chester, Ralph, and Herman rode out on horseback. James moved out on foot; time he got near Ruby's, they come for 'im. Ralph and Herman is trackin' the mens what took 'im. He ain't put up no fight."

"How many?" Elbert asked.

"I counted five guns on 'im," Chester said.

Josiah added. "Herman and Ralph is good at what they does–they won't lose 'em."

"Give me and Elbert a minute." Simon interrupted.

When the men backed away, Simon pointed with his chin toward the side of the barn. Elbert followed and once out of sight, he pressed his back against the building. He leaned over, hands to knees, trying to pull in air; he was feeling faint. Simon's black boots came into view as Elbert stared at the patched grass around his feet.

"Josiah is right–Herman and Ralph is good at what they does. We got to do our piece," Simon said.

Pushing himself to a standing position, Elbert took three cleansing breaths before locking eyes with Simon. He nodded when he was ready, and both men stepped away from the side of the barn to face the men. In his head, Elbert did a count of the saloon men versus their own men. Gazing about the space between the barn, the chicken coop, and the back of the saloon, he saw that everyone was waiting on him.

The whores were piled up on the porch and in the backdoor way, while the men were lined up in front of him. He was about to issue orders when Anthony, Frank and Lou came walking from between the establishments to join them. Elbert felt relief flood his person as he began to see the solution from all angles.

"Odell and Chester, take the men you came wit and secure the saloon," Elbert said.

"Yes, sah." Both men answered before they rushed off.

Elbert waited as everyone moved about; the women and patrons were herded back inside. When he was faced with the eighteen, minus E.J., Jake, and Jeremiah; yet, adding Virgil, Elbert spoke. His voice was low, causing the men to form a tight circle.

"Ant, Frank and Lou, send Black a telegram and wait for the answer."

Simon moved in to stand next to Elbert, his words lighting a fire. "We's organized and we got us a plan, even for dis shit."

The men were silent as they stepped toward their horses. Anthony, Frank, and Lou remained in place waiting for further instruction. Elbert walked away for additional privacy and once under the shade of the tree by the barn, he recited a carefully coded message for Black.

CHAPTER 9

HAMMER AND CHISEL

Black was standing on the porch of the cabin he shared with his wife. The sun was starting to fade behind the trees when Philip came running from the direction of the gate. Black couldn't say what it was that made him step from the porch and run toward the older man–meeting him halfway… but he did. Philip was breathless when he handed Black a telegram that read:

ONE FROM FOUR LEAVES THREE–ONE FROM THREE LEAVES TWO–HOW GRAND IT WOULD BE IF TWO AND TWO MADE FIVE

"Is everything, all right?" Philip asked.

Black's head snapped up at the sound of Philip's voice. He had forgotten the older man was waiting for a response. "Gather the women and send them to me."

"Sho thang."

When Philip would have turned to leave, Black added. "Ready yourself–we will leave in two hours."

"You wantin' me to gather a posse?" Philip asked.

"No. It will be you and me," Black said before striding back toward the cabin.

Behind him, he heard Philip running to do his bidding. When he reached the cabin, he didn't go inside. Black paced the footpath in front of the structure. He would wait for and speak with the women before leaving immediately. There was no room to overthink; he couldn't give in to his fear regarding the women and children.

Anna, Sunday, and Mary were the first to arrive. Black moved to stand on the porch once all his soldiers were accounted for. The weather was warm and the breeze that blew about them was caressing. Needing a moment to gather his thoughts, he stared up at the clear sky and quarter moon that was happening. Though night had newly fallen, the dark was complete save for the lantern light spilling from the window. He couldn't truly make out the women's features, and Black hoped they couldn't see his dread.

"I will be heading to Montreal, posthaste. Sunday and Morgan will lead in my absence. The gate will not be opened again until I return."

"Black…" Anna breathed. "Did something happen to one of the men?"

"I got a telegram summoning me." Black answered. "It isn't clear who sent the message. I will go and come back with the answer."

"How many of the menfolk will ya take?" Sunday asked.

"It'll be me and Philip. We'll make for the freight train that runs through town at midnight. If we miss the train, there will not be another until midnight again." Black was shutting down all questions and the women seemed to understand.

"We needs to meet in the study… right away," Morgan said.

The women moved toward the main house, until there was only Sunday left. He reached out a hand to her and his wife ran to him, hugging him tight. Pulling her back from him, he led her into the cabin. Black closed the door behind them and stood in the middle of the one room; a single oil lamp sat on the table by the window. Gazing down into Sunday's face, he saw her worry; he smiled to reassure her.

"What ain't you sayin'?" Sunday asked.

"I'm riding out for the train now–I fear missing it. We should reach Montreal by dawn. I will send word as soon as I can," he said, sidestepping her question to repeat what he had already told her.

"Is one of the men in trouble?" his wife asked, undaunted.

"The message was coded. I'm not sure who it came from–James or Elbert." Black lied.

His wife stared at him, and Black could see the moment she decided it was better if she didn't know what happened. Her tone was strong when she said, "Yo' saddlebag is under the table."

Black nodded and when she would have stooped to retrieve his bag, he grabbed her by the arm and pulled her against him. In her ear, he whispered. "I love you–go meet with the women."

Sunday pulled back to look him in the eyes. Slowly, she nodded, and turning for the door she quit the cabin. Once alone Black stepped to the wooden table and stooping, he retrieved his own saddlebag. At his desk he went through the leather sacks taking personal inventory. When he was satisfied, he took a last sweeping glance about the cabin.

The bed was made with a colorful quilt; the tub was empty, and his desk was piled high with parchments. The oil lamp offered steady lighting for him to give the place a once over. Turning the wick down, Black headed for the door. He stepped onto the makeshift porch to find Philip waiting; the men didn't speak.

They made their way to the cabin where Percy was being kept. Leaving Philip and his bag on the path, Black ventured up the stairs and into the cabin. He found the doctor seated to the table and Virgil's field hand fast asleep. Upon seeing him, Shultz stood and moved to the door in silence. Once outside, the doctor asked.

"Something wrong?"

"I can't say," Black answered. "We're headed to Montreal."

"I will come with you," Shultz said.

"I need you here with the women and children. If you have a problem with Percy…"

The doctor cut him off. "He is agreeable and still weak from his ordeal; his sputum is green. You needn't worry–what of the man James sent back? What would you like me to do with him?"

"He is dead." Black responded. "I must go–I will send word as soon as I can."

"Safe travels," Shultz said, his dislike at being left behind evident.

And with that, Black stepped from the porch and faded into the night with Philip at his side. At the gate, torches were lit and a black carriage waited. Black didn't stop to give direction, instead he climbed into the cab and Philip did the same from the other door. The gate yawned as two of the fort men drove the carriage while two men covered them on horseback.

Black sat opposite Philip in the cab and still no words passed between them. They rode for a little over an hour before being dropped off on the outskirts of town to await the train. There were no lampposts, only underbrush and night. As the carriage pulled away, Black slapped the side of the vehicle twice causing Zeke to call out.

"Whoa… whoa!"

When the carriage stopped moving, Black handed Zeke a slip of parchment. "See to it this gets sent tonight. The owner of the dry-goods will be happy to assist as I have helped him a time or two."

"Yes, sah." Zeke answered. "Me and Albert finna stay close by til the train come and you's on ya way."

"Yeah," Black said.

The sound of the harnesses jingling and the cab bouncing signaled Zeke's and Albert's departure. Throwing his saddlebag over his shoulder, Black moved out on foot to get closer to the tracks; Philip followed. It was roughly two hours until midnight when the men settled in to wait. The temperature had dropped, still it was spring. Black could smell the overgrown vegetation; dirt and a coming rain taxed his senses as the cicadas added a rhythm to the night that drowned out his thoughts.

"Can ya tell me what happened now that we ain't at the fort?" Philip asked.

"If I'm deciphering the message right–James has been taken hostage. Elbert ain't sure if he still alive," Black said, his tone deadpan.

"Shit."

"Yeah," Black replied.

Less than two hours passed when a tremor started under his feet long before Black heard the whistle announcing the train's approach. They stepped back into the vegetation for safety purposes as the locomotive blew by in a gigantic gust of wind; the odor of burning coal and iron scraping iron assailed as they waited for the train to come to a complete stop.

Black and Philip remained in the underbrush as men carrying torches walked along the side of the railcars, calling out numbers to one another. Some of the cars were open and empty while others were closed. Standing on the edge of darkness, they waited patiently until the torch holders disappeared. And when the train started moving, Black grabbed Philip by the collar of his overcoat. Throwing his saddlebag in first, he hurled himself inside. Philip stumbled, but Black kept hold, dragging him up into the rolling railcar.

Both men slumped against the wall and didn't move; they couldn't see. Black wished they could travel faster but it seemed their speed was no greater than a horse and carriage. The train made lots of noise as it journeyed along the rickety tracks toward Montreal. Allowing thoughts of his sweet wife to flood his senses, Black found that he was pained by the stilted goodbye they shared.

He would make it up to her. It was his last thought before he was lulled to sleep by the rocking motion of the train.

* * *

James spit blood before he slowly glanced about the cabin where he was being held. His right eye was swollen shut from the beating he had sustained and his left eye... well, he couldn't focus. He had been hit so many times that his thought process was hazy. Twice he had passed out, and they had revived him with what felt like ice water. When he could grab a thought, he had been confused to note that the focus for this group was the ambassador–not Black. It was the same three questions that he refused to acknowledge.

"Is the slave Black and Hope Turner one in the same?" The newcomer and the tallest of the men asked.

When James refused to answer, he heard a voice say, "Douse him again."

He wasn't strong like Elbert and Black, James cried out when the freezing water splashed over him. It also registered that he was naked, even as he heard the next questions swirling around in his head. "Why would an ambassador partner with niggers? Is Bainesworth working for the queen of England or is he rogue?"

James heard someone ask the man who appeared to be in charge. "What are you saying, Camp? You think the queen duplicitous?"

"Not now, Renfro." The man called Camp snapped back.

The wooden chair he occupied had been overturned from the force of a blow to his head. James lay on his side still tied to the chair. There was a lantern on the floor in the corner, only the boots of his captors visible. The room itself was tilted... James hoped for oblivion.

"You ain't going to get shit from him," another man said from somewhere in the room.

Someone chuckled. "What would a slave know about the queen?"

"All of you... stop damn talking." Camp snapped. At least James thought it was the one called Camp.

"We fixin' to kill 'im. What it matter–what he hear?"

James wanted to focus on the conversation happening around him, but his earlier wish had come to pass; he blacked out.

* * *

Campbell allowed his eyes to bounce from man to man. His level of disgust was high; it was now evident what caused the fail in the organization's previous endeavor.

"I am going to ask this question, and I want you all to truly figure on it before responding." Campbell paused before he went on. "You all realize these slaves have run and managed to remain free, correct?"

Renfro tried to speak, but Campbell raised his hand to silence him. He continued. "Think–please before you speak."

As he glanced about, Campbell couldn't say what was driving him, anger or jealousy. He acknowledged that his emotions bordered on unstable, if the unconscious slave laying at his feet was any indication. The goal had been to extract information from his prisoner, not beat him until he couldn't speak. His ability to always call on his self-control was a source of pride for him; but this night Campbell did not recognize himself.

Turning his back on Renfro, Styles and Clinks, he was trying to give himself a moment. In the corner on the floor sat an oil lamp, its light climbing the wall at an awkward angle. The smell of dampness permeated the air. The cabin was old and sparsely furnished, save for several chairs that didn't match the wobbly table. Campbell walked to the window to stare out, but the darkness plus the lantern equaled his own reflection. He looked over his shoulder to Styles who appeared puzzled.

"Are you sure you weren't followed?"

"We clanked him on the head and carried him through the tunnel. Ain't no one followed us." Styles replied.

"You think we are underestimating the slaves?" Renfro asked.

Campbell let the tattered drapes slip through his fingers as he turned to look Renfro in the eyes. "What do you believe?"

"You think England is double dealing?" Styles asked.

Clinks stood to the left of his cousin offering no words. Renfro took a step forward. "We were being followed by two slaves. The men we hired applied the right amount of pressure. It gave us time to get away."

Styles chimed in. "This cabin is hid pretty good, figure we kill 'im and be on our way by the time they find it."

Campbell could only nod his head. "Gentlemen, Canada is home to thousands of runaways. You have to assume they have some organizational skills. To underestimate is to lose our way of life."

Clinks finally asked. "You think this Bainesworth… this Brit is the intelligence of this rogue slave group?"

"I am unclear on what to think." Campbell lied; he couldn't expose the confederate president. It was common knowledge that England sold weapons to the south. But was the queen selling guns to the north? Had England been recruiting slaves?

Campbell's focus fell to the naked slave still tied to the chair. The runaway knew something, it was in the way he tried to remain expressionless. As the leader of this band of misfits, Campbell needed to find a more controlled way to apply pain. The slave's eyes held a perception that was hard to miss. He had witnessed the same look in Penny's eyes. It was a look that challenged his whiteness, but from Penny, it lit a fire within him–from this male slave it spelled mayhem.

"I will arrange to have him moved," Campbell said aloud. "The other runaways will expect us to hide him out here somewhere.

When the time comes, we will kill him and dump him at that eatery. In the meantime, stay alert."

"I think we should kill him," Clinks said looking anxious.

"Do you know why the south is on the brink of ruin?" Campbell asked the room at large.The question was met with silence. He didn't elaborate on the posed question. "You will move him to an establishment near the hotel when I give the signal."

Turning for the door, Campbell walked out of the cabin into the chilled night. He was careful in his maneuvering of the rotted old porch. Climbing into the awaiting carriage, he sank into the plush black velvet seats. When the carriage lurched forward his thoughts turned to Penny. The very notion of her in the arms of another caused his blood to boil.

The carriage ride allowed him to collect himself before he dealt with her. He thought about the slave and realized that his handling of the runaway was a direct reflection of the angst he was feeling about Penny. The runaway took the beating he could not give her; she wouldn't have survived such a lashing. He would get to the bottom of her defiance, thereby getting his life and this damn mission back on track.

Campbell felt his control coming back; he had a plan. He would resolve this problem with Penny, then deal with the runaway. And if he couldn't get the slave to talk at their next encounter, he would kill him. He needed to locate the Brit, which translated to more time spent with that useless actor. As the carriage came to a slow rolling stop in front of the hotel, he didn't wait for the driver to set the stairs. Pushing the door open, he hopped down onto the roadway. He was stepping up on the boardwalk when he spotted Booth speaking with the merchant to the left of the entrance. The merchant's two niggers stood together opposite them.

It was after midnight, but well before dawn. Booth and the merchant acknowledged him, the slaves did not. Campbell could feel it, the unease of the merchant and his slaves.

Booth, who appeared to be in his cups, greeted him. “Camp, my good man.”

Campbell eyed the slaves while addressing the actor. “Booth.”

The merchant nervously stepped forward introducing himself. “The name is Hunter Edwards.”

Avoiding anything that appeared friend like, Campbell didn’t reciprocate. But he did let it be known what he thought of the merchant’s control over his slaves. “You ought to sell those two to someone who can handle them.”

Campbell turned to walk away and behind him, the merchant squeaked.

CHAPTER 10

TROUBLESOME TIMES

Once on the train, Black did not ponder, so he would be fresh in the head when he faced his men. He could not allow himself to dwell on or engage in thoughts where he was without another brother. As the train rumbled along, his only thoughts were of a naked Sunday. It was the best way to get through the dark hours as they sped toward Montreal.

The intermittent but violent jerks of the railcar as it adjusted on the track was his first signal that they were nearing their destination. When Black opened his eyes, dawn was happening. He stood making his way to the door facing the countryside; the natural light had not yet leaked to the land. The sky was a combination of night mixed with hues of orange, yellow and gold. In his periphery, he noted Philip getting to his feet and stumbling to the opposite door.

As the locomotive came to a grinding, screeching halt, the sun broke through the darkness. Black's eyes scanned the countryside and lined up in plain view were his men. Jumping down from the railcar, he turned back to assist Philip. The track was at the top of a slope, and it took some balancing to keep from tucking and rolling. Once on level ground, Black looked up to find two white conductors ambling his way. But when his men were spotted, the railroad workers disappeared back into the train. Giving the men his undivided attention, Black stood still allowing himself to be surrounded. Philip blended in with the crowd.

A mental count confirmed they were down four men: E.J., Jake, James, and Jeremiah. Black surveyed his posse and found pain etched on the men's faces; he felt the same. Save for the train letting off steam and the birds cawing overhead there was nothing from the men. Black's gaze bounced around the gathering until his focus fell on Elbert and Simon. Offering a curt nod, Black moved toward Elbert. Simon stepped forward taking Black's place at the center of the men.

Simon had maneuvered the men until he and Elbert stood alone facing each other. Black smiled reassuringly. Elbert broke the silence; his voice was thick and his eyes glassy.

"I failed–he's prolly dead already."

"Did you go to Ruby's?" Black asked stepping over his brother's misery.

"Spike, the poor bastard, is in a carriage out back. Shit, a little more time and he'll be an unknown."

Black looked toward the sky as he spoke. Elbert's hurt was hard to witness. "He ain't dead yet–they would have dumped him where he could be found."

Elbert's head snapped up. "What makes you so sure?"

"They mean to distract us. I'm sure he's been beaten like Virgil's field hand, but he ain't dead yet. Collect yourself, brother–we will get him back."

Elbert nodded and Black went on. "I brought match sticks."

"Yeah."

Turning, Black walked back to the center of the circle. Simon and Elbert moved in to stand at his back. Staring from man to man, he noted the guns, the single black carriage, and the horses. When he was sure he had every man's attention, Black spoke, his tone oozing authority.

"You all think you have failed. Let me reassure–you have not. Until James' body is recovered you are to consider him alive. Make no mistake... This. Is. A. Rescue."

In the background the train hissed and still there was no sign of the conductors. Truth be told, Black didn't care what they saw or overheard. He and his men were about to raze Montreal to the ground. His words were controlled as he continued.

"You all know what I don't. Each man will be given three minutes to tell me anything he feels is important. If you have nothing to offer, see Simon. He will set up the groups."

Seven men stepped forward while the others followed Simon. Ephraim and Josiah spoke at once, causing Black to hold up his hand in an attempt to calm them. "We have three minutes–organized. There can be no other way."

"Me and Jos moved out by carriage. We rode out ahead of 'im–shit happened too fast. It was six of dem," Ephraim said. He was dark of skin and wore a tan knit cap pulled down to meet his troubled eyes.

Josiah added. "Three of 'em was standin' in front of Ruby's, two was cross the roadway and then the one what shoved a gun into James' ribs. We thought to keep from a shootout... I sees the misstep now."

"Me and Chester went for help. I counted the same–but it was some mens on the roof of a bakery," Odell said. "Couldn't get a count of da ones on top."

"Ralph and me tried to track dem what got James. But when we got to the barn, it was a real posse," Herman said, his brown skin making the redness of his eyes prevalent.

Black reached out and grabbed his shoulder. "How many?"

"I say 'bout twenty." Herman answered, his exhalation shaky.

"They carried James away by a hole beneath the barn behind

Ruby's place," Ralph said. "Did ya know it was a way under the barn?"

"There is a tunnel, but it wasn't big enough for a good size man–only women and children." Black answered as he thought aloud. "They must have widened the passage."

When Ralph would have turned to walk away, Black clapped him on the back. Tears spilled from the other man's eyes, so emotional was he. His brother was the last of the men waiting to speak with him. Black cut Elbert off to keep him focused.

"Did Odell speak to you about Campbell Penn and room 225 at the Grand Hotel?"

"Yeah, the smithy told me. But I ain't had no time to chase what you sent back." Elbert answered. "Leading... it ain't for me."

Black shook his head before asking. "You ready?"

"You got a plan then?"

"I want all the establishments in close proximity of the hotel and theatre gone through. We want to make certain James isn't nearby when we execute the plan," Black said, his tone cryptic.

"I left E.J., Jake and Jeremiah in place."

"We need to burn that damn theatre," Black said. "Our message must be clear."

"When?"

"Now," Black answered.

Elbert pointed over his shoulder at the carriage. "Inside... I got us some black powder."

Black couldn't help it, he grinned.

It was still early when the twenty-six began moving through Montreal. The men were divided into two groups. Philip took the lead over the ten men from the fort. Simon and Elbert took control of fourteen men breaking them down into seven and seven. Black would slide between the groups when needed, but he had his own tasks to complete.

The goal was to shake down all the establishments surrounding the theatre before moving to the businesses attached to the hotel on the opposite side of the roadway. The men would follow a checklist while working within the time constraints of one hour. Montreal was still asleep, but Black and the men… well, they were woke.

* * *

Simon stepped into the backroom of a small barbershop. The place was divided into two separate spaces by a thick red curtain. A thin white man with brown hair parted in the middle and a clean-shaven face was busy readying himself for the day. He was wiping down a brown leather barber's chair when he realized he wasn't alone.

The proprietor stood to his full height of five feet, seven inches and paled. He looked to the front of the shop where the door was locked; a sign hung in the window that read–closed. The man trembled in fear, and when he opened his mouth–no words came out. He was dressed impeccably in a white shirt, blue trousers, and a matching bow tie.

Simon assessed, then ignored the owner as he took in the front room. There were three barber chairs and a small black stove in the corner. The wood flooring was polished to perfection and the natural light fell through the display window exactly right. While the place was inviting, there was no sign of James. When Simon spoke, his words were clipped and to the point.

"You ain't finna do business today. Go home." The proprietor nodded, and Simon glared. "Say words."

"N-no. I will not open this morn."

* * *

Gilbert caught the bootmaker at the backdoor and shoved him over the threshold. He was a bruiser of a man standing about six feet. When the man tried to put up a fight, Frank was on hand to clank him upside the head with his gun. They only had six minutes to go through the shop.

"Ya ain't kill 'im, did you?" Gilbert asked.

"Naw… he still takin' in air," Frank said.

The bootmaker's set up was simple and unorganized. Gilbert took in the scuffed wood flooring, the many shelves of unfinished footwear and the fumes. The lighting was dismal, and what he knew for sure–James was not here. Frank and Gilbert stepped over the bootmaker and quit the workshop. The whole exchange took five minutes.

They pressed on.

* * *

The confectioner was pulling a pan from the oven when Elbert stepped through the backdoor. She wore a blue dress, and her black hair was piled high on her head. The space she occupied smelled of cherries, nuts, and sugar. There were three large stoves, and along with the great aromas, the shop was rather warm. She hummed as she worked, and never did she look away from her task.

Elbert coughed and the sound caused her head to whip around. Upon seeing him, her blue eyes widened. Clutching at her chest, the woman made a request in French; her fear was evident.

"Ne me faites pas de mal… s'il vous plait."

Elbert stared, not because he didn't understand her words. He had six minutes and he was striving for efficiency. Her plea was simple – *Don't hurt me...please*. After offering the correct amount of intimidation, he allowed his eyes to scan the backroom; there was no sign of James.

"Asseoir," Elbert demanded; the woman moved with quickness to a wooden chair in the corner.

Stepping past the brown curtain to the front room, the sunlight made the place magical as he observed the glass cases which housed all manner of confections. There were muffins, chocolates, candies, and many intricately decorated cakes–but no James. Retracing his steps, Elbert found the woman where he left her.

"Aller… Tranquillement." Elbert demanded and the woman did his bidding. She stood and left quietly.

* * *

Black was sweating as he and Philip maneuvered the carriage around to the back of the theatre. Odell and Chester were inside the cab steadying the kegs to keep them from rolling or banging into each other. Elbert said he had *some* black powder, but what he actually had was *too* much black powder. Philip rode shotgun, and Black could feel his anxiety.

There was a bit of an incline and still Black did some fancy driving to get the carriage right up to the backdoor of the theatre. Behind the Buckingham were several tall trees and patched grass; the morning was warming up as the sun settled high in the sky. Black pulled the brake, then hopped down from the bench. Philip followed suit; his stance was unsteady.

Black opened the carriage door to find both Odell and Chester dripping with fear and perspiration. The two older men's reaction to traveling with explosives would be comical if the matter weren't so severe. Odell had explained that Elbert went back to the railroad town and negotiated for the black powder… so this was his second time riding with the barrels. Chester was so nervous he could hardly gather himself enough to climb from the vehicle.

Black was about to head for the backdoor of the theatre when Elbert, Simon and the men stepped through the trees.

"No sign of James," Elbert said when he was close enough.

"Cain't tell whether that be good or bad," Simon said as he joined the discussion.

Black didn't engage. Instead, he kept them on task. "Did the messages get sent?"

"Yeah," Elbert said.

"Get the supplies from the carriage. The tradesmen from the fort are to get moving, they know where to wait." Black ordered.

As the men carefully unloaded the carriage, Black, along with Anthony, Frank and Lou stepped to the backdoor. Banging on the wood three times in rapid succession caused the door to swing open. An elderly white man stood in the frame, and Black thought him feeble.

"Who the hell are you?" the man asked.

Black pushed the muzzle of his gun to the man's nose and walked him to the left of the door. "Who is inside?

"Just me and Mave," the man answered, and it seemed he would burst out crying. "We keep the place."

"The Preservers of Southern Life?" Black asked.

"They come at night and on the days when we have no shows. That actor brings the trouble," the old man said. "Please, don't hurt Mave."

Black nodded toward the carriage. He ordered the man. "Get in."

The men moved through the theatre while Black waited outside. Soon, Anthony appeared with a white-haired woman. She wore a blue dress with a matching shawl. Her hair was pulled back in a bun and her brown eyes were wide with shock.

"Miss Mave," Black said. "This way, please."

The old woman didn't utter a word, but she did step to the carriage and allow Black to help her in. Chester and Odell climbed in on either side of the couple, and when Black slapped the door, the carriage lurched forward. Lending his focus back to the matter at hand, Black turned in time to see Ralph stumble as he helped Anthony carry a barrel of black powder. Frank moved in, catching Ralph before he could go down.

"Easy!" Simon yelled.

Black shook his head; they were all on edge. Simon continued. "Tim, the ambassador, and Virgil is keeping watch."

"I'm going in," Black said, pointing over his shoulder to the door.

Simon nodded. "We has it out here."

Following the men, Black stepped over the threshold into a long dim corridor that led to the auditorium; the stage was to his left. The theatre was quiet save for his men moving about. Walking up the middle aisle, Black pushed at the double doors. He found himself in an empty lobby with an awful color scheme of brown and burgundy. The next set of doors leading to the roadway were locked up tight and on the right was a small window.

Peering out, Black assessed the goings on in front of the theatre, confirming that Tim, Bainesworth and Virgil were indeed in place. There was no foot traffic, but that would change when the shop owners began sounding the alarm. Retracing his steps, he saw that the men were waiting for him at the mouth of the corridor. As he walked the center aisle, he noted the powder keg laid on its side. It was wedged between the podium and what appeared to be three carved stairs. The other barrel was placed on a chair in the third row to the right, and the smell of kerosene was thick in the air.

"Move out," Black yelled, and the men shuffled back up the corridor. Elbert waited. When he reached his brother, he said. "Imma give you men four minutes to scatter."

"I'll wait."

Black nodded as he reached for his pocket watch. "How we leaving?"

"Backdoor."

The brothers waited together for the allotted time before Elbert handed him an oil lamp. Black lit the lamp and placed it in the first chair–in the first row. Turning, he and Elbert took off running down the corridor until they reached daylight; the men had already dispersed.

They kept up the sprint until they reached the roadway facing the Grand Hotel. Black and Elbert crossed the thoroughfare with haste, then made their way down the narrow alley between the dressmaker and hotel. Once behind the building, they strolled right into the kitchen. The men were greeted by the sounds of dishes clinking, kettles whistling and people chatting. But all activity ceased when Black was spotted. He hated ignoring the people, but time was of the essence. As he and Elbert maneuvered between the white countertops ladened with all kinds of deliciousness, it occurred to him; the people needed direction.

"Go about your day–answer no questions."

The noises and chatter restarted as the men pushed through the black doors that led to an empty dining area. They avoided squeezing between the dainty tables and traveled the perimeter of the eatery until they came to the entrance. Black stepped into the lobby of the Grand Hotel giving the thin white man behind the counter minimal consideration.

Other than the man's navy-blue uniform with the big brass buttons, Black was uninterested. Elbert held the bellboy at gunpoint before backing away to take the steps two at a time to the second floor. The brothers were standing in front of room two-twenty-five when the first explosion hit. At the second blast, Black felt the vibration even from across the roadway.

Patrons began spilling into the hall and running for the stairs. The chaos was real, and Black had a moment of doubt regarding their plan when the door to room two-twenty-five opened. A tall white man with brown hair and eyes came into view. He was trying to jam his arms into a blue suit jacket, as Elbert stepped forward shoving the muzzle of his gun between the man's eyes. The brothers walked their newly acquired hostage backwards into the room.

"You Campbell?" Black asked, and the man refused to reply. Elbert shot him in the foot.

Their prisoner fell to the floor howling in pain. Black continued, his tone even. "We mean to have our man back."

Black looked up as a tall, dark skinned woman came running

into the common area. When she spied them, she stopped short and clutched at her throat; her fright was apparent. Stepping over the moaning man, Black moved toward her. The woman backed away as if trying to fend him off.

He stopped advancing and spoke. "Is his name Campbell?"

"Yes."

"And your name?" Black continued to press.

"Caroline."

"Who else is here, Caroline?"

"Just me."

Black nodded. "Please have a seat."

"Yes, sir," she whispered.

Turning back to the man, who was now panting in an attempt to manage his pain. Black stooped to his haunches giving the man time to focus. "I want the whereabouts of my man."

When the man closed his eyes as if to avoid answering, Elbert shot him in his other foot. The woman screamed, but Black never looked her way. He continued in his assessment of the man named Campbell. Their prisoner was sweating, and his hair was plastered to the side of his face. Black leaned in to gain eye contact when he gritted out.

"Where. Are. You. Holding. My. Man?"

Elbert cocked his gun and Campbell mumbled. "In a cabin by the old sawmill… five miles out."

"He is still alive then?" Black asked, fearing the answer.

"Yes… he… yes." Campbell answered.

"Which way is this sawmill?" Black pressed.

"East," Campbell grunted in pain. "Stay east."

Black drew back his fist and slammed Campbell in the face, outing his light. Behind him, the woman wept uncontrollably. His tone was minus threat when he advised. "Hush, woman… I can't think."

Elbert started for the door, then stopped to look back at him. But before he could speak, Black directed. "Go–I got it here."

His brother turned his lifeless eyes on the woman, and Caroline shook–visibly. Black's tone was calm when he reiterated. "Head out."

Elbert nodded before yanking the suite door open and joining the unrest in the corridor.

CHAPTER 11

GUN PLAY

Once on the opposite side of the door, Elbert held onto the knob until he heard and felt the bolt being thrown. This was no easy feat given the noise level in the hall. He was jostled along toward the stairs in a mixture of colored staff and white patrons trying to make an escape. When he reached the landing, he had to wedge himself into the flow of foot traffic.

The madness happening on the stairs leading to the lobby made it difficult for Elbert to watch his own back. Anyone could knife him, then fade into the crowd–vigilance was impossible. He considered doubling back for Black. He felt torn with the realization that he could not be in two places at one time. Keeping his eyes forward, his pace was slow.

A light cloud of smog had drifted into the lobby with the opening and closing of the main entrance. Some people stepped outside only to rush back indoors to avoid the billowing smoke. Mapping out an escape, Elbert decided to go back the way he and Black had come–exiting through the kitchen. He was nearing the bottom of the staircase when a strong hand landed on his shoulder.

Elbert was prepared to do violence when he looked over his shoulder and into the face of the black cracker. Jake moved in on his side, and E.J. had crammed himself in front of Elbert. The men didn't speak; but once on the lobby carpet, they moved toward the dining area. Elbert took the lead as he headed for the back swinging doors. Patrons and staff alike were glued to the windows as the Buckingham Theatre went up in flames. Trekking back through the kitchen, Elbert was happy to find it almost deserted. Although there were people gathered at the backdoor.

A pantry door to the right of the kitchen sat ajar and Elbert pointed, then headed for the closet. Stepping into the dark space, he waited for E.J., Jake, and Jeremiah to do the same. Jake pulled the door shut, and Elbert gave what was necessary.

"James has been taken." And to his shame, his voice broke. "Black is in room two-twenty-five."

Elbert couldn't get his thoughts together; he was worried for both his brothers. There was also the possibility that James was dead. He was wallowing in misery and what ifs–when Jeremiah spoke.

"E.J.–Jake, go to Black. Imma back Elbert."

"You all should go to Black." Elbert managed.

"Ain't no time for talkin'," Jeremiah snapped. "E.J., go to Black and take Jake."

Jeremiah opened the pantry door allowing E.J. and Jake to leave. Elbert was about to follow. He had no energy to argue. But the black cracker placed a palm in the middle of his chest. Jeremiah shut them back in the darkened pantry.

"My gun hand is your gun hand. We will get James back alive."

Elbert took a breath. "Shit."

"You ready?"

"Yeah," Elbert replied. "I'm going to meet the men. We headed to the old sawmill about five miles out."

"Lead the way."

Elbert burst from the pantry with Jeremiah on his heels. He felt a little stronger; he could now focus on James and not worry for Black. They pressed themselves through the crowd clogging the back entrance. At the mouth of the narrow alley were more people, mostly the colored staff who cleared the way for them. When they made it to the roadway, Elbert had to collect himself.

The morning sun was bright, but mixed with the smoke and flames, the day appeared overcast. Elbert noted the people lined up in the roadway with buckets of water. The goal was clear for all to see, the only option available was to stop the spread; the theatre was going to burn to the ground.

Elbert tried to work at shallowing his breathing so as not to take in too much smoke. He started moving east on Sovereign Way when the sharp sound of someone whistling caught his attention. Across the roadway, and a little further up the boardwalk, the men stood waiting for him. Picking up his pace to a light jog, he headed toward Simon with Jeremiah in tow.

"The old sawmill," Elbert yelled. "It's about five miles out. We need to stay east."

The men scrambled to their horses, then headed for James.

Black stepped forward locking the door before heading to the window. There was pandemonium on the roadway below as the people of Montreal lined up to douse the flames shooting out the front doors of the Buckingham Theatre. As he gauged the madness, he spoke to the woman.

"Caroline, please bring me a sheet."

When he didn't hear any movement behind him, Black turned to see that her face was wet with tears. She was trembling, and if he were being honest, he felt like she looked, so large was his worry for James. He sighed.

"The sheet, please."

She nodded and stood heading for the open door to the right of the suite. While she was gone Black surveyed his surroundings, the blood red carpet, the mint-colored furnishings and the large bowl of fresh fruit that sat on the well-polished table. When she returned with the sheet, Black laid it on the table. She had been about to go and sit down again, but his words caused her to freeze in place.

"Please empty your pockets, Caroline."

Black kept a straight face when her head snapped up, and her huge, brown eyes widened as they met his. Her breaths were hurried as if she'd been running; she didn't move right away. After an intense moment, her slender fingers disappeared into the pleats of her blue skirts. Black waited patiently as she pulled from her right pocket a gold letter opener. Laying the would-be weapon on the table, she then extracted from her left pocket a shiny pair of silver scissors.

"What else are you hiding?"

Dropping her gaze, she whispered. "I have nothing else."

He didn't bother to pat her down. "Have a seat."

When she was seated in one of the armchairs, Black turned his attention back to the window. He worked at cutting the white sheet into strips while monitoring the activity below. Once the sheet was shredded, he walked over to his unconscious prisoner and tied him up. Campbell moaned as if to wake and Black tagged him again, sending the man back into oblivion. Caroline yelped, but she remained unmoved.

Removing a straight razor from his own boot, Black cut the boots from Campbell's person before tying the white strips tightly around his feet to stem the blood. He needed this man alive, he meant to get answers. Black meant to see how far this plot went. Once he secured his prisoner, he stood and eyed Caroline. He felt bad for intimidating her, but he'd seen her type before. She had embraced bondage because she lived better than most; he would leave her on edge.

Although he didn't speak to her unless necessary, he was engaging her. Black offered the right amount of body language and eye contact to make clear her situation. His female hostage was beautiful with large brown eyes framed by thick lashes. Caroline was dark of skin with full lips and a plump nose. She wore her hair pulled back from her face which only added to her appeal. But what made her absolutely stunning, she was nearly six feet, and her carriage was graceful. Black ignored her while at the same time studying her.

He moved about the suite to see what he could glean. The backdrop to their situation was the muffled sounds of shouting in the hall and the commotion coming from below even as the windows were closed. In the smaller bedchamber was a well-made, full-size bed with maple wood furnishings that shone in the sunlight. The bed dressings were peach and there were many pillows on the bed. On a nightstand to the left of the room was a white porcelain basin and pitcher. The closet door sat open displaying an assortment of brown, blue, gray, and black dresses. Crossing to the opposite side of the suite, he stepped into the master chamber where a huge bed dominated the space.

The bed was unmade and both sides appeared used. Red drapes were drawn together to ward off the brightness of the day. On an armchair in the corner was a pink dress haphazardly tangled up with blue trousers. The color of the room and its furnishings were brown and beige. Pushed into the corner was a large, copper tub; the fireplace held much soot.

Black had stepped back into the common area to make eye contact with Caroline. She was sitting with her eyes to the floor and her hands folded on her lap. He was about to step into what he was sure would be an office when someone knocked on the door. The woman jumped as the sound of five knocks, two times in quick succession alerted Black that it was one of his men.

Pulling the door wide, Black found E.J. and Jake staring at him. The hallway was clear, but the sound of people gathering in the lobby said much.

"Where is Jeremiah?" Black asked.

"He went with Elbert." E.J. answered.

"Elbert was wantin' E.J. and me to back you," Jake said.

E.J. entered first; Jake, being the last man over the threshold, shut and locked the door. Black was standing between the armchair and settee. He saw the woman look up at the sound of Jake's voice, and when E.J. stepped to the side... she gasped.

* * *

Jeremiah rode at Elbert's side and their speed was breakneck. His son popped into his head, and he knew they could not go home without James. Abby was his next thought and Jeremiah shut down the worry of facing her. They would not leave Montreal empty handed.

As the posse made for the old sawmill, the black cracker vibrated in the saddle. It was the clumps of dirt sent flying as the horse's hooves came in contact with the earth; it was the way the world shook as they rode down on their target, then fanned out to meet the challenge. It was the way his mind slowed allowing him to see everything more clearly. Jeremiah had never felt more alive than he did at this pitiful moment.

What the black cracker understood was gun play. He appreciated the directness with which the fifteen men he was riding with approached the situation. They would engage their opponents by ambush leaving their enemy no room to contemplate anything other than self-preservation. It would be the difference between life and death for all of them.

Three white men stood on the porch and five were gathered in front of the mill. The men scattered trying to take cover when they realized they had company. Elbert drew his gun while still in the saddle and let off two shots. Jeremiah swung down from his horse and drew both weapons at his hips. The black cracker dropped to one knee and let off two shots. Both rounds hit their marks dropping two of the three men on the porch.

Elbert rode his beast right up to the brown four-story structure, and Jeremiah kept him covered. Swinging from the saddle, Elbert charged the porch as the last man standing ran for the door; he tried to slam the door shut. Elbert shoved at the wooden barrier and Jeremiah helped him. The man gave up and tried making a run for it. But Elbert brought him down with a bullet to the back of the head. Guns drawn, Jeremiah assessed the threat as Elbert kept moving.

Simon suddenly appeared in the doorway, and Jeremiah turned drawing on him–all in one motion. Upon seeing it was one of their own, the black cracker moved about looking for James; he did not let Elbert out of his sight. Outside the morning was lit with men yelling and gun smoke.

"How many?" Elbert asked.

"'bout twenty," Simon answered. "The men done found another cabin behind here."

"Cabin," Elbert repeated before he ran for the door.

"Ain't you gon check here first?" Simon asked.

"Our prisoner said James was in a cabin." Elbert countered.

Stepping back onto the porch of the dilapidated structure left the men vulnerable. Someone took a shot at them causing the doorframe next to Elbert's head to shatter. They all took cover as best they could. Simon stood sideways behind a beam that ran from the planked floor to the overhanging roof. Jeremiah shoved Elbert back into the house as he scanned the area and came up with nothing. In the distance there was constant gunfire, and Jeremiah couldn't separate what he was hearing to isolate their shooter. They both covered Simon so he could get back inside, while more bullets whizzed their way.

The black cracker looked about the room taking in the

cobwebs and grime on a desk and chair that sat in the corner. A staircase to the left of the room wasn't going to be helpful. At the opposite end of the room was an open doorframe that led to a hall. Jeremiah headed that way and ended up in another room that looked the same with no furniture. Three other rooms were empty and dim. The last room he entered had a large window that overlooked a small creek.

He could see Anthony and Lou taking cover behind trees as they let off a few shots then ducked. Breaking the glass with his gun, Jeremiah brought down a man that was moving in on Anthony and Lou. The place began to vibrate as more men on horseback splashed through the creek headed their way. Jeremiah was relieved to see the fort men; more gunfire joined the fray as he yelled.

"Elbert–Simon, this way!" They came running as Jeremiah pointed to the backdoor. "The fort men are here."

The backdoor was stuck, so Jeremiah shot the knob off. When the men got the door open, the gunfire had moved west and the cabin they were seeking was to the east. Elbert went to step out and Jeremiah spoke.

"Have a damn care, man. What sense is it to save James if you get yo' head blown off."

Elbert didn't respond verbally, but he did nod. Simon moved into the doorway and looked about. "Me and Jeremiah gon cover ya… head for the cabin."

At Simon's signal–Elbert stepped through the doorframe and took off running. Jeremiah let off shots to the west and Simon to the east; but the best part of the situation was watching the tradesmen from the fort close ranks around Elbert. Behind them came the sound of booted feet and Jeremiah turned to deal with the danger, while Simon watched their front.

The black cracker sighed in relief at the sight of Josiah, Herman, and Frank. It was Simon that maintained leader quality when he asked. "How many we got left?"

"Two hostages," Frank said.

"Hired hands… if'n ya ask me." Josiah added.

"James?" Jeremiah asked. They all froze in place trying to hide from reality as long as possible.

The black cracker turned heading out back; but he hadn't cleared the exit good when Elbert came rushing from inside the cabin. At this distance, Elbert's expression was unreadable and without thinking Jeremiah took off running toward him, a sense of dread filling his chest. Wind whipped up the dirt as he ran; the tall grass around the cabin swayed and the smell of damp vegetation lingered in the air.

When Jeremiah got close enough, Elbert yelled out. "Help me… please!"

The black cracker didn't break his stride as he followed Elbert back inside the cabin. It was a one room structure with dirty windows that blocked the natural light. There was a chair turned over on its side in the far corner. Upon closer inspection Jeremiah saw the lifeless body of a man still tied to the chair; the black cracker's steps faltered at the vision.

James lay naked and still as death. His hands were tied behind him–around the back of the wooden chair. Even in the dim light, Jeremiah noted that his face was badly bruised and both eyes were swollen shut. His torso, wrists and ankles were bloody; around his neck were burn marks from a rope and there was what looked to be a slash across his shoulder. Elbert's request shook him from the murkiness of his pain.

"You got a knife?" Elbert asked.

"Is he alive?"

Elbert's voice shook. "Barely."

Jeremiah pulled a straight razor from his boot and handed it to Elbert. Behind them, the men started piling into the cabin. Simon issued orders.

"We needs a wagon and some blankets."

"We has supplies," Odell said as he ran back out to the carriage.

"Me, Frank and Ant will be back wit' a wagon," Lou said.

"The rest of ya need to secure the place whilst we get him ready to be moved," Simon said as Odell reappeared with blankets and other supplies.

Jeremiah helped cut James loose, struck by Elbert's steady hand. But what concerned him was the fact that James never showed signs of life. The black cracker worried James had died, and they weren't qualified enough to see it.

* * *

Elbert, Jeremiah, and Simon had taken great care to move James to the middle of the blankets provided by Odell. James' breathing was shallow and from what Elbert understood, it was the first sign of death. He wished Black or Shultz were here; they would know what to do.

Anthony backed into the cabin carrying the end of a board; Lou was at the other end. The younger men placed the makeshift stretcher on the floor next to James. Elbert adjusted his head and shoulders. Jeremiah supported his back, and Simon lifted his feet. On the count of three James was hoisted up enough to move him.

Elbert took the head of the stretcher and Simon the foot. The men spilled out of the cabin first, offering protection as they moved James to the covered wagon. His brother was swaddled like a baby in the pea green blankets used at the barracks. When the sunlight hit James' face, Elbert stumbled at the sight. His knees buckled, but Jeremiah was on hand.

"Let me."

Elbert stepped back allowing Jeremiah to take over. He had been about to turn away and take a minute, when his brother opened his eyes. Elbert could tell James was disoriented; he looked as though he were going to try to sit up.

Leaning down, Elbert whispered. "I'm here, brother–rest." James focused in on him as best he could, then nodded.`

Simon and Jeremiah resumed moving toward the wagon. Once James was settled in the back, Elbert climbed in. Frank drove and Lou rode shotgun, while the carriage driven by Odell followed. The rest of the men closed ranks as they traveled. Elbert sat at the back flap of the wagon covering staring at the old sawmill. The brown, four-story building was on the verge of collapse and in truth, so was he. At this point, all he wanted was to collect Black and go the hell home.

* * *

Black sat to the table in suite two-twenty-five reading through the correspondence he found in the office. The stacks of parchment fell into several categories–coded, decoded, and mundane. Black couldn't say for certain, but it appeared Campbell Penn was answering to Jeff Davis himself. There were several telegrams that greatly resembled his own exchanges with Lincoln. He made no move to gain information from his prisoner. In the meantime, Campbell had been bound, gagged, and propped up against the green settee; his indignation echoing about the common area.

The mood was intense as they waited for word of James. Black had moved the woman to the smaller bedchamber with Jake standing guard over her. It was tactical and meant to provoke his hostage. E.J. stood at the window monitoring the situation across the roadway, while Black continued to read as if his prisoner didn't exist. He sat to keep from pacing and revealing his doubt. Periodically, he would ask Campbell a question, and of course his prisoner couldn't respond–being gagged in all.

"I see you have a receipt for two other rooms on this floor. Who are the occupants?"

Black's inquiries were met with silence. Undeterred, he turned to E.J. and asked. "Have you met Carlton Renfro, Roderick Styles or Jared Clinks?"

"I have met Styles and Clinks–not Renfro. I've also spent time with that pompous actor, John Booth." E.J. responded in disgust.

"I haven't met Styles or Clinks, but I have had the displeasure of encountering Renfro," Black said with a chuckle. "His plantation is Magnolia Hills in Alabama."

"I guess… I have heard of Magnolia Hills." E.J. responded.

"Did you know that I have a strong dislike for the words plantation, magnolia, and cotton?"

"I can understand your aversion." E.J. answered. "Would you like me to check out the other two rooms?"

"Hmmm, no." Black replied. "They will not be there. I'm afraid they are aware of my presence."

As Black participated in polite conversation, he also employed intimidation. In his mind there was nothing quite like well-mannered coercion. It had been his experience that affluent sitting parlors in the north and south were filled with those who were savage and polite; he had learned from the best.

Shaking his head, Black stood and walked over to the window to survey the activity below. Smoke filled the air as men gathered in the street with buckets and no organization; the Buckingham was no more.

"How many ways are there out of this place?" Black inquired.

"Jake and Jeremiah reported five exits. Two for patrons and the other three for servants, merchants and the rubbish."

At the base of the windows, E.J. and Jake set wet sheets to catch the smoke, but that was becoming ineffective. The patrons and staff were preoccupied; still, it was the middle of the day and moving his hostage could prove difficult. *It was time,* Black thought *to collect his brothers, his men, and head home.*

CHAPTER 12

FLOWERS, HOSTAGES AND GUNS

Caroline kept her eyes downcast to avoid any connection with the man called Jake, who was both shorter and younger than she. He had flawless dark skin, discerning brown eyes, thick lips, and a wide nose. His eyebrows, mustache and goatee enhanced his maleness while highlighting his undeniable beauty. Danger radiated from him and where she had missed this fact during their first encounter, she realized now it was wrong to have thought him a slave.

If she were admitting truths, thinking this man a slave had given her license to get a closer look and feel safe doing it. As she reassessed, Caroline recognized it was her own desperation that caused her to see what wasn't there. While the man called Jake wore high quality clothing, and this was surely a sign of bondage; his gun holstered to his upper left side was not. In her experience only white men carried weapons.

Campbell Penn had been a deterrent to all male suitors in her life. No man, slave or free, had ever openly shown interest in her.

This man's attention made her feel not too tall, not too old, and not too awkward. Caroline felt shame at how much she needed to feel beautiful. At the risks of physical punishment, she had dressed up to stroll the boardwalk. Jake had been in the lobby that day watching as she descended the stairs. He stood to the left of the great room as she made for the entrance. She didn't have to look his way to feel his eyes on her; the sensation had been intense.

Unbidden, Caroline's thoughts wandered back to the unwanted conversation with a young, colored maid; she was more Jake's match. *"The man what be wit' that white merchant asked after ya. He named Jake."*

Caroline wasn't friendly with the waitstaff. Campbell would never have allowed such interactions. When she didn't respond, the maid placed her hands on her narrow hips. The right side of her black uniform rode up as she sneered. *"I told 'im you's a uppity wench and too old for 'im to boot."*

The woman had stopped her as she made her way through the lobby. Jake was nowhere in sight; the maid's unwelcomed dialogue stung. Still, Caroline held her head high as she stepped past the skinny woman to the staircase. Behind her, she heard the woman hiss. *"Heffa."*

Jake's voice snatched her from her musings. "Why you have two names? Which is yo' name?"

"My name is Caroline," she whispered, lifting her eyes to meet his.

Jake stood with his back against the bedchamber door; his demeanor in direct contrast with what was going on around them. He had taken the liberty of drawing the drapes and lighting an oil lamp. This action did nothing to quell the anxiety rolling around inside her. The commotion from the street below, the smoke and the yelling in the corridor added to her panic.

"Will they kill him?" She finally got up the nerve to ask.

"Who?"

"Master Campbell."

Jake's eyebrows drew together but when he would have spoken, there came a knock on the door. He stood for a moment, his eyes locked with her own before he abruptly turned and yanked on the knob. The large, bald black man appeared in the doorframe.

"Time," the bald man said.

"Yeah," Jake replied.

The bald man walked to the window and pulled back the drapes. Both men stared out, then Jake nodded. A thin mist of smoke was starting to fill the bedchamber causing her to cough. Each man turned to look at her.

"Bring her back out here–less smoke." The bald man ordered.

"This way," Jake said motioning to her.

In the common area Campbell was propped against the settee; her master was bound and gagged. Caroline covered her mouth at the amount of blood smeared on the furniture and the helpless spectacle Campbell made. Her master was pale, and his hair was wet with sweat; his eyes widened at the sight of her. She would have rushed to his side, but Jake stepped between her and Campbell.

"Please sit, Caroline." Jake instructed.

The bald man stood to the left of Campbell with his arms folded over his chest. When she would have pleaded for his life, she heard the scrape of a skeleton key in the lock. It was then that she noticed the white man was missing. The door opened and three men stepped over the threshold. She was holding her breath as she witnessed the exchange between the men.

The first man through the door was the man who shot Campbell–the man with the lifeless eyes. He and the bald man stared at each other and their exchange though silent was grim; the bald man nodded, and his anger was apparent. Next into the suite was the white man, his black hair was pushed behind his ears, and his dark eyes were assessing everything. The last man to enter was the black-skinned man with the inky mane of wild curls. This man stood out; he was strapped with three guns. Caroline watched as the men systematically moved about, and while their tasks appeared separate–they were all in one accord.

"Is Imma need to tie you up, Miss Caroline?" Jake asked, his tone matter of fact.

The activity in the suite stopped, and it seemed all the men were waiting for her response. "N-No... that won't be necessary."

Once she answered, they all went back to the tasks at hand. The large bald man gathered all the correspondence from Campbell's desk. The man with the mean eyes punched Campbell out, then wrapped him in the bed dressings from the master chamber. It was the white man who stepped in to help with Campbell. The man with the wild hair pulled the two guns at his hips–stepped to the right of the door and nodded.

The bald man opened the suite door and stepped into the corridor without a care. Caroline was certain of two things. One: they wouldn't harm her and two: her master was as good as dead.

Black stepped into the empty hallway followed by the woman, then Jake. Elbert and E.J. handled their prisoner. Jeremiah brought up the rear–guns drawn and ready for business. The corridor held a light haze of smoke that would only worsen. Black led them to a door hidden at the opposite end of the hall. Floral wallpaper dressed the door the same as the wall; the setting was to make the removal of chamber pots unintrusive for the high paying guests.

Pulling the door wide, Black noted that the stairs before him were crooked, and it was dark. Jake spoke up. "Twenty steps... the floor gon be slick. The railing is on yo' left."

"Last step is higher than the rest of 'em. Push at the wall once you at the bottom," Jeremiah said.

"When you reach out back...go left." E.J. added.

The odor in the raised corridor was foul. Jeremiah went on.

"When you reach outside, don't breathe in too deep... just more waste."

Counting down the stairs until the last, Black pushed at the door. They found themselves on the edge of a fenced in lot. There were about thirty wagons filled with what Black thought could only be rubbish. The system was simple; when a wagon was full it was hitched up, then towed away. There were men working with mules to clear out the waste and trash for the establishment.

Once on the outside, Black kept the group moving. They continued until they came to a grove of trees and high grass. Out in front of them were two carriages, one driven by Philip and the other driven by Chester. Odell, who was riding shotgun with Chester, hopped down to help with their prisoner. There was no talking as the group split up.

Jake, the woman, and E.J. got into one carriage. Elbert tossed Campbell into the other vehicle none too gently, then climbed in. Black and Jeremiah followed. As the carriage started rolling, Black looked up at the sky from the window. A plume of blue-black smoke hovered in the distance; a sign that Montreal would be working for days to keep the flames in check.

Black sat opposite Campbell who was uncovered, but still bound and gagged. While he and his prisoner eyed each other, Black directed his conversation to Elbert. "James?"

"Not good." His brother answered. "I sent the men ahead so we could get him home."

Black nodded. Jeremiah spoke up. "The men won't enter the gate without us... I'm concerned for Abby and the children."

Turning his attention to Campbell, Black asked. "Who else at the saloon works for you?"

Elbert's head snapped up, but their prisoner never looked his way; Black went on as if Campbell's mouth weren't stuffed with a handkerchief. "You will answer me... to be sure."

Lending his attention to the great outdoors, Black disengaged. In his head, he went through a list of issues that would need tackling given the circumstances. But Jeremiah was correct regarding first things–first, he would see to his brothers, Abby, and the children. It was late afternoon when they met up with the wagon carrying James. The men stopped near a sizeable pond to rest the horses and themselves.

The temperature was warm, and Black was certain that would change when the sun went down. Stepping into the bushes he undressed and submerged himself in the water. Cleanliness would be essential in his dealings with James. When he came out of the pond, Philip was there with a change of clothes. Elbert was next and when they were both scrubbed up, they headed for the wagon carrying James. Anthony and Lou took their place in the carriage with Jeremiah and Campbell Penn. Crammed in the second carriage with the other two hostages were Jake, E.J., and Caroline.

When Black climbed into the back of the covered wagon, the fading sunlight only added to the dimness happening. James lay swaddled in pea green blankets surrounded by several pillows and more blankets; his brother was still as death. Black scrambled over to James as Philip handed a small lantern to Elbert through the backflap.

"Shit," Black breathed as he stared down into his brother's face. The firelight and the soup green blankets turned James' pallor to the shade before death. Reaching out, Black pressed two fingers against his throat. He was relieved to find a heartbeat. Turning to Elbert, he said, "He is still alive."

"Shit," Elbert repeated... he was feeling the same.

James' eyes popped open at the sound of Elbert's voice. His eyeballs were bright red, and the lids were severely swollen. Black spoke to James and his words were emotional. "Me and Elbert are here. We're taking you home... try to hold on."

James' eyes drifted shut; turning to Elbert, Black ordered. "You rest first."

Elbert didn't argue, instead he laid down next to James throwing his left arm over his face. The wagon was small for three grown men; still, the brothers made it work. They didn't engage the other men in an attempt to keep down infection. The men rode all night stopping only to rest the horses and themselves. Simon took charge of navigating them home.

Black never did find rest, and Elbert who shared James' pallet didn't sleep either. A lantern was wedged in a hole of the planked flooring, and it remained lit with a low flame. The wagon cover itself was brown and to Black's surprise it was a bit stifling. His saddlebag was thrown haphazardly in the corner along with Elbert's bag and three water canteens. Travel was rough and even Black's body hurt from the constant rocking.

Outside the wagon, Black heard the squeaking carriage springs and the thunder of horse hooves. The wagon was protected by the men on horseback with each carriage placed at the front and rear of the procession. Lanterns dangling from both sides of the vehicles helped to light the way. The men normally traveled in complete darkness, but Black meant to cut time off the trek home; they would deal with ambush if it happened.

The caravan was about three hours out from the town and fort when James began writhing in pain. Immediately, Black reached for his saddlebag while Elbert turned up the wick on the lantern. The firelight bounced and wobbled, but Black managed to grab the sleeping powder he had in a small blue jar. He mixed it with the water in the silver canteen and shook it. Pressing the spout to his brother's lips, Black forced the water down James' throat. James tried to fight, but he was no match.

Water spilled on the blankets and Black removed the swaddling to redress his brother in new blankets. James was naked and the bruising was serious; seeing his brother's battered body made Black's eyes smart. When James began trembling, Black wrapped him in fresh blankets before sagging to the floor in a heap of roiling emotions. Elbert turned the wick down and placed it back in the holder before laying back and throwing his arm over his eyes once more; it was Elbert who broke the silence.

"I was tryin' not to manhandle the people."

"What I would have done," Black said.

"I should have stayed at the railroad town... shouldn't have moved into the saloon."

"If this was James' task to check out Ruby's... how would where you stayed have made the difference?" Black asked.

"I ended up managing the saloon instead of the issue of Ruby's death."

"That would have happened in the railroad town as well." Black answered.

"You figured out someone at the saloon worked for the Preservers of Southern Life."

"That was in the papers in Campbell's office." Black countered.

"We accomplished nothing."

"The message we sent was clear to Montreal and to our people," Black said and his tone was even.

"Shit," Elbert said. "I needed you."

"And I came." Black replied.

"Some of them bastards got away."

Black's tone was matter of fact when he responded. "Part of being a great leader is putting your men and people first."

"Don't you see–I failed," Elbert said.

"That too is part of being a leader." Black shot back; the brothers fell quiet as the wagon rumbled toward home.

About two hours passed when the posse rode through the town nearest the fort. The animals were exhausted and so were the men, but they pressed on. As the group rounded the bend on the last leg of the journey, the night sky began blending with the early morning sun. The small caravan broke free of the overgrown vegetation heading straight for the gate.

Black was seated near the backflap of the wagon. His eyes bounced about the landscape as he worried for Abby and the children; the wagon slowed then stopped but didn't pass through the gate. Hopping down, Black walked to the front of the vehicle and his breath caught at the sight of fifty armed white men; their guns were drawn–their formation aggressive.

Stepping out in front of the wagon that carried James, Black faced this new conflict head on. Behind him, he heard the click, click, click of his men drawing their weapons. At his upper left was more of the same with the men of the fort posted up at the top of the gate–guns drawn. Black moved to the center of the chaos and folded his arms over his chest.

As the sun took hold of the morning, Black watched as the white army before him parted. A large fellow walked toward him and from what he could see the man looked agitated. Black didn't wait for the man to reach him; instead, he dropped his arms and moved forward with purpose. When he stood among his would-be adversaries, he asked.

"Who the fuck are you?"

"Lincoln sent us." The man with blue eyes, shaggy blond hair and thick neck replied.

"The question I asked is… who the fuck are you?" Black repeated to the much taller man.

"My name is Miles Glendale, your president sent me."

"You are mistaken, Glendale. I have no president. You and your men will stand down or there will be bloodshed to mark this morning." Black promised.

"And you are?"

"Not pleased," Black said. "Your president's problem is in Montreal. Why would he send you here?"

"Stand down!" Glendale yelled over his shoulder.

Black didn't give the same instructions to his own men. He waited for the situation to become neutralized and when Lincoln's men lowered their weapons, he said. "Now–why are you really here?"

The man named Glendale looked away for long seconds before answering. "We have orders to take possession of any prisoners you might have."

Black chuckled, mirthlessly. "I'd like to see you try."

Glaring at his unwanted guests, Black spun on his heels and strode away. The sight before him was one for which he felt immense pride. His men stood at the ready and over the top of the gate he could see more guns drawn. He had wasted enough time and he had critical matters to address.

"Open!" Black yelled.

When the gate groaned open, his men spilled out blocking all views of the caravan as it entered the fort. Black walked with Elbert and when the gate closed firmly behind them, the brothers climbed back into the wagon. They worked fast pulling James' listless body onto the makeshift stretcher and pushing him toward the backflap. The vehicle rolled to a stop the long way in front of the house. Jeremiah stepped into Black's view, but his attention was focused on the path at the bottom of the small hill.

Black hopped down first, his boots disturbing the dry earth. He turned in time to see Abby running at them, her legs getting tangled in her brown skirts. She was screaming and as she drew nearer, her pain evident. Tears streamed down her cheeks; her black skin glistened with sorrow.

"I ain't see James." She sobbed. "Where James?"

"Get 'im in the house," Jeremiah said as he moved toward Abby. "I'll bring her inside."

Black barely had time to register that the other women were with her. The sun had become brighter as if to make clear there would be no hiding. Elbert pushed the stretcher through the flap and Black had no choice but to catch it. Abby's screams of agony caused his blood to stop in his veins. Frank and Lou appeared to help with the stretcher while Elbert hopped down from the wagon.

The men didn't hesitate; they jogged for the stairs leading to the porch and the house. Elbert yelled, "Get Shultz… Now!"

"We sent for 'im." Philip hollered back.

At the top of the landing, Big Mama, Cora, and Iris stood to the left of the door. The older women showed no emotion, while the backdrop to the morning was Abby's screams. In that moment Black saw two sides of colored women. It was moments like this that made him uncomfortable with his attention to detail. In the faces of the older women, he saw a calm understanding that colored lives would never truly matter; in the younger women, he saw resistance to such a notion–even as they were being suffocated by a fact the older women had already come to accept.

As Black walked backward past the older women, his eyes fell on their mama. "I put him out wit' sleeping powder… figured that would be best for traveling and pain."

Mama directed. "Last room on the end."

Black glanced one last time to the path in front of the house. The people were starting to spill from their homes. Abby was still hollering, and Jeremiah was trying to manage the women.

* * *

The black cracker moved toward Abby as she stumbled and cried out for James. Jeremiah reached her just as she collapsed in a tangle of brown fabric. Pulling Abby's body flush against his own, Jeremiah cradled her head to his chest. His wild black curls created a curtain around their faces; still, he could feel the bright sun and the eyes of the people on them. Placing his mouth to Abby's ear…

"Shhh… we will see to James and the children together."

At his words, Abby went limp against him. She was trembling and weeping softly as she worked at trying to calm herself. Jeremiah didn't let go and when Abby wrapped her arms about him, he hugged her tighter.

"I cain't lose him." She whispered.

He didn't address her words. "You ready?"

Jeremiah didn't wait for her to give an answer to his question. He scooped Abby up in his arms, and she nuzzled into him. Jeremiah carried her up the porch stairs, into the house and up to the second floor. There was a lot of activity in the corridor and when he placed her back on her feet, he held her at the waist until she was steady.

Abby looked up at him, her body still trembling. "I's ready."

He didn't get a chance to respond. Shultz came rushing up the stairs, his words clip and sure. "I am here, Abby."

And with that, the two disappeared into the commotion spilling from the third room on the left.

CHAPTER 13

FIRST IMPRESSIONS

Once inside the gate Jake climbed from the carriage, then helped Caroline down. Travel had been grueling with two hostages and a woman all in the same vehicle. But when night fell and there was only the light from the lanterns swinging outside each door, she nuzzled into him, seeking his protection. All night her body trembled against his own and when the carriage stumbled, she started. Caroline didn't rest and it was the same for him.

The sun shone down on the fort like James wasn't near death and like there wasn't an army at the gate.

Standing in the center of the activity, Jake realized he had nowhere to take a woman; he lived in the barracks. In the face of threat, Simon was left in command of the gate. Placing Caroline under the shade of a small tree, he sought Simon's council.

"Wait here."

Caroline didn't speak but she did nod her acknowledgement. Simon stood to the right of the gate speaking with the men. Spying Jake, he waved him forward.

"Ya needs somewhere to put her?"

Jake was thankful for Simon's ability to read a situation. "Yeah."

"Take her to one of the cabins near where Shultz got Virgil's field hand." Simon said. "Imma leave her to you. Black got his hands full... Elbert too. Philip, Odell and Chester got the prisoners."

Jake wanted to protest; instead, he gave a curt nod. Simon continued. "Get wit' the women and they'll help ya."

"Yeah."

Simon turned away from him and was on to the next matter. It appeared Caroline would be his responsibility until life got sorted out. Jake looked over to where she stood under the tree, and he assessed. She looked lost, afraid, and tired, but what got him was his own emotions. When he first laid eyes on her, he had to have her; he had even pondered stealing her, now he felt...

The temperature was mild. Still, if the way she wrapped her arms about herself was any indication, Caroline looked chilled. Jake sighed before moving in her direction. The idea of being stuck with her chafed, and he wandered if he could trade duties with one of the other men. He would bide his time and he would treat her as he would any woman.

A breeze blew just as he reached her, and Caroline shivered. His words were short and to the point. "Please follow me."

Jake ignored how wide her eyes had gotten in response to his tone. He walked them in the direction of the vacant cabins Simon had spoken of. They took the long way, ending up three cabins over from where Shultz was housing the field hand. There was no one on the path but he and Caroline; the hour was still early.

Stopping in front of the cabin, he explained. "This here is where you gon be stayin'."

Again, she nodded; Jake added. "Come."

He climbed the stairs of the makeshift porch and pushed at the door. Stepping aside, he allowed her in first. The cabin was plain like all the structures on this side of the fort–more storage than cozy. Still, there was a full-size bed, a wooden table, three chairs, a fireplace and a small wood burning stove. Pushed into the corner was a large tin tub.

Caroline stood by the door staring about as if she couldn't comprehend how she had come to be there. The cabin was dim causing Jake to step to the window and pull back the homespun curtains. The sun spilled into the cabin highlighting how much the woman before him didn't fit in this space.

"I'll have supplies brought to ya," he said before turning to leave.

"Jake!" her voice was panicked.

Looking back at her, he found her wringing her hands in her skirts. She looked travel weary and on the verge of tears. He waited for her to speak.

"What will become of me?"

Caroline's southern drawl was dainty–throaty. Jake felt his balls tighten, but he reminded himself that she was not for him. "You ain't gon come to no harm. Imma be outside."

Her chin quivered and he grabbed at the back of his neck. His discomfort made the exchange difficult. He was about to try to exhibit better manners, but her words…

"Is my master dead?" she asked.

"Miss Caroline, why don't you rest?" Jake snapped before quitting the cabin.

Outside, he gazed about as he paced the dirt path in front of the cabin. He shoved his hands in his pockets, then removed them. His agitation was such that even the crunching of gravel under his boot rankled. He would still, then abruptly resume pacing. Shaking his head, he looked to the trees that lined the path and then to the blue sky.

Finally, he allowed his thoughts to settle on James. But when he envisioned Black and Elbert without their brother, he turned his mind away from such musings. Shit, he wanted to cry; he loved James. Clearly, he was tired, hungry, and needed to take a piss.

There was no other way. He wouldn't think about James–he would wait to hear from Black.

A stray branch stabbed him in the side as he stood in the fat bushes relieving himself. At the pump he washed his face and hands trying to wake up. He'd just made his way back around to the front of the small structure when he noticed a flat wagon driven by Anthony heading his way. When the vehicle stopped, Anthony hopped down to help Emma, his wife and Molly, Lou's woman down from the back. They had come with items for Caroline, and he was thankful.

"Mornin', Jake." Both women greeted.

"Ladies..." He responded.

He and Anthony were still in a difficult place where Emma was concerned, and Jake couldn't understand why. There had been next to no interaction between he and Emma. Today, however, he was happy for their arrival; he needed help.

The women went on ahead leaving he and Anthony to carry two crates each. Following the women up the porch stairs, they all waited while Emma knocked.

"Come in," Caroline's voice was thick.

Emma pushed at the door, stepping over the threshold first. Molly was next and Jake last. Anthony set the two crates he was carrying on the floor under the window. Jake placed his load by the window as well. Standing once more, he glanced over Molly's and Emma's heads to see Caroline standing to the right of the table. The damn sunlight splashed her dark skin magnifying her pain and her inability to control her emotions.

"Good mornin,'" Emma said softly. "This here is Molly."

Molly whispered. "Nice to meet ya."

"I'm Caroline." She sniffled and tears rolled down her cheeks.

"I cain't cook, but Molly here can." Emma explained.

Jake watched the exchange, and it was all wrong. Caroline was much taller than both women, the blue dress she wore though dusty from travel was fancy. Emma and Molly wore brown dresses that were conducive to cooking and cleaning. Jake wondered if there would ever be a setting in which Caroline fit. While he was busy contemplating the scene before him, Emma stepped forward giving Caroline a hug. The action broke something within her, and the taller woman wept. Jake exited the situation in a hurry to pace the path.

It was a few moments before Anthony appeared on the porch with two buckets in his hands. Anthony's tone was… something.

"You wanna grab the other buckets. Dis will be faster if you help."

"Just give me the damn buckets." Jake replied as he walked over and snatched the pails from Anthony's grasp. He didn't wait for a response as he headed to the pump.

Anthony soon appeared with a large black pot. He didn't speak, but he did hold it under the spout. Once the buckets and the pot were filled, both men headed around front. When they reached the porch, Anthony spoke.

"Why don't you get some rest? You gon be out here through the night. Black say to leave her in yo' care."

Jake stared at Anthony, nodded then walked away.

* * *

Virgil was seated on the second to the last step in front of Black's house. He had helped bring water to the room where James was taken. The house was a bevy of activity with people rushing about to assist in any way possible. Virgil hung his head to avoid eye contact–he was positive that he couldn't handle polite conversation at this moment.

In the last weeks he had cried more than he had in his entire life. Digging the heels of his hands into his eye sockets, he tried to wipe away his tears. His very spirit ached with all he had seen over the course of a fortnight. Helplessly witnessing the agony of others uncovered frailties within himself that he had not known existed. Virgil had been unable to escape the shit that was his life.

He was contemplating finding a bed at the barracks. Now that he was back at the fort, he couldn't face Percy. An awkwardness had settled into his person, and it was accompanied by pain. He thought about being forced to leave at a time when Percy needed him most; still, he understood Black's plight–how could he not with this dilemma? Hadn't he seen with his very own eyes Ruby's demise?

He was still pondering his next move when a long shadow fell over him. Virgil reared his head back to find Tim, E.J., and Jeremiah standing over him.

"You ain't lookin' so good," Tim said.

Virgil snorted. "Thanks."

"You sick?" E.J. asked.

"How's James?" Virgil asked stepping over the question.

All three of the men standing before him shook their heads and to Virgil's horror, his eyes watered. He heard rather than saw an approaching carriage and Tim waved it over–calling out.

"Whoa...whoa."

"Key man," Jeremiah called out to the driver.

"Jeremiah," came the old man's response.

Tim directed. "Give Virgil a ride around to his cabin."

"Sho' will." The Key man answered.

Virgil wanted to decline but he feared bursting into tears in front of this bunch. He truly couldn't take another humiliation. He stood on unsteady legs and walked over to the black carriage that waited. His gait was that of a person who had indulged in too much drink. The older man looked as though he were about to get down to set the stairs, but Virgil waved him off. He climbed into the carriage and didn't look back.

The black leather seats smelled of saddle polish and the red curtains were pushed back to allow the natural light; once alone his tears flowed. His business came to mind, and it too was one more thing that had gone to hell in a handbasket. The rattle of the carriage, the horse hooves plodding along and the old man yelling soothing words to the animals almost broke him… almost.

"Whoa dere… whoa."

Virgil didn't linger or the old man would have attempted to help; instead, he pushed at the door and hopped down. Time stood still as he stared at the cabin, while behind him the carriage rolled away in a symphony of rattles and squeaks. Looking up and down the pathway, he spied Anthony standing in front of a cabin three doors down. It showed Black's level of efficiency for he had not been left unattended.

Sighing, Virgil ambled up the porch and shoved at the door. As always with this man, all his senses were immediately engaged. Percy was seated to the table, a cup of coffee before him. Virgil noted that he was shirtless, his ribs were bound, and his right hand was bandaged to just beyond the wrist. The faint smell of cinnamon clung to the cabin; it was familiar–it was him.

Percy's brown skin was still marred by deep cuts and abrasions, but it didn't subtract from the beauty of his maleness. His arms and chest were packed with muscle–his body carved from years of physical labor. Raising his hand, Percy rubbed at his clean-shaven jaw. A sign that he was feeling stress. Virgil's breath caught when their eyes met. It hadn't been noticeable at first glance, but he saw it now and his jealousy became hot. Dropping his eyes, Virgil tried to gather himself.

"You're back." Percy said, his voice rich–deep.

"We're just back."

Percy shuffled at the table before Virgil heard his chair scrape the floor. He, himself was six feet, but the man before him was taller and outweighed him by a few stones.

"You don't look well, Beau."

Virgil's eyes snapped up at the use of his pet name. "They got ahold of James. It ain't good."

"Damn. Will he be all right?"

"This whole matter is a nightmare." Virgil breathed.

Percy had moved to the center of the cabin. He had the right amount of hair that trickled from his navel into his brown trousers. On his feet were a pair of new black boots. Today, Percy resembled the man he met six years ago.

"Why don't you come sit, Beau?"

Virgil really did need to sit, but he couldn't manage to move his back from the support of the door. And there was also the jealousy that was choking him. He swallowed hard, then asked in an even tone.

"Who… ah… who braided your hair?"

Percy stared at him for seconds, then folded his arms over his chest. His muscles bulged with the movement. It was brief but Virgil saw his hurt and annoyance. He was certain Percy would back away, but he answered.

"Miss Abby braided my hair. She and the doc thought it better than shaving. Dr. Shultz was worried that I might catch my death with a bald head."

"I don't wanna fight." Virgil lied.

"Yes… you do, Beau." Percy contradicted. "Come lay down and rest. We can pick up where we left off once you've slept."

"You are casual with your words because your sentiments toward me have changed." Virgil said, his voice rusty.

Percy dropped his arms and moved into his personal space. His tone was minus the agitation that showed in his expression. "The people here know that Virgil and his field hand engage in unnatural acts."

"Have you been mistreated in my absence?"

"We were all once slaves here, Beau. Our sensibilities have endured much." Percy responded.

"You find humor in my hurt."

"I sidestep your insults." Percy countered.

He looked away, but Percy grabbed his chin forcing eye contact. Virgil whispered. "I mean no disrespect."

"Rest, Beau, you need it."

Percy's grip slipped around to his neck. Virgil's eyes drifted shut when Percy leaned in and kissed his cheek; the contact suspended time. He reveled in the roughness of Percy's touch and the softness of his lip. Desperately, he wanted to ask if Percy still planned on leaving him, but he feared an honest reply. Unable to help himself, Virgil reached up and palmed the back of Percy's head, touching the neat rows of braids. His heart hurt with the knowledge that someone could perform a task for this man that he could not.

He hadn't known how much he missed the intimacy they shared until Percy pulled him into a full body hug. It was the many months of trying to decide if they would remain together. It was Ruby, James, and Percy himself. Shit, it was Abby having braided Percy's damn hair that did it. Virgil wept, and Percy held him.

He remembered being led over to the bed where Percy removed his boots then helped him undress. Virgil fell asleep as soon as he laid down.

* * *

Black stood on the side of the large four poster bed staring down at the battered, bruised, and naked body of James. The chamber was overtaken by some concoction that Big Mama had mixed in the bathwater. He and Elbert were present to be the brawn. Black didn't know which bothered him more, James being unconscious or seeing his brother staring about as if unaware of his surroundings.

A small table was moved into the chamber. Three oil lamps sat on its surface, two were lit. The pale rose colored drapes were pull back and to Black's way of thinking there was too much light. Abby and Shultz slowly moved their hands all over James' body trying to discern the extent of his injuries. Black could do nothing but look on in admiration, for Abby did not resemble the screaming woman from an hour ago.

Shultz had shaved the right side of James' head and Abby sewed the gash herself; her hands were steady. Like Virgil's field hand, two of his fingers were broken. The doctor splinted the fingers together then wrapped the whole hand just beyond the wrist. Elbert had backed away from the bed and Black suspected it was to give himself a moment.

"Mama, is you ready for us?" Abby asked.

"Black, you and Elbert bring your brother to the tub–hear."

Following the instructions of their mama, Elbert took his feet and Black supported his head. The brothers shuffled their feet rather than stepped, so as not to jostle James too much. Once at the side of the black tub, their muscles were strained as they lowered him in. James cried out when his body came in contact with the warm water and Black's heart squeezed. Abby hovered on the edge of the situation, her eyes never leaving James. The water lapped over the side of the tub, wetting both men and the floor.

Black knelt beside the tub while Elbert did the same opposite him. They held his head above the water and Black was thankful when James gazed at him with awareness. James' eyebrows drew together before he croaked out.

"Is you all right, Hope?"

"Yeah," Black answered.

"Elbert?"

"Right here," Elbert answered.

James turned at the sound of Elbert's voice and once he laid eyes on Elbert, he smiled.

"Sleeping powder is still on him." Shultz explained when James' eyes drifted shut.

The doctor pulled a chair next to the tub and the women draped towels over it. Black and Elbert were soaked by the time they heaved James out of the water and into the chair. Abby dried him. Shultz applied the tight binding about his ribs and forced more sleeping powder in him. Mama readied the bed. Black and Elbert moved the chair and James to the bed before lifting him. The women swaddled him and so it began, the wait to see how this would play out.

"You and Anna take Cora's bedchamber. She can sleep wit' me," Big Mama said.

"Yes, Mama." Elbert replied.

"Black, go on and rest causin' we gon need ya both directly. Ya both got to rest when James rest for now."

"Yes, Mama." Black answered, but to Abby he said. "Come get me and Elbert if you need us."

"I will." Abby replied as she seated herself in the chair near the bed.

Black turned to leave. He needed a break; he needed Sunday. Trying to escape Shultz, he quit the bedchamber. Still, the doctor followed him into the empty corridor.

"He will make it," Shultz said. "They beat him worse than Percy."

"They were busy killing Ruby," Black said with a grunt. "That's why Percy didn't get worse–they were focused on Ruby and Spike."

Elbert closed the door and stood facing the stairs. He didn't speak, just listened. Shultz asked in a low tone. "Hostages?"

"Three," Black answered.

"Do you have who did this to James?" Shultz asked, his anger apparent.

"We have who ordered it," Elbert said.

"I read the papers." Black answered. "We have who did it."

Elbert looked at him, and Black went on. "I didn't want you to kill him during travel."

The three men were quiet for a time when the doctor said, "Imma stay with James."

When Shultz turned walking back into the bedchamber, Elbert and Black were left staring at each other.

"I believe what we have is the man who ordered the deaths of Ruby and Spike. Campbell Penn is also the man that beat James," Black said.

"We have resolved nothing," Elbert said before he started pacing. "That actor got away again; he is who kept the shit going at that damn theatre."

"The Buckingham is no more. I will find out how far this plot goes. Elbert, this was not a waste. James will live."

"Lincoln sent men to the fort... why? Why didn't he send men to Montreal?" Elbert asked.

"The president wants our hostages."

"I believe what we got in the other two are hired help. I think we only got one real prisoner," Elbert said. "Question them and turn them over–keep Campbell."

Black nodded. "Get some rest."

"Yeah," Elbert said before he headed for Miss Cora's room.

Black took the stairs and headed to his room. It wasn't lost on him that Elbert was a real leader. His brother was constantly thinking. These were his thoughts as he trekked down the hall, through the kitchen and into his own bedchamber; his discomfort finally registered because of his wet clothing. Sunday stood in the center of their bedchamber and when he entered, she ran to him. She was shaking and crying.

"Shh. James will live and I am well."

The lovers never moved away from the door. Instead, they held each other reveling in the fact that they were both alive. His mind wandered to Ruby and Spike... to Virgil's field hand and James. Unable to ponder a moment more, Black pushed everything from his thoughts except Sunday.

* * *

Elbert stood in the center of Miss Cora's bedchamber thankful that Anna and the children weren't present. His emotions were all over the place, and he needed a moment to collect himself. When he thought it was safe to venture out of the room, he took the steps straight out to the porch and kept moving until he came to his cabin.

Climbing the little porch, he shoved at the door. Anna was getting up from her sewing chair when he entered their humble abode. The lighting was dim and in direct contrast to the morning sun at his back. The natural light splashed in around him as he stood in the doorway.

"I have water on the stove." She greeted.

Elbert didn't speak, but he did begin filling the tub. He also filled and refilled the buckets at the pump. Tasks complete, he closed the door and undressed. On the table sat his silver flask and once he was naked, he drank deeply before settling his weary bones in the too hot water.

He was dazed and it seemed his wife knew it. She had removed her gray dress and was kneeling beside the tub in a white shift. Reaching in the water she scrubbed his back with the red cloth floating about and then washed his hair. When she spoke, her words were soft.

"What is Dr. Shultz sayin' about James?"

"He's gonna make it."

Shaking his head, he continued. "When Simon told me James was taken, his words stole my breath."

Elbert raised his eyes to meet Anna's gaze. He had avoided giving her his full attention; he didn't want her to see his pain. She nodded, then leaned in and kissed him. Anna never questioned him about the goings on; it was what he needed, instead she discussed the practical.

"I'll pack for the children. We can come back and forth to bathe."

"Yeah," he answered.

When she would have stood, he reached out a large hand dripping with bathwater and placed it over hers. The action stopped his wife from going about her chores.

"You and the family mean everything to me."

"I know," she whispered.

"Where are the boys?"

"Dennis is with Callie. Junior and Otis are with my mama," she said.

"Who has Jamie?"

"Callie has Jamie too. I think she and Jeremiah are going to be in the other room at the house. They will help me care for James and Abby's baby."

"Yeah," Elbert answered before washing his face and standing.

His wife was quick with a towel for him to step on, even as she handed him another for drying his body. Elbert's eyes scanned the cabin and at the foot of their bed lay a pair of black trousers with a matching shirt. Next to his clothing lay a blue dress with a white chemise and pantaloon set. Turning back to his wife, Elbert saw that she had removed her wet underdress. Hanging it over the side of the draining tub, Anna dried herself with a white cloth.

The sight was familiar, he needed comfort from this woman. Walking over to his wife, he lifted her into his arms. Anna wrapped her legs about his waist and her arms about his neck. He groaned at the warmth of her brown skin against his own. He was rougher than intended when he pushed his tongue in her mouth.

He smiled as the flavor of peppermint flooded his senses. Pulling back from her, he said. "Little Otis and his peppermints."

"Me, Abby, Callie and Sunday had to start eating some of the candy or the boy would have a belly ache." Anna giggled.

Chuckling, Elbert buried his face in her neck. But his voice was sober when he whispered. "Anna, I need you... please."

His lovely wife leaned her head back to catch his gaze. "Take me to our bed, Papa."

He palmed each cheek allowing his fingers to graze her core. At the side of the full-size bed, he set Anna on her feet. Lying down in the center of the multi-colored quilt, Elbert stared up at her; his wife didn't hesitate. Anna crawled onto the bed and straddled him, pinning his dick between them. As she sat above him, she smoothed her hands over his chest.

Leaning in, she kissed his lips one at a time and he could feel how much she missed him. Elbert felt the same. He needed for his wife to take control. His eyes drifted shut when she began placing open mouthed kisses across his chest. Elbert didn't want to think; he wanted to feel. When Anna bit his right nipple, the action caused him to hiss and grunt.

His wife licked a trail down his belly as she slid backwards exposing more and more of his body. She now sat astride his legs. Elbert opened his eyes in time to see Anna take him into her hot wet mouth. The effects of grief and lust on his person took him by complete surprise. His eyes rolled back up in his head.

"Shit, Anna… too close." He groaned.

But his wife did not heed his warning. Anna sucked him harder, pulling him all the way to the back of her throat. When he felt his dick pulse, she released him. Elbert was trying to calm himself as Anna's frantic fingers positioned him until she was above his shaft. Sliding down onto him, she threw her head back in absolute ecstasy and moaned. He had been about to warn her to go slow. But Anna started throwing that ass, wiping his mind clean of all thought.

Sunlight spilled through the crack of the drawn curtains into the dimness of the cabin and onto Anna's lovely brown skin. Her movements were slow and deliberate. Elbert felt drugged by their joining. She leaned in giving him a stormy kiss.

"I love you… so much, Papa." she whispered against his lips.

Anna's leg muscles clutched at his hips as she rode him. Elbert grabbed her rear, assisting her angle and helping her to pleasure him. When she clamped down on his dick, the sensation shoved him toward conclusion. His testicles tightened and his breath caught as he shot wave after wave of his hot seed into her. Reaching her peak, Anna slumped over him while still grinding herself against him. Their kisses became as turbulent as their lovemaking. Elbert could taste her worry, her love, and the salt from her tears.

In the aftermath, the lovers lay holding each other for a few stolen moments. Having his wife in his arms gave Elbert the courage to turn his mind to James, the hostages and Lincoln.

CHAPTER 14

FINDING THE FACTS
MAY 1864

The sun was going down when Jake spied Black and Elbert on the path striding toward him. Inside the cabin were Emma and Molly, who seemed to have taken pity on his hostage. Jake had to admit that Caroline cried less in the company of the younger women. Today, however, had been better than the last two days. But as he watched Black and Elbert moving toward him, Jake was clear about one thing. The day he thought would be better than most, might be his worse day yet with his prisoner.

He stood leaned against the post of the makeshift porch staring at the brothers when they came to a stop in front of him.

"James?"

"Slow going," Black answered. As was his way, Elbert didn't speak allowing Black to do all the talking. "The woman, has she spoken with you about anything?"

"She ain't done nothing but cry." Jake countered, while trying to hide his displeasure at being stuck in this position. "We don't say much to one another. Emma and Molly might be the ones to ask. Miss Caroline is better when they come."

"You say she speaks with Emma and Molly, but not you?" Elbert finally asked.

Jake shrugged. "Might be that Miss Caroline is 'fraid of menfolk."

Elbert stood with his arms crossed over his chest, and Black stood next to his brother with his hands clasped behind his back. Both men wore all black and Jake shook his head. This wasn't going to go well. As his eyes bounced between the men, Jake felt studied.

"I put you in charge of her because she is fond of you." Black said.

And there it was, Black's ability to see all. Clearing his throat Jake said, "Cain't say for sure why you would think such a thing. She ain't done nothing but weep at the sight of me."

Black eyed him and Jake had to maintain the contact. He had never been the single focus of Black's scrutiny; it was an uncomfortable place to be.

"After you," Black said.

Turning for the door, he walked into the cabin followed by Elbert and Black. The sight before him was cozy. Molly was standing at the stove stirring a large pot, while Emma and Caroline worked at the table rolling out dough. Emma and Molly smiled, Caroline did not.

The conversation and giggling stopped between the women. Jake made certain not to look at his prisoner. Molly moved the pot from the fire, then placed the metal lid over the flame to snuff it out. Emma draped a towel over the dough and stood. Both women wiped their hands on their aprons as they moved toward the door.

"Me and Molly gonna fetch the spice we forgot. We be back directly," Emma said.

"Yes, of course." Caroline whispered.

Jake watched as Molly and Emma exited the cabin in a flurry of brown serviceable dresses and stained aprons. Caroline remained standing behind the chair she had pushed up to the table. The fading natural light offered nothing to the situation, but two oil lamps made up for it. His prisoner also wore a brown dress that was ill fitted in length. Her hair was braided in two fat cornrows and when Jake met her gaze, he found that Caroline's eyes were bright with unshed tears. She was stunning.

He thought Black would do the talking, but it was Elbert that stepped forward addressing her. "Miss Caroline, how many men traveled with you and Campbell Penn to Canada?"

Jake stood across the room from the table watching the exchange. Elbert stepping forward caused Caroline to retreat. She didn't answer, so Elbert repeated his question while taking another step forward. Before Jake could think on the matter, Caroline rushed over to him wedging herself between him and the wall behind him. She was trembling against his back. Jake looked to Black for help only to be met with a smugness so sharp he dropped the contact. Damn Elbert for being scary and damn Black for seeing too much.

"Miss Caroline has been under the weather since we been back. Today is the first day she felt better. Please give us time." Jake requested. His every word binding him to the situation and her.

"I can assign another man to the matter," Black said, his tone void of emotion.

"The master and I traveled alone to Canada," she said, trembling at his back.

"How many men did you see once ya got to Canada?" Elbert pressed.

"It's difficult to say." Caroline answered. "I wasn't allowed in the company of many. If there was a gathering in our suite, I remained in my bedchamber. I was there to meet the master's needs."

Jake couldn't help it, he flinched at that statement. Black sensing Jake's discomfort stared around for a bit, and then he and

Elbert quit the cabin. Jake couldn't say which was worse, facing Black and Elbert on the path or staying to deal with Miss Caroline. Still, he found the manners enough to say.

"Have a seat. I won't be but a minute."

Stepping out onto the porch, he found Elbert and Black waiting for him. Elbert walked away leaving him and Black.

"You want me to assign someone else to Miss Caroline?" Black asked without preamble.

"No."

Jake thought Black would push the issue, forcing him to face himself. Instead, Black said. "Find out what she knows about the theatre. I'm sure she hadn't been there, but maybe she met people from the Buckingham."

"She said he ain't allow her around others. What is I'm lookin' for?" Jake asked.

"Anything," Black said before striding away in the direction of the cabin Virgil occupied.

Looking back to the cabin where Caroline waited, Jake shook his head. Damn Black.

* * *

The fort was filled with a tension that had not dissipated even though the men were home. Black suspected it was because James was still out of it and the people didn't know what to think. If he were gauging truth, he didn't know what to think either. In order to gain control of the matter, Black sifted through all the issues. He would address them in order of importance, much had been delayed to help with James.

Simon and Gilbert had questioned the other two hostages and they did indeed appear to be guns for hire. Still, he would see them before turning them over to Lincoln. When Black arrived at the first storage building, Lou and Sunday stood guard. Black behaved as if it didn't bother him that his wife and the other women kept up their duties. He thought with James being down the women would flock around him, but that had not been the case. The women managed to do both and though Black had not said, he was impressed.

"What have we got?" Black asked.

"They ain't said they names," Lou said.

Turning to his wife, Black asked. "Your thoughts?"

"These prisoners knows less than Petey," Sunday said.

Black nodded and climbing the stairs he disappeared into the storage building to face his first hostage. The man before him was pale of skin with black kinky hair; his prisoner was passing for a white man, but Black knew better. He was disheartened by this turn of events, still he had encountered worse in his dealings with the people. The prisoner was shackled and cuffed.

"Let us start with your name."

It was as Black suspected; the prisoner didn't speak. In fact, the man stared past him to the door. His prisoner looked to be about forty summers and thin of frame. Black judged him to be no more than five feet, ten inches. The type of men that took this kind of work were loners. They made life hard on men with plenty to lose.

In his head, Black went over the paperwork he took from Campbell Penn's suite. It was clear that Penn saw matters based on class and Black was certain the man thought himself a participant of high society. What Black found interesting was Penn's attachment to Miss Caroline, for she was considered low in the world. Penn hadn't even listed his hired guns in his paperwork. It was an indication that he didn't know the men carrying out his orders. Styles, Clinks and Renfro were the men Penn worked through to get matters handled.

Refusing to repeat his question, Black pulled his weapon and cocked it. This action caused his prisoner to take notice.

"My name is Myron," the man said without further prompting.

Black noted that Myron's speech was learned. He didn't engage verbally, leaving Myron to sweat and talk. "I took this work for the coin. I know naught."

"Your friend… what is his name?"

"Marvin," Myron answered.

"How many men were there working with you?"

"I am unsure." Myron whined as the chains at his hands and feet clanked. There was blood on his white shirt and dried mud on his brown boots.

Black stared at the man seated before him and promised. "If yo' partner gives me a different name. Imma kill you."

Myron nodded, and Black spun on his heels quitting the cabin. Sunday and Lou stood on the path dressed in all black, and the two were almost invisible. Stepping down from the porch, Black joined them, and together the three moved on to the next situation and the next hostage.

Black didn't tarry, he kept on straight into the cabin. Seated before him was a white man with brown hair and a swollen right eye. He too was shackled and cuffed. This storage building was empty save for his prisoner, the chair on which he sat and an oil lamp that hung from a hook in the ceiling. The man tried to ignore his presence.

"Marvin," Black said, using the element of surprise. The man's eyes bounced up to meet his own. "How many men worked with you in Montreal?"

Instead of answering the question, his prisoner spat on the floor. And to Black's great shock he felt nothing for the defiant display. There was a melancholy that seemed to surround him and after staring at his prisoner for long moments, Black exited the cabin. Elbert had been correct; these men were of no value to him. He would turn them over to Lincoln, but Campbell Penn belonged to him and James.

When he stepped from the cabin this time, Horace and Emmet were in place to guard the prisoners. His wife and Lou were gone. Black greeted both men before walking away. On this side of the fort, the darkness was all encompassing. He would deal with the trouble at the gate in the morning, for now he would deal with his family.

The temperature was warm, and the spring season was in full swing. No breeze was happening, the air was still and thick. Summer was upon them. Around him were the sounds of insects and the crunch of his boots on the dirt and gravel path. When his home came into view, Black's stride slowed. Many of the windows were lit up, a sign that no one slept. Caring for James was happening around the clock.

Reaching the porch, Black smelled cigar smoke before noting the shadowed form of Elbert standing to the left of the front door. The red-hot end of his cigar pinned down his location in the newly fallen night. Climbing the stairs Black stood next to his brother as he gazed at the full moon.

"James?" Black asked.

"Still out of it."

"Abby?"

"Mama finally made her go rest. She's in Mama's bed."

"Who is with James?"

"Anna and Callie."

The brothers fell silent until Black said, "I will deal with the gate in the morning."

"Campbell Penn?"

"When James is back on his feet." Black replied. He paused then went on. "I will turn the two over to the men at the gate."

Elbert chuckled. "Lincoln wishes to run with the twenty-two."

"Lincoln wishes to have a yes man and I am not that man." Black snapped.

More silence fell between the brothers, and Black could see when the red-hot tip of the cigar fell to the porch before disappearing under Elbert's boot. His brother bumped his arm to offer the flask. Black drank deeply before handing it back.

"Which one of us is on duty?" Elbert asked.

Black never answered the question. Both men strode into the house and went upstairs. Elbert stepped onto the landing first. As Black made the landing, Callie came rushing from the room where James was laid up. Elbert started for her meeting her halfway.

"What is it?"

Black moved in behind Elbert, but he couldn't bring himself to ask any questions. The reason was simple, he never really believed James would make it. He just never voiced such an opinion–not even to Elbert.

"It's James," Callie said. "He is asking for you, Black."

He couldn't move. Black's eyes bounced to the oil lamp on the table to the right of the hall. His mind seemed to get fixed on the fact that Paul had made his rounds to light the house.

"Black?" Elbert's tone was one of concern. "You ready?"

"Yeah."

He moved around Callie to the door of the bedchamber. James lay propped up on many pillows, his eyes were closed and his form still as death. Anna stood over him wiping his forehead with a cool cloth. She looked to the doorway and smiled. It seemed to Black that James had drifted back to sleep, but Anna leaned down and spoke to him.

"James... James, open your eyes. Black and Elbert are here."

Black was surprised when James turned his head in the direction of the door. Now that a few days had passed, the bruising looked worse not better. Although his eyes were open, they were so severely swollen that Black had to move toward the bed to make it easier on his brother. James being light of skin didn't help matters any.

James focused on him and croaked out. "You alright?"

"I am well." Black answered. "It's you I'm worried about."

"I feels like shit." James answered. He closed his eyes and Black thought he fell back to sleep. "Where Elbert?"

"I'm here." Elbert answered.

James looked between them and drifted again. Black was about to back away from the bed when James groaned. "No more sleepin' powders... I cain't. No more please."

"Shh," Anna soothed.

"Rest," Black said. "Me and Elbert are here."

Elbert paced back and forth to the window. Black sat on the side of the bed. Callie appeared with Abby, Shultz, and Big Mama in tow. Joining Elbert at the window, Black watched them work. When the doctor was finished examining James, Shultz came to stand with them.

"James wants the sleeping powder stopped," Black said, his tone low.

"The powder is what's keeping the pain at bay." Shultz responded. "He is pretty bad off."

"Cut the dose and see how he manages," Black said.

Shultz nodded. "Percy requested the same. He still spitting up green shit, but he's much better."

Black was staring over the doctor's shoulder observing the women. When they had James all tucked in, Big Mama said.

"Abby, you come on wit' me. Come see 'bout yo' baby for a bit."

Black could see that Abby was going to protest, but when Mama spoke of Jamie, she gave in. Shultz gained his attention when he said, "Things could take a turn as with any person who is under the weather. But he will make it, that's my honest medical opinion. Time is what is needed here."

Refocusing on Shultz, it was Black's turn to nod. The doctor read his thoughts and his fears. He avoided Elbert's stare. It looked as though Shultz would say more, but they all turned at the sound of little feet running down the hall. Elbert started for the door in time to catch Lil Otis before he could enter the bedchamber.

"Mama..."

"Come wit' me." Black heard Elbert saying as he stepped into the corridor and firmly closed the door behind him. Lil Otis had not seen James. Everyone was keeping the boy occupied, but he was still asking for his papa.

The room cleared out, and Black suspected Anna went to see how Otis managed to sneak upstairs. Snuffing out one of the oil lamps and dimming the other, he pulled a chair to the side of the bed and relaxed. Hearing James request to stop the sleeping powder helped him start believing the shit he told his men and family. His worry for James, Abby and the children kept his mind on the larger issues. Now that James was on the mend, Black could see through to the smaller details where the real trouble lay.

It was almost midnight when the door to the bedchamber opened, and Abby appeared. James started moaning and thrashing about as she stepped over the threshold. Black stood as Abby rushed to the side of the bed. James was flushed with fever and his eyes were bright with pain. He tried to sit up but Black gently pushed him back down into the pillows.

Abby brought a canteen filled with water to his lips and James did drink, though not much. He was panting when Black whispered. "We will cut the dose."

James nodded. Abby mixed one spoonful into some water and James tried harder to get the liquid down. He coughed and Black raised his torso to keep him from choking. When James was propped up again, he stared around the room as though he were sightless. His voice was raspy from no use, still his words and sentiments were clear when he spoke.

"You got… hostage?"

"I have *the* hostage." Black clarified.

"You and Elbert finna wait…"

"I will save this treat for you… Rest, man." Black promised.

When James drifted off to sleep once again, Black looked to Abby. "I can stay through the night so you can rest."

She smiled. "The whole house on James time. Ain't none of us resting, even the children is wide eyed."

Black chuckled. "Send for me if you need me. I'll be back in the morning."

Abby moved around the bed, hugging him. Black stepped into

the corridor to find Jeremiah pacing while carrying Jamie. His niece was a sweet little thing with a complexion that matched James' and a head full of curly black hair. Elbert was doing the same with Dennis, his youngest. His nephew looked like Anna with a chuff of black hair on top and none around the sides. Both babies were sleeping. The door was open to the bedchamber next to where James was resting. Black saw Anna rocking Otis. Callie sat holding Elbert Jr. and Miah. He hated that the children were feeling the strain.

Black wouldn't attempt conversation over the children's heads, he took the stairs to the lower level and headed for the porch. He needed air because the entire matter was stifling. The house was still well-lit as if the hour were early. At the bottom of the stairs, he could hear the voices of the older women. The gathering in the kitchen made the porch that much more appealing.

Pulling the door wide, Black was surprised to find his men standing about. They didn't speak for a time. Black played his words with James over and over in his head. The exchange made his blood thrum, for even in a battered state his brother saw the matter with Campbell Penn the same. It was Gilbert who stepped into the light cast by the front door sitting open.

Gil rubbed at his face, causing Black to notice his anxiety and his missing fingers. His hair was braided in two fat cornrows, and he was dressed in brown homespun clothing. It seemed all the men felt some kind of way about James. Luke crossed Black's mind, and he experienced a stab of regret. Gil looked hurt; still he waited patiently for some kind of reassurance.

"James will make it," Black said.

Nodding, Gil stepped to the side. All the men took a turn speaking with him and Black realized, he needed this as much as they did. Little by little the men dispersed, until there was just him. The mildness of the night air added to his peace. In the morning he would begin dealing with the details and there would be some who would not be pleased.

When he finished reflecting, Black turned and headed back into the house. In the sitting room Elbert and Jeremiah stood by the window in the dark. The black cracker spoke first.

"My ass tired, but sleep won't come."

Elbert chuckled. "The children won't rest, so we ain't resting."

"Where are my children?"

"Daniel and Ben-Ben is sleep. Nattie is laying in Mama's bed with Ms. Cora. She ain't sleep."

Two oil lamps lit the hallway leading to the kitchen. Black stepped into the gloom with his brother and Jeremiah.

"We need to go back to Montreal," Jeremiah said. "We need to keep our eyes on the goings on."

"Yeah," Elbert agreed.

Black listened but offered nothing. It was better to keep his thoughts to himself. He had to swallow down feelings of revenge to see his way through to the details. There were too many people who depended on this life. Still there were the victims: Ruby, Spike, Percy, and now, James. At his silence both Jeremiah and Elbert ended the discussion.

"I'm going to bed," Black said on a sigh. "Wake me if anything changes with James."

Both men answered in unison. "Yeah."

In the kitchen Mama and Iris were cooking something that made the house smell delicious. Black greeted both women.

"Mama–Iris."

"Hey, baby." His mama replied.

"Good mornin', sweetie." Iris answered.

He stopped before stepping into the connecting corridor leading to the bedchambers and his study. "Where is Sunday?"

"She at the gate; she be along directly. Sunday, Morgan, and the others done kept to they duties. Anna, Abby and Callie is workin' wit' the children and James. Otis is beside himself wantin to know why he cain't see his papa," Big Mama said.

Black had disconnected from the conversation, his mind

wandering to his wife. When his mama stopped talking, he looked up to find her staring at him. "I'm sorry… I'm exhausted."

"Is ya well?" Big Mama asked.

"I am."

"Go on and rest," Mama instructed.

Black nodded and headed for his bedchamber. He almost detoured for his office since Sunday was still out. He peeked in on his children and found everyone fast asleep–even Miss Cora. Once in his bedchamber, Black snuffed out the oil lamp on the table, undressed and climbed into bed. Slumber claimed him immediately.

It was almost dawn when he was awakened by the warmth of his wife's body lying next to him. As he became more coherent, he realized Sunday had her hand wrapped about his dick and she was stroking him. Black groaned.

His wife climbed on top and angling his dick she slid down onto him. Sunday took control of their lovemaking; the darkness caused his sense of feel to be overtaxed. Sunday smelled of lavender and when she leaned in to kiss him, Black thought he would lose it. His wife never stopped fucking him and he understood that they weren't trying to prolong the sensations.

"Damn… Sunday," he choked out.

"Ohhh, Nat. I never wants to waste a moment showin' you love." Sunday panted.

At her words, his orgasm slammed into him. Sunday's channel tightened around him and there was no holding back. His dick started pulsing and his seed burst from him in sensations so sharp, Black felt his world tilt. The lovers didn't disconnect, instead they held each other and allowed sleep to claim them once more.

CHAPTER 15

THE DETAILS

Virgil woke to the early morning sun streaming through the window, the sound of water sloshing around and the scent of cinnamon soap. He opened his eyes to find that Percy had crammed himself into the tin tub. And while the tub was large, it was way too small for him. Virgil also noticed that though he was better, his lover was still under the weather. He appeared to be in pain, but refused the medicines offered by Shultz. Percy's cough had improved, but his sputum was still discolored.

These were the awkward moments between them; the times when they both tried to ignore intimacy. Still, Virgil suspected they were avoiding each other for different reasons. He was dodging familiarity to hide from rejection, and Percy was avoiding bringing finality to their life together. The uneasiness of polite conversations was taking a toll on his mind and heart.

When he could wait no longer, Virgil climbed from the bed and ambled over to the chamber pot. He took a piss, closed the lid, and strode over to the green water basin and pitcher on the table. After washing his hands and face, he reached for the floral printed towel hanging on the back of one of the chairs. He dried his face with vigor and when he lowered the cloth, he found Percy staring at him.

"I brought extra pails in for you. There's warm water on the stove."

Virgil turned his back when Percy stood. He was trying to give them each room to breathe. Clearing his throat, he managed. "N-no… I'm fine."

The sound of a low chuckle caused Virgil to turn back to him. Percy had wrapped a towel about his waist and even battered, his mahogany skin was hypnotizing. Virgil continued warily. "You mock my discomfort."

Percy stepped over his statement and asked the real question. "Do you still have affection for me, Beau?"

Virgil grabbed at the back of his neck. His long red underwear suddenly becoming itchy and hot. Everything in his world was reduced to this moment. But what was strange… Percy was asking about his feelings.

"Yes, I still have affection for you. I have gone mad with my fondness for you."

"And yet, you spent all your time at your establishment. Seeing me only when I complained." Percy said, his tone flat. "I stopped protesting your time away and you stopped coming home."

Virgil stared at him and for the first time, he was truly seeing the hurt between them. Living at the fort and being forced into this small living space was eye opening. He cleared his throat again, but words failed him. In the past, Percy had been good at hiding his pain; but now, everything was amplified.

"I love you." Virgil managed and to his credit, his voice was steady. "I had not meant to make you feel unwanted."

"I don't come to the store because I don't wish to draw attention to our situation. Life is dangerous enough as an ex-slave; an ex-slave practicing buggery could mean death."

Silence hung in the air until Percy turned away from him. An urgency to stay connected kicked in and Virgil whispered and pleaded. "Please don't leave me."

Percy's eyes widened. Virgil went on. "I'll sell the business if you wish."

"Virgil—"

"Please," Virgil hissed, cutting off Percy's dismissal of their life.

"You love being a merchant. I would never ask such a thing."

"I love you more," Virgil said, his voice tight–emotional. "Seeing you hurt, and the woman killed…"

Percy closed his eyes and Virgil feared his response. Seeing the bruises and contusions along Percy's torso was all too much. Taking three long strides, Virgil's clothed body collided with Percy's nakedness. Tugging him by the back of the neck, Virgil pressed his lips against Percy's mouth before begging.

"Please, Heart, stay with me."

When Percy inhaled, Virgil offered his tongue and both men groaned from the contact. Their dynamic had always consisted of Percy setting the limits, but today Virgil was drowning in anxiety and heartache. This made him press for more than he would have in the past. He shoved Percy against the back wall–hard. The cabin shook on impact.

In his quest to be skin to skin with this man, Virgil became frantic. Popping the buttons on his long underwear, he shucked the fabric and rubbed himself against Percy. When their erections brushed, Virgil buried his face in the crook of Percy's neck–the intensity nearly buckling him at the knees. Time stopped as he breathed in cinnamon and man; he needed this.

Virgil thought he would be denied–turned away; instead, Percy reached between them. Desperate to witness the beauty of his lover's skilled grip, Virgil dropped his forehead against Percy's chest and peered down in wonderment. He placed a hand over Percy's to demonstrate his needs. The hardness of their bodies clashed and strained into one another. Virgil broke out in a delicious sweat. Percy was relentless in his chase for orgasm; each of his delightful strokes had purpose.

Being taller, Percy adjusted for a better angle. "Kiss me, Beau... I'm almost there."

"Shit," Virgil whimpered as he kissed Percy with reverence.

Time restarted as quickly as it had stopped, and Virgil felt alive. Percy let go first and his warmth sent Virgil over the edge. He held tight to the web of sensation cocooning them until Percy pulled away. His fear reasserted itself when his sex haze began to recede. Rejection tore through him, but Percy leaned in and kissed him.

"I don't want to be without you, Beau."

"Shit." It was all Virgil could manage.

Percy placed a palm to his cheek then kissed his forehead. "You have to trust me."

"Let's clean up," Virgil sidestepped.

They fished the cloth from the bathwater and wiped off. When they were both dressed in long underwear, Virgil walked to the table and Percy to the side of the bed. They stared at each other for seconds before Virgil backtracked the few steps to the bed. Percy climbed in first. The men lay on their sides facing each other. Unable to handle his feelings, Virgil's gaze fell between them. Percy lifted his chin with two fingers. Virgil understood that Percy would not allow him to retreat.

"I want no one but you. You have to trust me, Beau."

"You have an appreciation for women that I don't have. It worries me."

Percy didn't deny his words and Virgil felt the sting of reality. He tried to look away again, but this time Percy gripped his chin. "Sometimes, Beau, you are so green you stink."

Virgil nodded; he knew his jealousy was a problem for them. They had never spoken of it, for the topic was embarrassing. Still, he admitted. "I worry you will leave me for an easier life... a woman."

Percy's smile dawned bright. "I will try to help out at the store, and you will try your hand at trust."

Virgil swallowed hard. "Yeah."

They kissed and caressed each other until Percy asked. "How long do you think Black will keep us hostage?"

Virgil had the last few days to mull over Black's actions. There was much to consider in the face of Ruby's and Spike's death. Having known Black for years, he realized they weren't prisoners. If Black had found him duplicitous, they would both be dead. No, he was certain they were being considered hostile guests.

"I'll try for an audience with Black today." Virgil promised.

"I'll come with you."

"If you wish," Virgil answered, but he preferred facing Black alone.

Percy and Virgil laid about for another hour before readying themselves for the day. They didn't try for more intimacy; the fear someone would come to the cabin at an inopportune time was real. Virgil didn't want to flaunt their relationship. In fact, after witnessing the treatment of Ruby, Spike and Percy, he downright feared for their well-being as a couple. He would bow down and ask for Black's help.

* * *

Black stood in his study facing his men and it was difficult without James. Elbert was leaning against the door to keep the women out and Black felt no shame at excluding them. He wanted to know what the men may have gleaned in Montreal. There had been no time to meet for the purpose of exchanging information. The priority had been James.

Elbert was the first to speak. "My guess is you know more than us."

Leaning back against the edge of the desk, Black replied. "We must go back."

As his eyes bounced around the room, the men's expressions

were readable. They didn't want to leave the women and children. Lincoln's men at the gate and the James issue only added to the apprehension felt by all of them.

"We need to keep Montreal under our boot." Black said when his words were met with silence. "Life at home will be addressed before anyone rides out."

He could see the collective nodding of heads. Simon, who stood at his back asked. "What we gon do wit' Miss Caroline?"

Black's eyes found Jake's and he repeated the question. "What is to be done with Miss Caroline? Is she to stay or go?"

Jake cleared his throat. "I ain't for sure. I was needin' to speak wit' you in private, Black."

"See me later. In the meantime, she is to be treated as a guest. If she wishes to leave, she will not be allowed to do so until Lincoln's men are long gone from the gate. She is not allowed to see Campbell Penn under any circumstance." Black instructed.

Jake winced at the mention of their prisoner, but he nodded in agreement. Elbert inquired. "Virgil and his field hand, what will we do with them?"

Black sighed, "They too are to be treated as guests. It troubles me that our actions have caused hell to be brought down on them. I have weighed the matter from all angles. Virgil and Percy do not appear to be mired in deceit."

"So, we finna let them go?" Anthony asked. "Is it safe for 'em?"

"I will speak with Virgil. If he wishes to leave, I will not stop him. But I will try to encourage him to stay. It is not safe right now for any of us." Black explained.

"Who at the saloon was the traitor?" Elbert asked, bringing the real matter into focus.

Black looked around the room before answering. "They all were."

His words hung in the air until Elbert spoke. "We were there for days… what was in Campbell's damn papers?"

"It's what was missing from his journal. There was no distance in regard to the saloon in his writings. Campbell spoke of the establishment as if it were his base of operations. He also understood the watering hole and the women were making no coin. His musings were fixed on Freddy, Spike, and his intimidation of the people. The real clue was the mention of how the coloreds separated from the men at the saloon."

Simon chimed in. "I sees it now, but not then… suppose our men movin' about was too much for them to pin us down."

Elbert stared off as if deep in thought. "You sayin' Fenton is the cause of this? You tellin' me he caused his brother Freddy's death?"

"I'm asking questions too, Elbert." Black replied. "Why wouldn't the men bury Spike… if they were acquaintances? Fenton had the most to gain."

His brother stared at him, and Black had no doubt there would be some discussion later. It appeared Elbert was struggling with his thoughts, but Black kept the meeting on task. "Did any of you see Booth, the actor? He is unaccounted for… again."

"We were supposed to see him the morning the theatre went up in smoke. He had invited me to breakfast. I lost focus when we spied Elbert." E.J. admitted.

"Understandable," Black said. "Campbell worked with Renfro, Clinks and Styles. Do any of you know them and were they accounted for when you retrieved James from the old sawmill?"

"Shit… guns was poppin'." Jeremiah answered. "But I ain't see the three ya speak of. They time was spent nannying the actor. Can't say I understood it."

Black moved into the circle of men and lowered his voice. "Campbell is to be kept under guard until James is back on his feet. Together, my brothers and I will deal with the deaths of Ruby and Spike. The women are not to deal with this prisoner."

The men offered a collective, "Yeah."

"That's all for now," Black said.

The men exited the study leaving only Jake, Simon, and Elbert. His brother spoke first.

"I thought the men in the saloon strange, but I never suspected."

"Me neither," Simon said.

"At the church… the older folks trusted me. The young folks were angry, and their distrust was visible." Elbert added. "They knew what I did not. We gotta go back."

"I agree," Black said.

"Imma figure on it." Simon added.

Black turned his attention to Jake. "Walk with me."

Leaving Elbert and Simon in his study, Black followed Jake. They trekked through the quiet house and out the front door. The morning was chilled, but the bright sun held the promise of a great spring day. Both men kept on until they reached the dirt path. When he was certain they were out of earshot, Black turned to Jake. His intention was to encourage conversation, but Jake cut him off.

"I ain't for sure what to do wit her."

It was the first time Black felt like smiling in weeks. But he didn't of course, Jake looked troubled. He started walking and Jake fell into step beside him. They headed for the cabin that housed Miss Caroline.

"May I ask the issue?" Black inquired.

"She loves him." Jake bit out.

"Ah… you want her."

"The moment I seen her, I wanted her." Jake answered. The muscle in his jaw ticked. "But she callin' his ass Master… I cain't take that shit."

Black stopped walking. They were on a piece of the path where there were no people, tall trees, and overgrown grass. Black looked up at the sun to give himself a moment before letting his stare fall to Jake.

"You're angry." It was a statement not a question.

"Y-yes," Jake stammered.

"You been mean to Miss Caroline?"

Jake looked to the ground. "I ain't been mean, but I ain't been nice neither."

"You ain't been mean." Black gritted out. "But you ain't been nice. Explain."

Jake cleared his throat. "I… ahhh ain't spoke to her or made her feel welcomed. She cries when it be just me and her. I leaves her to Molly and Emma."

"I thought I instructed you to speak with her. You were to see what you could learn."

"I ain't wantin' to hear her call his ass Master." Jake shot back.

Black folded his arms over his chest and glared. Jake squirmed. "You are dismissed from your duties to Miss Caroline."

Jake opened his mouth, but this time Black cut him off. "Send Lou and Anthony to me. Tell them to find me at Miss Caroline's cabin."

And with that, Black turned his back on Jake and walked away. What he did not need was more trouble added to the long list of issues he was currently dealing with. He surely didn't need the younger men making more work for him. Black shook his head, most of the men were older than him, but most days he felt ancient. When he reached Miss Caroline's cabin, he had to remain outside. He was too perturbed to engage with her.

Black stood on the path for about fifteen minutes, when Anthony, Emma, Lou, and Molly rounded the bend.

"Mornin', Mista Black," both women greeted.

"Ladies."

The women kept on into the cabin, leaving the men to talk. Black got down to business informing Lou and Anthony of their new duties. "Both of you will guard Miss Caroline. She is to be moved from this cabin to one near you all."

They didn't question, and Black didn't offer explanation. Turning, he walked away so that he could start with the details. He reached the cabin housing Virgil and Percy as the door swung open. Virgil stepped out onto the makeshift porch first and Percy moved in behind him. Black noted that both men appeared nervous. In his quest to address the details, he observed Virgil's pallor was better.

"Good morning, Black." Percy greeted.

Virgil's field hand was still pretty banged up, but he too looked better. He was dressed in brown trousers and a white shirt–black boots on his feet. Virgil was dressed the same.

"Percy–Virgil."

"Black," Virgil said, trying for nonchalance and failing.

Going right to the heart of the matter, Black said. "You are both free to go. But I hope you will stay on. It isn't safe."

Percy stepped from behind Virgil and off the porch. "I haven't had the chance to properly thank you for allowing me to convalesce at your home."

"You are most welcome." Black replied.

The field hand was a bruiser standing equal to Simon's six feet–five inches. Black read him well, and he was certain Percy lived a rough life before Virgil. The even demeanor he displayed meant nothing if riled. The morning was warming up and there were other problems Black needed to address before noon.

"I can't leave Everything closed," Virgil said voicing his concerns. "I could end up with looters, or worse yet squatters."

"Me and the men will be returning to Montreal. You can leave after we return," Black said.

"I wish to ride out with you," Percy said, his statement shocking Black. It appeared to have taken Virgil by surprise as well.

"Percy—" Virgil pleaded.

"Can you shoot a gun?" Black asked.

"Of course," Percy replied and to Virgil, he said. "What, Beau…? I wish to see the men who killed the woman in front of us. Even you, who has been unshakeable in our time together, cannot rest after what we saw."

"The doctor still has your ribs wrapped." Black said, stating the obvious.

"When will you leave?" Percy asked. "I will allow the doctor to put me out so I can rest."

Black stared at Percy, then gazed up the path toward the gate. Turning his attention back to Virgil, Black could see his old acquaintance coming to life. He had been about to take his leave, but Virgil spoke. "I was worthless in Montreal."

"Times are tough for us all." Black responded before heading for the gate and his unwanted guests.

As he rounded the bend, his mind turned to the external problems that were making the fort uptight. When the entrance came into view, the sight that greeted him was perfect. There were men hunkered down at the top of the gate–weapons drawn. There was no chatter or joking between the men. Everyone was at the ready. At the door to the right of the massive gate stood Simon, Tim, and Elbert, with them were the tradeoff prisoners for Lincoln. Their shackles had been removed, but the prisoners were still cuffed.

When Black stood among the men, Elbert and Tim each took a prisoner; both men cocked their guns. Tim jammed the barrel of his weapon in Myron's back, and Elbert did the same with the prisoner called Marvin. Horace was about to pull the door wide when the one called Myron broke from the group and took off running.

At the same time, Simon broke from the group and stiff armed their hostage causing him to topple over. Myron landed face first on the gravel path.

"Get his ass up," Black snapped.

Simon grabbed the man by the seat of his trousers and bloody neck of his shirt. Once he was on his feet, Elbert slapped him upside the head. "Hold yo' ass still."

Myron eyed Elbert, but he didn't speak. Black nodded to Horace, who pulled the door wide for he and Simon to exit. Out in front of them, Black noted that Lincoln's men had set up camp. There were twenty blue tents and shelter for the horses. Once the soldiers spied them, a sharp whistle pierced the morning.

Black, followed by Simon, moved to the middle of the clearing, and waited. Miles Glendale, who appeared to be the commanding officer of this outfit, strolled forward stopping about five feet in front of them.

"Good morning, gentlemen," Glendale said.

"Morning," Black returned.

Glendale was dressed as a union soldier though his uniform had seen better days. His blond hair was wet, and his jaw scraped clean; there was blood on his cheek. His men hung back, and Black suspected it was done that way so as not to antagonize.

"We will turn the prisoners over this morn. You are to be gone by noon," Black said.

Glendale smiled. "So, these are the hostages you are willing to part with. Is that the way of it?"

Black stared and Glendale sighed. "I have been directed to extend an invitation to Washington."

"An invitation or an order?" Black asked.

"The president wanted me to reassure you. This is not an order, but a request." Glendale explained.

"Please inform Mr. Lincoln that I am unable to fulfill his request at this time," Black said.

"The president has proclaimed your people free, yet you are unmoved," Glendale said with a hint of sarcasm.

Black smiled. "The president can't gift me with something I have already taken."

Simon chuckled, and Black continued. "My men will escort you and the prisoners to the border."

At those words, Simon called up to the men and the gate yawned open. Elbert and Tim walked the prisoners out. The man called Marvin was the problem this time, but Lincoln's men were on hand to subdue him. Gilbert, Horace, Emmett, Simon, Elbert, Tim and Bainesworth walked their animals out. They would stand around and see the soldiers to the border.

Black turned to walk away but stopped when Glendale called after him. "Is there a message for the president?"

"No," Black said before disappearing through the gate.

Once inside the gate he was pleased to see the extra twenty men moving out to back Simon and Elbert. The escorts would be gone about five hours. Odell and Chester were preparing to man the gate, but Black had other plans.

"Please see me in my study in one hour."

"Yes, sah, Black," both men said in unison.

The men rode out and when the gate was securely shut. Black headed home to see about James. Elbert, Simon, and Tim would handle the Lincoln debacle, and he would handle the fort. Back at the house, Black climbed the stairs and stepping into the gloomy corridor, he headed for his study. Mama was seated to the kitchen table enjoying her morning coffee. Stopping only to kiss her cheek, he kept on to his study. He prepared a message for the president – its contents simple.

FAMILY MATTERS THERE WILL BE NO POSTHASTE

When Chester and Odell appeared in the doorway of the study, Black waved them in. "I need you both to see that this message is sent from the dry-goods."

"Yes, sah," Chester replied.

Odell nodded and the small action caused the smell of burnt metal to collect in Black's nostrils. When the men left to do his bidding, Black wandered back down the hall toward the kitchen. Mama was gone, so he kept on to the stairs. Climbing them two at a time he found Abby, Sunday, Callie, and Anna in the corridor. The women were speaking in low tones to one another.

In the room Anna and Elbert were now sharing sat Cora, Iris and Mama. They were dealing with the children. Sunday looked up and separated from the women to approach.

"Is ya all right?"

"I am," Black replied and bending down he kissed her cheek.

"I see ya locked us out of the meetin'," his wife said.

Black grinned and stepping over her observation, he asked. “James?”

Sunday didn’t smile and he noted that she appeared tired. “It’s a betta day.”

“Go get some rest.” He ordered his wife.

“I plan on goin’ back to our chamber,” Sunday said on a yawn. “I was seeing ‘bout the children.”

“Go… I will see to James first and then the children.” His wife turned her face up to his and as always, he was moved. “I love you.”

James lay flat on his back staring at the familiar ceiling. The sound of his family chatting beyond the closed door was comforting. He had been in and out of oblivion, but he was certain that Abby, his brothers, and Mama had been by his side. What gave him pause was the number of times he opened his eyes to find the black cracker seated at his bedside. His body hurt all over and still, it was better than the nothingness of sleep.

In his periphery, he saw the chamber door open, though he couldn’t see the person. James closed his eyes and swallowed as he prepared himself to face his visitor. He needed to look alert, or they would drug him again. The footsteps were heavy and slow. Soon, Black was standing to the left of the bed staring down at him. His brother looked concerned.

Black wore brown trousers and a brown shirt, his gun harnessed at his upper left side. James saw his brother’s eyes widen.

“You are awake.” Black said. “How you feeling?”

“Like shit.”

“You want me to get Shultz?”

“He just left.” James managed; his voice still rusty from lack of use.

Black pulled the chair up and James found himself looking to the door for Elbert. Reading his thoughts, Black explained. "Elbert is handling a matter. He'll be along directly."

James nodded. "I cain't remember how I got home."

"Elbert and me brought you home."

"How you come to be in Montreal?" James asked.

"Tell me what you do remember."

James turned his head, glimpsing the pale rose drapes floating on the mild breeze from the open window. The fireplace had a small black pot that hung over a low flame. Chicken soup clung to the air in the chamber. Though the day was bright, the sun had shifted leaving the chamber dim.

"Me and the men was headed to Ruby's. We was wantin' to know fo' sho' if it was Spike in the carriage… but when I stepped up on the boardwalk, they was waitin' on me."

"Can you remember how many?"

"Shit fuzzy," James answered. "They's wantin' to know 'bout Bainesworth. They's askin' if Hope and Black was the same slave."

"Campbell?" It was all Black could muster.

"You has Campbell? I cain't see his face… too blurry."

"Yeah," Black said.

"Do we has them all?"

"No," Black answered with honesty.

"Ya has to go back." James said, turning his head on the pillow in Black's direction.

"I know."

The brothers stared at each other for moments. James said, "Ya cain't wait on me. The women gon' look after me. I'm good."

Black offered no reaction, this made James feel anxious. His brother stood stepping out of his line of vision. When Black offered him some water, he asked. "Half dose?"

"Less than half," Black answered. "You need rest."

"When will you and Elbert leave?"

"Soon."

CHAPTER 16

CONVERSATIONS

The day was overcast as Black stepped out behind the barracks to a small woodshed built by the men for Campbell Penn. The prisoner had been removed from a cabin and taken to the one-man structure based on the need for constant security. The twenty-two had business in Montreal and Black couldn't leave the women and children exposed.

Three men stood guard with one man pulling the door wide to reveal Campbell himself with a fresh shave and haircut. The prisoner had been given a set of homespun clothing and his wounds were tended by Shultz. Black also gave orders to keep the Campbell situation as tidy as possible. This last order was important for the health of the men in the barracks.

Though the day was cloudy, Campbell squinted when his eyes met with daylight. Black had avoided engaging the prisoner so that he could stay the course. Looking upon Campbell brought visions of Ruby into the forefront of his mind and there was also Spike to consider. James and Percy were on the mend, but even the interruption of life for Virgil had been a problem for Black.

The guards backed away to give him and his prisoner privacy. Campbell was seated in a large wooden chair that filled the darkened space awkwardly. He was collared, cuffed, and shackled. Times like these were invaluable to Black for it marked the instance when one had to face reality. It was the very moment when a slaver was forced to realize that he or she was not as strong as those they deemed themselves better than.

"Where is Penny?" Campbell asked, the question displaying his brokenness.

"Caroline is resting. I'll tell her you asked after her."

"Her name is Penny." Campbell growled.

"She answers to Caroline just fine." Black countered. "You are working for Jeff Davis, correct?"

Black had not expected an answer, but he was attempting to gauge Campbell's reaction. His statement about Davis was met with silent resolve. Black would have beat the answer from him if not for James.

"I am Black… and Hope too." At those words Campbell's eyes widened. "Surely you are not shocked."

"I wish to see Penny."

Black smiled. "She has not asked for you."

"You lie."

Crossing his arms over his chest Black stared at Campbell. "Don't ask me about Caroline again. She is no longer yours."

The goal was to agitate Campbell until he became desperate enough to give away the farm. He intended to use Caroline without ever letting him see her. It was all he had; any other tactic would see Campbell Penn dead before James got on his feet. Elbert was smarter, deciding not to venture behind the barracks. His brother feared killing Campbell before time.

"You have come for information, and I wish to see Caroline." Campbell said as he adjusted himself in the chair. He couldn't move his neck; the collar gave nothing. The chains at his hands and feet clanked and jingled. "You will get nothing unless I see Caroline."

Black stepped forward dropping his arms, he was pleased to see dread in the other man's eyes. His words were deliberate–calm. "You will control your tongue, or I will cut it from your fucking head."

Campbell paled and after calming himself, Black said. "Careful."

Black turned on his heels, entering the barracks from the back-door. He moved down the center aisle with purpose, stopping when he stepped through the front door. Elbert and Simon were waiting.

"Shit… you alright?" Elbert asked.

"Yeah," Black answered.

"Yo' ass ain't lookin' too good." Simon countered.

Black debated no further. "Have the men meet at my cabin now."

He walked away to gather himself before the meeting. When he reached the cabin, it started raining and the weather matched his mood. Soon the men filed in, shaking the rain from their persons. Some stood and others sat, but once the room settled Black spoke.

"The time has come to ride out."

It was Gilbert who asked, "What the plan is?"

"We finish what we started." Black answered.

"When?" Elbert asked.

"Midnight–two days," Black replied. His eyes bounced from man to man. "That will be all–go rest."

The men quit the cabin until only Jake remained. He cleared his throat twice before he spoke. "Black… I… Sorry for how I handled thangs."

Crossing his arms over his chest, Black leaned against the edge of his desk. Jake went on. "I… ahhh would like–I means to say, I wanna work wit' Caroline."

Black glared at him. "Are you ready to take orders?"

"I'm is."

"Good. You will not ride out with us. I need someone other than the women to manage Miss Caroline. You will work with the women and keep them safe."

"Yes, sah."

Black never dismissed Jake, he simply turned his mind to the next issue.

* * *

As Jake headed for the cabin housing Caroline, he thought of the exchange between he and Black. There could be no mistaking, Black had been expecting him.

* * *

Caroline stood back from the table staring at the bread she'd just pulled from the oven. The little cabin was hot, but she preferred the heat to the cold. She had to laugh because her baking skills were subpar next to Molly's abilities. Her creation was lopsided and there was no other description for it.

A deep voice changed her focus. "Never mind how its lookin'–what it taste like?"

Zeke sat opposite from where she stood, and he too was staring at the bread. They were almost equal in height with him being a smidge taller. He was muscled and dark of skin with a splash of gray in his well-trimmed beard. His hair was a mixture of salt and pepper, though he appeared to be before forty summers. The brown of his eyes was so dark, they seemed black; the man called Zeke was kind and beautiful.

"You would eat this?" Caroline laughed and her tone was comical and grim.

"Smells good," Zeke said on a chuckle. "Is you 'fraid of yo' own cookin'?"

"We need to let Molly and Emma see it first."

"What for?" Zeke protested. "Molly the one what told ya it was gon be crooked."

Zeke's words made her giggle, and she didn't think it possible to feel lighthearted in the face of all that had happened. The one called Black and his brother with the mean eyes evoked feelings of apprehension. Still, she had come to no harm in their presence. Emma and Molly, though much younger, were wonderful, and they managed to keep her sorrow over Campbell at bay. She'd asked after the master, but never got a straight answer. Both Molly and Emma would clam up whenever she tried to find out if he was dead or alive.

If she were being honest with herself, she cared for Campbell's well-being. But she absolutely felt different toward him after he didn't come back to the room one night. And when he'd shown up the next morning, he smelled of that Beacham woman's perfume. It was just one more hurt between them, for she had not been allowed to wear fragrances of any kind. The master claimed they displeased him.

Jake had been the first man to openly show interest without fear of Campbell's wrath. But now that Campbell had been removed from the situation, he had not looked at her the same again. Perhaps, she mused, she was too tall, too old, too dark...

"Miss Caroline?" Zeke said breaking her thought pattern. "You alright?"

"Oh—"

There was a knock at the door and again her focus shifted. Caroline was thankful for the interruption for she was experiencing both sadness and joy.

"I'll get it," she said. "At least Molly and Emma will see the loaf before we cut it."

Caroline was giggling and overthinking when she pulled the door open to find Jake standing on the makeshift porch. He was wearing a black slicker and a matching wide brim hat. She couldn't help it, her smile faded at the sight of him. Jake symbolized loneliness for her. Behind him the rain came down on a slant, and while it wasn't cold, there was a damp chill hovering about the threshold.

Rainwater beaded on his dark brown skin and his nostrils flared when he spoke. "Aftanoon, Miss Caroline."

"Mista Jake," Caroline found herself saying. "Won't you come in out of the weather?"

She stepped back and pulled the door wide enough to allow him entry. Zeke's chair scraped the floor as he stood and came to stand next to her.

"Jake," he said with a grin.

Caroline noted that Jake did not return his glee, but he did respond. "Zeke… thought Ant and Lou was standin' guard."

"Sometimes they has me stand in." Zeke answered. "Ain't no bother–Miss Caroline is easy companionship."

"I has it from here," Jake said, his tone rude and dismissive.

Zeke leaned his head to one side and truly stared at Jake. It was as if he were deciding whether to engage in the pissing match happening. He must have felt it wasn't worth aggravating his soul because he stepped around Jake to the peg beside the door and donned his slicker.

"Thank ya, Miss Caroline, for a wonderful mornin'."

"Thank you, Zeke, for the help. Won't you take a piece of bread for your trouble?"

"Ain't been no trouble–next time on the bread," Zeke said before he disappeared into the downpour.

Turning her attention to Jake, she stared at him while he stared at the door. Caroline's eyes watered which represented the constant state of upheaval she was dealing with. When Jake finally turned his attention to her, Caroline saw the muscle tick in his jaw.

"Why are you here?" she asked, trying to manage a steady breath. "When will Zeke be back?"

"He won't."

Caroline found that in a matter of moments, Jake had changed her mood from happy to sad. Most disheartening, the fact that he and Campbell were alike. Both men were unable to meet her needs while trying to block potential suitors. Jake might even be the worse of the two. He didn't want her and yet he ran Zeke off. There was nothing between she and Zeke, but he had been dismissed just the same.

"Can't you ask to be elsewhere?" she whispered. "The whole matter is stifling enough without you being my guard. You don't even like me."

"You ain't a prisoner." Jake grunted. "You's a guest and I has been told to help you. And… I… I likes you plenty, Miss Caroline… *plenty.*"

She didn't bother to acknowledge his words. "My master, what has become of him? Is he alive or dead?"

"Campbell Penn ain't none of yo' damn master." Jake gritted out.

"Do you know what has become of him?" she asked ignoring his ire. "Please…"

Jake stared at her as if vacillating between whether to tell her or not. "Penn had a woman kilt and dumped at the gate. He ain't dead but neither is he long for this world."

Caroline stared at Jake but not in disbelief. His statement brought several pieces of a moving puzzle together for her. In her mind she could see and hear the hushed conversation between Campbell and the other plantation owners. She had to look away for shame engulfed her. Heaven, help her, she still cared for the well-being of Campbell Penn. It was what she had done her entire life.

Jake broke eye contact as he removed his hat and slicker. He hung the garments on the peg next to the door and kept his back to her for a few extra moments. He was giving them both a much-needed reprieve. It was during this small space in time that her mind latched on to several thoughts. Jake had said she was a guest;

he had said she was free and that she no longer had a master. In all her travels with Campbell, the one thing she had never been considered was a guest. The very concept was frightening.

The emotions she felt overwhelmed, and Caroline burst into tears. Jake spun on his heels and rushed to her side. "Come sit."

He reached for a cup and poured her some water from the pitcher on the table. She took a sip and coughed. "I don't have a home. I don't have coins. How will I live? I know nothing but the south."

She was seated now, and he was standing. "You cain't go back into the south. War is happenin'."

Caroline figured she must have looked faint. Jake rushed over to the door and yanked it open. "It's hot as hell in here."

The breeze helped; Caroline had to admit. But she also hated the cold. Jake was back at her side within seconds. He stooped before her. "Is that betta?"

She could only nod as she attempted to suck in air. When she started to calm, he said. "You can stay on here… be with me."

Caroline snapped her gaze up to meet his. Her face must have showed what she was feeling because he smiled. "I'm sorry… I ain't been agreeable–been too busy being jealous."

He dropped his forehead to her knee, and she was struck by his masculinity and youth. His youth gave her pause. "How many summers are you?"

Jake lifted his head, shrugged, then beamed. "What is you needin' to hear?"

"You don't know how many summers you are?"

"I say–I'm 'bout thirty summers… give or take."

It was the give or take Caroline was worried about. She shivered and he moved to shut the front door. The cabin warmed immediately. Had she ever had a man apologize to her? Had she ever engaged with a man other than Campbell on this level? There was Jasper, but they had never been alone–not like this.

She must have taken too long in her musings. Jake stood in

front of her, and his tone was pleading when he asked. "Try wit' me. We can go slow... please."

Caroline's nod was slow as she thought through her circumstance: Had a man ever used the word *please* with her? Jake's tone and words made her belly roll. She was certain that she cared for Campbell, but she had been tired of life with him. He had always been vicious, and the woman Jake spoke of was not the first person to meet their demise at Campbell's direction.

* * *

Black sat at the side of the bed watching as James dozed. His brother was having longer bouts of awareness though he only engaged Abby. When he or Elbert attempted conversation, James would feign sleep. The bruising got much worse before getting better, still Black could see he was on the mend.

"You angry with me?" Black asked in the quiet of the room.

James opened his eyes and glared at him. "I ain't mad wit' you or Elbert. Tryna figure on why I ain't see shit 'fore it happened."

"What do you remember?"

"Not enough... they whipped up on me pretty good." James answered. "They kept askin' 'bout you and Bainesworth. Guess they figured out the queen shit."

Black nodded. "It seems our prisoner is the confederate president's man. The southern government has something cooked up, but I can't see it. I think this chaos has been orchestrated to make fuzzy the real target–Lincoln."

His musings fell on deaf ears, James had started snoring in earnest. Black sighed, stood, and exited the room. He found Callie and Jeremiah speaking in low tones in the corridor. The black cracker was holding his daughter and Callie was reaching for the baby. She disappeared into the room with Abby after taking the baby. When they were alone Jeremiah spoke.

"They waitin' for you."

Nodding, Black headed for the stairs with Jeremiah in tow. The house was quiet and the hour late. At the bottom of the stairs, it was dark, save for the lit oil lamp midway down the hall. They stepped onto the porch and Jeremiah closed the door behind them. Black couldn't see, but he recognized the voices.

"Something has been troubling me," he said. "I feel as though we've missed something."

"This ties up neatly to my way of thinking." Bainesworth replied.

Shultz added. "It's seems to me... the goal here is to stop Lincoln. We hindered the process for those that want the union president dead."

"They were attempting to distract us," Elbert said.

"It worked," Black said with disgust.

"The men we chased were not of one goal." E.J. added.

"The actor," Black said. "What was his purpose?"

"He is a southern enthusiast hoping to make a name for himself. The actor is a fame whore, who doesn't appear to be serious about anything," Tim said.

"I see it the same," E.J. said, agreeing with Tim.

"This is the second time we didn't catch the actor." Elbert reasoned.

"The damn actor was too chatty to be taken serious," Jeremiah said.

There was laughter from the men, but Black couldn't see the humor in all that had happened. The front door opened, and Sunday appeared in the frame. The lamplight was behind her making it difficult to read her expression.

"Nat."

It was her tone and the use of his real name that gave her anxiety away. Black moved toward his wife and over his shoulder he said, "In the morning, gentlemen."

"Yeah," the men chorused. "Evening, Sunday."

"Evenin'," his wife replied.

Shutting the door behind him, Black asked. "You alright?"

"Yes... I missed ya–is all."

He stared at his wife for seconds before reaching his hand out to her. "Come show me how much you miss me."

Their bedchamber was cast in the soft glow of flickering light. Steam rose from the tub and Black smiled. There was a small fire in the hearth that fought off the chill that came with the night air. On a small tray table beside the tub sat a plate with sliced chicken, cheese, and fruit. Placing his gun on the nightstand by the bed, Black undressed.

"So, you really did miss me."

Sunday giggled. "Yes."

When he was naked, Black stepped into the tub and sank down into the water. Sunday followed suit removing her dress, shift, and pantaloons. She climbed into the welcoming water and settled between his powerful thighs. Black wrapped his arms about her.

"I love you... wife," he said against her ear. "More than words can say."

Sunday sighed as the water lapped the edge of the tub and spilled over. All that could be heard was their breathing and the crackling of the small fire.

"When night come again, you gon leave me."

He turned her face up to his and kissed her deep and rough. The water sloshed between them and when he released his hold, he spoke. "You are not to worry. I will be gone for only a few days–all will be well."

Sunday turned in the water sitting astride him. She cupped his face with her wet hands to gain eye contact. "Ya promise?"

"I do," he said.

Sunday was serious when she asked. "What will you do in Montreal?"

"Tie up the loose ends."

"So... you ain't finna tell me." She responded, her worry evident.

He had attempted easy conversation. His tone was grim when he answered with honesty. "Imma finish teaching Montreal a lesson."

Later when the water cooled, the lovers dried themselves and fell into bed. Black was desperate to be inside her. There was no foreplay. Pushing her thighs apart with his knees, he plunged into her to the hilt. His wife cried out, so intense was their connection. Giving her no time to adjust, Black rode her hard. Their kisses were like a storm happening and he couldn't get enough.

On every stroke, Black shoved himself into her until he could go no further. This extreme rhythm brought their joining to an abrupt end. He did not try to prolong the act, instead he let himself be overtaken.

Breaking the kiss–he grunted. "So damn good."

"Nat... oh, Black." Sunday chanted. "I loves you."

He reached for her twice more before dawn and when the sun rose into the sky, Black was certain his wife was sore. Being physical with his woman meant much; he felt no regret.

Two groups gathered at the gate, ten men from the fort took control of two carriages and a covered wagon. The twenty-two now included Virgil and Percy, with James and Jake sitting this one out. Percy rode in the carriage to keep from being jostled on horseback. There was no great show, the gate yawned open, and the men rode out.

Black took the lead as they made for Montreal. Elbert brought up the rear. It was time to address the needs of the people.

CHAPTER 17

THE PEOPLE
JUNE 1864

Black and the men rode for a day and a half, stopping only to rest the animals. As the posse drew nearer to Montreal, he could feel the thrum of violence that vibrated in conjunction with the pounding of horse hooves. A light but steady rain accompanied the men on their journey. It was early June, and the weather was too warm.

When they made it to the edge of the railroad town, the sound of metal striking metal greeted them. Black and Simon flanked Elbert as they brought their horses to a stop. Out in front of them steam seemed to rise right up off the little town. The smell of hot metal, damp earth and animal saturated the air about them. Black's thought pattern was grim, and the dimness of the day did nothing to help the situation.

The men fanned out around the settlement, and it wasn't long before three men came forward on foot. They were all dark of skin wearing brim hats and slickers to ward off the rain. All three men were of average height, and each looked to be more than thirty summers.

"Mista Elbert, I ain't expect to see you 'gain."

"Toby," Elbert replied, his tone void of emotion. "This here is my brother... Black."

"Toby," Black added. Toby's eyes fixed on him.

"Heard a ya, Mista Black," the man said, and there was awe in his voice. "I got me two daughters. They's five and six summas. My wife tells 'em stories 'bout how you means the best for coloreds."

Black forced a smile. He was on this mission because he had not done enough for the coloreds in Montreal. "May I ask the name of your wife?"

"She name Ethel."

"Ahhh," Black replied. "Moses and me helped her get free from North Carolina. Glad to hear all is well."

Before the man could continue in the same vein, Elbert asked. "You got more black powder?"

"I has what you need," Toby said.

"What you know that I don't." Elbert pressed.

"I knows Montreal thankful for this here rain." Toby said, chuckling. "Been a heap of white folks running for the states–like coloreds running from the plantation."

"Toby!" A man called who was working at laying tracks.

Looking back over his shoulder for the briefest of moments, Toby said. "I has to get back to work. Tell me if'n ya needs me."

Elbert nodded, and Toby walked away followed by the other men from the town. Tim wandered up. "Town ain't where we come across it last."

"It ain't." Elbert confirmed.

The men gathered around a lean-to as the people of the railroad town went about their day. Though it helped nothing, the rain had stopped. Simon broke the men down into groups. Black stood off to the side allowing the process to happen. Jeremiah moved in on his left and Black noted that he never took his eyes from the activity.

"You vexed?" Black asked.

"I feel watched... don't like it." Jeremiah answered.

Black let his eyes follow Jeremiah's gaze. "Your gun hand is accurate... you worry for naught."

Jeremiah chuckled and Black went on. "Maybe I should learn to shoot with both hands."

"Ain't no need... we all an extension of yo' gun hand. You need to lead." The black cracker replied.

The men from the fort moved in to care for the horses, and Black changed the subject. "Walk with me."

They moved about casing the settlement. There were lean-tos and tents all over. The ground was soft and the mud thick. Under a large, half shelter stood a group of women. They were cooking and tending children, while their men laid railroad tracks. Black's gaze bounced to a young, dark skinned woman with a shaved head. She appeared both hard and soft; her beauty held an innocence that was marred by the swelling of her right eye.

"Shit," Jeremiah hissed and Black noted that he too was staring at the young woman. "Imma need a moment."

Black nodded and turning his attention to his surroundings saw the steel workers headed his way. They crowded around and he began to speak–direct.

Jeremiah walked over to where the women were cooking and waited; black, cast iron pots sat bubbling. The smell of the beef cooking turned his gut. The young woman didn't hesitate coming to stand in front of him. He looked down at her and winced when she smiled. Up close, he could see that her lip was busted. This sight angered him.

"What is yo' name?"

"Fern," she answered without inquiring about his name.

He pointed with his chin in the direction furthest away from the crowd of men speaking with Black. They walked over to a tree stump to the right of the women. Fern wore a brown, short sleeved dress; her boots and hem were mud splashed. The white apron she wore over the dress was so white it made the day appear that much more gray.

Once out of earshot, Jeremiah asked. "What happened to ya?"

"I ain't have dinna ready when my man come in from workin'."

"How many summers are you?" he asked.

"I's twenty summas–give or take. Errol don't mean no harm, he just like thangs one way."

Jeremiah had been about to speak when he saw her eyes widen as Fern stared over his shoulder. He was sure the man he had seen with her the first time they were here was awaiting his attention. The black cracker turned to face the man called Errol, who upon closer inspection was larger.

"Fern… get on to our tent. And don't come out till I says."

"Errol—" she attempted.

"Do what the hell I say, woman," her man said.

Jeremiah never took his eyes from the man. In his periphery, he watched as she did her man's bidding. Black stepped in on his left and E.J. appeared on his right. Errol's attire was homespun and brown. His eyes were mean; still, he wasn't addle minded. Jeremiah allowed the other man to assess and see that he was strapped. His would-be opponent stalked off in the opposite direction from the woman.

Black chuckled and E.J. said, "I thought I told you to mind yo' own business."

"Imma kill his ass on the way home." Jeremiah mumbled.

* * *

Standing on the edge of the railroad town watching his men interact with the people, Black repeatedly turned the issues over in his mind. A thought bloomed in his head that led him to consider insult. He acknowledged that his emotions had gotten the better of him and it was all rooted in his fear for the women and children. Still, his enemies had put forth little effort where he was concerned.

Campbell Penn had bested him with the deaths of Ruby, Spike and Sidney, the beatings of James and Percy, the disappearances of Freddy, the hotel kitchen girl Lucille, and the old piano player, Jimbo. His need to keep the people safe had been expertly used against him and his actions brought mayhem to the doorstep of Fort Independence.

Before night fell over the railroad town, the sun came out adding no comfort to the situation. When the natural light faded into an inky blackness, the men broke down into three groups. Each man had a task and Black was no exception. He rode hard for the township called Niggerville with ten men at his back. The hour was early and there was much to do before midnight.

Travel took about forty minutes before they came upon a place much like the fort. Candlelight flickered from the windows of a few homes making visibility a step above complete darkness. Black felt his heart squeeze when random windows went dark, and no one took to their porch to greet him. The men thundered to a stop in front of an old house at the end of the lane. Anthony, Frank, and Lou lit the torches as he swung from the saddle.

The door opened before Black could step into the front yard. A thin man moved into the frame and though the house was well lit, his features were shadowed.

"Clive."

"Hope," the man returned. "You finally come."

"I'm sorry that it took me so long, my friend."

"Won't ya come on in?"

Clive went back inside, and Black followed. Once in the house he was greeted by two sets of accusing eyes. He knew Clive's wife, Wilma; she was light of skin with two fat braids pinned at the top of her head. Next to Wilma sat an elderly woman with deep brown skin and a silver cloud of hair. The old woman wore a black dress, which made her cotton-like hair stand out. Black didn't know her, but he got the impression she knew him.

"Good evening, ladies."

"Hope… Clive say you would come. I's glad ya here. Thangs been a mess," Wilma said.

The old woman grunted, and her displeasure was evident. Clive added. "Dis here is my mama, Miss Etta Mae."

Black didn't get a chance to speak before the old woman boxed his ears. "They done kilt Ruby. She loved Spike, but she ain't love him like she loved you. Spike knowed but wasn't nothin' he coulda done 'bout it."

Unable to maintain eye contact, Black let his gaze drop to his boots. Miss Etta Mae went on. "Ain't yo' fault you ain't feel the same. White mens showed up to her bidness askin' 'bout you. I told her to send for ya, but Ruby say she ain't wanna disturb yo' life. I believes Spike ain't want you here–why he ain't send for ya himself."

The front door was wide open, and Black could hear his men moving from house to house. His men were instructed to start with the homes where there was no candlelight. Those were the places where he'd lost the faith of the people. When he could gather himself, he spoke.

"I didn't know what was happening, no word came." Black was hurt by her description of Spike. Surely, he wouldn't have allowed Ruby to perish because of jealousy.

"The youngins tell me they seen Spike. Ain't no one found Ruby." Miss Etta Mae said, and Black could hear the hope.

"I have Ruby…" Black admitted. "She has been laid to rest at my home."

The old woman leaned her head against the table and burst

into tears. Wilma pushed back from the table and went to her, rubbing Miss Etta Mae's back as she sobbed.

Black shook his head trying to clear the nightmare happening. "I am late, but make no mistake, I care. It won't bring Ruby back, but I will see this through."

He tried to lend his focus to the mundane; he took in the roughly made table and matching chairs. There was a wide framed door that led to what he assumed were the bedchambers. On top of the large black stove, sat two pots and in front of the fireplace were two rocking chairs. Clive's home was modest and clean.

Wilma helped Miss Etta Mae to her feet, and the old woman spoke at him… wringing a promise from him. "Make sho' they pays for what they done to Ruby."

"Yes, ma'am." Black replied as he watched Miss Etta Mae hobble away.

Clive wore tan overalls with work gloves sticking out his front right pocket. The oil lamps on the table gave off enough light to see a man's honesty. Black asked. "Why didn't you send for me?"

"I let the talk get in my head." Clive answered.

"What talk?"

"Folks said we's on our own." Clive explained. "They said Hope ain't care no mo'."

Black glared at him, then turned on his heels heading for the door. He could hear the thinner man's quick steps as he tried to keep pace. Stepping onto the porch, he found the glow of lanterns, oil lamps and torches. The people were gathered shoulder to shoulder in anticipation of his words. As the firelight danced, Black waited patiently, and right on cue came the thunder of more horses. Along with the men on horseback came the squeak of wagon wheels. The crowd shifted making room for the animals, wagons, and extra men.

The night air was thick. Black felt the fabric of his homespun shirt clinging to his skin as sweat rolled down his back. His discomfort kept him grounded as he addressed the people. Frank and Lou came forward to stand on either side of him, giving a better visual of the matter. A hush fell over Niggerville, and Black spoke.

"I have come to extend an invitation. You are all welcome to settle with me at my home."

The silence that blanketed the crowd didn't ease. Black lingered in the quiet giving the people a moment to digest his offer. He clasped his hands behind his back, so as not to appear threatening. The homes were spread out, yet in close proximity. Nightfall prevented him from seeing everything; it was why his men were among the people. After a time, a man stepped into Clive's yard, stopping at the stairs leading to the porch.

Lou moved to stand to the man's right, so Black could see with whom he spoke. The man was average in height and weight; his hair was shorn close, and the firelight danced on his spectacles.

"My name Lloyd, Mista Black. I sho' do thank ya for openin' ya home. But wit' all due respect, I ain't wantin' to leave my land. I needs help from where I'm is–and that be right here."

It was Black's turn to ponder in silence while the man–no, the people waited. Another man stepped up. "I be Colin, Mista Black. I ain't wantin' to let up off my land neither. A piece of land to work ain't easy to come by."

Torchlight showed Colin to be light of skin and about thirty summers. Several men stepped up behind the first two and they all had the same words. A conversational buzz took over the crowd and Black allowed it for a time. Lou took his place back on the porch and Black lifted his hands indicating that he was ready to speak.

"I would be remiss if I didn't ask. What kind of help are you all wanting from me?"

A woman stepped between the men. She was short, plump, and dark of skin. Her hair was plaited in several braids that were pulled away from her face. "My name Willie Mae, Mista Black."

"Good evening, Miss Willie Mae."

"We is wantin you to see 'bout us like you do the folks where you live." She answered and explained.

"How could any of you want such a thing–if you didn't send for me?" Black asked holding them accountable. "How could you all want my help if you don't trust me?" His voice boomed with authority.

Behind him, Clive said. "I's sorry, Black. I let fear get hold of me."

The consensus in the gathering was the same. Black lifted his hands again and the crowd quieted. "Your apologies are accepted. I hope you all can see that I too have regrets in this matter."

"Will ya help us?" Colin yelled.

Humbled, Black answered. "Yes."

The crowd did not cheer at his answer. There was much to be done and they all knew it. Lloyd asked the question everyone was figuring on. "Where do we go from here?"

Black was prepared. "Over the next few months there will be plenty to do. But tonight, we have four issues to address."

He paused to give the people a moment. "You will be subject to my complete authority. Who among you does not see it the same?"

More waiting and silence ensued. When no man or woman refuted his words, Black continued. "You will accept the extension of my power through my men."

The twenty-two stepped forward lining up on the porch behind him. Elbert and Simon came to stand on either side of the doorway and Black. "To my right is my brother, Elbert and on my left is Simon. Both men are trusted with the safety of my woman and children; they will do the same for you. The men you see before you will help keep you and your loved ones safe."

The men at his back dispersed and the crowd parted. Black gave orders. "Please divide up into two groups. Those who can shoot a gun and those who cannot."

He waited as the people did his bidding and he was pleased to see that it was mostly the women who fell into the cannot category; Black gave the people hope. "My men and I will arm you this night with better weapons. Those who can shoot will be responsible for those who cannot."

There was shuffling in the crowd as the people formed a line. While Elbert and Simon handed out the guns, Black had one last order of business.

"I will not..." he said, his voice strong and sharp, "be the leader of a township called Niggerville. I decree from this day onward–this settlement shall be forever known as Blacktown."

And the people cheered.

CHAPTER 18

LOUDER THAN WORDS

Black had to modify his timeline for the next leg of the journey. He ended up seated to the table in Clive's home while the people with concerns and information lined up. Settling in, he embraced their worries and circumstances. He offered his patience, and he hoped the people would do the same for him. In his head, he had much to atone for.

A brown skin boy on the brink of manhood stepped into the house. Anger rolled off him in waves causing Black to adjust in his chair and lean in. The boy wore tan overalls and no shirt to mitigate the heat. On his head was a matching hat which he pulled from his head when facing Black. His words were clip and laced with shame.

"My name Clem, Mista Black."

"Won't you sit, Clem."

The younger man plopped down in the opposite chair and glared at him. "My grandpa loved ya."

"It was the same for me. I loved Jimbo."

"He say he used to write songs 'bout you to make you vexed," Clem said.

"Yeah, he did." Black chuckled. "Jimbo was good to me."

"Overseers come to the house and dragged 'im off." Young Clem dropped his gaze in disgust.

"Did you hide?"

"Yes, sah. Did what my grandpa say for me to do," Clem said.

"These men–did you get a good look at them? Have you been to town? Have you seen them still going about?"

"I seen 'em–don't know 'em." Clem answered. "It was Fenton what got my attention."

"So, you recollect seeing Fenton?" Black asked.

"I do," Clem said. "They woulda kilt me too if'n I ain't hide. Fenton don't know I seen 'im."

Jeremiah, Elbert, and Simon stepped into the house and Black stood. When he spoke, he addressed his men. "Clem will be riding out with us."

The young man grew wide eyed and stood in a rush. "Thank you, Mista Black."

"Let us be about business." Black answered and to his men, he asked. "Is everything in place?"

"It is." Elbert answered.

Black addressed Clive. "We'll return later."

"Yes, sah."

Once in front of the house the men saddled up and rode out. The distance was small as they made for the saloon. It was earlier than Black had intended, and he was certain he lost the element of surprise. This fact made him ride straight up to the swinging doors. Dawn was upon them and so was the answer to many of his questions. At his back were Elbert, Virgil, Jeremiah, Simon, and the twins.

When Black pushed through the saloon doors, the scene was as he expected. Zeke, E.J., Philip and Percy were involved in what looked to be an intense card game. Percy and Zeke each held a scantily clad woman in their laps. All activity stopped and the barkeep's eyes snapped up to meet Black's perceptive stare. Fenton tried to reach up under the bar, but Elbert drew his piece.

"Get yo' damn hands up top."

Fenton did as warned, bringing his hands up with his palms visible. Black was still as his men drew their weapons. Next to him, Clem spat. "Fenton a snake. Prolly kilt Freddy wit' his own hands."

"You's a damn lie!" the barkeep yelled.

Black placed a hand on Clem's shoulder, the gesture meant to calm. His eyes never left Fenton even as the situation around the saloon became volatile. Black studied the barkeep and found him to be unfamiliar. Yet, Elbert said Fenton spoke of him with confidence. The boy was correct… a snake indeed.

"Who is in charge of the women?" Black asked, his voice filling the quiet.

"I's in charge of the women business." A dark-skinned woman said as she stepped forward. "My name Trudy."

All the women moved behind her as she spoke. Trudy had been Elbert's hostage; his brother had not trusted this woman. In his search of Campbell Penn's personal musings there had been no mention of a whore named Trudy. She must have been Petey's preference.

"Which one of these men do you work for?" Black inquired.

"I ain't never needed a man to show me how to trade pussy for coin." Trudy replied while holding eye contact.

"Fair enough," Black said. "Petey?"

"I did–kept an eye on that one." She answered, raising her hand to point at Fenton. "The damage was done–wasn't no sense in me or the other girls gettin' kilt for the likes of him. Petey give me coin for my troubles, and I shared it wit' the other girls."

Behind Trudy, the other women nodded, and she continued. "Look about–ain't no other coin comin' in dis place. The patrons stopped visitin' when Spike left. He wanted that Ruby woman. Tried to tell 'im that she ain't want 'im. It did no good."

A bright skinned woman with a slender build and green eyes stepped up beside Trudy. Her face was heavily painted, and the blood red lipstick made it appear as if she were sneering at him. She wore her hair pulled back in a bun. Both women were dressed for their profession, their red gauzy gowns were almost see through. Still, Black wasn't ready for her words.

"I's here when you come last, Mista Hope," the woman said. "Trudy, here, is new. Spike wasn't never the same afta ya left way from here."

"What is your name?" Black asked.

"Martie."

Black waited appearing almost disinterested in what was being said, but he was vibrating with the need to know. Martie went on. "Before the white men come here for Fenton, they come lookin' for Spike. I knowed it was gon be some trouble."

Elbert, who must have sensed his need to ponder all that was happening, barked out. "Men to the right side, women to the left."

Virgil pointed to the corner with his chin and Black followed. "I was useless when I first came here with the men. But I did see her giving money to the other women. The Trudy woman speaks the truth."

"So, you were paying attention."

Noticing that Virgil's attention was fixed on something across the room, Black allowed his eyes to drift over to where Percy sat with a woman in his lap. When his eyes fell back to Virgil, he saw that a muscle ticked in the thinner man's jaw. Virgil cleared his throat.

"I am present."

Black's tone was matter of fact. "Focus."

Nodding, Virgil replied. "I saw Miss Trudy and Fenton having an intense discussion in the kitchen. Their words weren't clear to me, but I could see that Fenton might have killed her had Elbert not been in charge."

Elbert's voice rang out when he said to the women still seated to the table with Zeke and Percy. "Ladies… you can move on yo' own steam or I will do it for you."

Black spoke to the room at large. "We will start with Fenton."

Frank and Lou, who were dressed in all black, rushed the bar lifting the countertop. Together they grabbed Fenton and dragged him kicking and screaming into the back office.

"Turn me loose!" the barkeep hollered. "I ain't done nothin'. How ya listenin' to some whores?"

Jeremiah moved in front of him making certain the office was safe before Black entered. On the desk sat a lantern. The chair was pushed to the center of the office. There were crates in the corner of the office next to the large, uncovered window. Black noted the bullet holes in the door as he had on his last visit.

The twins left to watch Elbert's back; Percy took their place. Black watched as Jeremiah, Virgil and Percy secured Fenton. The men tussled with him until Jeremiah became agitated and clanked him upside the head with his weapon. It grew quiet in the office with the distant sound of Simon and Elbert maintaining the saloon. Fenton groaned and opened his eyes.

He tried to fight against the restraints to no avail. Jeremiah and Virgil moved to watch the window. Percy stood to Black's right glaring at the barkeep. Black's concerns were great, and he desperately hoped he was wrong.

"Campbell Penn?"

Fenton's spectacles were crooked on his face. His forehead was wet with perspiration and his knotted black hair stood on end. The barkeep was afraid. Black could see the moment when he decided to cooperate. Fenton thought he could save himself–but he could not.

"Spike sold the bar to dem white mens. He made a blood deal for us all."

Black stared at Fenton for a time. "You telling me Ruby's death was Spike's fault?"

"I's sayin' Spike struck a deal and when Ruby found out, she wasn't happy 'bout it," Fenton said. "Spike wanted her but she ain't want him–he blamed you."

"Jimbo?" Black asked and he was afraid to know the truth.

"He tried to send for ya and Spike ain't want that. They got Jimbo cause Spike told 'em the old coot knowed too much."

"And yo' part?"

"I made sho' Freddy met with that Campbell Penn." Fenton stopped talking for a moment. "Spike say we could share the bar and the coin if'n I get Freddy to be still. I ain't know they was gon kill 'im."

Black didn't know what hurt worse, Ruby's death or Spike's betrayal. He didn't give Fenton a reprieve. "You trying to save yourself, but you haven't told me anything I don't know."

"I ain't got nothin' else." Fenton whined. "I ain't seen Mista Clinks, Mista Renfo or Mista Styles since that theatre was blown to hell."

"The men in this bar?" Black asked never acknowledging that Fenton was on the emotional edge.

"The men out there worked wit' me and Spike… the people knowed about it somehow and stopped comin'."

At Fenton's words, Black turned and walked out of the office. He could never unhear this conversation… *The men out there worked wit' me and Spike.*

In the short corridor Black stood for a moment in the dark, then moved on toward the flickering light of the saloon. He stared beyond the swinging doors and saw that the light of day was coming. In this circumstance there were only two orders to give.

Black addressed Philip when he said. "Move them to the fort."

Next, he addressed Trudy. "The bar and saloon belong to you women."

"We ain't got no papers… what if…" Trudy said.

"Make a list of your full names and give it to Clem. He will deliver the proper deeds." Black replied.

Elbert helped the fort men move the prisoners out back to the awaiting vehicles for transport. Black wandered through the dim kitchen, until he stood in the backyard. As the early morning sun shone down on him, he had to fight off his last memories of Ruby and Spike.

"I'm guessing you would prefer I not be alone with Miss Ruby." He had asked Spike.

"You would be guessin' right," Spike shot back.

Black found that perception truly was everything. Philip broke his thought pattern to ask. "What is you wantin' done wit' these prisoners?"

Black stared around the yard at the patched grass, the faded barn, and the mended chicken coop. What he wanted was to kill these men and leave them where they fell, but the women deserved better.

"Take them to the quarantine area and put them all down–one hole."

Philip didn't flinch. "Sho' thang."

Black rode shotgun as Jeremiah parked the carriage at the entrance of the Grand Hotel. Hopping down from the bench, he set the stairs and pulled the door wide. E.J. jumped down onto the boardwalk and headed for the hotel. Black, who took Jake's place followed in his wake. Behind them, the carriage rolled a few feet, so as not to block the walkway.

Glancing about, Black's eyes fell to the Buckingham Theatre. The playhouse was destroyed and sat as a shell of its former self. Turning his head back in the direction of his feet, Black kept moving. The Buckingham was now a combination of rubble and charred wood. Several of the businesses on that side of the roadway burned with it and Black felt no remorse. He would not allow Montreal to peacefully be seduced back into the slave trade.

Inside the hotel, a chubby white man of about forty summers stood behind the counter. His face was clean-shaven, and his cheeks were ruddy. He was dressed in a blue uniform and his graying hair was combed over to cover his bald spot. The man looked only to E.J. when he spoke. Black glanced about as if he were watching E.J.'s back. Other servants noticed him, but his stance caused them to continue as if they had not seen him.

"Do I have any messages?" E.J. inquired, his southern tongue dragging exactly right.

"No, sir."

"I take it my room has not been disturbed." E.J. continued.

"No sir, everything is as you left it," the man said. "We received your message and the coin."

E.J. nodded, about to walk away when he turned back to the man. Afterthought clear in his eyes. "I see the Buckingham is in a dreadful state. No one was hurt, I hope."

"No sir, no one was inside." The man answered. "The old couple that tended the place barely escaped with their lives. They say they are unclear what happened."

"Thank the Lord." E.J. mumbled and tsked to himself. "Booth… John Booth, is he still here at the hotel? I'm sure my friend is heartbroken about the state of the theatre."

"I have not seen Mr. Booth, sir. Some say it was the actor that kept up the ruckus regarding the war between the states. Patrons of the theatre say this is all Booth's fault. Now Montreal is paying the price."

"Hmmm," E.J. responded. "I had heard such rumors, but never believed them to be true. Mr. Booth is talented. I so enjoyed his company."

Black watched the colored servants in the dining room. The early hour was the reason there were so few patrons. He listened as E.J. continued his questions.

"Is Mr. Styles or that Mr. Clinks available? Maybe they could help me locate my friend."

The older man rubbed his chin. "I haven't seen them since the fire. Can't say I'm sad, they worried the staff."

E.J. appeared distraught when he ended the conversation. "I have belongings in my carriage."

"Would you like the staff to assist you?" the man asked.

"No… no. Herschel here is quite capable." E.J. replied, pointing to Black.

The man nodded and they turned striding across the lobby–back onto the boardwalk. Facing the theatre, Black shook his head at the sight. The next stop would be Ruby's eatery.

* * *

All of the men met at Ruby's and the mood was somber. Black climbed down from the carriage and stood in front of the restaurant, his eyes on the businesses across the roadway. Ephraim, Josiah, Odell, Chester, Ralph, and Herman gathered around him. These were the men that were with James the day he was taken. The rest of the men had task and time constraints.

The morning sun was bright and the weather, hot. It wasn't so early that the other establishments would be empty. Black could see someone moving about in the bakery. He stepped down from the boardwalk onto the cobblestone and noted that the stone was new. They crossed the street with purpose and when he stepped up on the boardwalk in front of the bakery, a colored man of more than seventy summers pulled the door wide and rushed forward speaking with jumbled words. The bell over the door chimed from his haste.

"It be me, my wife and granddaughter. They said I had to let 'em come and go as they pleased or we would end up like Ruby and Spike. I ain't tellin' no tales, Mista Hope. I's 'fraid for my family."

The abrupt opening of the door caused the men with Black to draw their guns. The old man was shaking and in the doorway was an elderly woman who seemed his equal. Holding onto her blue skirts was the prettiest little brown skinned girl with two braids on either side of her head and huge brown eyes. The woman's hair was white and pinned away from her face.

"Easy," Black said to his men.

The old man had no hair on top and thick spectacles. He wore brown trousers with a white shirt and white apron. The aroma of fresh bread hovered around the open door.

"What is your name?" Black asked.

"Walter," the man answered. "This here is my wife Berta and granddaughter Sylvie."

"Shall we step inside where it is safer for them?" Black said.

The men went ahead of him to make certain there were no surprises. Once inside, Black didn't have a chance to take in his surroundings as the other merchants from the surrounding stores piled into the bakery. A chair was placed between the glass display case and red curtain that separated the front of the shop from the back. Seating himself, Black waited as a line formed. There was no chaos; it was simply the people needing him and him needing the people. He turned off all thoughts of the men disposing of Spike's body.

"I'm the fur merchant. My name is George, Mr. Hope." A bright skinned man said stepping forward first. "I'm glad you's here–things were different when Mr. Spike moved in with Miss Ruby."

"Good to meet you, George. How can I help you?"

"I don't want nothing. I just wanted to say they pushed they way into my business."

Black nodded, and the man moved aside. A brown skinned man with a patch over his left eye said, "My name Ollie, Mista Hope. I's a carpenter, me and my sons make furniture. Those men did me the same. You's welcome in my bidness wheneva ya please."

Next, a young man stepped forward; he was dark of skin and

judging by the stick he carried he was blind. A woman held his hand; they both looked to be about thirty summers. The man spoke for them both. "My name is Arthur, and this here is Claudine. We run the boarding house... We glad you's here."

Things continued this way for one hour, and Black decided not to interrogate the people. Instead, he offered words of comfort and threat. "Let us wipe the slate clean while giving one another the benefit of doubt. Every man here this day will be judged by his actions–going forward. I offer you my protection and you will give me your loyalty."

The people gave a collective nod and Black went on. "In this situation there are only two kinds–those who are with me and those who are against me. I will let you decide, and you will be treated accordingly."

When the people dispersed, Black found himself alone with the elderly owners of the bakery. Looking about, he took in the paintings of flowers and the yellow walls. The place offered a type of appeal that made him think of Big Mama. There were cakes, cookies, and pies in the long display counter, yet his belly was not tempted. He had stalled long enough; it was time to stand in Ruby's last moments.

"I will be back to look in on you. You all will be safe."

Tears fell from the old woman's eyes as she offered. "Won't ya has somethin' to eat?"

Black spoke words of honesty. "I am about to deal with Ruby's home and Spike's body. My belly ain't up for it."

The couple nodded and Black spun on his heels, quitting the bakery; his men followed. Outside the sun had shifted in the sky. Turning the day to late morning–early afternoon. He crossed the roadway and when he stepped into the little eatery, he was assailed by sorrow. Some of the men from other establishments were present and helping with the cleanup.

Black walked straight through the dining area, ignoring the overturned tables and destruction that highlighted Ruby's demise.

He continued through the dim kitchen to the backyard. The men were digging the hole as he stepped up to the black carriage and pulled the door wide. The sunlight angled in as he stared at the decaying body of his enemy and old friend.

Elbert's voice blended into his thoughts. "It's a tragedy when a man dies before you can kill him."

"Yeah, it is."

Slamming the carriage door Black strode back into the house. He took the raised corridor to Ruby's personal space. It, too, appeared ransacked with clothes thrown about and the large bed flipped on its side. The white porcelain tub had dried blood at the bottom. Black rotated slowly, remembering better times spent with Ruby; his grief caused him to sigh aloud.

When he could gather himself, he backtracked to the corridor. Feeling along the wall, where the floorboard met the top step, he found the paperwork that he and Ruby had discussed on many occasions. The sounds of the men working and conversing below drifted up to where he sat on the top step. After a few more moments, he went out back and stood in the doorway of the barn, watching the men work.

Several of the women from the saloon joined them in their effort to make straight what was now crooked. Hours went by in a blur and when the sun went down, Black turned the key to the eatery over to the old couple for safekeeping. He and the men would backtrack through Blacktown to reassure the people before riding for home.

CHAPTER 19

LOVE AND LIBERTY

An hour passed since the posse had arrived in Blacktown. Virgil was exhausted, hungry, and jealous. The sun had gone down and as night settled, he found that he was thankful. He didn't think he could have watched that pretty brown doll of a woman from the saloon chase Percy another minute. Virgil wanted to make change, but his insecurities wouldn't allow it. He did his best to avoid Percy and the perfect little thing that dogged his heels.

Even though the sun quit working for the day, the heat remained. As he waited for his turn at the pump, Virgil had to fight the urge to punch something. After splashing cool water over his person, he moved to the shadows to don a clean shirt and ponder. Standing between Clive's stable and barn, he was trying to stay away from the torchlight and conversation.

He was plagued by unwanted images of his beloved Percy with a more dainty partner. His lover's deep voice interrupted his thoughts.

"There you are, Beau... What are you doing back here?"

Virgil was choked by his emotions. He kept his back to the man he loved and when he didn't respond, Percy reached out, touching his shoulder. "Beau..."

In the past when he felt like this, Virgil hid at his store and submerged his life in work. He stayed away averting his attention to prevent fighting with Percy... But right now, at this moment, he had no self-control. His lover was bigger, broader, stronger; still, Virgil grabbed him by the collar of his homespun shirt and slammed him up against the side of the barn. His voice was wracked with pain when he asked.

"Do you crave her... do you wish to fuck her?"

He had thrown his forearm across Percy's throat and leaned in applying pressure. His voice broke when he growled. "Answer me, damn you."

Percy coughed, then gasped and the sounds brought Virgil up short. He tried to back away from his anger and his partner. He had been about to slink off and wallow in his shame when Percy clamped a large hand to the nape of his neck, stopping his retreat.

There was patience in his words. "I want no one but you, Beau."

Virgil closed his eyes even as the darkness gave no visual. Percy rubbed his nose and lips against the side of his face. The action was filled with fondness. He wasn't ready for Percy's next words.

"It hasn't been our way, but seeing you like this... I wish to give you the bird's eye view of our next coupling."

Unable to help himself, Virgil's inhale was sharp and audible. Percy chuckled. "Come eat something before we ride for home, Beau. We will see to your temper later."

Virgil swallowed hard, then whispered. "Percy... I..."

"Don't apologize, Beau. I wish to feel your contrition."

In the background, there was male conversation and laughter. Against his cheek, Virgil felt the softness of Percy's lips and the roughness of his stubbled jaw. He nodded but did not continue.

They finally separated, and Percy whispered. "I love you, man."

"Not more than I love you." Virgil replied.

* * *

It was well after midnight when the men mounted up to leave Blacktown. Jeremiah stood between the horses while the men handled the last-minute details. Posted up on the edge of the torchlight, the black cracker turned his thoughts to a more pressing matter. He was going through all the possibilities when E.J. and Ephraim walked up.

Jeremiah smirked into the darkness, and it could be heard in his words. "I thought to do you a favor, Ephraim."

"You wants to do me a fava I ain't asked for. Sound like you finna hand me some cow shit."

E.J. laughed. "Your actions are suspect, brother."

"I'm wounded." Jeremiah replied before getting down to business.

While they spoke, Black walked up. "Ephraim–you in?"

"Is 'um in what?" Ephraim shot back.

Black was about to explain, but Jeremiah answered for Ephraim. "He's in."

E.J. laughed, then stifled his mirth when Black offered direction. "You have two hours. If this endeavor takes more than that, the posse will double back for you."

"Yeah," the black cracker said. "We fixing to leave now."

The three swung up into the saddle and rode out. Jeremiah's blood thrummed and it was his own excitement, the hot weather, and his need to separate the boys from the men. Giving the horse its head, they traveled in complete darkness for forty minutes. When the torchlights of the railroad town came into view, the black cracker smiled.

Leaving the horses in the underbrush they moved out on foot through the narrow pathways. Jeremiah was able to discern male voices in the distance; still, for the most part the settlement was asleep. He walked toward the chatter and found himself at the half shelter. The same place the women had gathered earlier to cook was now being used by the men. Jeremiah was certain Fern lived in a tent nearby.

Coming to an abrupt stop in front of the shelter, Jeremiah faced the railroad town's night watch. His brother stood to his right, while Ephraim remained invisible. Taking in the scene before him, the black cracker noted the large cast iron pot on a low flame behind the men. Their count was eight, and four of the men held a tin cup in their hand–whiskey, Jeremiah deduced. Still, he meant to have the answers he was seeking, so he started with a statement.

"I'm looking for Fern."

"What you's lookin' for is trouble," a fat man with dark skin said, though his tone held no malice. "Askin' for Fern gon cause her some grief."

Sticking out the wall to the left of the structure was a single torch that offered little visibility. Another man stepped forward and he held no cup. His features were shadowed, but Jeremiah could make out that he was light of skin. The second man's focus was on E.J. when he inquired. "Who the hell is you?"

Jeremiah stepped in front of his brother with the quickness and pulling his guns from his hip holsters, he placed the barrel of one gun against the speaker's nose. The black cracker then answered in E.J.'s stead. "I'm the man lookin' for Fern."

All the men surrounding the shelter raised their hands in surrender. The first man–the fat man, spoke. "One path back on da end is where she stay. Errol ain't pleased wit' her–she prolly sleepin' behind the tent."

The black cracker stared between the men, taking note, and reflecting on the scene before him. He was mentally and involuntarily transported back to the Hunter plantation. And like these men, he had been unable to empathize or understand the suffering of the female slaves. What was now painfully clear–Callie had been correct; he was the problem, rather than the solution.

Directing his words to the first man, Jeremiah said. "You look like a helpful soul. Come show me where Fern stay."

The man nodded, then stepped forward. Jeremiah had been about to threaten the remaining men when something in his side view caught his attention. Into the torchlight stepped Black, Elbert and Simon, behind them were the rest of the men. E.J. let out a shaky breath.

"I thought ya said… two hours," Jeremiah said to Black.

"I did." Black replied.

Turning back to the first man, Jeremiah waved him on with his gun. "After you."

Following the man behind the half shelter and away from the torchlight, Jeremiah's thoughts calmed. There had been a few seconds of complete darkness before their feet hit another dirt path. Several of the tents glowed from lantern light giving off an abstract sense of place. Two sets of boots crunched against the gravel on his left as the man in front of him came to an abrupt stop.

"Dis here where Errol be." The man whispered.

Jeremiah ignored the man and called out. "Fern!"

When there was no reply, E.J. said to the man. "Get us a lantern."

The man shuffled off to do E.J.'s bidding, returning in time for them to see the flap to the tent being shoved aside. Errol climbed out and stood to his full–towering height. He sneered at Jeremiah. "I see you done made a habit outta trackin' what don't belong to ya."

Ephraim stepped forward until he was nose-to-nose with Errol and growled. "Fern belongs to me now."

In his side view Jeremiah saw torches moving their way. His blood vibrated with the prospect of violence; the very notion excited him. He sidestepped and aimed both guns at Errol. This action was instigated by Ephraim, who ground out.

"Where Fern?"

A sense of relief blanketed Jeremiah when she crawled out of the tent and stood. "I's here."

"Get yo' thangs," Ephraim demanded.

Josiah moved in with the torchlight, and it looked as though she had donned her clothes haphazardly. Fern was holding the bodice of her dress together. The black cracker noted her disappointment that it wasn't him doing the demanding. But she recovered enough to answer.

"I ain't got nothin'... just myself."

Ephraim reached out a hand, giving her a nonverbal choice. The black cracker nodded his approval when she looked to him. Fern placed her smaller hand in Ephraim's, making the choice to be safe. Jeremiah couldn't help it; he stepped forward, outing Errol's light.

Turning to Black, Jeremiah said. "If we leave him..."

"Tie his ass up," Black sneered. "He will be yours to deal with as you please."

The sound of wheels, horse hooves and gravel became the background as a carriage stopped on the path in front of the tent. E.J. helped him tie up the man called Errol. Together, they tossed his ass into the awaiting vehicle before climbing in after him. When the carriage lurched forward, E.J. grumbled.

"It's hot as hell in here."

The black cracker had no words–he was too busy trying to understand who he had become.

* * *

Acts of Love

Jake was seated to the table in the cabin that Caroline occupied, and he was sweating profusely. She was learning to cook and like Anthony's woman, Emma, she wasn't good at it. He should know because it was he that had the unfortunate privilege of trying all that she prepared. Still, he had to admit, he was enjoying himself. Life for him had been rough but spending time with Caroline made him light of heart.

There *was* one thing that she did that drove him to utter madness. Caroline liked the summer heat, so between the weather and her stove always going, Jake felt like a wilted flower. As a result, when in each other's company, they were always half dressed to adjust for the temperature. This put the physical attraction he felt for her out of his reach.

"I think these will taste better than the last," Caroline said as she placed a pan on the table to cool.

The hour was late and though it did no good, both the front and back doors were open for a cross breeze. "What is they?"

Caroline beamed. "Gingerbread cookies."

He groaned and scrunched up his nose, causing her to ask. "You don't like gingerbread?"

"It ain't my favorite," Jake said while letting his eyes fall to the pan. "They looks more like biscuits."

She feigned vexation when she said, "Yo' honesty rivals the whip."

Jake frowned at her choice of words and her expression became closed. She whispered, "No."

And with that exchange the mood in the little cabin darkened. Jake noticed Caroline became anxious at night. At first, he thought her nervousness was due to her concern for Campbell Penn, but she no longer asked after him. It was the night after the men rode out that he realized she was struggling with her newfound freedom.

"Are you allowed... when you want to go outside this place—" Caroline stammered, gingerbread cookies forgotten.

"You ain't a prisoner."

"So, you have said," she replied. "But the gate is locked."

"My answer ain't finna change. Sometimes we locks the gate like now, but it's for ya own good."

"Own good..." She repeated.

Caroline stood on the opposite end of the small wooden table, a forced smile on her face. She wore a white shift with matching pantaloons. He was dressed in tan trousers and to ward off the heat, the legs were rolled up. His shirt was thrown over the back of the extra chair pushed up to the table. She kept the place hot as hell–she almost passed out twice causing him to insist that she strip down to keep from a heat stroke.

Emma and Molly came and went, but at night when it was just the two of them, they wore only their undergarments. Caroline's slender form and perky breasts kept him in a constant state of arousal. This coupled with the heat had him on the verge of crankiness. But after his exchange with Black about his attitude, he tried to manage that side of himself better. In truth he wasn't easily agitated, but he wanted Caroline and this added to his stress.

She was at first shy, but the temperature absolved her of any modesty issues. It was also clear that Caroline was unwilling to give up cooking. He couldn't be sure if she enjoyed the task, or if she was waiting for him to forbid it; thus, he put up with the uncomfortable heat. During the day, his time with Caroline was spent laughing about food, travel, and people. At night, their conversations became more serious, and he wondered if he were the right person to answer her questions.

In the wee hours, Caroline paced. She wandered between the bed and the table–then from the backdoor to the front. Jake didn't stretch his legs and his reason would have been obvious. His dick was hard, and this fact never wavered. He felt like a boy rather than a man. The whole matter was akin to a lit match falling on dry brush.

"You thanks I'm lyin' 'bout yo' freedom?" he asked. But Caroline shrugged, then looked away as if trying to hide. Adjusting his approach, he asked another question. "What is you wantin' to do that you thanks ya cain't?"

Caroline's large brown eyes collided with his own; her hair was pulled back from her face. Jake couldn't think. The glistening of her skin caused him to envision her in the throes of ecstasy. Trying to reel in his thoughts, he pressed her for conversation.

"Speak free wit' me."

"I'm thirty-nine–maybe–forty summers. Now that you say I'm free, the strangest of things tax my thoughts."

He nodded. "Tell me… I ain't finna mock you. I's like you when I first come free."

She stared at him as if weighing whether to trust him. Finally, she shrugged before saying. "I understand the perils of running for freedom. But when you're brought to a free place and there is no worry for safety–your mind will ponder the inconsequential."

Jake thought her intelligent, he also thought her above him in station. The fact that he was free, and she a slave didn't matter in this instance. He was pedestrian with nothing to recommend him; still, he couldn't let go. Where he was unpolished, she was refined. She had even caught the eye of the rich plantation owner–the word "master" hanging in the air between them on a metaphorical noose.

He must have missed some part of the conversation because he was stuck up in his head. When he came to himself, Caroline was staring at him as if waiting for an answer; she looked mortified, and the cabin pulsed with something he couldn't name.

"If it isn't something you want, I'll not take offense," she whispered.

"I'm sorry. I ain't sure what we' speakin' on." He admitted. "Say again."

"I want to be naked with you," she said holding his gaze and her breath. "I want to be naked with a man who has skin the same as my own–I want to choose."

Jake gave a slight shake of his head in an attempt to stabilize the pounding of his heart. Caroline read this action to be a refusal, and when she turned away from him, she mumbled. "I understand."

Bouncing up from his chair, Jake stepped to the front door

slamming, and then barring it. At the backdoor, he did the same. When he turned to face her, Caroline was standing with her hand defensively at her bosom. He allowed his gaze to float about the cabin, giving himself a moment to collect his less than proper thoughts. His eyes landed on the multicolored quilt, the scarred table, the two oil lamps and small black stove before looking back to her. He cleared his throat, but Caroline spoke first.

"Jake, I—"

"Ya test my limit, woman."

Jake had to cut her off. He watched as her eyebrows drew together and when she opened her mouth to speak, he held up his right-hand, palm out, as if to stem the flow of her words. She didn't take heed to his signal. Caroline spoke anyway.

"Am I too tall… too thin… too old… too dark?"

Setting his own shortcomings aside, Jake crossed the room to stand in front of her. When he spoke, he lowered and relaxed his tone, causing her to have to lean down a bit to hear him. Jake allowed his lips to hover about her ear as he whispered.

"I loves yo' black skin and yo' slender form… you is all I think about. What you makes me feel, you can be too young for, but you ain't too old for it." Jake chuckled when she breathed in sharply. He dropped his voice a little more and she further leaned in following his masculinity. "I'm man enuff, Caroline–I ain't pondered how tall you stand."

He stepped back to gauge her reaction to his words. Caroline's eyes were glassy as she held his gaze. Folding his arms over his chest, Jake regarded her for moments. His next statement appeared to have rattled her as much as it did him.

"Miss Caroline, I ain't gon be all right wit' you pickin' another after me. I want to keep ya… the thought of you wit'…"

Dropping her eyes to the floor, Caroline said. "I don't know if I will fit in here."

"You fit wit' me."

"Are you saying I have no right to choose what I am wanting?"

"I'm sayin' it pains me to think of you wit' another–I need more than the taste you's offering."

Her gaze swung back up to meet his, and he could see that she was trying to gauge his sincerity. Desperation seeped through his being when he whispered. "Please, woman… I want to be yo' onlyist choice."

Caroline burst into tears, and Jake stepped forward into her personal space. Cupping her lovely face between his scarred hands, he pulled her in for a soft kiss. The contact was chaste, Caroline tasted of ginger, sugar and need.

"Will you leave me and go to the barracks?"

"Imma stay, if that is what you is wantin." He answered before adding. "Hear me, Caroline, don't give yoself to me unless you means it."

Pressing her lips to his once more, she whispered between pants. "I'm choosing you, Jake."

Hearing her say his name caused his blood to heat and the world around him to slow. The urgency of wanting her fell away and something more basic filled him. He backed away to stare at her before crossing the one room and seating himself on the edge of the bed. Caroline looked both lost and found.

"Will you undress for me, Caroline?" She looked to the oil lamps and he reassured. "I wants to see all of you."

He thought she would refuse, but she didn't. Caroline brought her eyes back to his, and reaching for the hem of her shift, she pulled it over her head. The garment fell to the floor and she stood still–shy as if awaiting his approval. Caroline's skin was smooth and dark like coffee with no hint of cream. She had small breast with nipples like black berries. The vision before him made his heart sing. Pushing the pantaloons from her hips until they pooled at her feet, Jake took in the full sight of her loveliness.

She fidgeted, clasping her hands in front of the tight curls of her womanhood. Jake didn't speak, though he wanted to ask her to move her wringing hands, so he could see her unobstructed.

Instead, he stood, shucking the only bit of clothing he wore. When his dick sprang free and his trousers hit the floor, he sat, while continuing to hold eye contact with her.

"Come closer, Caroline." He beckoned and she did.

At this very moment, what he loved most was the way she glided toward him in all her naked glory. He was humbled by what she offered, and he would work hard to keep it. When she came to a stop in the middle of his thighs. Jake leaned forward nuzzling her belly, while placing open mouthed kisses against her hot skin. He wrapped his arms about her waist, and Caroline ran her fingers over his scalp as she held him close.

Abruptly, she released him and stepped back. Jake felt a new sense of urgency when he reached out to her in protest of the disconnect. Caroline knelt at his feet, and he was unable to stop the trembling in his hands as he once again cupped her face. He kissed her forehead, her nose and then her lips. As his need for her grew even larger, he pulled back to collect himself.

When he closed his eyes for the briefest of seconds, Caroline leaned forward and took him into her hot mouth. He grunted and hissed. "Ahhh fuck."

She gave a strong suck; he wasn't ready. "Wait… shit, wait."

His eyes snapped open, and he took in a cleansing breath. At his command, Caroline stopped, although she did not take her mouth or those huge eyes from him. He traced those beautiful lips with his thumbs, while they were wrapped about him. Jake was in awe at the vision. Still holding her face, he attempted to control the pace and the outcome. Caroline totally submitted to his nonverbal demands, licking and sucking him the way he directed, but it did no good.

She moaned and whimpered around him. He couldn't hold back, he tried to warn her… "I cain't … I'm fixin' to pop, woman."

Caroline rubbed her tongue along the sensitive underside of his dick and his mind went blank. There was a ringing in his ears, along with a tingling sensation that washed over him. His seed burst from him with such force, the edges of his sight went dark. She stayed with him until he was spent... Caroline stayed with him until the last drop.

"Woman... I cain't never share you."

She looked pleasure drunk and Jake was undone. Pulling her to her feet, he pushed her down onto the bed. Her skin held a light sheen of perspiration and it added to the sex haze happening for them. Climbing between her thighs, Jake leaned up over her. Caroline's lips were swollen and glistening from sucking him. Fusing their mouths together in a stormy kiss, he tasted his seed on her tongue. There could be no foreplay; he was too far gone.

His eyes drifted shut as he pressed into her tight, hot, hole. The friction was so intense, he feared their coupling would raze the little cabin to the ground. All his senses were engaged, she smelled of ginger, tasted like his pleasure, and felt like heaven. The noises she made while in the throes of bliss drove him crazy. Pushing up on his hands gave him a better view of her quivering body.

Jake pulled out, but not all the way. Unable to bear being separate from her, he ground himself back into her. "Ohhh my... Jake. I never knew it could feel like this."

And he didn't either. All he could do was grunt, hiss, and groan. His hips never stopped moving. Jake shoved into her, then yanked himself out, eager only to be back in her wet folds. Caroline tightened around him, and it was as if he hit a wall. Passion pulled him under as the orgasm was wrenched from his being. It was her pleas that caused his dick to give an extra kick.

"Don't leave me, Jake... please stay inside me."

Caroline felt so good that he tried to do what she was begging for–he pushed up into her one last time and stayed. Placing his face between her neck and shoulder, Jake wanted to hold on to the intimacy. He hadn't even realized that he needed this type of closeness until this very moment... No, he couldn't let go.

CHAPTER 20

A MAN'S HOME

When the men arrived home, the afternoon sun was still working. Jeremiah listened as Black, Elbert, E.J. and Simon spoke about all that needed doing. As the gate groaned shut, the black cracker's mind turned to the woman he took from the man called Errol. While he figured on what to do with his prisoner, his eyes fell on Ephraim and Fern standing in the shade of a tree.

Jeremiah couldn't look away, and the tension between the two could be felt even at this distance. Ephraim stood with his arms folded over his chest gazing down at Fern, who kept her eyes to the ground. There was a moment when Jeremiah worried that she might have felt forced. His concern eased when Ephraim grinned. Black's voice seeped into his thought pattern, and Jeremiah turned in time to see his brother and the other men walking away.

"She will be all right with him."

He glanced at Black, and when he looked back to the couple, Fern was pointing at him. Ephraim dropped his arms to his side and nodded. She began walking toward him and as if trading off hostages, Black moved toward Ephraim leaving Jeremiah alone with her. Fern stared up at him and the weariness that plagued her was visible. He waited.

"I guess you ain't want me," she said.

The black cracker chuckled. "I picked a better–more even-tempered man for you."

"Is you sayin' you's mean?"

Jeremiah thought her attractive. The tattered brown dress she wore took nothing away. Fern looked heartbroken at the perceived rejection. She never ended the eye contact, and he felt compelled to deliver.

"How many summers did you say you was?"

"Twenty… give or take."

The black cracker laughed. "Ephraim is closer to yo' give or take."

Fern smiled, then sobered. "Thank you, hear."

When she turned heading back over to Ephraim, Black made the tradeoff. The men fell in step, walking toward the small hill that led to Black's house. The background noise to their booted feet on the gravel path was children playing, men yelling, and hammering off in the distance. Black stopped as his house came into view, the action caused Jeremiah to do the same.

"When you came a few months back, you spoke of land that you and E.J. purchased."

"Yeah," Jeremiah answered, hesitantly. He wasn't ready to leave the fort. Black must have read his thoughts.

"We need to spread the fort out to encompass the town and the land you have with your brother. It would be wise to include Virgil's land."

"Oh."

"Will you and your brother consider my proposal?"

"Yes," Jeremiah responded.

"We will give the men time to rest, then we will meet."

"Yeah," Jeremiah replied, then he asked. "You goin' to James?"

"I am."

"I'll go wit' you."

Black nodded and they continued up the porch steps and into the shadowed hallway. The house was quiet as they took the staircase to the second floor. At the landing Jeremiah noticed that all the doors were open. The fading sunlight spilled into the corridor and as he passed the first bedchamber, he saw that it was empty. In the next room, he found Callie seated by the window reading.

Jeremiah stood in the doorway and waited for her to acknowledge him. Her dress was a pale green, and her hair was braided in several cornrows to the back of her head. Behind him, Black continued on to the room where James was being cared for. Callie smiled upon seeing him.

"You're home."

"Just got here a little ago."

She nodded and he asked. "Where is everyone?"

"Sunday and the other women took all the children down to the school. We trying to give 'em something to do. I stayed–cause Otis wouldn't leave James." Callie giggled. "The boy told us he don't want the doors closed."

Jeremiah shook his head, chuckling at the thought. Silence fell between them, until Callie said. "You been awful busy."

"Is you saying you missed me?" he teased.

"Yes, I miss you."

"I brought a woman home. Thought we might live like E.J. and his women," Jeremiah deadpanned.

Callie's smile was weak. "The black cracker would never do such a thing."

"Hmmm... you sound sure."

"Oh, I am," she said, pausing long enough to look him up and down. "I would poison you both."

"I figured on yo' answer, so I gave her to Ephraim."

Callie grew serious. "She doesn't feel forced–does she?"

"Ephraim was a good choice, just like ya thought." Jeremiah said, hearing her concern. He grinned. "She wanted me, ya know."

"How can any woman not want you?"

Jeremiah laughed. "You didn't want me when you first saw me."

"No, I didn't want you, but you have cast a spell over me."

He could hear conversation coming from the next room. Jeremiah tilted his head trying to listen. Otis was speaking animatedly, and James was answering. Turning his mind back to Callie, the black cracker spoke without missing a beat.

"I know a little magic–I can show you when I finish looking in on James."

Callie closed the book she was reading and stood. "I will be at our cabin waiting to see this magic you speak of."

"I'll be along directly."

She kissed his cheek in the doorway, then disappeared down the stairs.

* * *

James was seated in a wooden chair in front of the window. Otis was playing on the floor with his carved animals. It was just him and the boy. Abby had gone down to the school with the women and other children.

"Mooooo." Otis said, making like a cow. "You see dis, Papa?"

"I sees it."

Black stood in the doorway and James nodded, happy to see him. "You outta bed."

"Hardly," James countered. "Montreal?"

"Uneventful."

Turning back for the window, James had to fight the bitterness that welled up within him. Otis popped up, yelling. "Uncle!"

Black scooped Otis up, his rich laughter filling the room. "How's my favorite little man?"

"I's good." The boy answered. When he spied the black cracker standing behind them, he hollered. "Daddy!"

Wiggling down from Black's arms, he ran to Jeremiah. Lifting their son, the black cracker asked. "How is Daddy's boy?"

"Good!" Otis squealed before hopping down to tend his toys.

Both his brother and Jeremiah looked travel weary. James placed his focus back to the window dismissing them–absolving them, but neither man took the hint. It was the black cracker who pushed for conversation.

"You look well enough."

"Been betta."

Black added. "I intend to meet with the men in the morning."

"Thought you said ain't nothin' happen in Montreal."

"I did." Black replied.

"So, what you is sayin' is Montreal was too quiet?"

"What I'm saying is the actor, Renfro, Clinks, and Styles have fled, but they do not leave my thoughts. The coloreds in Montreal have become my responsibility. As a leader I can leave no stone unturned."

His brother was troubled, and James offered. "I can make it down to yo' study."

"We will meet in this room," Black said.

"Yeah," James answered and the black cracker agreed.

Black glanced between them, nodded, then left. James turned back to the window hoping to engage in more self-pity, but Jeremiah hadn't followed Black. Otis raced over to James and climbed in his lap to look out the window.

"Glad to see you movin' about on ya own steam."

"I only moved from the bed to the window," James said in disgust.

"Gotta start someplace."

Spinning to look at the black cracker. "I set thangs back and worried the womenfolk."

"We made shit right." Pointing to Otis, Jeremiah added. "The boy is wit' you and happy–nothing else matters."

"Thanks for lookin' after Abby."

Jeremiah laughed. "Miss Abby was too upset to realize it was me she was dealing wit'."

Elbert stepped into the room before James could respond. Otis ran to him. "Mama!"

"Why ain't you with the other children?" Elbert asked lifting him.

James had to smile because the boy's speech was much improved. "I's being wit' Papa."

"Oh," Elbert said, taking their son's words seriously before tickling the boy.

Otis squealed with delight, then wriggled down and led Elbert over to his scattered toys. Seating himself on the floor, his brother accepted the carved animals their son handed him. While Otis played, Elbert's eyes bounced between him and Jeremiah.

"Black ain't lettin' Montreal go," James said.

"Yeah, I saw it in his eyes." Elbert answered. "We gonna have to wait 'til he gets it worked out."

"Won't be too long, we meet tomorrow," Jeremiah said.

Otis was talking to himself and making sounds for his animals. Elbert leaned back against the wall and got comfortable before filling James in on Blacktown.

James was incredulous. "Black done took over Niggerville?"

* * *

As Jeremiah made his way to the cabin he shared with Callie, his thoughts wandered to their earlier interactions. He noticed it before, but he hadn't been sure of what he was witnessing. His chest tightened as he remembered Callie's reaction from weeks ago. He was seeing the exchange with new eyes. The setting, her facial expressions, and her pain were now all visible.

Callie had been folding clothes, while a vegetable stew simmered on the stove. She wore only a yellow shift. Their children were with Sunday giving them some much needed time alone. It was her cleverness that caused him to seek her thoughts on the matter of Fern.

"I met a young woman in our travels. The man she wit' beats her."

"Oh," she replied.

"I want to take her from him."

"Hmmm. What will you do with her?" Callie asked.

"I was hoping you would know what to do. If I don't take her–she won't live long."

When she didn't answer right away, he turned from the back window to stare at her. She shrugged. "Give her to Ephraim."

He smiled but looking back it was clear that Callie had not. The sound of a wagon rolling by brought him back to the here and now. Nightfall was happening as the last rays of light settled behind the tall trees. His cabin came into view, and Jeremiah couldn't wait to see her–reassure her.

Stepping onto the makeshift porch, he was sure Callie heard his arrival. Pushing at the door he found her kneeling by the large tin tub. The front of her pink shift was wet. She stood at the sight of him and smiled.

"I can shave you and cut your hair."

"Yes, please," he answered.

He undressed as she tended the stove. Their cabin smelled of vegetables and fresh bread. When his gun holster was hung on the peg by the bed, he dropped his dirty clothes in the basket at the foot. Wrapping a towel about his waist, Jeremiah sat in the chair and allowed her to work on him.

"Cut it all off," he said, chuckling when she gasped.

"I love your hair."

"I figured since… you like Black," he shot back.

Callie sighed. "I see your point."

"Do you?" he asked and there was a soberness to his tone.

She backed away and stared at him. The black cracker grinned, but he didn't accuse her of accusing him. Moments went by in silence until Callie dropped her gaze.

"All of me loves only you," he said.

Callie brought her eyes back to his and whispered. "I have been jealous."

Undoing the towel about his waist, he whispered. "Come ride me, woman."

Jeremiah reached out his hand and Callie accepted the invitation. She straddled him, then slid down onto him. Frantically, he wrapped both arms around her; he was stilling her… holding her. She pulled back to look into his eyes. He loved this position; it gave him access to all of her.

She panted. "I am so happy you are home."

His hand smoothed over her back until he was palming her ass and separating her cheeks. Leaning forward, he pushed his tongue in her mouth and they both groaned. The passion with which she returned his kiss rivaled his own.

"Ohhh, Callie," he groaned into the space between them.

When he was ready, he began lifting and dropping her onto him. Callie took over and he tried to stay focused, which added to his pleasure. He demanded. "Talk to me while you fuck me."

"I love it this way," she moaned.

"You feel good."

"Will you forgive my doubt?" she breathed between kisses.

"I shouldna taunted you... yes," he grunted.

"I love when you inside me," she whispered.

"Almost," he promised on a ragged exhale. "Take it from me."

Callie rolled her hips, grinding herself onto him at every other stroke. And he helped until he was mindless from all the sensations. Her lips and kisses were soft, her pussy tight and the hugs she offered loving. It was the perfect combination of lust and love that ripped his seed from him.

"Shit… Callie."

Following him to ecstasy, Callie pressed her face between his shoulder and neck. She tightened around him milking him to the last drop. Jeremiah couldn't get enough of her sweetness. The lovers stayed connected, kissing, and caressing one another until the sun found its way into the sky again.

* * *

The house was too quiet, Black thought as he stood naked and staring, unseeing out the back window. Change was coming to test his leadership and manhood. He could not afford failure, too much was at stake. Stepping away from the window, he walked over to the tub and eased in. Laying back in the cool water, he closed his eyes and allowed his mind to work.

A list of the businesses came to his head, along with distances and land rights. After an hour, Black got out of the water, dried off and pulled on some long underwear. He laid across the bed and dozed, exhaustion finally claiming him. As he was falling under a heavy sleep spell, it occurred to him that he had never cashed in on the deal he and the men made with the ambassador all those months ago. The time had come to see how much power Bainesworth had with the queen.

In his slumber he heard the laughter of children and the conversation of women. Black even heard his name from the depths of his sleep, still he did not stir. It was the wee hours when he woke to find his wife snuggled against him. Sunday must have felt the tension in his body for she nuzzled closer into his side. He didn't climb from their bed to dress and begin his day. Instead, he allowed himself to be lulled back into a peaceful rest. Black decided to let the sun happen before he left the sweetness of his wife's embrace.

The house had completed a cycle of night and morning with children laughing and pots clanking. Everyone was moving about and settling into their day. Sunday was gone tending the children, he supposed. Swinging his legs over the side of the bed, Black headed for the chamber pot in the corner and then the water basin on the table. Next to the white pitcher and basin, lay his shaving items.

His wife appeared in the doorway with a tray of food and a smile. Her voice was soft when she addressed him. "The mens is on they way upstairs. I come to help ya get ready."

"Come hug me, wife. This is the first I'm seeing of you since I been home."

Placing the tray on the table, Sunday stepped to him and squeezed him tight. Looking down at his wife, he could see her worry. She tried to step back, but he didn't let go. He asked. "What troubles you?"

"You was sleepin' when I come to bed. I been worried 'bout Montreal."

"The journey was uneventful." He replied.

"Why you and the mens lookin' like thangs ain't work out?"

Black sighed. "I will meet with you and the other women later. The issues at hand need a delicate touch."

"Then why is you meetin' with the men first if'n you needin us?"

"Trust me," he whispered.

Sunday stared up, then nodded. "Come sit so's I can shave you."

He sat in the black leather chair by the window and gave himself over to his wife and his thoughts. An hour later, Black stepped onto the second-floor landing to find the men spilling out of the last room at the end of the corridor. The tub had been pushed into the corner, leaving the center of the gathering empty. Black moved into the space becoming the focal point for the men.

There was no dallying with salutations, Black went immediately to the heart of the matter. "As you all know I have taken over in the colored sector in Montreal. In order to see to the people with efficiency, some things will have to change."

The men were quiet, but Black saw their doubt. He addressed

Bainesworth. "Ambassador, I wish to purchase the land between the fort and Virgil's farm."

"So, you are calling in your marker. The stretch between here and there is about ten miles."

"I am aware," Black said as he stood in the center of the men, arms folded over his chest. "I want the land between here and the town. E.J. and Jeremiah have land on the other side of the township–I want all that is between there as well."

The ambassador stared at him. Bainesworth breathed in slowly. "This is a tall order, my good man."

"So was warning the union president," Black shot back.

"Yes, it was."

Elbert chimed in. "What is happenin'?"

"The people of Fort Independence will begin practicing a freer existence and the men in this room will help me foster the concept." Black answered.

CHAPTER 21

AN EYE FOR TWO EYES
July 1864

The afternoon sun spilled through the back of the barracks and onto the desk where James sat handing out supplies. He was still not back to his old self, but he was much improved. Black had informed him that Campbell Penn had been moved back into a cabin. Around him the men chatted, yelled, and laughed. The beds were neatly made on either side of the great room. At the front of the barracks the door sat open too.

He had not gone to the cabin to deal with Campbell Penn for two reasons. One: he was seeing to Abby and his children. Two: He wanted his prisoner to stew. A third reason hung just out of his reach–it was hard facing a man that had bested him. The rage he felt was masked by polite interactions and work. He recalled Black's words.

"I will leave Penn to you."

"Yeah."

"Learn what you can."

"Yeah." There had been no variation in his speech or tone. He'd stared at Black as he sat behind the desk in his study.

That had been the extent of the discussion. His brother still trusted him, and he didn't know how that made him feel. Before he could fall into a hole with his doubts and emotions, Philip stepped up and spoke.

"James, I's here to take yo' place."

He stood, grinning at Philip before moving around the desk and heading down the middle aisle for the front door. Outside and to the left of the building were men working on several carriages. Further up the path the smithy could be heard plying his trade. James still hadn't decided whether he was going to pick up Abby from Black's house or face Campbell. It was a decision he made every evening when he left the barracks.

"James!"

Turning he found the black cracker striding toward him. Jeremiah continued. "Where ya headed?"

He wasn't sure where he was going. When he didn't respond, Jeremiah invited. "Walk wit' me."

James nodded and they started walking in the opposite direction of Black's house. They traveled down path after path until they came to the cabin where Zeke stood guard. He looked to Jeremiah and then the cabin.

"You ain't got to be boiling wit' anger to address shit."

"That ain't what rides me." James countered.

"We all been bested before. If any two men knows that–it's us."

James stared Jeremiah in the eyes for several moments. Turning he moved up the three stairs of the makeshift porch and addressed Zeke.

"We has it from here."

"Be at the barracks," Zeke returned.

He and Jeremiah stood on the porch for a time and when he was clear of mind, James turned and pushed at the door. The hinges didn't squeal and as he stepped over the threshold, he noted both windows where open. Still, it was stifling inside the cabin. On the floor lay a mattress, the only other furnishings were two old chairs. The backdoor was closed–barred.

In a chair placed against the wall of the cabin, sat his prisoner. The other chair held a wooden bowl and cup. At the prisoner's bandaged feet were a set of black shackles with no slack. Campbell would have to hop to get to the mattress. His hands were cuffed, and they too offered no give. When James allowed his eyes to meet his hostage, he felt it physically.

Penn had the beginnings of a beard and the hair on his head was shoulder length and knotted. James found himself grinning–for in the other man's eyes was fear and recognition. His own recall was foggy, but the prisoner's reaction meant Penn remembered him, and that was good enough. While he lingered at the front of the cabin with Jeremiah at his side, Penn broke the silence.

"I want to see Penny. You won't get shit unless I see her."

"I was hopin' you would say that." James replied, his voice flat. Turning to the black cracker he said, "Tell the smithy to bring his tools and be sho' to fetch the doctor."

"I'll get the shovels."

"No need–Ruby's grave is still open," James said never breaking eye contact with Penn.

Jeremiah walked off to do his bidding as he and Penn continued to size each other up. Once he evaluated his opponent to his satisfaction, James turned his back. He remained in the doorway with his right shoulder propped against the frame. There would be no questioning this man; Penn was dug in for the long haul. Tension settled over the cabin along with a disturbing quiet.

"I want to see her before I die."

James didn't respond. Penn went on. "I'm not hostile. I understand my plight–let me see Penny and I will tell you what you want."

There would also be no negotiating–this situation could go but one way. James kept his eyes on the landscape in front of him and his ears focused on the man behind him. A wagon rattled up the path and when it came to a halt, Jeremiah hopped down from the passenger seat. Odell was driving and Shultz was in the back.

"What will you get if you kill me before you can learn anything?" Penn asked.

James watched as Shultz got his black bag and Odell retrieved some scary looking tools from the wagon bed. One of the instruments appeared to be a huge pair of pliers. It felt as though his blood changed courses, so excited was he. There was no backing away from this matter; he was certain that when things concluded, Penn would be dead, and he would be a bit more violent.

A round table lay upside down on the back of the wagon. Jeremiah pulled it from the vehicle, carrying it up the three stairs and into the cabin. James stepped aside allowing the men entry. While he stood on the porch staring up at the fading sunlight, behind him Penn had stopped talking. James listened as the smithy, the doctor, and the black cracker set things to rights. After a time, silence blanketed the men inside the cabin and on the outside–not even a breeze blew this day.

James felt constricted by his gun holster, still he turned making his way inside. Shultz had opened the backdoor and it did nothing to dissipate the stuffiness that wrapped about them; but he had worked in worse conditions. The smell of burning wood drifted in from the back of the structure, it was the signal. James addressed his hostage.

"Shultz is gon try to keep you alive, and Imma try to kill yo ass." His tone was matter of fact. "We'll see how it go."

The color drained from Penn's face and it occurred to James that it was dimmer in the cabin than on the porch.

"Imma need mo' light."

"I'll see 'bout it." Odell hollered from beyond the backdoor.

On the table in the center of the cabin sat two crudely made pairs of black pliers. If he had to guess, the purpose of the larger instrument was to squeeze a man's head until his eyes popped. The smaller of the tools were more suitable for teeth. James had seen the latter used–it wasn't pretty. Next to the pain devices lay a white towel.

As he studied the items displayed, James contemplated the best method to inflict serious pain while sustaining life. He was drawing a blank when Penn spoke.

"This will stop nothing."

James stared at the man for moments. "What is you thankin' I'm tryna stop?"

"The Lincoln situation."

James let his focus climb the wall behind Penn landing on a small imperfection in the wood. His mind wandered to Black. He could see his brother's heartache and stress; James could see the shit Black didn't say. Penn had very nearly collapsed the black settlement in Montreal, while simultaneously organizing the murders of Ruby and young Fred. Black had also faced the knowledge of Spike's betrayal and he had done so without words.

"What hand you uses for letter writing?"

"You won't get shit." Penn sneered.

It was the audacity and hostility of this man that drove James to rage. He looked to Jeremiah who nodded. Picking up the smaller pliers, James took three swift steps and grabbed Penn by the hair. His prisoner tried to shove him away, but the black cracker was on hand to help subdue his quarry. Jeremiah climbed between them pinning Penn's legs and arms.

Even with all the tussling and flailing about, James managed to secure the pliers around a front tooth. He yanked hard, pulling the incisor from Penn's head. The man cried out causing James to punch him in the face for good measure. When he and Jeremiah backed away, Penn spat blood on the floor as he glared at them; still, the prisoner was dazed.

Turning his back on the situation, James tossed the pliers on the table causing the tooth to bounce and skid across the surface until it disappeared over the edge; blood and thick spit snagged on the wood. He ignored everyone in the situation as he emptied the contents of his pockets. The doctor moved into his periphery and placed his black bag on the tabletop. James stepped out onto the porch to give Shultz a moment to check the prisoner.

Jeremiah followed, but they did not engage in conversation. Neither man wanted to give the prisoner anything to leverage. When Shultz posted up in the doorframe, James went back inside; he kept on to the backdoor and peered out. Odell was gone but the fire burned steady in the pit between the storage cabins. Sticking out the small blaze were two long rods.

James looked up as Odell rounded the curve holding a lantern. He moved down the two stairs meeting the smithy halfway. Taking the light from him, James turned and walked away. Over his shoulder he called out.

"Be back."

"Sho' thang," Odell returned.

Inside the cabin, James sat the lantern in the corner; his goal–to keep shit from burning to the ground. Penn eyed him as he moved about the cabin. James had nothing in mind but killing this man. Still, he made a show of it to create dread. Black wanted information, but all he could see was Penn beating his ass, so an explanation of events wasn't high on his list. James stood in front of the prisoner. The black cracker moved in behind him but remained silent.

"Is we still in the same place?"

"Nothing has changed." Penn countered, his tongue falling in the empty space left by his tooth.

James felt himself easing into the role of nightmare and it was only fitting. As a man he had sustained a true besting–but how had it been for Ruby? Unlike his brother, he had been able to avoid what she must have gone through. But now–in this circumstance, it was all he could figure.

Abruptly, he turned and walked out the backdoor. He knew he had Penn's attention, so he lingered speaking in low tones with

Odell. The smithy did as he requested, pulling out the long-padded gloves. Back inside the cabin, he offered Jeremiah some instruction.

"I wants him pinned to the floor."

At his words, Penn stood and attempted to take a step. His prisoner must have forgotten that the shackles at his feet offered no slack. When Penn would have taken a step, he toppled over, and the black cracker put boot to his back to keep him in place. James moved to stand in front of where Penn was sprawled out. He squatted, then grabbing the chain that joined the cuffs, James yanked.

Penn had nothing to aid him, he was laid out flat. On his right Odell stepped into the side view. The smithy carried an iron rod–the end red hot and shaped like the letter "F". James would have liked the metal to be hotter, but this would have to do. Looking to the backdoor, he nodded at Odell. As if on cue the blacksmith came forward and placed the brander to the back of Penn's hand.

Instead of crying out, Campbell Penn passed out. James spoke into the quiet of the cabin. "He ain't never say which was his letter writing hand–do both."

The branding of the other hand caused Penn's body to shake, but he didn't wake from oblivion. James was disappointed. When he and Jeremiah stepped back, it was in time to see Elbert and Black step through the front door. His brother looked about, assessing the situation.

"You get anything?" Black asked.

"No."

"You tryna get anything?" Elbert asked.

James shrugged.

"What is the damn Lincoln matter?" Shultz asked.

Penn started moaning. Shultz moved in close to see about him. James followed his brothers and Jeremiah out the front of the cabin, while the smithy exited the back to tend the fire. The sunlight was almost gone when the men formed a circle on the porch. Behind him, James heard Shultz and Odell rushing about trying to get his prisoner right. In front of him, Black spoke.

"We need to ride out."

"Blacktown?" Jeremiah asked.

"Three days."

"Imma finish wit' Penn tonight." James promised.

"Yeah," Black replied. "Drop his ass in wit' Ruby and close the hole."

His brother stepped from the porch and walked away. Elbert didn't follow. Shultz appeared in the doorframe and the doctor's words brought peace.

"I think he's ready to talk."

James moved around the doctor and walked back into the cabin. On his heels were Elbert and Jeremiah. Penn had been propped up in one of the chairs. His eyes were wide with pain and both hands were bandaged. Except for the bruising–his face was minus all color. When James moved in to get a closer look at Campbell Penn, the man leaned over and tossed up his belly.

Jeremiah jumped back and cursed. "Nasty shit."

He and Elbert held steady, eyeing their prisoner. It was Elbert that issued the next threat. "You want me to take it from here?"

James found himself shrugging again. The cabin now stank from the puke seeping into the planked floor. Elbert reached down lifting the right leg of his brown trousers. Pulling a razor from his boot, Elbert stood and flipped his wrist. The razor snapped open and so too did the prisoner's mouth.

"I was sent to distract." Penn wheezed.

"We know that." James countered. "You done good–you has my attention."

Behind them the black cracker laughed, and Elbert spoke. "Imma need something I don't know."

"Work for... Davis." Penn groaned. "...kill Lincoln and his vice president."

Their hostage was out of his head. Turning to Elbert, James said. "His ass drunk wit' pain–he tellin' the truth."

He looked back to his hostage in time to see Penn keel over and fall face first to the floor. Elbert shook his head. "Shit... he been shot, burned and had a tooth yanked from his head."

They stepped back when the smithy threw water on him. Penn was lethargic. James stooped down next to the felled man and grabbed him by the hair. "When Lincoln 'posed to be killed?"

Penn grunted. "Don't... know–not yet."

And there it was for all to see. Penn had been yanked from the plan before the final decision could be made in this so-called Lincoln Affair. Still, James was clear that Penn's disappearance could bring about more danger for the fort and Lincoln.

"Odell!" James hollered toward the backdoor.

The smithy appeared. "Yeah."

"Take us to the graveyard."

"The wagon out front," Odell said.

Jeremiah grabbed the prisoner's feet and James grabbed his torso. The men followed the smithy outside tossing Penn on the wagon bed. James climbed up and Jeremiah rode shotgun. Elbert and Shultz remained on the makeshift porch. His brother was lighting a cigar as the vehicle lurched into motion. Penn moaned and tried to sit up. Under the cloak of darkness James set upon his victim and slit his throat.

When the vehicle entered the cemetery, Odell lit the torches. James pushed a lifeless Penn from the back of the wagon. The black cracker was on hand to drag their quarry to the open grave. His prisoner was still gasping and choking on his own blood when they pushed him into the hole Ruby occupied. The sound of shovels hitting earth became rhythmic as they closed the grave and the problem of Campbell Penn.

James walked from the cemetery back to the cabin he shared with Abby. The darkness was complete as he moved along the path. He stopped at the pump behind his cabin and removed his blood-stained shirt. His body ached, which was all part of the healing process–per Shultz. He wanted his old self back and he worried it might not be possible.

Rounding to the front of the cabin, he faltered before taking the few steps to the porch. James pushed the door open to find his front room empty and the wick turned down to a soft light. He could hear shuffling coming from the backroom. On the table was a plate covered by a yellow towel. A large pot of water sat on a low fire at the back of the stove.

Dropping his blood-stained shirt by the door, he retrieved the buckets and headed to the pump. Back in the cabin, he dumped the water into the tub and went for more. When he refilled the buckets and stepped into the house, Abby appeared from the bedchamber. She wore a blue wrap and it looked as though she had been braiding her hair. The two cornrows were neatly done. James noticed everything about her.

He poured the extra water into the tub, then placed the buckets at the door. His head was filled with clutter and his woman knew it.

"James… you's home." Abby greeted. "How you feelin'?"

After mixing in the warm water from the stove, he shucked the rest of his clothing. Placing his gun on the table next to the plate of food that awaited him, James answered her question with the truth.

"My body hurts," he said easing into the water.

"You hungry?"

"No."

Abby nodded, and he watched her head for their bedchamber. The light beyond the curtain went dark. He closed his eyes to hide from her concern. She didn't push and he was thankful. He was managing the shame at the scare he gave Abby and his mama.

After an hour he climbed from the tub and dried off with the towel she left for him.

James sighed as he strode into their backroom and slipped into bed behind her. "I'm sorry… I ain't been myself."

Abby didn't hassle him, instead she turned and hugged him. His eyes smarted, but he managed to hold his emotions in check. He kissed her and she accepted his love. What started as a chaste connect soon burned hot. They had not been physical, and he felt the loss.

James deepened the kiss by pressing his tongue into her mouth. His sweet woman burst into tears, while hungrily returning his passion. Needing no further encouragement, he pulled her to him until she was under him. Abby wore no pantaloons, and he was thankful.

She wrapped her arms and legs about him as he shoved into her to the hilt. He was clumsy in his desperation, but Abby… she was graceful and welcoming. Opening her legs, she allowed her palms to slide down his back until her little hands were gripping his ass. Abby was assisting him, and it made him call out.

"Ohhh, shit… you gon end this if you don't ease up."

He thought the warning would calm them down, but it didn't. Abby was frenzied when she moaned. "Please, James… kiss me."

She had begun clenching and releasing almost as soon as he entered her. He wanted it to last but she pulled him along with her. The ecstasy they shared pushed his pain in the margins of the moment. James felt her body stiffen and it was the shove he needed. His hips stuttered and faltered as pleasure consumed him.

"Abby… Fuck, I love you," he groaned.

James allowed himself to be held as he came down from the high of their sex haze. He worried he was too heavy, but Abby took his full weight and didn't let go.

CHAPTER 22

BLACK THOUGHT

Staring around his study Black could see the confusion on the faces gazing back at him. The women were seated in the front two rows; the twenty-two sat behind them. On the couch between Miss Cora and Iris sat Big Mama, who held Elbert's youngest boy, Dennis. The ambassador stood to his left, E.J. and Jeremiah stood together on his right. The door to his office was open and when he looked to the back of the gathering, Black found Simon standing in the doorframe.

It was early morning and the sun shone through the window signifying new beginnings. He had been careful in his word choice when discussing his plan for the people and himself. But judging by the expressions of those looking at him, he had not done a good job. His wife asked the first question, her bafflement evident. She did not call him Black as she did in the company of others.

"Nat… is you wantin' us to live somewhere else?"

"We will continue to live here." Black answered and he could see the women visibly relax. "You in this room will help me with the people of Fort Independence–you will help me set a liberated mindset. The leaders in *this* room will help me release the people from their fear and the past."

There was more silence and so Black waited. The ambassador spoke up. "As the queen's man, I have managed to secure the land rights you requested. It was no easy task, my good man."

"Me and E.J. will be raising horses," Jeremiah said.

"The farmland will be yours to do with as you please." E.J. added.

Black nodded. His eyes landed on Virgil, who sat next to Percy with his head down. It was the field hand that spoke. "We are ready."

Virgil's head popped up and he smiled. "Sally Lovelace contracted with me and sold her women's apparel establishment."

Black smiled when he saw Anna's face light up. Virgil went on. "The innkeeper was all for buying new dishes cooked here and transported there. Nigel stated the women can come and take over his kitchen whenever they wish. He will split the profit."

"When we gon start this change?" James asked.

"Now."

This time, sidebar conversation did start, and Black didn't try to stop it. When there was a small pause, he added. "We will travel by rail to Montreal. Simon will stay back to run the fort. Sunday and Morgan will travel with me."

Both his wife and Morgan looked surprised. Black gazed about before dismissing the women, but his wife and Morgan remained. The twenty-two stayed as well and when the door to the study closed, Black offered direction.

"As we seek to expand… as we look to live in unrestrained freedom, there will be those who try us. We as men will attempt harmony, but not in the face of aggression. The goal here is as it has always been–you are to remain upright."

The men nodded as Black paced in front of his desk. He had one more order. "Should we ever face ambush, my wife's safety and that of any woman traveling with us will come before mine. Am I clear?"

"Yeah," the men chorused.

* * *

Sunday and Morgan were seated opposite of her husband in a carriage that rocked and swayed as it moved toward town. She watched the countryside roll by, and Morgan did the same from the other window. Her husband called her name, and his voice broke her train of thought.

"Sunday."

"Yes."

In the dimness of the carriage, she could see Morgan turn her attention to them. Her husband smiled, then asked. "Do you have questions for me?"

"I ain't sho' what to ask."

Chuckling, Nat responded. "Travel time is the best time to ask questions."

Nodding, Sunday turned back to the window. She felt lost and this was yet another time when she realized that her husband was bigger than she could comprehend. Morgan chimed in.

"I ain't understandin' what we doing."

Sunday wanted to kiss Morgan; her friend had summed up all that troubled her. As they rocked along, her husband offered patience and direction. "The people of Fort Independence will spread out–they will help me control the land and the coin that flows."

"How is we gon be safe if we spread out?" Sunday found herself asking.

"The gate doesn't keep you safe. It's the men that work the gate that keeps the people safe, and they will continue to do so."

"Is we still gon live together?" Morgan asked.

"The twenty-two will, but we will move about to help the

people. Everyone's burden will be lighter, for even the farmer will take up arms."

"We has another fort in Montreal?" Sunday asked.

"There are more coloreds who wish to join with us. They seek protection, and I have agreed to give it to them."

"Niggerville?" Morgan asked.

"Blacktown," Nat corrected.

After about an hour of riding, the carriage rattled to a stop. Odell set the stairs and her husband hopped out before handing both her and Morgan down. The afternoon sun was bright as she stood on the boardwalk. Two wagons pulled to a stop alongside the carriage, one driven by Philip and the other by Chester. A combination of twenty-two men spilled from the back of each vehicle.

Sunday noted some of the men were dressed in black, others were dressed in brown. What was uniform–the guns they carried. The men didn't smile or even speak among themselves; the twenty-two were about business and they did not resemble the men she interacted with at home. She had to admit, her husband was correct–the gate wasn't what kept the fort safe.

When Sunday turned her attention to Morgan, who was wearing a pastel blue dress, she too was staring about casing the joint. And for all her prettiness, Morgan's black gun holster was visible for all to see; her friend was about business as well.

Black carried his wife's valise, while Gilbert carried Morgan's travel bag. The train could be heard in the distance and the ground shook with its approach. His wife was nervous, but the trip was necessary. The men closed in around them as they made for the clearing. There was a station that served as a resting place for weary travelers, but there was no backdoor. One had to walk around to the back of the building to meet the train.

The land surrounding the little structure could turn an ankle, but the women had on the proper footwear. As the train rushed into the station, it carried with it a grass bending gust of wind. They all stood back from the tracks as the train slowed, then stopped. Fifteen minutes floated by before a colored man appeared on the steps of the railcar in front of them.

Elbert and James climbed the metal stairs first, causing the porter to move back from the doorway. Black lifted Sunday and Morgan up onto the train, then climbed in behind them. Once inside the train, he looked about pleased to find the accommodations fitting for his wife and Morgan. The benched seats were covered in plush black velvet. The carpeting was blood red, and the windows were large allowing in plenty of natural light. There were five sets of benches that faced each other on either side of the railcar.

Black led the women to a middle set of benches on the right side of the car. Sliding in opposite them, he sat facing his wife and Morgan; the men set up around them providing an extra layer of protection. The porter disappeared leaving them to their own devices. It was warm in the railcar–even with the doors open at either end. Thankfully, and also the reason Black had chosen this seating arrangement, two of the big windows opened at the middle benches.

The train let off a loud hissing sound, and his wife jumped; her anxiety was apparent. Black wanted to comfort her, but he was sure that would get him a proper set down. As the train lurched forward, Morgan reached for Sunday's hand giving it a reassuring squeeze. His wife reciprocated. It occurred to him that it was his job to instruct his wife, thereby enhancing her life–as she had done for him. But what was closer to the truth, given her reaction to being outside the fort, he had caused life for his wife to become stagnant in his attempt to keep her safe. The very thought shamed him.

Maybe because Sunday was taking this journey with them, the

men remained quiet. Black settled in across from the women and like the men, he didn't engage. Sunday and Morgan spoke in low tones about the countryside. They ate whatever Big Mama packed for them, and he ate the rations packed by the men. Black dozed when the sun went down. The hour had grown late when he felt his wife crawl into his lap.

Against his ear she whispered. "How much longer, Nat?"

"Dawn."

Sunday snuggled into him, and he found that he needed it. Black was troubled, and it was the anticipated conversation about Ruby that was sure to come. He didn't speak on it–he would let the chips fall where they may.

"I love you, Sunday."

"I's sorry 'bout being so nervous."

"You're doing good."

When his wife found sleep, he remained awake holding her tight to him. This was how dawn found them. Sunday woke when the brakes were applied to the big mass of steel. The screeching woke everyone. He looked up when the porter entered the railcar. Black gave his attention to the brown skinned man with the thick glasses and bald head. The railroad worker, who looked to be about forty summers, smiled as he came to stand next to where he sat with his wife on his lap.

"Morning, Orange."

"Mawnin', Mista Black." The porter answered. "They's waitin' to carry you all to Blacktown."

"Thank you, Orange. This here is my wife, Sunday and Morgan, Simon's wife."

"It be a pleasure, ladies," the porter said while bowing to them.

"Good morning," both women said in unison.

Around them the men readied themselves to get off the train. The porter backed away and the men exited first. Sunday and Morgan stayed on the train to relieve themselves and freshen up. When they emerged from the train, both women looked travel weary. Black lifted them down from the metal stairs. Elbert helped Morgan, and Black helped Sunday maneuver the uneven landscape until reaching level ground. Out in front of them were two wagons and one carriage.

Elbert, James, and Gilbert closed in around the women. Black moved forward approaching the vehicles first. Clive, who drove the carriage, hopped down to set the stairs. Task complete, the older man turned to greet Black and the men. His brown weathered skin and graying hair amplified his tired eyes.

"Hope, glad to see ya."

"Clive," Black nodded. Sunday's presence had him strung tight.

"We has ever-thang ready for you."

Black stared about checking for ambush. Clive's voice conveyed his hurt when he said in a tone meant for Black's ears only. "The peoples is wantin yo' forgiveness–same as you is wantin' ours. We wouldn't neva hurt you or yo' woman."

Time stood completely still as Black stared at Clive. He could find no response to such a statement, but the older man's honesty glowed like the morning sun. Black nodded, and to his men he yelled out.

"Let's move."

Elbert and James escorted the women to the carriage. James climbed in next to Morgan, while Black sat next to his wife. The hour ride was uneventful and when the little caravan rolled into Blacktown, the people were standing about waiting for him. This greeting was far different from when he was here last. The carriage came to a stop in front of a modest house with two chairs on a white porch.

Black and James exited the carriage from opposite doors. Both men closed the women in the vehicle out of habit as Black allowed himself to be approached by the people. Only the men of the settlement came forward to greet and shake his hand. The twenty-two were experiencing the same treatment. He was tired but not too weary for the people–there was much to be done.

A dark-skinned man named Mitchell came forward to shake his hand. The man appeared equal in age, standing about five-feet, ten-inches. He wore tan overalls and smelled of smoke. His eyes were perceptive, and his stance sure.

"You the smithy?" Black asked.

"Yes, sir. Me and my brother Jonah is both blacksmiths."

"Come see me when the sun goes down," Black said.

"We will."

When the smithy backed away, and before anyone else could come forward, Black turned and opened the carriage door. Sunday squinted against the morning sun as she allowed him to lift her out of the cab. James did the same for Morgan. Black didn't linger. Instead, he took his wife by the hand and walked her up the path to the porch of their new home.

Turning back, he addressed the crowd. The twenty-two stood among the people, blending in… showing unity. His words flexed his influence over the settlement dubbed Blacktown. "This day I bring my wife to you. She is an extension of my authority–should you challenge her, it will be looked upon as aggression to the order I have put in place. Matters will not go well for those who test me."

His eyes bounced to the collage of faces, and when no one spoke, Black smiled. "People of Blacktown… my wife, Sunday Turner!"

The people cheered. Sunday stepped forward and waved. When the crowd quieted, Black went on. "There is much to be done, but we are up for the task."

A buzz started in the crowd as Black walked his wife and Morgan into the house. Along the back wall sat a brown square table with two benches on either side. A black stove sat in the corner and the fireplace was swept clean. On the planked floor was an orange throw-rug that sat in front of a brown couch. By the window sat a white rocking chair placed invitingly in the sunlight; the little house was welcoming.

In the bedchamber was a large platform bed, and Black could

tell whoever crafted it did so with his size in mind. There was a privacy screen in the corner of the room for the chamber pot, and in front of the fireplace was a large white porcelain tub. The tub had been his only request. Across the small hall was another room with a full-size bed and chest. On the nightstand was a basin and water pitcher. Black was pleased.

"I will bring water for you and Morgan." He promised.

"Thank you."

When the women were settled, he stepped back onto the porch to give them privacy and time. Elbert was seated in one of the chairs smoking a cigar. James was standing at the top step looking about. Black moved down the stairs to mingle with the people and get a better understanding of their set up. Elbert remained posted up, but James followed. Anthony and Jake stood guard at the back of the house.

Black and James were given horses, and they rode for hours seeing the land and the people. James was weak and tired, but he wouldn't admit it. When they returned to the house, Elbert was where they left him. A stablehand took the horses, and when Black stepped onto the porch, he noticed that it wrapped around to the right side of the house. At the back of his home the porch spilled out to a small courtyard facing the barn. The space was converted into a mini barracks for the twenty-two.

By mid-afternoon, Black was seated on his porch observing the goings on. The people went about their day in much the same way they did at the fort. Black noted repairs being done to some of the homes. Women, both young and old, rushed about carrying baskets. Children played, gardens were tended, and the fields were being worked. The small tracts of land butted up against each other for the most part and the men labored together. Blacktown was smaller than the fort, still he was impressed.

On his agenda and before this night ended, Black would assemble another twenty-two men; their jobs would be protection, and it would be achieved by any means necessary.

* * *

Nightfall was complete in Blacktown and to ward off the darkness, many lanterns were lit. Black kept working even while suffering silently from lack of sleep. The twenty-two followed his lead and engaged with the men being chosen to protect Blacktown. It seemed the settlement had about two hundred residents; the men chosen were eager to do their parts.

After choosing the smithy and his brother Jonah, who was light of skin and quiet, Black continued in his quest to get this undertaking finished. He chose a man named Booker, who was roughly six feet and brown of skin. He had intelligent eyes and dialogue. And so it went, Matthew, Jackson, Homer and Hobart were chosen by James. Andrew, Julius, Abel, and Teddy were Elbert's choice.

Black and Anthony decided on Isaac, Robert, Ben, and Elijah. All four men were after thirty summers, but before forty. These men all had wives and children. Black saw it in their eyes–they all had something to lose. His options tapped out after Wesley, Noah, Leo, and Johnny. The last men were all before thirty summers.

As the men stood about speaking in low tones, laughing, and getting to know each other, Black sat on his porch observing. He was cataloging his tasks for the following day, the duties falling together in his mind like puzzle pieces. He needed to send a message to Lincoln, but before he could get on to the next thought, a woman began screaming Booker's name. She was running and stumbling toward them, causing several of his men to reach for their weapon. Like his men, Black also reached for his peacemaker.

Mitchell laughed. "It's Sweetie, she come to tell us that it's her sister's time."

"Time?" James asked.

"Margaret is having her little one on this night." Jonah explained. "Booker is our doctor."

The young woman named Sweetie was out of breath when she

reached them. Booker stepped forward and took control. "Sweetie, I'm here."

"Margie ready... she ready."

Booker took the shrieking woman by the arm and led her away. Black noted that Shultz followed, so they all did. The lantern lights appeared to be floating down the pathways as the men carrying them followed as well. Finally, they came to a small house with a picket fence in front. The men piled into the front yard, while the woman named Margie hollered her head off.

Shultz rolled up his sleeve as he trailed Booker into the house.

* * *

Inside the house the air was still and hot. Shultz hung back giving Booker the lead, the younger man was so focused, he was sure Booker didn't even realize he was there.

"Where Margie?"

"She in da back." An old woman with gray hair answered.

Sweetie turned as if her job was complete. She ran from the house slamming the door in her wake. Booker stepped into the back room and began issuing orders.

"Open the window–it's hot as hell in here."

Three lanterns sat about the small space: one on a chair in the corner, the other on the nightstand and the larger of the three lamps hung from a hook in the ceiling. This only added to the stuffiness of the chamber, Shultz thought. The set up that was in place appeared planned. Two big wooden bowls sat on the stand side-by-side. Both bowls were filled with water.

Booker removed his shirt, then washed his face and hands before donning a clean shirt. Shultz was about to back out of the chamber when Booker looked directly at him.

"Miss Velma will get you a clean shirt and fresh water."

"Come wit' me... overseer." The old woman instructed.

He wanted to tell Miss Velma that he was no overseer, but this was not the time. She set him up with fresh water and a clean homespun shirt before walking away. The doctor was pulling the shirt over his head when he heard the younger woman scream. He knew the sound; the patient was exhausted. A birthing could end on a sad note if the woman was too tired to labor.

Shultz felt useless when he stepped back in the small room. Old Miss Velma had encouraged the woman to the edge of the bed. Booker was checking her while speaking softly.

"What you eat today, Margie?"

"Velma baked apple pie," she panted.

"You ain't send for me." Booker accused.

"We has some left for you. Don't we, Margie?" the old lady said.

"Velma saved you some." Margie groaned and it seemed she was trying to concentrate. "She say you wouldn't see 'bout me if'n I ate all the pie."

Booker stepped back from the patient and accepted the cloth the old woman gave him. While wiping his hands, he moved to the side of the bed to look Margie in the eyes. His expression was determined.

"You sapped out?" he asked.

"I cain't do no mo'," she whispered.

The younger man stared at Margie, waiting until she breathed and panted through her next pains before he spoke.

"Everything look like it should. I think I have it figured out."

Shultz noticed the woman was hanging on Booker's every word. He too was enthralled. The younger man went on. "I see the head. Seem like when ya push–you stop right at the point of progress."

"The pain too much." Margie panted.

"I'm sure it is but you strong enough."

"All right," Margie whimpered.

"On yo' next pain I wants you to bear down wit' all yo might."

Booker walked back to the end of the bed and throwing the

bloody cloth over his shoulder, he leaned into the problem. As if on cue the pain started, and Booker spoke.

"Each pain that comes is a chance to get out of this here problem. Push and don't let up."

Turning his attention to Shultz, Booker nodded toward the bed and Margie. Taking the hint, the good doctor stepped in to help the screaming, grunting woman sit up.

Booker grinned. "We got the head–rest for a time."

When the next pain hit, the woman yelled. "I's dying."

Shultz knew the shoulders burst free when Booker announced. "Almost."

Poor Margie screamed until she was hoarse, and then the wonderful sound of a baby crying made the cabin a little less suffocating. Booker set about separating mother from child as he said in a clear strong voice.

"Got us a baby girl."

Miss Velma took the baby as Booker finished up with Margie. When Sweetie appeared, the men moved into the front room. Booker headed for the backdoor and the pump. He removed his shirt and washed up. There was no conversation, and when he finished the younger man disappeared through the back of the house. Shultz freshened up and met the men in the front.

Upon seeing him, the man called Jonah asked. "How is Margie?"

"Good… good." Shultz replied. "She has her a brand-new baby girl."

Black and the men moved back up the path toward his house. They found Elbert seated on the porch, the front door was open. A single lantern sat at his foot, and it was the only source of light until the other men carrying the extra lanterns joined them. Shultz stood off to the side with Black, his mind falling into thoughts of Blacktown and its people.

"Did the woman called Margie fair well?"

Turning to catch Black's shadowed features, Shultz answered. "The young miss fared well. Booker is more than competent."

He could barely make out that Black was nodding his head. The doctor asked. "Have you slept?"

"No, strung too tight."

"These people love you and us by extension. Go rest, my friend," Shultz said.

"Yeah," Black replied before he stepped around Elbert and entered the house.

The men from Fort Independence and Blacktown stood guard while Black slept.

* * *

Black woke to the sound of nothing happening around him. He was disoriented for a bit until he remembered where he was. Swinging his legs over the side of the bed, he made for the chamber pot. Donning his trousers, he went in search of Sunday. He felt panicked as he moved toward the front door and porch. His hand shook as he pulled the door open to find James seated on the porch alone.

James looked up at him as he stepped outside. "Sunday went to see the new baby."

"Who is with her?"

"Morgan... Elbert is following them."

Nodding, Black had been about to turn for the door, when his brother added. "Sunday got her own duties. We cain't stop that."

"Yeah."

Once back in the house, he grabbed the buckets by the fireplace. He headed out back to the pump. There was a mix of men from both settlements present; they greeted him. After making three trips to fill the tub. Black sank down into the cool water and pondered.

When he finally stood from the water and dried off, his wife appeared as he was wrapping the towel about himself. Sunday closed the door behind her with her foot. In her hands was a tray of food: scrambled eggs, grits, sausage, and warmed bread. Next to the plate was a glass of water and a cup of black coffee. His wife placed the tray on the small round table in the corner. There were two chairs on either side.

Sunday wore a peach dress with a snug fitting bodice. The sun streamed in through the window, and he was aware of the makeshift barracks behind the house. Still, it was a good distance away and the house was raised to stop prying eyes. Taking his wife by the hand, he sat on the side of the bed, pulling her to stand between his legs.

"Thank you," she whispered and leaned in kissing his lips.

"For?"

"Thank you for not comin' to fetch me."

He chuckled. "I almost did. Why didn't you tell me you were leaving to go visiting?"

"I ain't been tellin' you I's leavin' when we at the fort."

"Yes, but the fort is home—"

"We's home here too, ain't we?"

"Yes, but I'm not ready."

She kissed him again. "I won't do it again."

"Thank you."

"For?" Sunday giggled.

"Thank you for letting me think I'm in charge."

His wife smirked. "I ain't in charge, Elbert is. He followed us, and he ain't care that I told him not to."

"Everyone has a job, Sunday."

"Come eat for yo' food get cold." She said changing the subject. "Margie is lovely and little Nelly is beautiful. Booker is good at doctoring."

They sat to the table enjoying each other and when he was dressed, Black headed out to the great room of the small house. Although it was afternoon when he woke, he accepted that his schedule was off. On the bench table, he found the items he requested: ink, parchment and a ledger with the names and issues troubling the people.

Black settled into his day, while checking off all the tasks on his list. Most important, he sent three telegrams; still, he was certain he would only get back two responses.

CHAPTER 23

OUT MANEUVERED

The confederate president was entertaining dinner guests when his secretary, Burton appeared on the edge of the formal dining room. In his right hand he clutched a piece of correspondence. Davis pushed back from the table, dabbed at his mouth with the white cloth and stood. A slave came forward placing the chair back to the table.

"Please excuse me, duty calls." The president said. "Continue enjoying yourselves, I shan't be long."

Davis rushed over to Burton and they both stepped into the dimness of the corridor. The secretary handed him the telegram and the president moved toward a table with an oil lamp. Leaning into the meager light, his eyes scanned the message and his breath caught.

SLAVER I WATCH YOU AS YOU WATCH ME–PENN HAS SUCCUMBED TO MY CHARMS

"Who sent this message?" Davis asked and his voice shook like his hands.

"The keeper of the dry-goods establishment delivered the message himself." Burton replied as he grabbed at the back of his neck. "What is happening?"

The president stared at him for long seconds not hearing what his secretary was saying. "Burton, please make my excuses."

Davis strode away without a backward glance. It seemed his plan to kill Lincoln and his vice president had been compromised.

* * *

The union president was still in his nightdress when his manservant, Jonathan entered his bedchamber. One of the maids followed him placing a tray of food on the table by the window. Ignoring the servants, he made for the table.

Next to the pot of tea was a telegram. Lincoln waited for the servants to leave before opening the message. The words were to the point.

TWO BIRDS CAN BE KILLED WITH ONE STONE

Lincoln rushed to his closet and dressed. He had much to do.

* * *

Simon was seated at the desk in front of the barracks. The afternoon was slow going as the men moved about in their duties. He missed his wife, and his daughter missed her too. They were staying at Black's house to be near the womenfolk in case he needed help. He was thankful for Callie who a had a tender hand with the children.

Philip strode up to the desk to relieve him. When Simon stood to greet the older man, he was handed two telegrams. He walked out the backdoor for privacy and once alone at the oak tree, Simon opened the messages.

ALL IS GOOD

The second message read:

I LOVE YOU

Simon grinned.

* * *

Black sat to the table studying the ledger while eating a slice of apple pie. It had been nearly two weeks since he and the men arrived in Blacktown. He timed his stay this way on purpose; and though he hated that his wife was with him, it was the perfect way. Sharing Sunday meant he cared for and was in partnership with the people.

Yet, he felt real fear where the women were concerned; still, he tried not to be led by trepidation. In the face of what happened to Ruby, it was difficult to let them out of his sight. He understood that he had to live by his words and the people needed to witness the action. Black needed to demonstrate liberty and all that the concept encompassed. Allowing the stay to last a fortnight gave them all hope.

They had razed the theatre to the ground in the spring. Black realized that the warmer weather would be accompanied by the anger of the privileged. He wasn't delusional about the shopkeepers or their cries of indignation. Black was positive the white sector would regroup, then head to the closest colored settlements.

He was laying the fork across the dish when the thunder of horse hooves sounded outside the open window. Blacktown was a maze of dirt paths and large trees. The settlement boasted of cabins, medium size homes, barns, and wheat fields. Black pushed back from the table, wiped his mouth, then stepped out onto the front porch.

The sky was overcast, and the threat of rain made him happy. It meant if a match were struck, fire wouldn't take hold. Sunday was in Morgan's room chatting, and he was thankful the women hadn't gone visiting. As he took his lone position on the porch, Black offered no reaction to the twenty white men on horseback. They appeared to be lawmen, and he knew why they had come. It seemed this day was as good as any to address the burning of the Buckingham Theatre.

Leaning his shoulder against the beam that supported the small overhang of a roof, Black waited. The leader pushed his horse forward, and offering a forced smile, he spoke.

"Hope… I hadn't known you were a resident of Niggerville."

Harvey Michaels was about fifty summers with brown hair and silver sideburns. This was a man who could be mild mannered and dangerous all at once. Harvey was an example of opposing concepts occupying the same space. Black had a history with this man. It was neither good nor bad, but it made the circumstance all the more hazardous.

"Can I assist you gentlemen with something?"

Harvey's voice shook a bit when he asked. "You and sweet Miss Ruby back together? Is that why you here?"

Standing to his full height of six-feet, three-inches, Black crossed his arms over his chest. He stared at Harvey until the older man squirmed. Allowing his gaze to pass over the men before him, Black presented as bored. When his eyes bounced back to the leader of his unwanted guests, his tone was flat.

"Is there something I can assist you with, Harvey?"

The lawman wore clothes of high quality. Sweat stained the armpits of his expensive white shirt. Harvey wore two guns at his hips. Clearing his throat, the older man explained. "I'm sure you are aware that the theatre was burned to the ground."

"I am."

Harvey continued. "We have come to question the people of Niggerville. Campbell Penn has disappeared, and we wished to question him. The niggers at the hotel say Penn had slaves doing his bidding. We want to question Penn or anyone who might know of his whereabouts."

Black shook his head ever so slightly. Silently, he gave an unseen Elbert and Gilbert the signal to stand down. His eyes never left Harvey when he corrected. "The people of *Blacktown* have encountered no such man. I'm afraid we cannot be of service in this matter."

Harvey stared at him as if gauging his sincerity. "Several of the shop owners stated they were accosted by niggers."

Black showed nothing because he felt nothing. "Are you accusing us?"

"I am trying to investigate a serious matter."

"And I have answered your questions." Black replied.

"We wish to speak with the residents."

"No need, your inquiries have already been addressed."

The men stared at each other until Harvey nodded and turned his horse. When the posse thundered away, Black stared after them. He would have to give them some real incentive not to come back. They would see to this matter when night fell.

After the unwanted guests took their leave, the people of Blacktown continued on with life. Black watched as the men appeared from the different houses and the children ran about playing; he had to fight the urge to erect a gate, thereby caging in the people. As the men walked around the side of the house, he turned retracing his steps. Black continued through the great room and out the backdoor.

Forty men stood about waiting for direction and there was no defeat in them. In the small courtyard, several trees kept the activity private. The barn that was converted to a barracks was beginning to show signs of life. A shift change was happening as the men rotated duties for the day and night watch. Behind the barn was another gray storage building. The weathered structure had become the place where Black held private meetings.

There was no real furniture, just chairs and plenty of floor. Black stood while everyone sat. He spoke freely and it was for the benefit of himself as well as his men.

"How many of you know Harvey Michaels?"

All of the men from Blacktown raised a hand. Elbert, James and

Bainesworth were the only ones to raise their hands from the fort. He allowed his gaze to bounce about from man-to-man. Black went on.

"What we have is a lawman that ain't so just in his actions. He is asking after Ruby and the slaver Penn. This is not happenstance–this..." Black turned about in place, "is threat."

Booker who was seated to his left said what they all were thinking. "They will be back to molest the people."

"Shit gotta be dealt wit' or the line of bastards lookin' to do violence against us will be long," James said.

"I have a plan." Black replied.

"I'm in." Booker added.

"We all in." Elbert confirmed. And so it went.

The men took their leave to rest up, this night would be long. Black headed back into the house and the moment he stepped over the threshold, it started raining. He closed the door and barred it. In the corridor leading away from the bedchambers he could hear movement. Following the sound, he found Sunday folding the clothes she must have pulled off the line in anticipation of the rain.

"Where is Morgan?" he asked.

"She on the porch wit' James."

His wife looked up, offering a weak smile and Black felt his heart squeeze. The women were a perceptive bunch. Morgan had stepped out to give them some privacy.

"I came to Montreal with the men when Lincoln first became president. I did see Ruby." He admitted.

Sunday nodded, but didn't speak. Black continued. "I didn't... I wouldn't... shit, nothing happened."

Sighing, Sunday said. "Nat—"

"I have not broken faith with you—"

"Nat, I believes you."

Black stared at his wife for long seconds trying to assess her pain and disappointment with him. He saw the things that he had in the past tried to avoid. Having his wife with him clouded the issues. A clear mind was essential to staying upright, still this was his home. Sunday was present because this was her home as well.

"Come with me," he demanded.

Leaving the clothes and the basket by the table, Sunday moved to stand in front of him. She held eye contact and he found that his heart needed such a connection. He turned heading back down the small dim corridor to their bedchamber. Pushing at the door he stood to the side allowing her in first. When he crossed over the threshold, he closed the door and locked it.

"Nat—"

"I wish to spend time speaking with you," he said.

"Is you really gon speak wit' me?"

"So, you are disappointed with me?" he replied.

Sunday was about to speak when he spun her to face away from him. Black made quick work of the buttons at the back of her dress. He helped her from the gray garment, laying it over the back of a chair in the corner. Grabbing the hem of her white shift, he pulled the fabric over her head.

He undressed while Sunday removed her pantaloons. Black smiled down at his wife's loveliness. Her brown skin was hypnotizing and therein lay the problem. Sunday's breasts were full, her hips wider and her belly flat. His wife was a distraction. He had to make the adjustments that spoke of their new life.

As the summer storm raged on, the wind blew into the bedchamber from the open window. Droplets of water collected on the floor under the sill. After shucking his weapon and clothing, Black moved to the side of the bed. He pulled back the multicolored quilt revealing a white top sheet. Folding the sheet back, he let his wife climb in first.

Sunday lay back amid the pillows staring at the wooden beams in the ceiling. She was avoiding him.

"I had not seen Ruby since before you came to the fort." He explained as he stared at her profile.

There was a moment of silence that happened before his wife

turned her head to look him in the eyes. She continued in this vein until he felt compelled to say. "You are my everything."

"The woman what was found… was she yo' Ruby?"

"Yes."

His wife caressed his face and whispered. "I's sorry for you, Nat."

"I have guilt." He admitted.

"Causin' you ain't feel the same?"

He felt uncomfortable discussing this matter with his wife, but he saw no other way. "I did care for her… it was different than this–than what we are."

Sunday turned on her side and leaned in kissing his lips. He had grieved for Ruby, but the hurt he felt about Spike was submerged in betrayal. The double cross was real, and it was that part that he couldn't reconcile. When he first discovered Spike's treachery, the rage had consumed him. Now, time had left him emotionally injured.

His wife's touch was in direct contrast to the violence coursing through his veins. In his dealings with Sunday, he kept the roughness that was him separate from her. The aggressive brute that was him was normally restrained so that he could be a husband, a father, and a leader of men. But this day, he reveled in hostility; his last bit of control snapped when his wife invited.

"Just be who you is… I wants it all."

Pushing the many pillows from the bed, he climbed over his woman and pressed inside her hot hole. The kiss he offered was searing, all lips, tongue, and teeth. He pulled out, then slammed home three times before stilling. His wife was panting and chanting his name.

"Ohhh, Nat… Nat."

Orgasm was off in the distance for him, but Sunday was nearing her peak. Against her ear, he instructed. "Not yet, woman."

He pulled out and flipped her over. His demand was spoken between gritted teeth. "Hands and knees."

"Yes, Nat."

Lining his dick up to her sweetness, he pushed into her from behind. He groaned and his wife moaned. As he stroked her, his mind let go of the shit he couldn't control. Black released Ruby's death and Spike's betrayal. His fails evaporated as he chased orgasm... and when he thought he would spill his seed, he backed out of her snug channel.

Scrambling to the left of the bed, Black scooped his wife up. He wanted to feel spent... he wanted his muscles to shake with fatigue. Black wanted his wife to cling to him as he was doing to her. Pressing her back against the far wall, he entered her and none too gently.

He palmed her ass to keep her pinned in place. The friction and rhythm were glorious, but it was the way she held on to him. It was the delicious burn of his straining body that pushed him to euphoria. Black crushed his mouth over hers as she milked him for all he had. His hips couldn't stop the rutting motion as he fought to stay up in her.

"Sunday... Sunday, you so damn sweet." He whispered against her mouth. And when the sex act was done, the real affection began. He carried his wife back to their bed and snuggled close to her while she rubbed his back. Sunday didn't push for conversation, she allowed him to be.

He stayed wrapped up in her until night fell. But when total darkness happened, he untangled from his wife and dressed. He didn't light a candle, though he knew his wife was awake. Once his gun was strapped in place, he spoke into the darkness.

"Anthony and the twins will remain. You and Morgan are to watch over them."

Sunday giggled. "We will."

"Get dressed. I have cleaned your gun... you are to wear it."

"I will do what ya tell me."

Black nodded his approval–even though his wife couldn't see

him. Stepping to the bed, he leaned down and found her lips. When he backed away, he reassured. "Everything will be well."

Exiting the master bedchamber, he headed for the front of the house. Darkness and silence greeted him as he closed the door.

"We ready," James said into the night.

Black smiled for he too was ready.

"It's finna be a long night," Jonah said.

"Gon be a fun night," Elbert added.

"Yeah," Black said to no one in particular.

The residents were also doing their part–not a candle was lit. Black descended the stairs and mounted up. Forty men broke down into four groups of ten and those groups would break down into two groups of five when needed. As the leader Black would move between the groups. Elbert, James, Booker and Jonah would head up the groups.

Elbert's group took the saloon/pussy parlor. James took his group to the Grand Hotel. Black was part of Booker's group, and they rode hard for Harvey Michaels' land. Jonah and his men posted up on the edge of Blacktown as the night watch. The last ten men, headed up by Robert, would blend with the men from the barracks and field hands–they would maintain safety at all costs.

James and the men rode their horses right up to the Grand Hotel, leaving the animals in the shadows of what remained of the Buckingham Theatre. They took the alley on the side of the hotel leading to the back of the building. The kitchen doors were thrown wide revealing a beehive of activity. There was food and utensils being tossed between the colored staff. As for communication, there was plenty of yelling above the clanking of pots and dishes.

It was the same as the night when Spike brought them to meet Freddy. The weather was hot and the courtyard leading to the kitchen smelled of rotted food and chamber pots. James surveyed as far as the light coming from the open doors would allow. His men fanned out as they watched the colored staff work. The ten-man posse consisted of five men from the fort and five men from Blacktown.

Mitch stepped from the shadows heading for the kitchen door. James moved around the edge of the light as his man walked into the activity. At the entrance way Mitch lingered for moments until a young woman spied him and approached. Their facial expressions were shadowed given the circumstance, but James saw the woman turn and point to something or someone.

As the woman spoke, Mitch looked over her shoulder. He raised his hand as if to wave over whomever they spoke about. James saw Mitch step back from the woman, his stance aggressive. He was still thinking when Mitch ran into the kitchen. The woman moved away from the entrance, and James lost his visual on both. He ran forward to assist his man. Ephraim and Jackson backed him up.

At the entrance James could see that Mitch had run a white man down. With his quarry pinned against the wall–nose first, the colored staff had backed away . A young colored man dressed as a waiter stood to the right of the door. His dark skin gleamed with perspiration; the kitchen of the Grand Hotel was hot.

"You's from Blacktown?" the man asked.

"Yeah."

The younger man stepped in front of James and yelled out. "We has work to do and guests to serve."

And with that, the staff went about the business of keeping up appearances. Ephraim and Jackson helped Mitch tie up the prisoner, who tried to yell for help. His men carried the struggling hostage from the building. James stood about staring at the gathering of brown faces. The woman who had been speaking to Mitch came to stand in front of him. Up close she was tiny in stature and older than he first thought.

"See to it he don't come back. Two of the girls got a belly full cause he don't understand the word no. He invites his friends; the women needs the work, they cain't say no."

"What he name?" James asked. He assessed her anger, and it was like the weather–hot.

"Folks calls him Dansby," she said with disgust. "Got him a friend the peoples call Barney. They works for Harvey Michaels, the lawman. They's drunk wit' power."

"Campbell Penn?" James inquired.

"He ain't at the Grand no mo'. We ain't seen this man or the uppity slave woman he keeps."

James had been about to walk away when the woman said, "It's that damn theatre. They's askin' who razed it."

"Do you know who burned the theatre?"

"Naw…"

James dipped his head a smidge to offer eye contact. She didn't back away from his assessment. Her complexion was a bit darker than his own. Though the kitchen was well-lit, he couldn't make out her eye color.

She continued. "If'n any of us knowed, we wouldn't speak on it. The whites here done changed since the south come beggin' for help."

Nodding, James turned and walked back into the darkness. They regrouped at the horses with James offering direction.

"Mitch, Jackson, Ephraim and Tim will ride on wit' me to meet Black. Ralph, Able, Herman, Homer and Andrew will take this hostage home to Blacktown. Leave him at the barracks… meet us on Harvey Michaels' land."

His words were met with silence until the men moved to do his bidding.

* * *

Elbert didn't hesitate when he pushed at the swinging doors of the saloon and stepped inside. The scene that greeted him was base, yet lighthearted. Two scantily clad women had replaced Fenton at the bar. A young man banged out a tune on the piano, he wasn't as good as old Jimbo, but neither was he bad.

The cheer didn't stop at his appearance. There were a combination of erotic sounds and people laughing. Trudy, the head woman in charge, stepped from the throng of patrons to greet him. She wore a yellow corset and wrap that worked well with her dark skin.

"Mista Elbert, how can I help you?" Trudy purred.

As Elbert stared down at his former hostage, it appeared she had forgiven him for his past transgressions. His tone was low when he asked. "Miss Trudy, what do you know that I don't?"

She answered, her smile forced. "Plenty."

Trudy headed for the office and Elbert looked to the door. Gilbert and Ben stood at his back; his other men invisible. He nodded to both men before following. The office was a different place now that the women were running things. There was a large brown couch with a deep orange rug beneath it. The desk and chair had been replaced with two wooden chairs that faced the new sitting area. Thick orange curtains covered the window and aided in hiding the goings on. The place could have been considered cozy if not for the business at hand.

When Elbert entered the office, he found Trudy seated on the couch legs crossed and staring at him. The smile was gone from her delicate features.

"A lawman and his posse come here. He named Harvey Michaels. I ain't seen him but one other time. He come one afternoon to speak with Fenton. He was wit' that slaver Campbell Penn and his men."

"When? What was the lawman after?" Elbert asked.

Trudy sighed. "White men think colored pussy is free. But we won't be givin' no free ass at this here fine establishment."

Elbert nodded and Trudy went on. "They come during the daylight asking after Penn. I only know what Petey told me and it wasn't much."

"And what did Petey tell you?"

Trudy threw her hands up in disgust. "Petey say we was all gon be slaves again, but he could make life easy for me if I helped him. I spoke on this to Fenton, hoping he would protect me and the other women but…"

"But what?"

"Fenton was workin' wit them. Harvey Michaels ain't cross my thinkin' until yesterday. I told Michaels we don't know nothin' 'bout nothin'. His men wanted the women, but we made it clear–no coin–no pussy. They was angry when they left, we all worried they gon come back."

"Anything else?" Elbert asked.

"Naw."

"Miss Trudy, I will see to it that these men ain't yo' worry no more. You and the women are under our protection."

She nodded. "Some of the men do come in from Blacktown. They looks in on us. Thank ya, hear."

Elbert nodded before he turned and quit the office. When he stepped back into the bar, Gilbert and Ben were right where he left them. He kept on to the swinging doors; his men followed. Outside, the darkness swallowed them whole and when they were mounted up, Elbert spoke.

"We will break down into two groups. Teddy, Ben, Gilbert, Jesse, and me will head toward Black. The rest of you will watch Blacktown and its people… Go."

* * *

The house of Harvey Michaels stood like a beacon in the night. The two-story structure was surrounded by acres of land. Black and the men fanned out in an attempt to see the situation from all angles. Putting his new men to the test, Black remained still, offering nothing but silence. He was the eleventh man in this posse, and he would move between the groups as needed.

Jonah, Jake, Emmett, Leo, and Wesley were armed with sweet meats laced with sleeping powder. The Michaels spread had several large hounds that roamed the property day and night. Behind the main house were six cabins and a bunkhouse. Three of the cabins were occupied by white families. In the bunkhouse lived eight men–all colored. The rest of the workforce for this property were day laborers, who came and went with the sun.

Black and the men stood long enough to see the bottom of the main house go dark. Aside from the whimpering and snoring of the hounds, the night was quiet. Interrupting the inkiness, James spoke.

"We took us a hostage from that hotel. The women say this one don't take no for an answer. They calls him Dansby."

"Elbert?" Black asked.

"I'm here. Michaels and his men went to the pussy parlor. Miss Trudy wasn't pleased."

"What they wanted?" James asked.

"Michaels and his men wanted to know about Penn." While Elbert wasn't visible, the shoulder shrug could be heard in his voice. "They also wanted some pussy."

"How many?" Black asked.

"I sent five back to Blacktown."

"Same," James added.

"It's time." Booker said.

Black mounted his stallion and nudged him to a trot that headed straight for the front of the house. Jeremiah, James, Elbert, and Booker followed, and no one lit a torch. The gallop of many horses sounded like thunder, so Black wasn't surprised when Harvey Michaels stepped onto the porch with five men; three held shotguns and two held torches.

"Been expecting you, Hope."

"I'd be hurt if you didn't." Black responded. "Shame about the rain."

Harvey's head moved about as if trying to place Black's location. Reluctantly, the lawman offered explanation. "We were investigating is all. Why the hard feelings? Me and you crossed paths in the past–ain't been no issue with us."

Black didn't verbally respond; instead, he swung down from his horse and stepped into the torchlight. Climbing the stairs, he moved to stand nose to nose with Harvey Michaels.

"This ain't the past."

Behind him, Black tensed when one of the gunmen sneered. "Harvey, how you letting niggers threaten us?"

A shot rang out followed by one of the torch holders howling in pain. Black didn't flinch and now with only one torch burning, the situation grew dimmer. Jeremiah and James stepped to the bottom of the stairs and the pair was barely visible given the lighting. It was the black cracker who barked out.

"You will stand down or we will put you down."

Booker brought two lanterns up onto the porch. Every man was quiet while he lit both wicks, brightening the matter. When the flames began to dance, Black turned his attention back to Harvey Michaels, who spoke first.

"You must want something cause I ain't dead yet."

Black could smell the lawman's fear. Both men were distracted by Elbert, who stepped from the darkness. Climbing the stairs, his brother took the guns from Harvey's men. Black asked a question.

"Who's in the house?"

"My wife and young son." Harvey answered.

"What is the man's name who thinks niggers should be threatened–but shouldn't issue threats?"

"His name is Bill... Bill East." Harvey replied.

Over his shoulder, Black ordered. "Tie Bill up."

A scuffle ensued and the nigger-caller was thrown to the planked floor of the porch. Elbert tied him up. When the chaos settled and the downed man could be heard grunting and moaning, Black spoke over his hostage's discomfort.

"Were you working with Penn, Harvey?"

"I wouldn't call it workin' wit' Penn, no."

"What would you call it?"

In the flickering light, Black noted the glassiness of Harvey's eyes. All the men present knew where this was headed. "Penn and I had a few business dealings."

"Did you know Penn killed Ruby and Spike?" Black asked while watching the other man's reaction.

Harvey gasped. "Spike was good for himself. But Miss Ruby..."

Black stared at the older man. He noted Harvey's remorse for Ruby and not Spike. "Where did you think Ruby was–if not in her eatery?"

"I thought she left Spike and was with you."

"Did you bring Penn to the eatery?" Black inquired.

"No," Harvey said, and his reply was swift. "Penn paid me to look the other way while they used the theatre."

"So, you helped the Preservers of Southern Life." It was Black's turn to sneer.

"I just made a little coin. I ain't helped them at nothing." Michaels explained.

"You exploited colored folks' fear of recapture." Black ground out. "Then you accused the people of Blacktown."

Behind him, the torch holder whimpered, and Black suspected that Elbert still had his boot to the felled man's back. It was a lucky thing for Harvey Michaels that everything around them was still wet from the earlier storms and the intermittent drizzle. Black found that he was angry enough to burn the house and the land around it. He gathered himself and stayed the course.

"Michaels, you will report to me all things concerning this war, colored folks and the Preservers of Southern Life." Black's voice dripped menace. "Should you even think to slight me, it will be your last thought."

"Penn and John Booth were my contacts, both men are gone. I have nothing to report." Harvey whined.

Black stepped back from Harvey Michaels and staring into the night, he shouted. "Men, we are done here."

Out of the darkness, the black cracker, James, Noah, Leo, and Ephraim ascended the stairs dragging the gunmen and the torch holders away. Harvey's men put up a fight, but Jeremiah pulled his weapon and put the nigger-caller out of his misery for all to see. Black wanting the message to be clear added.

"Consider your wife and child, Michaels."

Harvey nodded as he watched Jeremiah drag the dead man from the porch. Black continued. "We have nothing to lose; we will come back for you if needed. You will report to the pussy parlor once a month–alone. A man from Blacktown will meet you there. If you miss a meeting, we will kill you."

"Yes…" Harvey said. All the fight had left him.

Black applied the rules. "You will not engage the women at the pussy parlor or the colored staff at the hotel. All I speak of is an extension of Blacktown. You understand?"

"Yes… I understand."

Staring at the defeated man, Black said. "Consider this our first meeting."

The finality of Black's statement caused Elbert to out the lanterns. Darkness overtook them as Black descended the stairs and mounted his horse. The men followed and they rode hard for home. On the edge of Michaels' land, three men from Blacktown waited with a carriage to transport the hostages and dead man.

The ride home was uneventful giving Black time to contemplate Harvey's next move. He was certain his unwilling informant wasn't pleased with his high-handedness. But he did have one thing working in his favor. Harvey Michaels was a coward of the first order. The show of force displayed this evening would be enough to keep him in line for a time. Eventually he would have to kill Harvey, and he hoped it would be after the lawman served his purpose.

There were still a few hours until dawn and like his men, Black felt strung tight. Booker, Jeremiah, and James would handle the hostages. They would be questioned, put down, and then buried in an unmarked grave. All of this activity would take place behind his home.

Bringing his horse to a stop in front of his house at the center of Blacktown, he allowed the beast to be taken away. Climbing the few steps of his porch, Black seated himself in one of the chairs to await dawn. The backdrop to this morning was the sound of men hollering in agony, gunshots and shovels hitting earth. It was the sound of control.

Black contemplated his next move as he observed his men working by torchlight. The goal had to be stability but not routine. As a people, they would have to practice being random. Their ability to appear chaotic, while being organized and productive was a matter of safety. The front door opened behind him, and three sets of booted feet stepped onto the porch.

"Miss Sunday in Morgan's room," Frank said.

"Ain't been no issues," Anthony added.

"Miss Sunday say you left her and Morgan to protect us." Lou said on a chuckle.

"I did," Black admitted.

"Shit, I been at ease knowin' they's watchin' over us," Frank said.

Black laughed. Frank, Lou, and Anthony walked to the back of the house by way of the wraparound porch. When he was alone again, Black continued in his thoughts regarding the well-being of the people. It was before dawn when the door opened again, and his wife stepped out. Sunday climbed into his lap and snuggled close.

"I miss the children."

"Me too," Sunday said on a sigh.

"I'll get the people settled and then we will journey."

Sunday kissed him before whispering. "All right, my love."

They sat in a peaceful quiet as the rays of dawn broke through the darkness. Black was not into public displays of affection, but this felt good... right. She kept her face between his neck and shoulder, while he watched Blacktown come to life. When exhaustion wrapped about his mind and body, Black stood and carried his wife to their bed.

* * *

Black's constant worry about security, coupled with his attempts to promote a freer existence, made the next few days busy. He worked tirelessly with the people to address their concerns and his own. As the leader of two settlements, he understood that he could not journey back and forth until the proper precautions were in place. He had a vision, and he would see it realized through his men... and the people.

It was late afternoon, and the July heat was relentless. Black stood at the center of his men, spinning in place. The only sound was the shuffle of his booted feet as he attempted eye contact with each man. In the building behind the barracks, they stood shoulder to shoulder awaiting his words–his direction. But today he would offer something more; this day he would offer this elite group–authority.

"I have a plan," Black said, before pausing for effect. "We have to give the people more."

When no man spoke up, Black continued to spin in place. He noted the subtle changes which gave him hope. The fort men were mixed with the men from Blacktown, a sign they saw themselves as one.

"Some of you have women and children from either the fort or Blacktown. The men who are unattached–form two lines and do so by settlement."

Black waited as the men moved about. He knew which men were unattached from the fort but not from Blacktown. Jesse, Emmett, Ralph, Josiah, John, and the ambassador were his unattached men from back home. His unattached men from Blacktown consisted of Booker, Mitchell, Jackson, Leo, Isaac, Homer, and Wesley. When Black spoke, the chosen men stepped into the circle with him forming a smaller one around him.

"The men from the fort will remain here in Blacktown. You will run the barracks and see to the safety of the people. We will do things the same way we do at the fort. Jesse, Emmett, Ralph, Josiah, and John, you will all answer to me, and the people will answer to you."

Black gave the men a moment, allowing his words to seep in before continuing. "Ambassador, you will set up at the Grand Hotel and report to me any suspicious activity. The men of Blacktown will watch your back."

"As you wish," Bainesworth replied.

"Booker, it seems you are the only doctor. How will the people fair without you?" Black asked.

"The older women are good at doctoring. But yes, I am all we have." Booker answered.

"You and Shultz will see to the people before we ride out." Black instructed. "This task needs to be completed in three days–no more."

"Yeah," Both Booker and Shultz responded.

Black stepped through the plan. "Every month for the next three months–the chosen men will move between the fort and Blacktown. When you are here you will lead–when you are at the fort, you will learn."

"Three months?" James asked.

"Yes," Black responded. "Everything will be done in three-month timing. When the time is up, we will switch to a new group. The men with families will be added into the rotation to keep everyone sharp. It is my goal to make all of you leaders."

Elbert whistled and shook his head.

Black chuckled before continuing. "Every day a telegram will be sent about the weather. You will see to it that I get it at the same time. If I don't receive a message, we will come to you."

"I ain't for sho' I understands. Me a leader..." Emmett said, his stress visible.

Choosing his words, Black stared at Emmett for moments. The shorter man's brown eyes were troubled–sincere. "All will be well… we will labor together to make this thing work. I will move back and forth every two months. You will not be alone."

Reluctantly, Emmett nodded, and Black went on. "You will all remain upright–this will ensure the safety of the women and children."

In unison they answered. "Yeah."

When the men dispersed, a few lingered to engage him. Black wasn't in a rush to head back into the house. Sunday was hosting a sewing party, where he was sure the women would discuss their own concerns. His wife would come to him if she needed his help. Leaving the little building, he strolled into the courtyard as the men from the barracks were changing shifts.

"Hope!" One of the men called out.

Black stopped walking, allowing the men from the barracks to approach. A dark skin man greeted.

"How is ya, Mista Hope?"

"I'm good, Lenny."

"I's glad you here." A brown skinned man named Walter said. "My woman is sleeping betta."

Black smiled. "This is our goal; the women and children will always come first."

He knew many of these men already from his travels into the south. Black stayed in the courtyard until the men completed the change and only the men from his meeting remained. His brothers, Jeremiah, E.J., Tim, Percy, and Virgil stood about with confusion on their faces.

"So... you finna travel every two months?" James asked.

"I am."

"Who will run the fort if not you?" Elbert asked.

"Simon... you, and James." Black answered.

"I ain't finna stay behind. Imma go wit' you," James said and there was challenge in his voice.

Black stared at his brother. He saw the worry James tried to hide. In his head, he fought back the feelings of dread that owned him when he discovered James was missing. He wouldn't fight with his brother. Instead, he directed. "Get us some horses. We have to check on a few things before we head home."

James stared at him, then nodded. "Meet you 'round front."

Elbert followed James. Jeremiah, E.J., Percy, Virgil and Tim followed Black around to the front of the house. There was no conversation, a stablehand came forward with several stallions. James and Elbert were already mounted up. Black swung into the saddle and took the lead.

The sun was still working as the posse rode away from Blacktown. An hour went by before the Michaels' land came into view. Black didn't hesitate, he rode right up to the porch, stopped his animal, and waited. Harvey Michaels stepped into view and his hostility was evident. Black spoke first.

"Michaels, I wish to have words with you."

Even at this distance, Black could see the red blotching the lawman's face. Harvey didn't offer a verbal response; instead, he made his way down the stairs. Black climbed from the saddle and walked away from his men. Harvey followed.

"Hope."

"You knew Spike had betrayed Ruby... Where is Jimbo's and young Fred's body?"

The color drained from Harvey's face. "Hope, I ain't involved myself in no killings. I knew Jimbo was missing... I knew Freddy was gone, but I ain't had a hand in no killings."

Black glared at him, not to gauge sincerity but to intimidate. He wanted to drive home the fact that colored lives mattered. Black meant to convey a message of threat and follow through. He meant to make clear that what he did in the dark, he was man enough to do in the light. When Harvey dropped his gaze, Black took stock of his surroundings.

He noted the vegetation, the corral and white men standing in the distance observing. Pointing with his chin, Black asked. "Your men know not to test me… yeah?"

"We don't need no trouble."

Black added. "On the last day of August, you will meet my man to report what you have gleaned… oh, and, Harvey."

The lawman cleared his throat. "Yeah."

"Don't come to me empty handed."

The men stared at each other for moments before Black turned to his horse and swung up into the saddle. He eyed the elegant white house as the curtain fell back into place at the front window. Nudging his horse to a trot, Black took his leave. It was time to journey on to the fort.

CHAPTER 24

FORT INDEPENDENCE
AUGUST 1864

The railcar rocked and swayed as it moved through the night. Black remained awake and as they neared their destination, he readied himself to lead. It was all new, but the people trusted him, and he was humbled by the notion. The train hissed and slowed as the first rays of dawn pushed through the large windows. Black saw the small town of Independence as the train came to a complete stop.

His brothers stood first, each going to separate ends of the car for security. Eleven men followed Elbert; the others followed James. They filed out giving the women a moment of privacy. Black waited by the iron stairs until Sunday and Morgan appeared. Turning his mind to his surroundings, Black spied the carriage and two wagons that awaited.

Taking both women by the elbow, he led them to the carriage.

The men handled the bags as they piled into the wagons. A breeze blew giving the August morning a slight chill. It was a far cry from the heat and discomfort of the railcar. He listened as Sunday and Morgan spoke about missing the children.

"The children ain't gon know us," Morgan said.

"Oh, they gon know us all right. My Daniel ain't finna let me outta his sight."

"He sho' ain't." Morgan giggled.

Black eventually tuned the women out as he watched the countryside. He was looking for signs that signified life had changed for the better. As they neared the fort, he saw men working at clearing back the vegetation. In some places full cabins had been erected and it was as he had envisioned. Fort Independence now extended beyond the walls.

He wanted to stop the carriage and speak with the men–labor with the men. But the women were tired and the twenty-two had not seen their families. He would rest today, tomorrow would be soon enough to witness the expansion of his vision. They rode for a half hour more when the fort came into view. The gate was open and welcoming; still, the men stood at the ready–prepared to stand and deliver.

There was a crowd at the gate causing the vehicles to slow. Black understood what the people wanted. As he gazed out the window, he spoke, directing the women.

"We should get out here; the people want to see us."

"All right," both women answered.

Black opened the door and hopped down. Turning back, he lifted Morgan down first and then his wife. The people created a semi-circle and they all started speaking at once. Black smiled before raising his hands. He waited, and the crowd grew hushed.

Chuckling, he said. "I am most happy to be in your company. Please help me make the new men feel at home."

Once more, the people started speaking at the same time. Black answered the best he could; he would make a more formal statement once everyone was rested. As he gazed about, he noted that Simon had made his way over to Morgan. Carrie was holding Frank's hand. Molly was smiling up at Lou. Anthony was walking away with Emma. Hazel had accepted Gilbert's hug. Anna waited on the edge of the crowd for Elbert. Standing alone, regal, and proud, Miss Caroline waited for Jake by one of the storage buildings. Black smirked when he saw Abby, Sarah, Beulah, and Mary waiting for Shultz, Tim, Horace, and James.

Under the tree and to the left of the gate, Suzanne and Netti waited for E.J. Even Callie was out and about scanning the crowd for Jeremiah. She was with the new woman called Fern, who waited for Ephraim. Black took his wife by the hand and disengaged from the throng of folks. As he steered them toward the house, his wife started giggling.

"What is so funny, woman?"

Sunday sighed. "I guess it's a good thang the fort is gettin' bigger. We finna have us some mo' babies."

Throwing back his head, Black laughed. His wife's pleasantness only added to the lightheartedness he was feeling. The early morning sun was losing its orange hue when the house came into view. He carried his wife up the porch stairs and into the dim corridor before placing her on her feet.

Black whispered. "I want to bathe with you."

His wife was about to agree when the pitter-patter of little feet sounded in the corridor.

"My daddy!" Nattie yelled.

"Mama!" The twins hollered.

Sunday whispered, "Later."

Black groaned and chuckled.

* * *

Life at the fort had become jovial if Ephraim had to say so himself. As he stood with the men cutting back the high vegetation, he found that he was proud of what they had achieved as a people. A few yards in either direction, both Black and Simon could be seen doing the same. There was much work to be done and still the people were cheerful.

The women worked hard at keeping the men supplied with plenty of food and drink. Two wagons rolled out every few hours to give the men water. It was during one of these times when Ephraim noted his personal existence had changed. The men with wives were served directly. Ephraim had been prepared to get his own food when he spied Fern moving in his direction. She carried a small pail and a jug of water. She handed him a wet cloth. He wiped his hands and face.

Ephraim walked them to a large tree stump where they sat and avoided eye contact. The east wall of the fort loomed in front of them. Around them, the men yelled, a gunshot sounded and then laughter.

"Snake!" One of the women hollered and there was more laughter.

In his side view he saw Fern startle. Carrying on as if the situation were normal, Ephraim reached down into the pail and pulled out a drumstick. The bread was warm and the water cool. He was putting the jug to his mouth when Fern spoke.

"Ephraim?"

"Hmmm."

"If'n you don't want me–why you take me from Errol?"

Swiping the back of his hand over his mouth, he turned and assessed her. Fern wore a brown dress with black boots. The afternoon sun beat down on her lovely dark skin; her brown eyes were light in shade. Fern's hair was shaved close and brushed well. Her lips were dark like the rest of her face adding to her beauty. Oh… he wanted her, but he had not pushed beyond keeping company with her. He slept in the barracks and had done so since he brought her to the fort.

Before speaking his eyes landed on Jeremiah. Fern followed his line of vision; still, she waited for his response. Ephraim's tone was calm. "You want him, not me."

"I did cause ain't no one ever helped me." She answered. "I ain't wantin' him now."

"Don't mean you want me," he replied.

Fern nodded, then stood. She had been about to walk away when he pleaded. "Don't go."

She stopped and looked down at him. Her eyes teared up. "I has chores."

Ephraim ignored her and asked. "How old is ya?"

"I's twenty summers." She shrugged.

"Sit wit' me." He demanded in a polite tone.

Seating herself next to him, she stared off in the distance. He went on. "I want you, Miss Fern… tryna give you some time to think."

She looked up at him with those large eyes and he had to shake his head to stay the course. He reached out his hand with the chicken leg and commanded. "Take you a bite."

Fern laughed even as the tears fell from her eyes; still, she leaned in and took a bite. They ate together in silence until it was time for the men to get back to work. She gathered the pail and jug before racing off with the other women. Ephraim watched her go with a smile on his face. *Shit,* he thought, *he really did want her.*

When the women were out of sight, he approached the black cracker. "What you do wit' the man, Errol?"

Jeremiah grinned. "I put him down and threw him in the hole wit' the men from the bar."

Ephraim nodded. Jeremiah asked a question of his own. "You want Fern?"

Looking beyond the black cracker to the men working. Ephraim replied. "I do… but she young. Feels like she wants you."

Jeremiah laughed. "At least she ain't wantin' Black. You got a chance since it's me she fancy. She gon forget about me soon enough."

Ephraim shook his head and grinned. Jeremiah sobered before adding. "Miss Fern was thankful for my help is all. You about twenty- eight summers, ain't you?"

"Yeah," Ephraim answered.

"Well, she twenty summers... that too young for you?"

"No," Ephraim said. "I thought her younger."

"Naw... Fern is twenty summers. She figured me to be old–she added the give or take for me." Jeremiah chuckled. "You ain't old... you will do fine wit' her."

Ephraim smiled, nodded, then walked away to finish his workday.

When the sun started going down, the wagons appeared to carry the men to the front of the fort. Black was tired, but it was time to speak to the people. He could see uncertainty in the eyes of the women. The wagon was pulling through the gate when he hopped down from the back. He went in search of Philip and Chester.

"Please let the people know I wish to address them this evening."

"Yes, sah," both men said as they walked off to do his bidding.

He was happy to see that the men from Blacktown were faring well. They laughed and talked as they walked down the hill toward his home. His attire said much, he wore brown trousers and a brown homespun shirt–the sleeves hacked off. Black wished he had time to freshen up, then thought it better if the people witnessed his exhaustion and grime from honest work. He would give the people his words, his encouragement, and his direction.

As they moved toward his home, he could see the women stepping from their gardens to join them. The men from the barracks headed their way and still others remained in place for security. His home came into view and on the porch were his wife, three children and his mama. In the doorway were Anna and Abby, along with his brothers' children. Iris and Paul stood to the left of the door.

There was already a small gathering at the bottom of the stairs leading to the porch. Black waded through the throng of people and took the steps two at a time. When he reached the landing, his son Daniel reached out for him. Taking the baby from his wife, he turned and faced the crowd. As Daniel hugged his neck, Black stared out at the sea of brown faces.

The sun, which was in the process of setting, splashed hues of orange and purple over the gathering. He moved to the edge of the landing, alerting the people that he was ready to address their concerns. Black cleared his throat.

"In the coming days we will bring down the east wall." As expected, a conversational buzz started up. He waited and when the gathering quieted, he went on. His voice was sure–gritty. "A dry day and a matchstick can change our very existence. We can no longer live caged and call it liberty. The wall is not what keeps you safe; it is the men who do this job. The people of Fort Independence will live a truer existence. Me and the men standing among you will see that you do so unmolested. As a man, I have helped many to freedom. As a leader, I am tasked with uncaging your thoughts, emancipating your way of life and unshackling us all from fear."

The crowd grew hushed. Black took a deep breath and raised his fist. "I ask for your trust. In exchange I will lay down my life for your protection."

"We trust ya, Black." A light skinned woman in the front yelled.

"Sho' do," an elderly man in the middle of the gathering hollered.

Black's voice softened when he added. "In our quest to live freer, we will strive for harmony. But we will meet acts of aggression accordingly. Me and the men will do violence before we allow you to be separated from freedom."

At his last declaration, Black turned and walked into the house. His family followed and the people cheered.

* * *

Fern was seated at the backdoor of her cabin; she wore white pantaloons and a matching shift. The summer heat settled on the one room and had not eased, even as the sun disappeared behind the hills. She was trying not to sweat. The soap from her bath had the scent of gardenias in the air. She bathed on the back porch and hadn't emptied the large tin tub. There was a great possibility that she would have to bathe again before Ephraim came to fetch her.

In the background one oil lamp flickered, the wick turned down low. Living in a cabin was a bit of a luxury. She had spent the last three summers living in tents. Her winters had been spent in cabins with groups of people who resented the presence of her and Errol. They had come to Canada in the spring to be part of the railroad town. Errol started beating her shortly after they arrived.

She wondered briefly what had become of Errol, but she had not asked after him. The need to separate herself from him was real. She didn't want Ephraim to think she was pining over another. It was nice here and the little cabin felt secure. Fern hadn't felt safe since she woke one morning and found that her mama had walked off. These last few weeks had been the best of her life. Ephraim's voice pushed her from her thoughts.

"Why is you sittin' in the dark?"

"It ain't dark, the wicks turned down is all." She whispered.

Ephraim stood in front of her at the bottom of the stairs. His form was shadowed given the lighting. "You ain't wantin' to come with me?"

Fern found herself leaning forward in the chair. "Yes, I'm wantin to be wit' you."

"Why you ain't dressed?"

"It's hot as blazes. I ain't want to sweat." she said, her tone soft.

Ephraim stepped back from the light and chuckled. Fern searched the darkness but couldn't see him. There was a smile in his voice when he said, "Ladies don't sweat–they perspires."

"I must ain't no lady… I'm sweatin'." Fern grumbled, then laughed. The sound of his mirth warmed her.

"Go dress. I'll wait for ya."

Fern rushed inside the cabin and donned the pretty green dress Molly gave her. The bodice buttoned in the front and pushed her small breast upward. She never looked so fine. On her feet, she wore a new pair of stylish black boots. Outing the oil lamp, she stepped back onto the porch, closing the cabin door behind her.

The darkness complete, Fern was about to step to the edge of the landing when two strong arms lifted her. Ephraim placed her on solid ground, then took her by the elbow. Her cabin was off the beaten path, and it was a bit of a walk to the next set of cabins. Ephraim, who seemed to know the lay of the land, led her to the path that took them to the gathering.

In the short distance, Fern could see several lanterns on the porch of the cabin that Emma shared with her husband Anthony. She could hear their laughter and it felt warm–safe. As she drew nearer, Emma called her name and waved her over. Anthony approached, and Fern thought him large.

"Ephraim–Fern." Anthony greeted. "Glad ya both come."

"Yeah," Ephraim replied.

Emma came to stand next to her husband, who placed a protective arm around her shoulder. She was bubbly when she said. "Glad you are both here."

"Emma," Ephraim said.

Fern allowed herself to be pulled along to where the womenfolk were gathered. In the clearing in front of the cabins, two tables were pushed together and weighed down by deliciousness. There were green beans, mashed potatoes, fried chicken, and sliced fruit. Pies, cakes, and several loaves of bread added to the heavenly smells. On either side of the table sat Molly, Caroline, and Carrie. Jake stood to the left of Caroline's chair speaking with Frank and Lou. The men laughed about something as Lou reached out placing his hand on Molly's shoulder.

Frank pulled out the chair next to Caroline for her. Fern liked the older woman; Caroline was the kindest of souls. She was tall, dark, and lovely. Carrie sat across the table, brown of skin and always smiling. Fern was thankful for the camaraderie. She fell into the discussion about cooking, sewing and the way life at the fort was changing.

Fern kept an eye on Ephraim and whenever he wasn't paying attention, he became her focal point. He was average in height with a thin build, still his muscles were well-defined. His hair was shaved close, his face free from hair. Ephraim had smooth black skin, thick lips, a small nose, and chiseled cheekbones. He was handsome for sure but what Fern found most attractive was his smile.

A few newcomers wandered up and Fern enjoyed watching the exchanges. A man named Horace came with his wife Beulah, he played the fiddle. All the women danced together except Caroline, who dropped her head and covered her mouth.

"You alright?" Fern asked.

"My belly is unsettled." Caroline answered in a weak voice.

Jake must have had the same concerns. He asked. "Caroline, is you well?"

The older woman looked embarrassed, but she answered. "My belly is rolling."

"Come," Jake said.

Caroline stood and Jake led her away by the elbow. Fern watched them go, tracking their figures until they were swallowed up by the night. Turning her attention back to the gathering, she smiled when Ephraim eased into Caroline's old seat. In his hand he held a tin cup.

"What is you drinking?"

Ephraim leaned in and against her ear, he whispered. "Moonshine–has some."

He put the cup to her lips. Fern sipped and panted from the strong drink. "Whoo."

"Too strong for you?" he asked.

"Yes... burns everything in me."

Leaning back in his chair, he smiled at her. They ate together and laughed at the antics of the others. When the hour grew late, Ephraim shook hands with the men. Molly, Carrie, and Emma came forward hugging her. Fern waved as Ephraim led her away. As the night swallowed them whole, he took her hand in his much larger one.

They strolled in silence until he asked. "How you come to be wit' the likes of Errol?"

"I was wit' my mama. She give me to him; she left me." Fern answered. "How you come to be here?"

"My story ain't much. I come from the Johnson plantation in South Carolina. I ran one night and ain't looked back."

"Did you has family on the plantation?" she asked.

"Naw... I was sold a few times," he replied. "The other plantations, I cain't recollect."

"Oh."

They reached the back of her cabin and Fern continued inside. Fumbling around she lit the oil lamp and turned the wick up a bit. Leaving the door open, she stepped back onto the porch. Ephraim was where she left him. He stood outside the light. She feared the evening ending, and she did not want him to leave. While she was trying to get up the nerve...

He said, "Imma go–"

"I ain't wantin' you to go." Her voice was soft–pleading.

Ephraim stepped into the light. He stared at her for long moments. She figured he was trying to think of a way to refuse her and still be polite. The silence was uncomfortable, and she was chiding herself for being too forward. Her thoughts raced.

"This man you was wit'… Errol."

"I ain't wit' child," she answered.

Again, he stood for silent moments assessing her. He nodded before stepping onto the porch. Seating himself in the chair closest to the door he stared out into the night. Like Caroline, her belly was unsettled now that he had agreed to stay.

His deep chuckle, splashed over her skin. "Now that you has me all to yoself– you 'fraid?"

"N-no."

More laughter from him caressed her. "Yes, you is. Come sit wit' me."

Fern moved to take the chair next to him, but Ephraim pulled her onto his lap. The rustle of her dress sounded as she got comfortable. His voice sobered when he promised. "You safe wit' me. I won't hurt you."

She leaned into him, placing her face between his shoulder and neck. He went on. "You hear me, woman?"

"Yes."

"Kiss me," he demanded.

She pressed her mouth to his and he pulled her bottom lip between his teeth. Fern gasped as he slipped his tongue into her mouth. She moaned and to her surprise so did he. Pulling back from her, Ephraim looked into her eyes.

"Shit," he grumbled.

"What is it?"

"You right, it's hot as hell back here. It ain't even no sun."

Fern giggled. "Don't I know it."

He stood carrying her into the cabin. Standing her on her feet, he turned the wick down. Ephraim undressed and Fern couldn't look away. He placed his holster and gun on the table. Pulling his shirt over his head, he laid it at the foot of the full-size bed. He removed his boots, then trousers to reveal a pair of white underpants that came to his knees. Ephraim's hard, black body was carved, and Fern thought him stunning.

She forgot to undress for watching him. His voice startled her when he asked. "You want some help?"

"No… yes," she whispered.

He laughed. "Which one is it?"

"Yes."

Ephraim stepped forward taking her dress by the hem and lifting it over her head. Placing the garment with his clothes at the foot of the bed, he took her by the hand. Guiding her to the edge of the bed, he removed her boots and stockings. Fern stared down at him in wonderment. He chuckled and she was coming to know him as even tempered. She knew he could be dangerous; she bore witness when he stood nose to nose with Errol.

"Come," he instructed. "Is you wantin' me to fill the tub for you?

"Yes," she answered, before asking. "You ain't minding?"

He didn't offer a verbal response. Ephraim held out his hand and without hesitation, she allowed him to lead her back outside. He didn't sit as she thought he would; instead, he tugged her along to the far end of the porch. The space was tight–dark. Pressing her back to the wall, he moved in rubbing himself against her. He was rough when he grabbed her by the chin. Ephraim kissed her, and it was all lips, teeth, and tongue. Her moans were soft; his grunts male. Fern wasn't familiar with the reverence that could happen before the sex act. She was awed.

As if attempting to engage all her senses, he directed. "Take dem bottoms off. I wanna touch you."

She nodded and moaned but did not speak. He was frantic in his quest to get her naked from the waist down. When her pantaloons fell to the floor, he backed away to remove his own underpants. Fern wanted to feel all of him against all of her. Peeling the shift from her body, she dropped it at her feet.

"Shit," Ephraim groaned.

Echoing his sentiment, she panted. "Shit."

Everything about her was strung so tight that her very being hummed with the anticipation of him. He palmed her breasts before rolling her hard nipples between his work roughened fingers. She cried out.

"Ohhh..."

He must have felt it too because he slammed his mouth down over hers. His leaking maleness poked at her belly. He dropped his hands from her breasts, and she whimpered in protest. Placing his left palm flat to the wall above her head, he broke their kiss.

"Open yo' legs," he commanded.

Mindlessly, she did as she was told, and he rewarded her by rubbing the head of his shaft against her sensitive flesh. "Ephraim... ohhh."

He whispered on a grunt. "Let go, woman; I has ya."

At his words, she fell into a sharp orgasm that caused her legs to tremble. He was deliberate and skilled with his touches; he pushed two fingers inside her and coaxed. "Give it all to me, Fern."

She was shocked at the grunts and moans coming from her. Fern thought she would pass out, but he pinned her in place and dropped to his knees. Lifting one of her legs over his shoulder, Ephraim slipped his tongue between her folds.

"Ohhh my... Ephraim... Ephraim."

He sought out her most secret of places. It was the heat of his breath, the texture of his tongue and the way he lashed her button over and over that caused her body to buck and jerk. When she was sure she would die from sheer pleasure, Ephraim stood, shoving his tongue into her mouth. He spun them until his back was to the wall.

"Hold on to the railing. Imma go slow... I wants inside ya."

Fern grabbed the railing and closed her eyes. Ephraim yanked her hips out to meet his straining body. Standing on a slant, he braced himself with the wall. He pulled her to an almost sitting position and entered her.

"Damn," he grunted as he rocked into her. "Yous snug."

Their rhythm was frenzied causing him to move away from the

wall and stand. This action changed his angle and pushed her to her tiptoes. They both called out, and so it went with him cramming himself inside her, and Fern pushing back to meet his every thrust. When she was positive she had nothing left to give, Ephraim did a reach-around, spanking her button with his big blunt fingers. Orgasm stole the very sound from her person; her lips forming a silent *O*... Behind her, he grunted, swore, then grunted some more.

"I likes this pussy." Ephraim groaned. "Mine, woman… all mine."

Wrapping his arm across her chest he pulled her to a standing position, lifting her to her tippiest of toes. And with one final shove, she felt his dick pulse as he filled her. Fern wanted sleep… Fern wanted more.

"Damn," Ephraim groaned.

He turned her chin to the side and kissed her. It was quiet save for their harsh breathing and the sounds of their lips connecting in soft smacks. He was still hard when he eased from her body. She turned in his arms and looked up at him. His features were shadowed and the flickering light inside the cabin didn't help. He pulled her into his arms and held her.

"Imma get you some fresh bath water."

She had been about to protest when he stepped back, donned his underpants, and walked away. He returned seconds later with boots on his feet and a bucket in each hand. Before heading to the pump, he stopped and emptied the water from the tub over the side of the porch. Ephraim then stepped into the night, walking back and forth to the pump until the tub was filled.

"Come," he said. "Get in the water."

His words and her shyness caused her to tremble. She didn't move as the very essence of him ran down her leg. He chuckled, the sound deep. "You shy now, Miss Fern?"

"Just a lil bit."

She thought he would tease her as she was coming to find was his way, but he didn't. He stepped into the cabin, and she noted that the light brightened. Ephraim reappeared after a time with her soap and a cloth.

"The sun will be up soon enough. Imma see what you tryna hide," he snorted.

"Did you turn the wick up?" she asked.

"I did."

"Oh," she breathed.

More chuckling. "Come to me, Miss Fern."

She inhaled deeply before stepping into the light and then back into the dark. The tub was on the opposite side of the little porch in the shadows. As she eased into the water, Ephraim pulled his chair next to the tub and sat. The chair was situated partially in the doorway. She could see the grin on his face. He leaned in elbows to knees.

"I ain't wantin you to be uneasy. I can stay at the barracks till yous ready for me," he said.

"I wants you here. It's... I ain't never..."

"You ain't never–what?" he asked.

"I never felt wanted."

"You's so sweet, woman," Ephraim said on a grin. "Miss Fern, I sho' wants ya."

* * *

Black stood with Elbert in the middle of the dress shop, while Anna and Miss Cora marveled at their surroundings. At the left of the door were shelves that were floor to ceiling. The cubby holes were stuffed with bright fabrics causing the women to ooh and aah. Two white sewing machines sat at the back of the store and both women couldn't take their eyes from them.

"Mama, you ever seen a sewing machine?" Anna breathed. "Imma have to teach myself."

"No... never," Miss Cora answered.

"Where did you get these?" Anna asked the men.

"Virgil helped me. I purchased the machines from Everything." Elbert answered.

Anna threw herself at Elbert, kissing him all over his face. When Miss Cora hugged him, Elbert was done. As the women went back to exploring the dress shop. Black laughed and his brother grinned. Turning their heads to the setup, the men wandered through the shop. They found that the backroom was sizable, but the red door had a flimsy lock. The room had white walls and Black knew the previous owner lived here.

"You will work from here some days?" Elbert asked.

"Yeah."

In the background, Black could hear the women chatting away in their excitement. Elbert interrupted his thoughts, his tone incredulous. "You will come all the way to town to work?"

"I will," Black responded. "Our women will not go unattended."

"Yeah," Elbert said.

Opening the backdoor, the brothers stepped outside to find Frank, Lou, and Anthony standing guard. The dress shop was jammed between the dry-goods store and O'Reilly's Inn. Behind the shop was a cobblestone courtyard that ran the length of the boardwalk in front of the establishments. At the very back, beyond the stone, were trees and high vegetation.

As the door swung shut behind them, Black said, "Have some of the men clear out the vegetation. We need to see this situation from all angles."

Anthony left to take care of Black's request, while Frank and Lou remained in place. The day was overcast as Black and Elbert walked the long way through the courtyard around to the front of the businesses. On the opposite side of the roadway was the public stables equipped with a smithy. There was also a bootmaker. The boardwalk ended abruptly and picked up again about a half mile up the thoroughfare in front of Virgil's establishment. Everything was the size of three establishments.

The brothers were making for Virgil's when E.J. and Jeremiah rode up in a wagon. On the back of the wagon were his men from Blacktown. Booker hopped down first, and the other men followed. Mitchell, Jackson, and Isaac came forward to greet Black. The men formed a circle around the brothers.

"Any problems?" Elbert asked.

"None," Jeremiah said. "We started building cabins on the edge of the land."

"Will you send men to tend the land?" E.J. asked.

"Yes," Black answered, but he kept his eyes on Booker who seemed agitated.

Percy and Virgil stepped onto the boardwalk. While Virgil and Elbert spoke about the sewing machines. Black watched the people and men moving about the small town. He noted that Virgil and Percy seemed happier now that they had moved into the store to live and do business. Black was thinking of other businesses that would benefit the people when Booker stepped to him.

"I have the list of supplies you asked after."

Black nodded. "Do we have it at the fort, or do you need to purchase some items?"

"Both," Booker answered.

The afternoon was hot, and Booker stood before him in overalls and no shirt. Black asked, "What troubles you?"

"Every damn thang," Booker winced. "Why does being free seem like a struggle that won't end?"

Black chuckled. "Because for colored men it won't."

CHAPTER 25

PLACING THE FACTS

Black was standing at the window watching the people go about their busy day. The east wall was being brought down in pieces and cabins of all sizes were being erected to fill the space. There was so much to be done, he simply couldn't afford distractions... even those that were anticipated. He sighed as he waited for the news.

Leo appeared in the study. He was thin of frame with brown skin and knotted hair. Homer, a brown skinned man with a bald head and a flat wide nose stepped into the doorway next. Both men were of average height. Black was relieved to see Simon rush into the study behind them.

"I come as soon as I heard," Simon said.

"Yeah," Black responded.

More men piled into the study. Booker was the last man to enter the crammed space. Since it was Leo's responsibility to collect the daily telegram from Blacktown, the men looked to him, and Leo confirmed the obvious. "Ain't nothing come about the weather."

Black issued orders. "We will ride out in one hour. I will meet you all at the gate. Simon, the fort is under your protection in my absence."

"Yeah," Simon agreed.

There was no discussion, the men left to ready themselves. Black went in search of his wife. He found Sunday in their bedchamber folding clothes while tending his brothers' children and their own. Jamie, Dennis, and Daniel were sleep on the bed. Ben-Ben, Nattie, Lil Otis and Junior were playing with blocks on the side of the tub. When he stepped over the threshold, his wife stood and moved toward him.

"Nat, what is it?"

"No telegram came."

Placing her hand to her throat, Sunday said. "You has to go?"

"Yes."

She nodded. He hated worrying her. Sunday wore a brown dress, her hair was braided and pinned to the crown of her head. She caressed his cheek, then whispered. "Go on... Me and the children is fine."

He searched her face before trying to explain. "Being the leader doesn't mean—"

"I chooses you Nat... all of you. Go now and know that it ain't no other choice for me but to love you."

Black stared at her for long moments before leaning down to kiss her. Wrapping his arms about his wife, he squeezed her to him before stepping back abruptly. Turning on his heels, he strode back through the house collecting the saddlebag that sat at the ready to the left of the front door. Jogging down the porch stairs, he met his brothers waiting for him on the path.

Forty-seven minutes later, Black and the men rode out. The fading sun was the backdrop to a grueling breakneck ride. The August heat was hard on the men and the beasts. Travel slowed as the hour grew late but it didn't stop. Black kept his thoughts on the issues and the people. He pushed his wife and children to the back of his mind. Around him the men spoke but they didn't engage him.

The pacing of this journey was made quicker by the fact that they left way before midnight. Black could not wait that long to begin travel; the train was not an option. He had promised the people he would come to them straight away in the event of an emergency. He kept his word. The route they took didn't include the railroad town for safety purposes. It was near dawn when the men made it to the edge of Montreal. The tension was tangible for Black and the twenty-three men who rode at his back. Another hour and a half passed before they thundered onto the pathways of Blacktown.

It was a scene much like from Beacon Hill. The residents appeared to be leisure, but nothing could be further from the truth. On the main path of the smaller settlement, cabins lined either side of the walkway. About midway down the lane, two larger structures sat opposite each other with three men posted up out front. When the men spied him, they stepped forward onto the path to greet him.

Black swung down from the saddle, the men at his back did the same. A few stablehands ran forward to tend the horses. Handshakes were exchanged, but no words. He surveyed the faces of his men; they seemed troubled, but not injured. Josiah, Emmett, and Jesse rounded the bend on the small footpath that traveled around his home at the end of the lane. They didn't move toward him, so Black walked in the direction of his home.

When he reached the side of his house, the three men turned and headed for the barracks. Black and his brothers followed. The men he rode into town with posted up on the porch and the footpath. They would rest, then break down into groups to relieve the men on duty by nightfall. The men watching over Blacktown went back to their responsibilities.

At the back of his house the courtyard was quiet, and the barrack's doors were thrown wide to mitigate the heat. Black followed Josiah, Jesse, and Emmett down the center aisle to the backdoors. There were cots on either side of the dorm and some of the men were sleeping. On the right side of the door was a large desk. Teddy sat in the chair softly speaking with the boy Clem. The man named Teddy was bright skinned with tiny eyes and a crooked nose. He stood and smiled when he saw Black, his front teeth were missing.

"Mista Black," Clem greeted.

"Clem–Teddy."

"Mawnin'," Teddy said.

Emmett, Jesse, and Josiah kept on to the backdoors. Black could hear his brothers greeting Clem and Teddy, still they all kept moving. Across the patched grass was the gray building he used to meet privately with his men. Jesse pulled the door open, and the stench of death was present. In the middle of the room was a pine box, the lid slightly askew.

Black's eyes bounced up to his men and neither man's expression was readable. He pulled a handkerchief from his back pocket to cover his nose and mouth before helping Elbert lift the lid. Inside lay the badly decomposed body of a white man. Black assessed the gruesome sight. The man in the box was over six-feet, his hair was brown. His clothing was of high quality, still the body was dressed in brown as if the man labored at something. The man was barefoot, which was common; whoever did this deed kept the boots. Nodding to Elbert they dropped the lid.

"Where did you come by this man?"

Emmett who looked exhausted, replied. "The whores woke to this. He was behind the pussy parlor betwixt the chicken coop and the tree."

"Who is he?" Elbert asked.

Josiah looked incredulous. "Bainesworth."

Black's head snapped up. "The man in the box is not the ambassador."

"How long y'all had 'im?" James asked.

"We carried him way from the pussy parlor night 'fore last." Emmett answered.

"So, the body was in this condition when you brought him here?" Black asked.

"Yeah," all three of his men answered.

"Why would you think it's the ambassador?" Elbert asked.

"Bainesworth ain't show for two times." Jesse explained. "The ambassador is always where he 'posed to be–when he 'posed to be."

"Dig a hole and drop him in, then get cleaned up." Black instructed before walking away.

The morning sun was high in the sky and the heat made matters difficult. Black needed sleep and time to think. Back-tracking through the barracks and then the courtyard, he entered his house from the back. He could hear his men in the great room and with his wife not in residence, his home would become the base of operations.

Black entered his bedchamber to find that the tub had been filled and there was sliced fruit on the tray in the corner. He bathed, ate, and fell asleep. It was late afternoon when the sound of someone knocking woke him.

"Give me a minute," he growled.

"Yeah," James hollered back.

The heat had loosened its grip on the bedchamber. In the corner the drapes flapped on the breeze. Black donned his trousers and boots. Shirtless, he holstered his gun to his upper left side. Stepping into the little corridor, he found the great room empty. He walked out onto the porch to find Tim, Elbert, James, and Booker. He tried to cover his mood, but James saw through him.

"Is you troubled 'bout the ambassador?"

Sighing, Black answered. "I don't know what happened to the ambassador, but the man in the box ain't him."

"How can you be for sure? I couldn't tell," Tim said.

"The ambassador's hair was thinning; the man in the box had thick hair." Black explained.

"Shit. I couldn't think for the smell," Elbert said.

"Well, that's good news... ain't it?" James asked.

Black shrugged. "Don't mean Bainesworth is alive–just means the man in the box ain't him."

The men stood about in silence until the barracks started going through a shift change. Black watched as the people began winding down their day. Off in the distance the sky was heavy with dark clouds even as the sun still worked. When night fell, he and the men would make their rounds. Though the theories were endless, the identity of the man stretched out in the box wasn't a total mystery. Still, he would investigate before musing aloud. He wouldn't further confuse his men by allowing them to witness the disorganization of his thoughts.

At the sound of booted feet on the planked flooring of the wraparound porch, Black looked up in time to see Emmett and Jesse join them. He remained unengaged as the men spoke with each other tossing out ideas. They were trying to solve the riddle of the man in the box.

"How many men we have at the pussy parlor?" Black asked.

"Four of 'em," Jesse replied. "Two what is seen and two what ain't."

"Who were the men on duty?" Black continued. "What did they have to report?"

"It was Robert, Hobart, Teddy and Andrew. They say they ain't see nothing," Emmett said.

"Tell them I wish to see them, posthaste," Black said.

All the men moved on to do his bidding, only James remained. Black walked back into the house, seating himself at the table. Miss Velma and Sweetie were taking care of him in the absence of his wife. A wooden plate was left at the head of the small table; it was covered by a red and white cloth. Black lifted the covering to see roasted chicken, cabbage, and potatoes. In the middle of the table sat a white pitcher. He helped himself to a cup of cool water as his mind placed the facts.

Black was wiping his mouth with the cloth when Emmett and Elbert appeared. The men who were guarding the pussy parlor the night the body was found were with them. Black dropped his fork and pushed his half-eaten food away; he addressed his men.

"Gentlemen."

"Black," the men replied at once.

"What can you tell me about the dead man?"

Robert, a man with skin so dark he was shiny, spoke first. "Me and Teddy was in the saloon."

"The dead man was out back when the whores went to see 'bout the chickens." Hobart added. He was about thirty-five summers and brown of skin.

Black stared between them. "Hobart–Andrew, exactly where were you?"

"We was standin' in the dark out front." Andrew responded.

Black sighed. If nothing else, they appeared sincere, and he was relieved. He could work with honesty.

"We knows the rules… we ain't fool wit' the whores," Robert said. "Looks like we ain't good at keepin' watch neither."

"Why is we watchin' over the whores anyhow?" Andrew asked.

"We watch over the whores…" Black replied. "Because colored pussy is worth protecting."

While it was clear Black wasn't in a joking mood, Elbert laughed before adding. "As a babe, every man in here done climbed up outta some colored pussy. As men, we each spend a good deal of time tryna climb back up in it. Yeah, colored pussy needs to be watched over. What would we do without it?"

The men laughed and Black found he needed the ease that was happening. It was better than ruminating over the possible demise of the ambassador. Had yet another in his camp been murdered in an attempt to topple the union president? He turned his mind away from his troubling thoughts and plotted his next step.

Black laid on the floor of the great room, while the men talked and speculated. When the house grew dark the men moved to the porch and then dispersed. He lay staring at the ceiling seeing nothing when Elbert's voice floated to him on the inkiness.

"The man in the box… you know who it is?"

Black sat up then stood. He didn't answer his brother. "The men?"

"They on the path waiting for you."

The brothers exited the house to find the men of Blacktown readying themselves for the night. Black left Emmett, Jesse, and Josiah in place. Meeting the men in the middle of the pathway, they waited while the stablehands brought the horses. Black rode out with nine men at his back. Their first stop would be the Grand Hotel.

* * *

There was a night life in Montreal that centered around the hotel. The hour being early meant people were still moving about. Frank, Lou, and Anthony were with the horses at the end of the thoroughfare. The lampposts had been extinguished offering the smallest amount of protection. Black and James took to the alley leading to the back of the hotel. Once between the buildings, Black looked to the theatre to find that it was in the early process of being rebuilt.

Five men followed them down the alley and into the courtyard. The kitchen doors were open as the colored staff moved about like swarming bees. His men remained on the edge of the light. Black walked forward, followed by James and Elbert. When the brothers stepped over the threshold, the staff nearest to the door stopped their work. A short woman who was light of skin walked up to James. His brother smiled.

"I ain't ask yo' name last time I was here. I'm askin' now," James said.

"Thelma."

"Well, Miss Thelma, I needs yo' help." James continued. "This here is my brother Black; we lookin for a Brit that stayed on here. We calls him Bainesworth."

The woman turned to Black and spoke. "I seen ya a time or two, Mista Black."

"Miss Thelma," Black greeted. "What can you tell me about the Brit or the room three twenty-seven?"

"I caint say, Mista Black. The fourth floor is the one I works," Thelma said. She held up her hand before rushing over to a woman and a man who were washing dishes.

He watched Thelma speaking with a plump colored man with hair on the sides of his head and none on top. Then, she pointed in their direction. The man smiled, dried his hands, and moved toward them. A thin, younger, brown skin woman with plaits all over her head followed. They both wore black bottoms and a white shirt.

"Mista Black," the man said. "I be Delmer. This here is my daughter, Louise."

"Delmer–Miss Louise," Black replied, and he was trying not to be clip–short. But they needed to move this along.

"You two work the third floor?" Elbert asked. "We wanna know about three twenty-seven?"

"We does." The woman answered. "Ain't no one in that chamber. It was a funny speakin' man in that chamber 'bout five days ago. The rich, they comes and goes."

"Is there a back corridor what leads to the floors above?" James asked.

"It is," Delmer said.

Turning to Elbert, Black advised. "Tell the men to watch the hotel. Me and James is going in."

"Yeah," Elbert replied before fading into the night.

Black followed James, who followed Delmer through the kitchen to a door in the far corner. The old man pulled the portal open, then grabbed a lantern hanging from a hook. The staff went on about their chores as if covering up their presence. The tiny flickering light only helped to ward off complete darkness where they stood. It did nothing for up ahead or behind them. The second problem: the old man huffed and puffed all the way to the third floor. When they stepped onto the landing, he was wheezing and coughing.

The raised corridor was suffocating, but it didn't reek. In fact, it smelled of food that had been trapped between the walls. Black could still hear the dishes clanking and the silverware clinking below. It was an indication that nothing was amiss. James pulled the door open and walked into the hallway first. The old man who finally gathered himself was second and Black brought up the rear.

"Down two doors on yo' right," Delmer said.

They kept moving while Black observed his surroundings. There were lit sconces in the wall on either side of the corridor to light the way. The carpet was blood red with a yellow royal emblem. Though the hall was well lit there was still a haze that kept everything from being sharp and in focus. James and Black stood on opposite sides of the old man while he used his key to open the door.

Black stepped over the threshold first, gun drawn. The dark suite was similar to Campbell Penn's except there was only a master chamber and a common area. James lit the two oil lamps on the table bringing the chamber out of the shadows. There was a brown couch with a matching chair. Behind the chair was a table that sat six. In the center was a white vase with no flowers. The hardwood floor boasted of a red area rug; the royal emblem sat dead center.

"Ain't nobody here," James said.

Delmer added. "Ain't been no one here in days."

Black walked into the master chamber and began looking about. His brother and the old man followed, bringing the light with them. It was simple; the furnishings consisted of a large bed, a chamber pot, a nightstand, and a desk. On top of the nightstand was an empty glass pitcher. The bed covering was brown as the color scheme of the chamber was earthy–masculine. In the corner the closet door sat ajar. The drapes were drawn.

James went through the desk. "Ain't shit here but blank parchment."

In the closet hung three suits, two blue and one brown. On the floor was one pair of brown boots that sat next to an empty saddlebag.

"Did you take what was in the saddlebag?" Black asked.

The older man was indignant. "Me and my child ain't gotta thief–we works hard."

Black stared at the man for long moments. When Delmer didn't squirm, he went on. "Who is the tailor around these parts?"

"He named Sir Worthington." Delmer answered. "The tailor make clothes for the mens and women. Ain't too many colored what like 'im. Worthy ain't right in the head. Some of the girls in the kitchen say he offer coins for company. It seem ain't none of the women hopeless enough to fool wit' 'im."

"Where is this tailor located?" Black asked.

"Worthy lives in his shop. You got to go like you's going to Blacktown. But when you get to the end of the thoroughfare, go right. His place 'bout a half mile up the road. It ain't too far from the public stable."

When Delmer stopped speaking. Black continued to stare at him. James understanding his brother said, "Old man... where is the gold watch what was in the saddlebag?"

"It wasn't no gold watch in them bags... a few coins were all.

We wasn't gon be rich from what we took," Delmer said speaking with haste.

"Who did you let in this chamber?" Black asked and his tone was flat.

If the slight rattle of the lantern he held was any indication, the old man was visibly shaken. "I let the tailor in to wait for the man what was here. He say they's friends. Worthy had the suits wit' 'im when he come calling."

"When did the man that was in this chamber go missing?" Black asked and his tone offered threat.

"After the tailor come," Delmer admitted and he was afraid.

"Who else tried to get in this chamber?" Black asked.

"Ain't no one else asked after this chamber but you all." Delmer whined.

Black reached out for the oil lamp James held then turned his back focusing on the room. His brother barked out to the old man. "Git yo' ass on the couch and be still."

Alone in the master chamber, Black moved the lamp and peered into the closet. He was trying to discern the facts. There was something smeared on the doorframe beneath his eye level. He assumed it to be blood. The room gave nothing else. When he joined his brother in the common area, James had removed a chair from the table. His brother was seated in front of the couch glaring at the old man.

"You have lied to me twice, Delmer." Black said. He paused for a moment then continued. "If you nor the staff likes this tailor, why do his bidding?"

"Cause he scary and white."

"You will speak about this to no one–do you understand me?" Black said. "Should anyone outside the hotel inquire about this room, you are to come to me posthaste."

"Yes, sah... right away, Mista Black."

"Let's go," Black said to James, who stood and followed him into the corridor. The brothers went back the way they came. In the kitchen, Delmer's daughter looked worried for her father. Black strolled by her workstation; she was up to her elbows in soap water.

"Mista Black," Louise whispered.

"You and your father are not to speak on this visit," he said and there was warning in his tone.

"Yes, sah," she mumbled.

James was speaking with Thelma, and Black knew he was advising her the same. They quit the kitchen and when they entered the alley, Elbert's voice floated on the darkness.

"What we got?"

Black sighed. "The ambassador has met with foul play."

"You still say it ain't Bainesworth in the box?" James asked.

"No... it is not the ambassador."

"What next?" Elbert asked.

"We already nearby–we're going to the tailor," Black said.

The brothers backtracked to the horses and the other men. They rode hard for a half mile until the public stable came into view. Many lampposts kept the area well-lit. Across the roadway were several houses that sat back from the street on a long drive. A few colored stablehands stood about. Elbert rode alongside Black and when they reached the men, his brother spoke.

"Which one is the tailor's place?"

A young man came forward and pointed to the only dark house on the lane. The men rode up the drive and into the shadows. Black, Elbert, James, Frank, and Lou swung down from the saddle. James hit the stairs first and the men followed. The rest of their posse fanned out to keep watch. Frank and Lou came with the torches and Elbert kicked the door in. They were greeted by the smell of death, and Black felt weak with the possibilities.

Frank and James entered first. Elbert and Black followed. Lou brought up the rear. When the men stepped into the great room, Lou almost tossed up his belly. Thankfully, Elbert was on hand to grab the torch when Lou would have dropped it. Moving into the house the men didn't have to go far before they found the source of the stench. On the floor in front of the couch was the decomposing body of a white man. There was enough of him left for them to see that it wasn't Bainesworth.

The men did a walk through while Black stayed in the front room with the body. There was nothing to do here, so the men backed out of the house. The goal–question the men at the public stables to see what they could learn. Black closed the door behind them and walked his horse back to where Elbert was already speaking with a young man. The stable worker looked to be light of skin and about twenty summers. His hair was braided in two cornrows on either side of his head.

"Folks call me Soup." The younger man was saying.

"The tailor?" Elbert asked.

"Strange man…" Soup said while shaking his head. "He was friendly enough wit' the coloreds here at the stables. But he was also one of them whites what supports the south in the war between the states. Don't make sense, his tongue say he was a Brit."

"When the last time you seen the tailor?" James asked.

"Been about a week," Soup said. "Figure he gone visitin'."

"Oh, he in the house," Elbert said. "It ain't pretty."

Black noted that the younger man looked away. He was trying to avoid more questioning. The other men from the stables had disappeared inside. Black understood their situation and so he asked. "Who have you seen coming and going from the tailor's home?"

Soup stared at Black, he shook his head, then stepped closer. "White folks do what the hell they wants. The men what works here got families. We don't see nothin' even when we sees something."

Elbert chimed. "We understand."

Soup nodded. "Five days back, Worthy and three other white men carried another white man into his house. They's all white, so we looked away. Hours later two white men left carrying a man out of the house. 'Bout three nights ago six white men come–they carried a white man away. Ain't been even a candle lit in that house since. Worthy sews for a living, so the candles be lit 'fore the sun go down… but nothing."

As Black listened, he was even more confused than when he started. He and Bainesworth had not been acquaintances, but the ambassador had grown on him. There had never been a reason to speak with Bainesworth regarding his past ventures. It was obvious now that he should have inquired. Exhaustion settled on his person along with a healthy dose of grief.

"Thank you," Black said, dismissing the anxious stablehand. When he was alone with his brother, he added. "I'm tired. We will wait for the sun to make the next two moves."

"Who is in the box?" Elbert asked.

"I can't be sure, but I believe the man in the box is Harvey Michaels."

"Hmmm," came Elbert's reply.

"You are vexed," Black responded, "because you see it the same."

"Shit," Elbert hissed.

The brothers swung up into the saddle, their destination, Blacktown. They rode for an hour making for home. Black went over in his head what he would do come daylight. But when the posse rounded the bend to the main path of the settlement, they were brought up short by the sight of a standoff. Seven white men on horseback were at the beginning of the main path. The men from Blacktown were visibly agitated even as they held their unwanted guests at gunpoint. At the edge of the crowd, Black climbed from the saddle.

Wading through the throng of men, he came face-to-face with Lincoln's man. Miles Glendale looked agitated as well, but his men had not drawn their weapons. Black also noticed that he looked relieved to see him.

"Glendale," Black greeted. All around them, the settlement men were quiet–assessing.

When the union soldier spoke, his vexation was evident. "We have your man."

"What man?" Black replied

"The ambassador."

Black narrowed his eyes. He asked the pertinent. "Is he alive?"

"Barely."

"How would the ambassador end up with you?" Elbert asked from behind where Glendale stood.

The union soldier turned for Elbert. "We were watching the tailor. He sent for us after receiving the telegram."

Emmett spoke to the men. "Back to yo' duties, we has it from here!"

The settlement dispersed. When Black and the posse he rode in with were alone with the union soldiers, Black said. "You may speak freely."

"The president sent us to Montreal to keep a look out. We helped your man because you all saved the president," Glendale said.

"You killed the tailor?" Black asked.

Glendale nodded. "And Harvey Michaels–he is who had your man picked up."

Black was incredulous at the turn of events. Folding his arms over his chest, he stared at Glendale. "Where is my man?"

"We are set up a few miles out," Glendale said in low tones. "He has come and wishes to see you."

Behind him, James whistled. Black stared at Glendale in the dancing torchlight. "Are you saying the union president is here?"

"I am," Glendale said. "As a matter of safety, we need to leave posthaste."

"Frank–Lou get a wagon!" Black yelled. "Anthony, fetch Shultz!"

As the men moved to do his bidding, Elbert asked Glendale a question. "How far?"

"Ten miles in the direction of the New Hampshire border."

Glendale responded. "After you all meet with him, we will move him by train."

Leaving Emmett, Jesse, and Josiah in place for the safety of Blacktown, the men rode out following the union soldiers. They would get the ambassador and head to the fort. Black allowed his mind to go blank. He needed peace to make the next few moves. When he addressed the union president, he needed to be clear and concise. He could not be Lincoln's puppet.

CHAPTER 26

THE BUSINESS OF LIVING
SEPTEMBER 1864

The men rode for fifteen miles, not the ten Glendale estimated or lied about. It was before dawn when they came upon a small settlement called Burgundy. The town was a mixture of whites and coloreds. It was poor by any standard, but the town was beautiful and so were the people. Black had come a time or two.

There was a general store and several small farms much like anywhere in Canada. A train came through once a week. Travelers were how the town made its coin. The posse rode almost to the other end of the settlement until they came upon a maze of dirt paths. On the porch of one of the cabins were four white men and per the torchlight, they appeared to be in deep conversation.

Stopping in front of the cabin, the union soldiers swung from their saddles first. Black watched as Lincoln's men greeted one another. Glendale kept on inside the house. Around him, his own men swung from their saddles to stretch. The last few days had been grueling. His men and Lincoln's men did not acknowledge each other, and Black supposed it was for the better.

Glendale was gone for about twenty minutes. Black was about to question the men on the porch when the captain reappeared.

"Black, this way please."

James and Elbert moved in behind him and though it looked as if Glendale wanted to protest, he didn't. The union soldiers stepped to the side allowing he and his brothers to pass. Lincoln sat to a large table with a cup of coffee in front of him. It was the end of the hottest August in years, and the president wore a sweater. To the left of the room was a brown couch placed over an orange area rug. The place was stuffy and uncomfortable, yet Lincoln looked cool. Black immediately broke out in a sweat.

"Mr. President."

"Black, your man is in the back room. I figure you'll want to look in on him first before we speak," Lincoln said.

Nodding, Black followed Glendale to a door at the back of the cabin. When he moved, so did his brothers. The soldier opened the door to reveal a black woman seated to the left of the large bed. In the center lay Bainesworth, and he did not look good.

Turning to Elbert, Black said. "Get Shultz."

His brother went to do as requested and Black went for the assessment. The woman seated at the bedside was plump and dark of skin. She looked to be about thirty summers–give or take. Her hair was cornrowed in two braids; her eyes held concern for her patient. The threadbare dress she wore was brown. She was dipping a cloth into the basin when her gaze met his own.

"Mista Black, I be Maybell."

Nodding to her, he managed. "How is he?"

"He gon make it, but they sho' beat on him," she said.

A lantern lit the room, but dawn was happening giving Black a better visual. Bainesworth was covered by a white sheet about the hips. There were bruises and contusions all over his torso. The ambassador turned his head and stared at him. His hair was wild, and he had not been shaved. His top lip was split, his left eye swollen shut. Bainesworth looked dazed–confused, still he spoke, and his voice was weak.

"Black… I knew you and the men would find me."

"Save your strength," Black answered. He didn't wish to speak in front of this woman.

Shultz stepped into the chamber and began issuing orders. Black had but one demand before he quit the room. "Get him ready to travel."

The doctor nodded and Black went to face Lincoln. In the front room, the president was where he left him. Stepping to the center of the great room, Black noted that the president looked exhausted. He recognized it to be the plight of a man who leads.

"Mr. President," Black said as he waited patiently for Lincoln's concerns.

"Black, I received your telegram. I took it to mean that you had learned of yet another plot on my life and that of my vice president."

"It seems the Preservers of Southern Life formed an alliance with Jeff Davis. Per our hostage, there was a scheme to assassinate you and Vice President Hamlin. We took him prisoner before he could learn the particulars. I have told you all that I know."

The president stared at him for long moments gauging his sincerity. When he was satisfied, Lincoln said. "I will be re-elected in November. The war is ending, and I believe the north will be victorious. There is much to be done. Reconstruction will be painful. I was hoping for your support."

It was Black's turn to stare for long moments. "Mr. President… I am no puppet. I will not be propped up in front of my people while promises are made and not kept."

Lincoln pushed his chair back from the table and leaned forward placing his palms to his thighs. His dark trousers bunched with the action. "I do not think you a puppet. I am looking for real help so the people can get what they need."

"With all due respect, Mr. President. The prospect of freedom for colored folks will bring about the staggering realization that we have toiled in the sun our whole lives with nothing to show for it. I have no concern for the slaver who will have to till his own land."

"You think I don't comprehend what you say?" The president's tone was one of annoyance.

"If you understand the concept of which I speak, then explain why you would pay reparations to the slaver and not the enslaved." Black replied.

Lincoln blanched. "There have been no easy decisions made…"

Black could do nothing but chuckle. It was either that or engage in behavior that could rile his men. Behind him, Elbert mumbled. "Shit."

Shultz picked that moment to burst from the back room. As he wiped his hands on a clean towel, the doctor gave his report. "They gave him a good thrashing. He'll make it, but it will be slow going. I'm going to give him some sleeping powder. The ambassador wishes to speak with you before he is dosed."

The doctor never missed a beat as he rushed to the front door. Once on the porch, he hollered for Frank and Lou, who came running with the stretcher. Turning his attention back to the president, Black nodded before going to see about Bainesworth. In the bedchamber, the ambassador, who was now propped up on many pillows, stared up at him.

Walking over to the bed, Black gave him the once over. The morning sun was unforgiving and to Black's way of thinking the ambassador looked aged. Bainesworth's words took him by surprise.

"I wish to keep Maybell with me... I don't want to leave her behind."

Black's eyes bounced to the woman, who also appeared shocked. "Do you wish to come with us?"

"Yes, sir," she whispered. "I works the dry-good store. The men sent for supplies, then asked me to stay on and tend the ambassador… I only has myself."

Nodding, Black turned to Bainesworth. "She has agreed. Is there anything else?"

"They were in my room when I got back from eating." Bainesworth grunted. "I am sorry to cause you this inconvenience."

"Save your strength, Ambassador." Black gazed out the window. He was weary, but he wasn't willing to stop moving.

Shultz appeared and Black watched as he dosed the ambassador before swaddling him in a clean white sheet. Maybell was anxious, and the doctor employed her help to give her something to do. When the ambassador was out cold, Black assisted Shultz in getting him onto the stretcher. Anthony held the doors, while they carried Bainesworth out to the awaiting wagon.

Outside the cabin his men readied themselves for travel. Lincoln had not moved from where he sat. Black addressed the president. "Sir, I appreciate your help with my man."

Lincoln waved a hand as if to dismiss the thought. "Black, I wish for you to come to Washington after I begin my second term. Please consider my invitation."

Sighing, Black offered hope. "I will consider your request. Stay safe, Mr. President."

CHAPTER 27

BLACK EXPANSION
NOVEMBER 1864

Jake stepped onto the porch of the little house he shared with Caroline. The lantern light spilling from the windows meant she was still awake. As he peered up at the moon a sense of accomplishment washed over him. Frank, Lou, and Anthony helped him build the house. Virgil assisted him with a few purchases. Caroline had been delighted and pleasing her made him happy.

August had been so hot that the warm weather continued straight through the fall. The workday had been exhausting and he was glad to be home. Pushing at the front door, he found Caroline stirring a pot on the black stove. She turned in time to see him step over the threshold.

"You're home," Caroline said, her voice soft.

The smile she offered was warm–genuine. She wore a pink shift and when she turned to him, it was plain to see she was with child. Caroline waddled over and kissed his cheek.

"You hungry?" she asked.

"I am."

"It's water on the stove for you," she said.

The house had a great room and two bedchambers; one room was a bit smaller than the other. Seating himself to the white kitchen table, Jake removed his boots, gun and then his clothes. He poured two large buckets of cold water into the porcelain tub that sat in front of the fireplace. He then added the two pots of hot water. When he sank down into the tub, he moaned. Leaning back, he closed his eyes as he listened to her moving about the house.

He opened his eyes when he heard the scraping of a chair against the planked floor. Caroline seated herself on the side of the tub. He loved when she engaged him. But what tickled him most was when she tested the limits of her newfound freedom.

"I plan on going to town wit' the womenfolk in the morning."

Jake smiled. "All right."

"I might stay all day wit' Anna and Miss Cora."

He knew she waited for him to object, instead, he inquired. "You gonna help at the dress shop?"

"You don't mind?"

"I don't."

She stared at him. "I baked some gingerbread cookies again."

"Oh," he replied. "I don't like gingerbread."

"Do you want me to stop baking them?"

"Not if you like them," he answered, smirking.

"Hmmm," she said. "I have decided to walk home alone."

"No," he replied.

"Am I not free to come and go as I please?"

"You are free," he explained. "But yo' safety is my job."

Caroline looked away, but not before he saw her smile. It was her way most nights and it thoroughly entertained him. He also understood that she was trying to gauge the magnitude of his love for her.

"How is you feelin'?" he asked.

"I am well," she answered, her voice soft.

There was a shyness that happened whenever he asked after her health. Caroline hadn't thought she could bear children. When she had taken ill, he worried. He had taken her to Shultz and waited outside pacing the path.

"Are you still happy about the little one?" she asked interrupting his musings.

"I love you both," he answered.

She breathed in sharply and he chuckled. Caroline gave him a different sense of family. He was unclear how he ever lived without it.

"Want me to scrub your back?"

"No," he replied as he washed his face and hair.

When he stood, she handed him a towel and tossed a second towel onto the floor. He stepped out. As he dried himself, Caroline looked away.

"I made stew," she said.

"I ain't hungry for food right now."

"Oh," she breathed.

He held out his hand and she placed her smaller one in his. Leading her to the back room, he stopped at the side of the bed. Cupping her face, he brought her lips down to meet his own. Caroline tasted of ginger cookies, and he loved it. Reaching for the hem of her shift he lifted the fabric over her head. The light from the front room spilled into their bedchamber illuminating her black skin and engorged nipples. He placed a palm over the roundness of her belly. It was a type of intimacy he never knew could exist.

Urging her to their bed, his voice was rough–emotional. "Get in."

Caroline climbed onto the large platform bed, and Jake felt a sense of pride at having built it with his own two hands. Dropping his towel, he scrambled in after her. She lay flat on her back. He moved in pressing himself against her. Lifting her long shapely leg, he pushed into her from the side and they both groaned.

Their coupling was slow, rhythmic, and filled with affection. He pulled a nipple into his mouth, while rocking into her. Caroline called out. "Jake… don't stop."

He palmed her belly as he made love to her. Caroline was tight, hot, and wet. Orgasm took him by surprise. Still, he didn't back away from the sensations that washed over him.

"Shit, Caroline…"

His dick remained stiff even as his balls emptied. And like he didn't back away from pleasure, he didn't back away from her. They continued in their quest for total satisfaction. Caroline was beautiful, their coupling was beautiful and their next orgasm… euphoric.

* * *

The ambassador sat in the dark on the porch of the small cabin he occupied. It had been a trying few months. He was older and he was not healing as he did in his youth. His hip was still paining him, though it was much improved. He planned to voyage back to England, but he had been procrastinating and the reason was plain. Fort Independence and its people were a wonderful experience.

Chuckling to himself, his thoughts traveled to a time when he had not liked Black. Now, he cherished the friendship. He suspected Black did too. Why else would he and the men have come to fetch him? There had been nightmares that followed regarding the tailor and being snatched from his rooms. In truth, he had been bitter about being bested. He wished they had killed him.

Lincoln having men in Canada had saved his very life. He could understand the union president wishing to employ Black and his men. They were an impressive bunch, but he also understood Black's stance and the fact that he refused to keep watch for Lincoln or become his puppet. It was all so intriguing.

What troubled him of late wasn't leaving the fort. It was the plump, chocolate beauty that had nursed him back to health. He didn't wish to leave her. Maybell slept on a cot brought in from the barracks, leaving the huge bed to him. Now that he was on the mend, he cursed that damn cot.

She had gone visiting with the women and while she was away, he had it removed. He understood that it had been forward to do so without asking her. The possibility that she would run screaming into the night was real. He could only hope the opposite would happen.

The sound of a carriage rattling on the path got his attention. It was time to face the fact that Maybell may not want him the way he wanted her. Sonny brought the carriage to a complete stop before hopping down to set the steps.

"Evenin', Ambassador," the older man said.

"Good evening, my good man."

Sonny pulled the carriage door open, and he could hear the women giggling inside. Bainesworth smiled as he listened to Elbert's wife Anna call out, "Thank you for your help today, Maybell."

"Thank you for lettin' me be at yo' shop."

The old man removed the steps, and the carriage rattled away before she noticed him. Lamplight flickered from the window, and she startled when she made her way onto the makeshift porch.

"Laverne, what is you doing out here in this chill?"

He stepped over her admonishment. "It seems as though you've had a lovely day."

She stared at him for moments. "Yes, today was nice."

He chuckled to himself. She didn't always catch his accent. This fact would only make it more difficult as he professed his love for her.

"Did you eat?"

"I had a little something."

"I brang ya some stew from Big Mama. We can share," Maybell said. "Come on inside."

When she would have continued into the cabin, his anxiety over his forward behavior got the better of him. His voice rose when he admitted. "I had the cot taken back to the barracks."

She stopped in her tracks and stared at him. Maybell stood outside the light cast by the window. He held his breath while he waited for her rejection. "Laverne, dear, speak slow. I ain't understandin' you."

Though he hated it, he stood and limped over to the door. He allowed her into the cabin first. His personal space was better suited for a man. The cabin consisted of a large tin tub, a brown table with two chairs and an enormous bed. In the corner there was a small desk that was added so the table could be used for eating. There was also a fireplace.

Maybell set the pot she carried on the table as she removed her blue coat while looking about. She stopped unbuttoning the garment and stared at him. He could tell when she realized the cot was gone and to his surprise, she looked stricken.

"I see my bed is gone," she whispered. "Is you wantin' me to find somewhere else to go?"

In the lamp light, he noted the smoothness of her dark skin and the glassiness of her huge eyes. Maybell had high cheekbones and juicy lips. She kept her hair in two braids pinned neatly at the crown of her head. She was full figured and sweet. Had he ever wanted a woman as much as he wanted Maybell? She was waiting for his response, which was ridiculous. His accent only worsened when he was nervous. This matter was going to get out of hand if he didn't clear matters up.

Stepping into her personal space, Bainesworth leaned in planting a chaste kiss on her soft lips. Maybell didn't pull away. "I want you to be mine."

Pulling back from her, he finished unbuttoning her coat. He hung the garment on the peg by the door, then turned to gaze at her. As he looked upon her beauty, he slowed his words down. He needed her to get his intentions on the first try.

"I want you to share my life… I beg you, dear woman, stay with me."

Maybell smiled. "Oh, Laverne. I ain't wantin' to be without you. I stayed on the cot cause you is on the mend. I'm tryna make sho' you don't strain yoself."

"Dear lady, I will bear the strain."

They both laughed and the tension eased from the cabin. But as fast as the tension lifted it was back and it settled with an awkwardness. She was going to sleep in his bed. Bainesworth worried his performance wouldn't be up to snuff. Maybell must have read his wayward thoughts. It was her turn to step forward and kiss him. Getting up on her tiptoes, she pushed her tongue into his mouth.

He groaned, then panted. "Food later."

She helped him undress and remove his boots and he did the same for her. Maybell was still wearing a white shift as she folded his clothes. He was dressed in long underwear. She was turning down the covers on their bed when he moved in hugging her from behind. Pulling at the hem of the shift, he helped her removed her last bit of clothing.

He shucked his underpants and when he pressed his body against her, he groaned in delight. She climbed on the bed, laying in the middle and he followed landing between her sweet thighs. He kissed her and the contact was all lips and tongue. Bracing himself up on his good hand, he backed away, kissing her collarbone and neck.

Maybell panted when he bit and sucked her nipples. He was drunk from the scent of peaches on her skin. He kissed a path down her belly and when he reached her core, he breathed in all that was her before wrapping his lips about her clitoris.

"Laverne…" she moaned.

He didn't bring her to orgasm, he needed to be inside her.

Climbing back over her, he entered her and stilled. Maybell twined her legs and arms around him. Bainesworth shut his eyes and allowed himself to feel loved and pleasured.

"Ohhh my...Maybell. Please, my dear, never leave me." He groaned.

She kissed him and to his utter shock, she promised. "I ain't finna go nowhere, my love."

Her words yanked the orgasm from him, and the ambassador surrendered.

* * *

Black was seated to his desk ordering supplies. In the background he could hear the women in the dress shop chatting with customers. It was his turn to watch over them, and thus his reason for being in town. There was a slight chill in the air and the fireplace was starting to make a difference when the backdoor swung open.

James stepped into the office and his arms were full of packages, telegrams, and a letter. All needing his attention. One brown package appeared to be from Frederick Douglass, the other from Lincoln. He suspected they held the same message.

"Imma walk down to Everything." James said. "Elbert is at the inn watching over Mama and Iris."

"Yeah," Black replied, his mind already on to the next thing.

He cut both packages open and indeed they both contained a newspaper. The headlines read different, though the meaning was the same. Lincoln had been reelected. Pushing his chair back from the desk, Black leaned back and read both from cover to cover.

When he was finished reading, he tossed both papers into the fire. Turning his mind back to ordering supplies, he left the letter and telegrams for last. Black knew what awaited, and he would tend it later; he was being summoned.

* * *

Sunday was still sleeping when he climbed from their bed. His mind was on the telegrams and letter that he hadn't addressed the day before. It was well before dawn when Black made his way to his study. Seating himself, he started with the letter.

My Friend,

I hope this missive finds you in good health. I am told that you have expanded your operations and are prospering. Please consider this an invitation to come share your knowledge. I hope to see you on April 11, 1865.

F.D.

Black placed the letter from Frederick Douglass to the side and moved to the telegrams. The first message read:

YOUR PRESENCE IS REQUESTED APRIL 11, 1865

The second message read:

THIS MATTER DESERVES ONLY THE BEST

Placing the telegrams from Lincoln aside, Black stood and paced his study. He wanted to be part of the reconstruction, but he didn't wish to be used to bring colored folks to heel. It was almost dawn and pacing the study was no longer satisfying the energy that rolled through him. Pulling the door wide he headed for the porch.

Now that the older women were spending time in town, they no longer woke early. The house was dark as he strolled through the kitchen and front hall. Once on the porch, he stared to the east and marveled at the new cabins and small houses that filled the space where the wall had been. Fort Independence was spilling over to town. Black was pleased.

CHAPTER 28

FORT INDEPENDENCE
JANUARY 31, 1865

The new year arrived and with it the bitter cold. Still, the people of Blacktown and Fort Independence were living off the fruit of their own labor. Life was good. As Black stood at the window of his study, the men filed in. There had been correspondence from Washington. When the men settled, Black walked to the center of the room and started the meeting.

"The constitution has been amended to abolish slavery."

"What is you sayin'?" James asked. "Coloreds is free?"

"It hasn't been signed yet." Black answered. "But the amendment passed through Congress."

"Who sent word?" Elbert asked.

"Douglass," Black replied. "I imagine the president is busy."

Silence fell over the room, and Black gave the men a moment. After a time, he added. "It's still only in the north. If Lincoln doesn't win this war–southern law will go back into effect."

"I ain't sho' how I feel," Gilbert said.

Black chuckled. "Me either, Gil."

The room fell into pockets of discussion as the men tried on freedom. As Black listened, the consensus was simple. The men in this room were free because they took a stand and it mattered. When the conversation lulled, it was Frank who spoke up.

"I ain't understandin'."

Black laughed. "What aren't you understanding?"

"Coloreds waitin' on white folks to say they's free," Frank said.

"It's a burden to be enlightened." Black answered.

The study fell silent under the weight of Black's words. Each man thinking on the fact that they had taken and maintained liberty for themselves and their families. Lou stood as if to end the meeting and Black had one last bit of instruction for this group.

"I will be leaving for Blacktown. February is upon us and as always, there is much to do. The men who are to move out with me, we have three days."

When the men were gone, Black waited patiently for the women. They had not gone to town at his request. His wife appeared in the doorway first, then the rest of the women piled in and there were at least two new faces. The tall beauty, Caroline, now with Jake and sweet Fern was now with Ephraim. It was a work around the home day, all the women wore brown.

The discussion with the women was in the same vein as the men. Black offered the facts as he knew them. "The constitution has been amended to abolish slavery."

"What that means, Nat?" his wife asked.

"It means Lincoln is trying to outlaw slavery." He answered.

"You saying coloreds everywhere is free now?" Hazel, Gilbert's woman asked.

"If Lincoln wins the war... yes." He replied.

"I feels some shame." Hazel continued. "Living wit' Gilly–being around you men, I don't thank about freedom no mo'. I's safe and I knows it for sho'– I done forgot what it is to worry about it."

"Me too," Molly said. "My Lou keeps me free from abuse."

As the women fell into pockets of conversation about feeling safe, Black was overcome with a sense of pride. He and his men were heroes in the eyes of their women. What more could he ask for? When the women went back to their chores for the day, Black left the house to handle some last-minute matters.

The day was cloudy, but the chill was bearable. Black walked along the path, surveying the new houses and cabins. When he made it to the barracks, the first person he encountered was Jake. Black was pleased, for Jake was his first order of business. The younger man greeted him first.

"Black."

"I want you to stay on at the fort. Simon and Sunday could use your help," Black said.

"I will ride out if you needs me."

"Miss Caroline is too close. I wouldn't ask that of you." Black replied.

"Thank you… I be happy to back Simon and Sunday."

"Congratulations," Black added, clapping him on the back.

Nodding, Black turned on his heels and walked away. He stayed on the path until he came to the ambassador's cabin. Stepping onto the makeshift porch, Black didn't knock. About three minutes went by before Bainesworth stepped outside. He was donning his coat when he turned to face Black.

"Morning, Black."

"Ambassador."

Bainesworth's cheeks were stained red, causing Black to ask. "Are you not well?"

Coughing, the ambassador answered. "Oh no… nothing like that. Maybell is still in bed, or I would have invited you in."

Black chuckled. "This is fine, Ambassador."

"I have done as you have requested and inquired about the land surrounding Blacktown. I think we could get a fair price and expand the settlement," Bainesworth said.

"Good… but that is not why I have come."

"Oh," Bainesworth said.

"I am headed to Blacktown in a few days. Are you well enough to travel?" Black asked.

The ambassador looked better, but the ass whooping he had sustained aged him. The older man looked away, causing Black to push the issue. "What is it? Maybell will be safe here with Simon."

"Yes… yes, I know she will be safe." Bainesworth answered.

"Then what…"

"I knew the tailor and quite honestly, I forgot about Worthy." Bainesworth managed. "When he appeared in my rooms, I didn't think it was to kill me. He wanted information… about you."

"But you gave them nothing," Black said.

"No, I didn't; but I was weak. I wanted the pain to stop," Bainesworth said as he dropped his gaze.

"They killed Harvey Michaels and Lincoln's men killed the tailor," Black said, then paused for effect. "I have the two men that worked for the tailor."

The ambassador's gaze snapped up to meet his own. Black noted that his stance became hostile. His words were clipped and to the point. "How long have you had them?"

"Two months."

"I can handle this, if you would rather not—"

"My good man… of course I will be ready to travel," Bainesworth said.

Black stared at him for long moments before saying. "Three days."

"Yes, I shall inform Maybell of my impending departure."

"Sunday and the women will look after her," Black said before climbing from the porch and walking away.

***

The men arrived in Blacktown five days later. It was almost midnight, and the darkness held a mean chill even without the presence of a wind. The sound of men hollering in pain caught Black's attention as he stood on the back porch gazing up at the stars. James passed him a flask and he drank for the heat and the buzz.

It grew quiet moments before the sound of a gunshot tore through the peace. Passing the flask back to his brother, Black waited. The echo of a second gunshot followed and still the brothers did nothing. Bainesworth and Elbert came walking from behind the barracks, both men bundled in heavy coats and hats.

"The deed is done," the ambassador said.

"Yeah," Elbert added.

"Y'all want help burying them?" James asked.

"Ground is frozen," Elbert said. "They asses will keep."

"They most certainly will," Bainesworth said.

Black nodded before turning on his heels and walking into his house. This was another problem solved.

CHAPTER 29

BLACKTOWN
APRIL 1865

Expansion was happening for the settlement and Black was pleased. He worked with the men to make some of the paths one way in and one way out. Black labored with the people to build new cabins and small houses. He also assisted in getting the land ready for seeding. His only hurt–being away from Sunday and his children.

The sun was lasting longer as the season changed. He stood on his porch listening to the men as they spoke about man shit. Young Clem came rushing down the lane hollering something Black couldn't make out at first.

"Da war over… da war over!" Clem was carrying a small brown sack. "The north done won!"

When Clem reached the porch, he was breathless. He handed the sack to Black and panted. "The north done gone and won."

While the rest of the men spoke with Clem, Black went inside. He needed to sift through the heap of correspondence that arrived.

All were telegrams and he suspected the dry-goods store was getting no peace this day.

The first message from Frederick Douglass read:

WE ARE VICTORIOUS–THIS IS A GREAT DAY

The second message from Moses read:

THIS HERE THE BEGINNING

The third message from Milford Church read:

THE WAR IS OVER

The fourth message from Lincoln read:

COME TO ME POSTHASTE

Black stood, rushing back out to the porch. He instructed the men. "We are headed to Washington."

The men dispersed to ready themselves and to the ambassador, Black said. "We need to go by train. Can you handle that?"

"If we ride back to Burgundy, there will be a train leaving at midnight." Bainesworth replied.

"We will move out within the hour."

* * *

Washington D.C.

They used Bainesworth's connections to get them into the states. Travel was slow as it always was by rail; still, he and the men were well rested when they switched trains in Boston. The closer they got to Washington the more crowded the streets became. The large windows displayed a war-torn country that would need much to heal.

When the men stepped from the train in the capital city, there was chaos. Black headed for the colored sector and took up residence in a rowhouse that Frederick Douglass was occupying. The older man was happy to see him. Douglass hugged him and clapped him on the back.

"This has been a long time coming… never thought I would truly see this in my lifetime," Douglass said.

"Same here," Black replied.

The rowhouse had two bedchambers and it was all on one floor. Black and the men would sleep in shifts in the common area. Gilbert and Booker moved the couch against the wall. Leo and Jeremiah got a fire going. Several lanterns were placed around the house and though the great room seemed threadbare, the house was clean.

It had been late when he and the men made it from the train station. Black hadn't expected Miss Lizzy, the dressmaker for Lincoln's wife to come walking out of the kitchen. She was dressed in brown skirts with a white apron tied about her waist.

"Black–James," she greeted.

"Miss Lizzy," James said stepping up to hug her.

Black followed suit. He was happy to see her. Tim moved in for a hug and she reciprocated. "Mr. Tim, how are you?"

"I'm fine, ma'am." Tim said, his surprise evident when she squeezed him again.

Miss Lizzy and two young women got the stove going and the smell of stewed chicken filled the air. As the late evening turned to early morning, the men ate and slept. Black couldn't sleep, so he posted up on the front stoop to watch the people. Spring in Washington held a chill without the presence of the sun. Still, Black remained outside pondering all that needed to be done.

In the distance, he could hear the madness happening in the streets. It was a combination of relief, celebration, and sorrow. The people seemed almost too weary to make merry. His brothers stepped out to be with him. It was James who broke the silence.

"Is you wantin' to be part of this rebuilding plan?"

"Don't know yet… have to see what Lincoln's made of." Black answered.

Frederick came outside as well. In his hand, he held a teacup that smelled of whiskey. The older abolitionist offered his thoughts. "Lincoln outlawed slavery; that has to count for something."

"It does..." Elbert said. "But this law—"

Frederick spoke over him. "Like you all, I too have taken my freedom–there are those who are not strong enough. See the value in what is happening."

The men grew quiet for a time until Douglass and his brothers fell into an amiable debate about what white folks don't have the right to give. And so it went, until Elbert and Douglass went inside leaving James to keep Black's company. It was almost dawn when Black found a spot in the corner of the great room and dozed off.

Men chatting and laughing woke him. Black stared to the window noting the brightness of the sun. Judging by its position in the sky, it was early afternoon. He couldn't believe how tired he was given the fact that travel to Washington was uneventful. The common area was empty save for Douglass walking in from the kitchen.

"I was coming to wake you."

"I am up," Black replied.

"The president is sending a carriage for us."

Black nodded. "I'll be ready."

Frederick was dressed in a gray suit, his usual wild hair and beard neatly cut back. Making his way to the vacant bedchamber, Black relieved himself and freshened up. He donned clean clothes and when he met some of his men in the kitchen, Black issued orders.

"Have Frank and Lou break the men down into two groups. Elbert and James, you are with me. We are to meet back here after nightfall."

The presidential carriage arrived about two hours after his men were deployed. Frederick stepped from the rowhouse first, then Elbert and James. Black brought up the rear. Colored folks lined the roadway, and they were happy to see them. While the men settled into the carriage, an elderly man stepped forward.

"Mista Black, when can we see 'bout our loved ones in the south?"

Smiling, Black answered. "We have to observe before we act."

The old man nodded, and Black climbed into the vehicle. As the carriage lurched forward, Douglass said. "That is going to be our main issue–reuniting colored folks with their loved ones."

"Yeah."

Black stared out the window, watching as the carriage maneuvered through the crowded streets of Washington, D.C. There were soldiers both white and colored, along with civilians, clogging the thoroughfares. The people looked bone weary as they celebrated the end of the war. When the carriage finally stopped in front of the war department, an hour had gone by. A colored soldier pulled the door wide and greeted them.

"Gentlemen."

"Young man," Douglass replied.

The group followed the dark-skinned younger man through the huge front doors, across the marble floors to an office overlooking the well-manicured lawn. A large brown table with about ten chairs sat in the center of the chamber. The secretary of war, Edwin Stanton, was the only person present. Douglass greeted the older white man, who stood when the doors closed behind James.

"Mr. Secretary."

Stanton spoke as his eyes fell on Black. "Gentlemen, the president will be happy you are here. The last few days have been busy."

"Yes... yes." Douglass answered.

The secretary moved toward the door and before disappearing into the hall, he said. "I will fetch the president."

Two hours passed and when the doors finally opened, it was a maid and butler pushing a tray ladened with all types of delights. Douglass partook–Black and his brothers did not. Another hour passed before Lincoln himself rushed into the office. The president looked pale and disheveled; behind him, Stanton looked the same.

"Gentlemen... Black, I am happy you have come." Lincoln greeted.

"Mr. President," they all said in unison.

Seating himself, Lincoln got down to business. "I need a reconstruction plan that will be well suited for everyone. This will not work if there is no voice for the ex-slave."

"I agree," Douglass said.

"Sir, your largest issue will be that coloreds will not know all their needs until they present themselves. Employing a free mindset takes time and there will be much pain in this transition. What are you proposing?" Black countered.

Lincoln nodded. "We need to offer land rights and funding to get the people back on their feet."

"Are we speaking about white folks or colored folks?" Elbert asked.

The president turned his attention to Elbert and Black looked on. Lincoln replied. "I am speaking for everyone."

James chimed in. "So, you thanks the slaver gon let go of free labor?"

The men fell into a discussion about what was needed. They all agreed that there was much to be cleaned up before reconstruction could start. Black saw the task as daunting. He worried that a country that consistently only addressed the needs of its white citizens would not be capable of hearing all voices. While Black pondered and the men chatted, a knock on the door interrupted their meeting.

A young white woman with black hair and dark eyes opened the door. She was dressed as a maid. "Mr. President, Mrs. Lincoln is asking after you."

The president nodded and the woman closed the door. Lincoln looked directly at him, and Black knew it was coming. "I have to tend my wife this evening or I will not have a marriage. Will you stay in the city for a few days? We will pick this discussion up in the morning and you will not have to wait as you did today."

Black sighed. "Yes, sir, Mr. President."

Lincoln clapped his bony hands together, then stood. "The carriage will take you back to your residence. In the morning the vehicle will fetch you at first light."

Black nodded and then Lincoln was gone. The same soldier escorted them to the awaiting carriage. As they rode for the colored sector, the sun went down. There were so many folks in the street where the rowhouses were, they climbed from the carriage and walked the rest of the way. Torches were lit to keep the activity going.

Children ran about and fiddlers played sweet music. Black loved seeing his people happy.

* * *

The last few of the men had returned, one hour before midnight and Frank looked troubled. Black, who had been standing on the stoop, went inside the house. He found Douglass in the great room speaking with Elbert. The men filed in after him. It was Anthony who broke the silence.

"Lincoln been shot."

"What did you say?" Douglass asked.

"They done shot Lincoln at that there Ford Theatre," Lou said.

Before Black could ask a question. E.J. added, "Booth shot him."

"Is he dead?" Black heard himself ask; still he was disconnected from his own person.

"Dats all we know," Gilbert said.

"Lincoln was taken to a boarding house across the roadway from the theatre." Jeremiah explained.

The house grew quiet. Lizzy appeared in the archway of the kitchen. "I must go to Mrs. Lincoln."

"We will go on foot," Black said.

They all moved out with Lizzy in tow. In the streets, word spread that the president had been injured. Black held out hope that Lincoln would survive. He turned off that part of his brain that tried to ruminate over the news that it was the actor, John Booth who did the shooting.

When they reached the boarding house, the streets were packed with coloreds and whites. People were sobbing, the unrest and sorrow large. Black and the men stood about with the residents of Washington, D.C., until the sun rose. The morning was well underway when a thin white man with glasses stepped onto the gray porch and announced.

"The president has died."

Lizzy tugged Black by the hand as she yelled and pushed through the gathering. "I am here for Mrs. Lincoln!"

The man waved her up to the porch. "Miss Lizzy, the first lady has been asking for you."

Black expected the man to block him, but Lizzy never let his hand go. Inside, the boarding house was cold and the lack of heat fitting considering the occasion. No candle lit the space leading to the rooms at the end of the corridor. Black could see the mourners huddled together, and he presumed the president's body lay beyond the door.

When the first lady spied Lizzy, she rushed forward and collapsed in her arms. Mrs. Lincoln wailed as Lizzy guided her to an empty sitting room. Black was left alone in the hall. He had been about to go back the way he came when the secretary of war called his name.

"Black… this way."

He didn't hesitate. Black wanted to see for himself that the president was gone. Stepping into the bedchamber, he noted the curtains were pulled back allowing the sun to spill into the window. The president was propped up on many pillows and blood splatter marred the white blouse he wore. One side of Lincoln's face was swollen. A young man sat holding the president's hand–weeping. Black walked to the foot of the bed, an attempt to get closer. He couldn't turn away from the sight. The president was indeed gone.

Nodding to Stanton, he turned on his heels and quit the boarding house.

* * *

The men didn't linger in the capital city. At midnight, they caught a train headed for Boston. Black needed to be away from Washington and the tragedy happening. They switched in Massachusetts for a train bound for Canada. The ride was uneventful and while the men interacted with each other, Black didn't engage.

After four days of travel, it was midnight when the men arrived in Burgundy. A wagon carried them to Blacktown, and the people greeted them as if they were heroes. The weather was mild for an early April morning. Black, who didn't feel sociable, headed for his house at the end of the lane. Climbing the porch steps, he went inside shutting out the world. He didn't wash away the dust from his journey, instead, he undressed and clambered into bed. Sleep overtook him, and he was thankful for oblivion.

The sun was high in the sky when Black finally opened his eyes. Disoriented for moments, he heard the men from the barracks moving about. Fetching the warm water on the stove and the buckets left by the door, he filled the tub. Later, he shaved and dressed. Still, he found that the need to be alone had not left him.

When he could find nothing else to procrastinate about, he left his bedchamber. On the table was a hot bowl of beef stew. While he ate, the front door swung open, and James walked into the great room.

"You alright?"

"I am," Black replied.

He thought his brother would push for more conversation, but he didn't. James said, "Imma get some rest."

Black nodded, he guessed everyone was feeling the effects of the last year. He finished eating; and dropping the spoon back into the bowl, he stood making his way onto the porch. Elbert was posted up alone watching the people as they went about their chores.

"Virgil and Percy are here," Elbert said. "They're at Ruby's… Virgil has decided to call the new store, A Few Things."

"Good."

Black was staring off in the distance when his brother asked. "What does all this mean?"

"I wish I knew," Black said.

The brothers fell into a comfortable silence and though Black wanted to hide in his bedchamber, he remained on the porch. As the people of Blacktown spied him, they gathered around. He knew folks waited for his encouragement–his words. But Black was unsure if he had anything to give. Life offered a type of melancholy that he couldn't shake. The situation with Spike, Ruby, Freddy, Jimbo, and now Lincoln didn't help matters. The bright spot in all this was the fact that James, Percy and Bainesworth had survived.

Black moved to the edge of the very top step and allowed his eyes to scan the people gathering. The pockets of conversation lulled when he walked forward. A dark-skinned woman in the front row called out.

"They done killed the union president. What this mean for coloreds? What of the loved ones we left behind?"

Clearing his throat, Black offered a dose of reality. "The war between the states and the death of Lincoln has given everyone pause. I can't speak on that which I do not know. I can only observe and offer assistance where needed."

Another woman, who was older and brown of skin, asked. "What is gon happen to us?"

Black sighed, thankful for a question he could answer. "You all will continue to live freedom–me and the men standing among you will see to your liberty. We will mark the emancipation of our people, but we will not step away from our quest to keep Blacktown safe."

The crowd was somber, and Black went on. "Let us prepare for the struggles ahead while celebrating the liberation of our loved ones."

As the people clapped and rushed about, they soon filled the pathways with merriment. The men set up several pits where goat meat and beef roasted over an open fire. Tables were set up with different dishes. The fiddlers played sweet music as the children ran about screaming and laughing. The women of the settlement danced and chatted. The scene did much to improve Black's attitude. He and the men did not partake in the activities. Instead, they did what he promised the people–they stood guard.

When the hour grew late, Black retired to his bedchamber; the men did a shift change. He didn't sleep, but he did ponder and figure on his interactions with the union president. There were moments of deep sorrow as he allowed himself to be cornered by thoughts of Booth. Later, his mind drifted to Sunday, and he found that he both needed and missed his wife. In the darkness, he wiped at his eyes and still more tears flowed.

Sleep claimed him in the wee hours and Black woke to the sound of male voices floating in from the great room. It was the familiar voice of a woman that caused him to shave and dress. Black wanted to see what was happening in his front room. He pulled open the bedchamber door to find Simon seated to the table eating and Morgan serving him.

"Black, is you hungry?" Morgan asked. "Miss Velma and Margie outdone themselves."

Seating himself across from Simon, Black asked. "What are you doing here?"

"Me and Morgan come sos'n you can head to the fort." Simon answered between bites.

"Sunday... my children?"

"They missin' you–same as you missin' them." Simon chuckled, then added. "Jake had him a girl wit' Miss Caroline."

Black nodded before dropping his gaze. Simon went on. "It's a train what leaves at midnight."

"Yeah."

"Three months… not two," Simon said.

"Yeah," Black replied. "If you need me…"

"We all knows that."

* * *

Black and the men boarded the train at midnight and exited the train after dawn. He sent word ahead and he was pleased to find Chester and Philip waiting for them. As the men piled into the wagons, Black could feel their excitement at being home. What he appreciated; the men didn't complain. He was proud to labor with them.

It was a lovely May morning; the weather was mild, and the scent of flowers was sweet in the air. Black sat at the opening of the flap gazing at the accomplishments of the people. New cabins peppered the landscape and there were people moving about at different tasks. A new stable had been erected and the sound of a smithy plying his trade was comforting.

When they reached the fort, the wagons pulled onto a path that wound through the newly built homes. And with the east wall gone–the fort was now a town rather than a prison. The men hopped from the wagons as some of their houses filled the void the wall left. Black jumped out by the barracks and with his brothers, he walked home.

He was the first one up the porch stairs and when he pushed at the door, he smiled. The sound of the women chatting warmed his heart. Moving down the long hall, Black found Sunday, Anna and Abby seated to the table with Big Mama and Miss Cora. Iris was standing at the stove stirring a big pot. His wife stopped talking at the sight of him.

Stepping into the kitchen, he kissed Big Mama. Black then lifted his wife into his arms and carried her to their bedchamber. Placing her on her feet, Black shut the door closing out his worries and hugged his woman. Sunday wept in his arms.

"I missed you so much."

"Same," she answered softly.

"Bathe with me?" he asked.

"Yes."

At her answer, Black set about filling the tub and he was thankful when he found the kitchen empty. Once he shut and locked the door to their room, he undressed. When he slid into the warm water, he watched as his wife shucked her clothing. Black groaned when Sunday climbed into the water and eased down onto his shaft.

It was what he needed, and he allowed his wife to take control. He laid back with his arms on the rim of the tub. Sunday placed her palms flat to his chest and began rolling her hips. Oh, how he missed all that she offered. The water sloshed over the sides and still she didn't stop bringing him pleasure. She changed her angle when she leaned in to kiss him.

He groaned and begged. "Woman, don't stop."

Sunday rode him until they were both mindless with ecstasy. The vision of her brown skin and deep chocolate nipples coupled with the sensations coursing through his veins undid him. And when she threw back her head moaning her satisfaction, she took him with her. Black closed his eyes and lingered in the haze of the sex act. He could feel his strength coming back from the weak moments spent with his wife.

She soaped his chest and rinsed him. Black opened his eyes when she whispered, "You is my king."

Black was humbled.

* * *

It was well into the afternoon when Black climbed from their bed. Dressing, he made his way to the kitchen. He could hear the chatter of women and children coming from the dining room. Black had been about to head that way as he had not seen his little ones, but when he walked past the front door, he could hear the sounds of a gathering happening.

The door was partially open, and he suspected it was because of the heat. Black stepped onto the porch to find the people of Fort Independence setting up tables. The smell of meat cooking floated on the air. Elbert and James walked out behind him as they had been staying on the second floor.

When the people spied him, it was the same as it had been in Blacktown. They huddled together looking to him for direction. Black didn't know what to say, for he too was baffled by Lincoln's death.

"We glad you's home." An old man in the crowd hollered.

"I'm glad to be here." Black answered.

"They done kilt Lincoln." A light skinned woman called out. "What of our peoples in the south?"

"This is going to be a long road." Black answered. "I cannot speak on the south right now."

"What will this mean for us?" A man at the back of the crowd asked.

"You all will continue in liberty, and it will not be taken from you. We will be vigilant in our stance against slavery–no matter the law. Our struggles will be many, but we will not stand down. Celebrate the emancipation of our loved ones and do so without fear."

The people cheered and went about commemorating colored life. Black stood to the left of the door thinking on the existence of their people in the south. His brother, Elbert stepped to him asking.

"You thought you would never see the first free black generation, but we as a people have arrived. Why can't you just enjoy it?"

"My thoughts keep wandering to Frank's words. There is something truly wrong when a law has to be passed to stop the enslavement of a people. But what troubles me most is the race of people who think they have the right to make such laws."

"Yeah," Elbert said.

"We are not free because white people deem it so–we are free because it is our right," Black said. "I worry for those of us who believe themselves liberated because white law says it's so. There is much bloodshed coming our way, but I am up for the task."

As the sun set over Fort Independence, Black and his brothers stood on the porch observing the people in their merrymaking. His heart was full as he envisioned the battles to come.